KU-273-429

TALES OF HORROR AND MYSTERY

TALES OF HORROR AND MYSTERY

DEAN

Horror Stories first published 1980
Mystery Stories first published 1981

This edition published 1993 by Dean, an imprint
of Reed Consumer Books Limited, Michelin House,
81 Fulham Road, London SW3 6RB
and Auckland, Melbourne, Singapore and Toronto

Line illustrations by Reginald Gray *(Horror
Stories)* and Sam Thompson *(Mystery Stories)*

ISBN 0 603 55222 6

A CIP catalogue record for this book is
available from the British Library

Printed in Great Britain by The Bath Press

HORROR STORIES

Contents

THE LANDLADY

Roald Dahl

Billy Weaver had travelled down from London on the slow afternoon train, with a change at Swindon on the way, and by the time he got to Bath it was about nine o'clock in the evening and the moon was coming up out of a clear starry sky over the houses opposite the station entrance. But the air was deadly cold and the wind was like a flat blade of ice on his cheeks.

'Excuse me,' he said, 'but is there a fairly cheap hotel not too far away from here?'

'Try The Bell and Dragon,' the porter answered, pointing down the road. 'They might take you in. It's about a quarter of a mile along on the other side.'

Billy thanked him and picked up his suitcase and set out to walk the quarter-mile to The Bell and Dragon. He had never been to Bath before. He didn't know anyone who lived there. But Mr Greenslade at the Head Office in London had told him it was a splendid city. 'Find your own lodgings,' he had said, 'and then go along and report to the Branch Manager as soon as you've got yourself settled.'

Billy was seventeen years old. He was wearing a new navy-blue overcoat, a new brown trilby hat, and a new brown suit, and he was feeling fine. He walked briskly down the street. He was trying to do everything briskly these days. Briskness, he had decided, was *the* one common characteristic of all successful businessmen. The big shots up at Head Office were absolutely fantastically brisk all the time. They were amazing.

There were no shops on this wide street that he was walking along, only a line of tall houses on each side, all of them identical. They had porches and pillars and four or five steps going up to their front doors, and it was obvious that once upon a time they had been very swanky residences. But now, even in the darkness, he could see that the paint was peeling from the woodwork on their doors and windows, and that the handsome white façades were cracked and blotchy from neglect.

Suddenly, in a downstairs window that was brilliantly illuminated by a street-lamp not six yards away, Billy caught sight of a printed notice propped up against the glass in one of the upper panes. It said BED AND BREAKFAST. There was a vase of pussy-willows, tall and beautiful, standing just underneath the notice.

He stopped walking. He moved a bit closer. Green curtains (some sort of velvety material) were hanging down on either side of the window. The pussy-willows looked wonderful beside them. He went right up and peered through the glass into the room, and the first thing he saw was a bright fire burning in the hearth. On the carpet in front of the fire, a pretty little dachshund was curled up asleep with its nose tucked into its belly. The room itself, so far as he could see in the half-darkness, was filled with pleasant furniture. There was a baby-grand piano and a big sofa and several plump armchairs; and in one corner he spotted a large parrot in a cage. Animals were usually a good sign in a place like this, Billy told himself; and all in all, it looked to him as though it would be a pretty decent house to stay in. Certainly it would be more comfortable than The Bell and Dragon.

On the other hand, a pub would be more congenial than a boarding-house. There would be beer and darts in the evenings, and lots of people to talk to, and it would probably be a good bit cheaper, too. He had stayed a couple of nights in a pub once before and he had liked it. He had never stayed in any boarding-houses, and, to be perfectly honest, he was a tiny bit frightened of them. The name itself conjured up images of watery cabbage, rapacious landladies, and a powerful smell of kippers in the living-room.

After dithering about like this in the cold for two or three minutes, Billy decided that he would walk on and take a look at The Bell and Dragon before making up his mind. He turned to go.

And now a queer thing happened to him. He was in the act of stepping back and turning away from the window when all at once his eye was caught and held in the most peculiar manner by the small notice that was there. BED AND BREAKFAST, it said. BED AND BREAKFAST, BED AND BREAKFAST, BED AND BREAKFAST. Each word was like a large black eye staring at him through the glass, holding him, compelling him, forcing him to stay where he was and not to walk away from that house, and the next thing he knew, he was actually moving across from the window to the front door of the house, climbing the steps that led up to it, and reaching for the bell.

He pressed the bell. Far away in a back room he heard it ringing, and then *at once* – it must have been at once because he hadn't even had time to take his finger from the bell-button – the door swung open and a woman was standing there.

Normally you ring the bell and you have at least a half-minute's wait before the door opens. But this dame was like a jack-in-the-box. He pressed the bell – and out she popped! It made him jump.

She was about forty-five or fifty years old, and the moment she saw him, she gave him a warm welcoming smile.

'*Please* come in,' she said pleasantly. She stepped aside, holding the door wide open, and Billy found himself automatically starting forward into the house. The compulsion or, more accurately, the desire to follow after her into that house was extraordinarily strong.

'I saw the notice in the window,' he said, holding himself back.

'Yes, I know.'

'I was wondering about a room.'

'It's *all* ready for you, my dear,' she said. She had a round pink face and very gentle blue eyes.

'I was on my way to The Bell and Dragon,' Billy told her. 'But the notice in your window just happened to catch my eye.'

'My dear boy,' she said, 'why don't you come in out of the cold?'

'How much do you charge?'

'Five and sixpence a night, including breakfast.'

It was fantastically cheap. It was less than half of what he had been willing to pay.

'If that is too much,' she added, 'then perhaps I can reduce it just a tiny bit. Do you desire an egg for breakfast? Eggs are expensive at the moment. It would be sixpence less without the egg.'

'Five and sixpence is fine,' he answered. 'I should like very much to stay here.'

'I knew you would. Do come in.'

She seemed terribly nice. She looked exactly like the mother of one's best school-friend welcoming one into the house to stay for the Christmas holidays. Billy took off his hat, and stepped over the threshold.

'Just hang it there,' she said, 'and let me help you with your coat.'

There were no other hats or coats in the hall. There were no umbrellas, no walking-sticks – nothing.

'We have it *all* to ourselves,' she said, smiling at him over her shoulder as she led the way upstairs. 'You see, it isn't very often I have the pleasure of taking a visitor into my little nest.'

The old girl is slightly dotty, Billy told himself. But at five and sixpence a night, who gives a damn about that? 'I should've thought you'd be simply swamped with applicants,' he said politely.

'Oh, I am, my dear, I am, of course I am. But the trouble is that I'm inclined to be just a teeny weeny bit choosey and particular – if you see what I mean.'

'Ah, yes.'

'But I'm always ready. Everything is always ready day and night in this house just on the off-chance that an acceptable young gentleman will come along. And it is such a pleasure, my dear, such a very great pleasure when now and again I open the door and I see someone standing there who is just *exactly* right.' She was half-way up the stairs, and she paused with one hand on the stair-rail, turning her head and smiling down at him with pale lips. 'Like you,' she added, and her blue eyes travelled slowly all the way down the length of Billy's body, to his feet, and then up again.

On the first-floor landing she said to him, 'This floor is mine.'

They climbed up a second flight. 'And this one is *all* yours,' she said. 'Here's your room. I do hope you'll like it.' She took him into a small but charming front bedroom, switching on the light as she went in.

'The morning sun comes right in the window, Mr Perkins. It *is* Mr Perkins, isn't it?'

'No,' he said. 'It's Weaver.'

'Mr Weaver. How nice. I've put a water-bottle between the sheets to air them out, Mr Weaver. It's such a comfort to have a hot water-bottle in a strange bed with clean sheets, don't you agree? And you may light the gas fire at any time if you feel chilly.'

'Thank you,' Billy said. 'Thank you ever so much.' He noticed that the bedspread had been taken off the bed, and that the bedclothes had been neatly turned back on one side, all ready for someone to get in.

'I'm so glad you appeared,' she said, looking earnestly into his face. 'I was beginning to get worried.'

'That's all right,' Billy answered brightly. 'You mustn't worry about me.' He put his suitcase on the chair and started to open it.

'And what about supper, my dear? Did you manage to get anything to eat before you came here?'

'I'm not a bit hungry, thank you,' he said. 'I think I'll just go to bed as soon as possible because tomorrow I've got to get up rather early and report to the office.'

'Very well, then. I'll leave you now so that you can unpack. But before you go to bed, would you be kind enough to pop into the sitting-room on the ground floor and sign the book? Everyone has to do that because it's the law of the land, and we don't want to go breaking any laws at *this* stage in the proceedings, do we?' She gave him a little wave of the hand and went quickly out of the room and closed the door.

Now, the fact that his landlady appeared to be slightly off her rocker didn't worry Billy in the least. After all, she was not only harmless – there was no question about that – but she was also quite obviously a kind and generous soul. He guessed that she had probably lost a son in the war, or something like that, and had never got over it.

So a few minutes later, after unpacking his suitcase and washing his hands, he trotted downstairs to the ground floor and entered the living-room. His landlady wasn't there, but the fire was glowing in the hearth, and the little dachshund was still sleeping in front of it. The room was wonderfully warm and cosy. I'm a lucky fellow, he thought, rubbing his hands. This is a bit of all right.

He found the guest-book lying open on the piano, so he took out his pen and wrote down his name and address. There were only two other entries above his on the page, and, as one always does with guest-books, he started to read them. One was a Christopher Mulholland from Cardiff. The other was Gregory W. Temple from Bristol.

That's funny, he thought suddenly. Christopher Mulholland. It rings a bell.

Now where on earth had he heard that rather unusual name before?

Was he a boy at school? No. Was it one of his sister's numerous young men, perhaps, or a friend of his father's? No, no, it wasn't any of those. He glanced down again at the book.

Christopher Mulholland *231 Cathedral Road, Cardiff*

Gregory W. Temple *27 Sycamore Drive, Bristol*

As a matter of fact, now he came to think of it, he wasn't at all sure that the second name didn't have almost as much of a familiar ring about it as the first.

'Gregory Temple?' he said aloud, searching his memory. 'Christopher Mulholland? . . .'

'Such charming boys,' a voice behind him answered, and he turned and saw his landlady sailing into the room with a large silver tea-tray in her hands. She was holding it well out in front of her, and rather high up, as though the tray were a pair of reins on a frisky horse.

'They sound somehow familiar,' he said.

'They do? How interesting.'

'I'm almost positive I've heard those names before somewhere. Isn't that queer? Maybe it was in the newspapers. They weren't famous in any way, were they? I mean famous cricketers or footballers or something like that?'

'Famous,' she said, setting the tea-tray down on the low table in front of the sofa. 'Oh no, I don't think they were famous. But they were extraordinarily handsome, both of them, I can promise you that. They were tall and young and handsome, my dear, just exactly like you.'

Once more, Billy glanced down at the book. 'Look here,' he said, noticing the dates. 'This last entry is over two years old.'

'It is?'

'Yes, indeed. And Christopher Mulholland's is nearly a year before that – more than *three years* ago.'

'Dear me,' she said, shaking her head and heaving a dainty little sigh. 'I would never have thought it. How time does fly away from us all, doesn't it, Mr Wilkins?'

'It's Weaver,' Billy said. 'W-e-a-v-e-r.'

'Oh, of course it is!' she cried, sitting down on the sofa. 'How silly of me. I do apologize. In one ear and out the other, that's me, Mr Weaver.'

'You know something?' Billy said. 'Something that's really quite extraordinary about all this?'

'No, dear, I don't.'

'Well, you see – both of these names, Mulholland and Temple, I not only seem to remember each one of them separately, so to speak, but somehow or other, in some peculiar way, they both appear to be sort of connected together as well. As though they were both famous for the same sort of thing, if you see what I mean – like . . . like Dempsey and Tunney, for example, or Churchill and Roosevelt.'

'How amusing,' she said. 'But come over here now, dear, and sit down beside me on the sofa and I'll give you a nice cup of tea and a ginger biscuit before you go to bed.'

'You really shouldn't bother,' Billy said. 'I didn't mean you to do anything like that.' He stood by the piano, watching her as she fussed about with the cups and saucers. He noticed that she had small, white, quickly moving hands, and red finger-nails.

'I'm almost positive it was in the newspapers I saw them,' Billy said. 'I'll think of it in a second. I'm sure I will.'

There is nothing more tantalizing than a thing like this which lingers just outside the borders of one's memory. He hated to give up.

'Now wait a minute,' he said. 'Wait just a minute. Mulholland . . . Christopher Mulholland . . . wasn't *that* the name of the Eton schoolboy who was on a walking-tour through the West Country, and then all of a sudden . . .'

'Milk?' she said. 'And sugar?'

'Yes, please. And then all of a sudden . . .'

'Eton schoolboy?' she said. 'Oh no, my dear, that can't possibly be right because *my* Mr Mulholland was certainly not an Eton schoolboy when he came to me. He was a Cambridge undergraduate. Come over here now and sit next to me and warm yourself in front of this lovely fire. Come on. Your tea's all ready for you.' She patted the empty place beside her on the sofa, and she sat there smiling at Billy and waiting for him to come over.

He crossed the room slowly, and sat down on the edge of the sofa. She placed his teacup on the table in front of him.

'*There* we are,' she said. 'How nice and cosy this is, isn't it?'

Billy started sipping his tea. She did the same. For half a minute or so, neither of them spoke. But Billy knew that she was looking at him. Her body was half-turned towards him, and he could feel her eyes resting on his face, watching him over the rim of her teacup. Now and again, he caught a whiff of a peculiar smell that seemed to emanate directly from her person. It was not in the least unpleasant, and it reminded him – well, he wasn't quite sure what it reminded him of. Pickled walnuts? New leather? Or was it the corridors of a hospital?

'Mr Mulholland was a great one for his tea,' she said at length. 'Never in my life have I seen anyone drink as much tea as dear, sweet Mr Mulholland.'

'I suppose he left fairly recently,' Billy said. He was still puzzling his head about the two names. He was positive now that he had seen them in the newspapers – in the headlines.

'Left?' she said, arching her brows. 'But my dear boy, he never left. He's still here. Mr Temple is also here. They're on the third floor, both of them together.'

Billy set down his cup slowly on the table, and stared at his landlady. She smiled back at him, and then she put out one of her white hands and patted him comfortingly on the knee. 'How old are you, my dear?' she asked.

'Seventeen.'

'Seventeen!' she cried. 'Oh, it's the perfect age! Mr Mulholland was also seventeen. But I think he was a trifle shorter than you are, in fact I'm sure he was, and his teeth weren't *quite* so white. You have the most beautiful teeth, Mr Weaver, did you know that?'

'They're not as good as they look,' Billy said. 'They've got simply masses of fillings in them at the back.'

'Mr Temple, of course, was a little older,' she said, ignoring his remark. 'He was actually twenty-eight. And yet I never would have guessed it if he hadn't told me, never in my whole life. There wasn't a *blemish* on his body.'

'A what?' Billy said.

'His skin was *just* like a baby's.'

There was a pause. Billy picked up his teacup and took another sip of his tea, then he set it down again gently in its saucer. He waited for her to say something else, but she seemed to have lapsed into another of her silences. He sat there staring straight ahead of him into the far corner of the room, biting his lower lip.

'That parrot,' he said at last. 'You know something? It had me completely fooled when I first saw it through the window from the street. I could have sworn it was alive.'

'Alas, no longer.'

'It's most terribly clever the way it's been done,' he said. 'It doesn't look in the least bit dead. Who did it?'

'I did.'

'*You* did?'

'Of course,' she said. 'And have you met my little Basil as well?' She nodded towards the dachshund curled up so comfortably in front of the fire. Billy looked at it. And suddenly, he realized that this animal had all the time been just as silent and motionless as the parrot. He put out a hand and touched it gently on the top of its back. The back was hard and cold, and when he pushed the hair to one side with his fingers, he could see the skin underneath, greyish-black and dry and perfectly preserved.

'Good gracious me,' he said. 'How absolutely fascinating.' He turned away from the dog and stared with deep admiration at the little woman beside him on the sofa. 'It must be most awfully difficult to do a thing like that.'

'Not in the least,' she said. 'I stuff *all* my little pets myself when they pass away. Will you have another cup of tea?'

'No, thank you,' Billy said. The tea tasted faintly of bitter almonds, and he didn't much care for it.

'You did sign the book, didn't you?'

'Oh, yes.'

'That's good. Because later on, if I happen to forget what you were called, then I can always come down here and look it up. I still do that almost every day with Mr Mulholland and Mr . . . Mr . . .'

'Temple,' Billy said. 'Gregory Temple. Excuse my asking, but haven't there been *any* other guests here except them in the last two or three years?'

Holding her teacup high in one hand, inclining her head slightly to the left, she looked up at him out of the corners of her eyes and gave him another gentle little smile.

'No, my dear,' she said. 'Only you.'

THE RIDDLE

Walter de la Mare

So these seven children, Ann and Matilda, James, William and Henry, Harriet and Dorothea, came to live with their grandmother. The house in which their grandmother had lived since her childhood was built in the time of the Georges. It was not a pretty house, but roomy, substantial, and square; and a great cedar tree outstretched its branches almost to the windows.

When the children were come out of the cab (five sitting inside and two beside the driver), they were shown into their grandmother's presence. They stood in a little black group before the old lady, seated in her bow-window. And she asked them each their names, and repeated each name in her kind, quavering voice. Then to one she gave a work-box, to William a jack-knife, to Dorothea a painted ball; to each a present according to age. And she kissed all her grand-children to the youngest.

'My dears,' she said, 'I wish to see all of you bright and gay in my house. I am an old woman, so that I cannot romp with you; but Ann must look to you, and Mrs Fenn too. And every morning and every evening you must all come in to see your granny; and bring me smiling faces, that call back to my mind my own son Harry. But all the rest of the day, when school is done, you shall do just as you please, my dears. And there is only one thing, just one, I would have you remember. In the large spare bedroom that looks out on the slate roof there stands in the corner an old oak chest; aye, older than I, my dears, a great deal older; older than my grandmother. Play anywhere else in the house, but not there.' She spoke kindly to them all, smiling at them; but she was very old, and her eyes seemed to see nothing of this world.

And the seven children, though at first they were gloomy and strange, soon began to be happy and at home in the great house. There was much to interest and to amuse them there; all was new to them. Twice every day, morning and evening, they came in to see their grandmother, who every day seemed more feeble; and she spoke pleasantly to them of her mother, and her childhood, but never forgetting to visit her store of sugar-plums. And so the weeks passed by. . . .

It was evening twilight when Henry went upstairs from the nursery by himself to look at the oak chest. He pressed his fingers into the carved fruit and flowers, and spoke to the dark-smiling heads at the corners; and then, with a glance over his shoulder, he opened the lid and looked in. But the chest concealed no treasure, neither gold nor baubles, nor was there anything to alarm the eye. The chest was empty, except that it was lined with silk of old-rose, seeming darker in the dusk, and smelling sweet of pot-pourri. And while Henry was looking in, he heard the softened laughter and the clinking of the cups downstairs in the nursery; and out at the window he saw the day darkening. These things brought strangely to his memory his mother who in her glimmering white dress used to read to him in the dusk; and he climbed into the chest; and the lid closed gently down over him.

When the other six children were tired with their playing, they filed into their grandmother's room for her goodnight and her sugar-plums. She looked out between the candles at them as if she were uncertain of something in her thoughts. The next day Ann told her grandmother that Henry was not anywhere to be found.

'Dearie me, child. Then he must be gone away for a time,' said the old lady. She paused. 'But remember, all of you, do not meddle with the oak chest.'

But Matilda could not forget her brother Henry, finding no pleasure in playing without him. So she would loiter in the house thinking where he might be. And she carried her wooden doll in her bare arms, singing under her breath all she could make up about it. And when one bright morning she peeped in on the chest, so sweet-scented and secret it seemed that she took her doll with her into it—just as Henry himself had done.

So Ann, and James, and William, Harriet and Dorothea were left at home to play together. 'Some day maybe they will come back to you, my dears,' said their grandmother, 'or maybe you will go to them. Heed my warning as best you may.'

Now Harriet and William were friends together, pretending to be sweethearts; while James and Dorothea liked wild games of hunting, and fishing, and battles.

On a silent afternoon in October, Harriet and William were talking softly together, looking out over the slate roof at the green fields, and they heard the squeak and frisking of a mouse behind them in the room. They went together and searched for the small, dark hole from whence it had come out. But finding no hole, they began to finger the carving of the chest, and to give names to the dark-smiling heads, just as Henry had done. '*I* know! let's pretend you are Sleeping Beauty, Harriet,' said William, 'and I'll be the Prince that squeezes through the thorns and comes in.' Harriet looked gently and strangely at her brother but she got into the box and lay down, pretending to be fast asleep, and on tiptoe William leaned over, and seeing how how big was the chest, he stepped in to kiss the Sleeping Beauty and to wake her from her quiet sleep. Slowly the carved lid turned on its noisless hinges. And only the clatter of James and Dorothea came in sometimes to recall Ann from her book.

But their old grandmother was very feeble, and her sight dim, and her hearing extremely difficult.

Snow was falling through the still air upon the roof; and Dorothea was a fish in the oak chest, and James stood over the hole in the ice, brandishing a walking-stick for a harpoon, pretending to be an Esquimau. Dorothea's face was red, and her wild eyes sparkled through her tousled hair. And James had a crooked scratch upon his cheek. 'You must struggle, Dorothea, and then I shall swim back and drag you out. Be quick now!' He shouted with laughter as he was drawn into the open chest. And the lid closed softly and gently down as before.

Ann, left to herself, was too old to care overmuch for sugar-plums, but she would go solitary to bid her grandmother goodnight; and the old lady looked wistfully at her over her spectacles. 'Well, my dear,' she said with trembling head; and she squeezed Ann's fingers between her own knuckled finger and thumb. 'What lonely old people we two are, to be sure!' Ann kissed her grandmother's soft, loose cheek. She left the old lady sitting in her easy chair, her hands upon her knees, and her head turned sidelong towards her.

When Ann was gone to bed she used to sit reading her book by candlelight. She drew up her knees under the sheets resting her book upon them. Her story was about fairies and gnomes, and the gently-flowing moonlight of the narrative seemed to illumine the white pages, and she could hear in fancy fairy voices, so silent was the great many-roomed house, and so mellifluent were the words of the story. Presently she put out her candle, and, with a confused babel of voices close to her ear, and faint swift pictures before her eyes, she fell alseep.

And in the dead of night she rose out of her bed in dream, and with eyes wide open yet seeing nothing of reality, moved silently through the vacant house. Past the room where her grandmother was snoring in brief, heavy slumber, she stepped lightly and surely, and down the wide staircase. And Vega the far-shining stood over against the window above the slate roof. Ann walked into the strange room beneath as if she were being guided by the hand towards the oak chest. There, just as if she were dreaming it was her bed, she laid herself down in the old rose silk, in the fragrant place. But it was so dark in the room that the movement of the lid was indistinguishable.

Through the long day, the grandmother sat in her bow-window. Her lips were pursed, and she looked with dim, inquisitive scrutiny upon the street where people passed to and fro, and vehicles rolled by. At evening she climbed the stair and stood in the doorway of the large spare bedroom. The ascent had shortened her breath. Her magnifying spectacles rested upon her nose. Leaning her hand on the door post she peered in towards the glimmering square of window in the quiet gloom. But she could not see far, because her sight was dim and the light of day feeble. Nor could she detect the faint fragrance as of autumnal leaves But in her mind was a tangled skein of memories

—laughter and tears, and children long ago become old-fashioned, and the advent of friends, and last farewells. And gossiping fitfully, inarticulately, with herself, the old lady went down again to her window-seat.

THE MONKEY'S PAW

W.W. Jacobs

Without, the night was cold and wet, but in the small parlour of Laburnam Villa the blinds were drawn and the fire burned brightly. Father and son were at chess, the former, who possessed ideas about the game involving radical changes, putting his king into such sharp and unnecessary perils that it even provoked comment from the white-haired old lady knitting placidly by the fire.

'Hark at the wind,' said Mr White, who, having seen a fatal mistake after it was too late, was amiably desirous of preventing his son from seeing it.

'I'm listening,' said the latter, grimly surveying the board as he stretched out his hand. 'Check.'

'I should hardly think that he'd come tonight,' said his father, with his hand poised over the board.

'Mate,' replied the son.

'That's the worst of living so far out,' bawled Mr White, with sudden and unlooked-for violence; 'of all the beastly, slushy, out-of-the-way places to live in, this is the worst. Pathway's a bog, and the road's a torrent. I don't know what people are thinking about. I suppose because only two houses in the road are let, they think it doesn't matter.'

'Never mind, dear,' said his wife, soothingly; 'perhaps you'll win the next one.'

Mr White looked up sharply, just in time to interrupt a knowing glance between mother and son. The words died away on his lips, and he hid a guilty grin in his thin grey beard.

'There he is,' said Herbert White, as the gate banged to loudly and heavy footsteps came towards the door.

The old man rose with hospitable haste, and opening the door, was heard condoling with the new arrival. The new arrival also condoled with himself, so that Mrs White said, 'Tut, tut!' and coughed gently as her husband entered the room, followed by a tall, burly man, beady of eye and rubicund of visage.

'Sergeant-Major Morris,' he said, introducing him.

The sergeant-major shook hands, and taking the proffered seat by the fire, watched contentedly while his host got out whisky and tumblers and stood a small copper kettle on the fire.

At the third glass his eyes got brighter, and he began to talk, the little family circle regarding with eager interest this visitor from distant parts, as he squared his shoulders in the chair and spoke of wild scenes and doughty deeds; of wars and plagues and strange peoples.

'Twenty-one years of it,' said Mr White, nodding at his wife and son. 'When he went away he was a slip of a youth in the warehouse. Now look at him.'

'He don't look to have taken much harm,' said Mrs White, politely.

'I'd like to go to India myself,' said the old man, 'just to look round a bit, you know.'

'Better where you are,' said the sergeant-major, shaking his head. He put down the empty glass, and sighing softly, shook it again.

'I should like to see those old temples and fakirs and jugglers,' said the old man. 'What was that you started telling me the other day about a monkey's paw or something, Morris?'

'Nothing,' said the soldier, hastily. 'Leastways nothing worth hearing.'

'Monkey's paw?' said Mrs White, curiously.

'Well, it's just a bit of what you might call magic, perhaps,' said the sergeant-major, offhandedly.

His three listeners leaned forward eagerly. The visitor absent-mindedly put his empty glass to his lips and then set it down again. His host filled it for him.

'To look at,' said the sergeant-major, fumbling in his pocket, 'it's just an ordinary little paw, dried to a mummy.'

He took something out of his pocket and proffered it. Mrs White drew back with a grimace, but her son, taking it, examined it curiously.

'And what is there special about it?' inquired Mr White as he took it from his son, and having examined it, placed it upon the table.

'It had a spell put on it by an old fakir,' said the sergeant-major, 'a very holy man. He wanted to show that fate ruled people's lives, and that those who interfered with it did so to their sorrow. He put a spell on it so that three separate men could each have three wishes from it.'

His manner was so impressive that his bearers were conscious that their light laughter jarred somewhat.

'Well, why don't you have three, sir?' said Herbert White, cleverly.

The soldier regarded him in the way that middle age is wont to regard presumptuous youth. 'I have,' he said, quietly, and his blotchy face whitened.

'And did you really have the three wishes granted?' asked Mrs White.

'I did,' said the sergeant-major, and his glass tapped against his strong teeth.

'And has anybody else wished?' persisted the old lady.

'The first man had his three wishes. Yes,' was the reply; 'I don't know what the first two were, but the third was for death. That's how I got the paw.'

His tones were so grave that a hush fell upon the group.

'If you've had your three wishes, it's no good to you now, then, Morris,' said the old man at last. 'What do you keep it for?'

The soldier shook his head. 'Fancy, I suppose,' he said, slowly. 'I did have some idea of selling it, but I don't think I will. It has caused enough mischief already. Besides, people won't buy. They think it's a fairy tale; some of them, and those who do think anything of it want to try it first and pay me afterwards.'

'If you could have another three wishes,' said the old man, eyeing him keenly, 'would you have them?'

'I don't know,' said the other. 'I don't know.'

He took the paw, and dangling it between his forefinger and thumb suddenly threw it upon the fire. White, with a slight cry, stooped down and snatched it off.

'Better let it burn,' said the soldier, solemnly.

'If you don't want it, Morris,' said the other, 'give it to me.'

'I won't,' said his friend, doggedly. 'I threw it on the fire. If you keep it, don't blame me for what happens. Pitch it on the fire again like a sensible man.'

The other shook his head and examined his new possession closely. 'How do you do it?' he inquired.

'Hold it up in your right hand and wish aloud,' said the sergeant-major, 'but I warn you of the consequences.'

'Sounds like the *Arabian Nights*,' said Mrs White, as she rose and began to set the supper. 'Don't you think you might wish for four pairs of hands for me?'

Her husband drew the talisman from pocket, and then all three burst into laughter as the sergeant-major, with a look of alarm on his face, caught him by the arm.

'If you must wish,' he said gruffly, 'wish for something sensible.'

Mr White dropped it back in his pocket, and placing chairs, motioned his friend to the table. In the business of supper the talisman was partly forgotten, and afterward the three sat listening in an enthralled fashion to a second instalment of the soldier's adventures in India.

'If the tale about the monkey's paw is not more truthful than those he has been telling us,' said Herbert, as the door closed behind their guest, just in time for him to catch the last train, 'we sha'nt make much out of it.'

'Did you give him anything for it, father?' inquired Mrs White, regarding her husband closely.

'A trifle,' said he, colouring slightly. 'He didn't want it, but I made him take it. And he pressed me again to throw it away.'

'Likely,' said Herbert, with pretended horror. 'Why, we're going to be rich, and famous and happy. Wish to be an emperor, father, to begin with; then you can't be henpecked.'

He darted round the table, pursued by the maligned Mrs White armed with an antimacassar.

Mr White took the paw from his pocket and eyed it dubiously. 'I don't know what to wish for, and that's a fact,' he said, slowly. 'It seems to me I've got all I want.'

'If you only cleared the house, you'd be quite happy, wouldn't you?' said Herbert, with his hand on his shoulder. 'Well, wish for two hundred pounds, then, that'll just do it.'

His father, smiling shamefacedly at his own credulity, held up the talisman, as his son, with a solemn face, somewhat marred by a wink at his mother, sat down at the piano and struck a few impressive chords.

'I wish for two hundred pounds,' said the old man distinctly.

A fine crash from the piano greeted the words, interrupted by a shuddering cry from the old man. His wife and son ran toward him.

'It moved,' he cried, with a glance of disgust at the object as it lay on the floor. 'As I wished, it twisted in my hand like a snake.'

'Well, I don't see the money,' said his son as he picked it up and placed it on the table, 'and I bet I never shall.'

'It must have been your fancy, father,' said his wife, regarding him anxiously.

He shook his head. 'Never mind, though; there's no harm done, but it gave me a shock all the same.'

They sat down by the fire again while the two men finished their pipes. Outside, the wind was higher than ever, and the old man started nervously at the sound of a door banging upstairs. A silence unusual and depressing settled upon all three, which lasted until the old couple rose to retire for the night.

'I expect you'll find the cash tied up in a big bag in the middle of your bed,' said Herbert, as he bade them good night, 'and something horrible squatting up on top of the wardrobe watching you as you pocket your ill-gotten gains.'

He sat alone in the darkness, gazing at the dying fire, and seeing faces in it. The last face was so horrible and so simian that he gazed at it in amazement. It got so vivid that, with a little uneasy laugh, he felt on the table for a glass containing a little water to throw over it.

His hand grasped the monkey's paw, and with a little shiver he wiped his hand on his coat and went up to bed.

* * * *

In the brightness of the wintry sun next morning as it streamed over the breakfast table he laughed at his fears. There was an air of prosaic wholesomeness about the room which it had lacked on the previous night, and the dirty, shrivelled little paw was pitched on the sideboard with a carelessness which betokened no great belief in its virtues.

'I suppose all old soldiers are the same,' said Mrs White. 'The idea of our listening to such nonsense! How could wishes be granted in these days? And if they could, how could two hundred pounds hurt you, father?'

'Might drop on his head from the sky,' said the frivolous Herbert.

'Morris said the things happened so naturally,' said his father, 'that you might if you so wished attribute it to coincidence.'

'Well, don't break into the money before I come back,' said Herbert as he rose from the table. 'I'm afraid it'll turn you into a mean, avaricious man, and we shall have to disown you.'

His mother laughed, and following him to the door, watched him down the road; and returning to the breakfast table, was very happy at the expense of her husband's credulity. All of which did not prevent her from referring somewhat shortly to retired sergeant-majors of bibulous habits when she found that the post brought a tailor's bill.

'Herbert will have some more of his funny remarks, I expect, when he comes home,' she said, as they sat at dinner.

'I dare say,' said Mr White, pouring himself out some beer: 'but for all that, the thing moved in my hand; that I'll swear to.'

'You thought it did,' said the old lady soothingly.

'I say it did,' replied the other. 'There was no thought about it; I had just—What's the matter?'

His wife made no reply. She was watching the mysterious movements of a man outside, who, peering in an undecided fashion at the house, appeared to be trying to make up his mind to enter. In mental connection with the two hundred pounds, she noticed that the stranger was well dressed, and wore a silk hat of glossy newness. Three times he paused at the gate, and then walked on again. The fourth time he stood with his hand upon it, and then with sudden resolution flung it open and walked up the path. Mrs White at the same moment placed her hands behind her, and hurriedly unfastening the strings of her apron, put that useful article of apparel beneath the cushion of her chair.

She brought the stranger, who seemed ill at ease, into the room. He gazed at her furtively, and listened in a preoccupied fashion as the old lady apologized for the appearance of the room, and her husband's coat, a garment which he usually reserved for the garden. She then waited as patiently as her sex would permit, for him to broach his business, but he was at first strangely silent.

'I—was asked to call,' he said at last, and stopped and picked a piece of cotton from his trousers. 'I come from Maw and Meggins.'

The old lady started. 'Is anything the matter?' she asked, breathlessly. 'Has anything happened to Herbert? What is it? What is it?'

Her husband interposed. 'There, there, mother,' he said, hastily. 'Sit down, and don't jump to conclusions. You've not brought bad news, I'm sure, sir'; and he eyed the other wistfully.

'I'm sorry—' began the visitor.

'Is he hurt?' demanded the mother, wildly.

The visitor bowed in assent. 'Badly hurt,' he said, quietly, 'but he is not in any pain.'

'Oh, thank God!' said the old woman, clasping her hands. 'Thank God for that! Thank—'

She broke off suddenly as the sinister meaning of the assurance dawned upon her and she saw the awful confirmation of her fears in the other's averted face. She caught her breath, and turning to her slower-witted husband, laid her trembling old hand upon his. There was a long silence.

'He was caught in the machinery,' said the visitor at length in a low voice.

'Caught in the machinery,' repeated Mr White, in a dazed fashion, 'yes.'

He sat staring blankly out at the window, and taking his wife's hand between his own, pressed it as he had been wont to do in their old courting-days nearly forty years before.

'He was the only one left to us,' he said, turning gently to the visitor. 'It is hard.'

The other coughed, and rising, walked slowly to the window. 'The firm wished me to convey their sincere sympathy with you in your great loss,' he said, without looking round. 'I beg that you will understand I am only their servant and merely obeying orders.'

There was no reply; the old woman's face was white, her eyes staring and her breath inaudible; on the husband's face was a look such as his friend the sergeant might have carried into his first action.

'I was to say that Maw and Meggins disclaim all responsibility,' continued the other. 'They admit no liability at all, but in consideration of your son's services, they wish to present you with a certain sum as compensation.'

Mr White dropped his wife's hand, and rising to his feet, gazed with a look of horror at his visitor. His dry lips shaped the words, 'How much?'

'Two hundred pounds,' was the answer.

Unconscious of his wife's shriek, the old man smiled faintly, put out his hands like a sightless man, and dropped, a senseless heap, to the floor.

★ ★ ★ ★

In the huge new cemetery, some two miles distant, the old people buried their dead, and came back to a house steeped in shadow and silence. It was all over so quickly that at first they could hardly realize it, and remained in a state of expectation as though of something else to happen—something else which was to lighten this load, too heavy for old hearts to bear.

But the days passed, and expectation gave place to resignation—the hopeless resignation of the old, sometimes miscalled apathy. Sometimes they hardly exchanged a word, for now they had nothing to talk about, and their days were long to weariness.

It was about a week after that the old man, waking suddenly in the night, stretched out his hand and found himself alone. The room was in darkness, and the sound of subdued weeping came from the window. He raised himself in bed and listened.

'Come back,' he said, tenderly. 'You will be cold.'

'It is colder for my son,' said the old woman, and wept afresh.

The sound of her sobs died away on his ears. The bed was warm, and his eyes heavy with sleep. He dozed fitfully, and then slept until a sudden wild cry from his wife awoke him with a start.

'*The paw!*' she cried wildly. 'The monkey's paw!'

He started up in alarm. 'Where? Where is it? What's the matter?'

She came stumbling across the room toward him. 'I want it,' she said, quietly. 'You've not destroyed it?'

'It's in the parlour, on the bracket,' he replied, marvelling. 'Why?'

She cried and laughed together, and bending over, kissed his cheek.

'I only just thought of it,' she cried, hysterically. 'Why didn't I think of it before? Why didn't you think of it?'

'Think of what?' he questioned.

'The other two wishes,' she replied, rapidly. 'We've only had one.'

'Was not that enough?' he demanded fiercely.

'No,' she cried triumphantly; 'we'll have one more. Go down and get it quickly, and wish our boy alive again.'

The man sat up in bed and flung the bedclothes from his quaking limbs. 'Good God, you are mad!' he cried, aghast.

'Get it,' she panted; 'get it quickly, and wish—Oh, my boy, my boy!'

Her husband struck a match and lit the candle. 'Get back to bed,' he said, unsteadily. 'You don't know what you are saying.'

'We had the first wish granted,' said the old woman, feverishly; 'why not the second?'

'A coincidence,' stammered the old man.

'Go and get it and wish,' cried his wife, quivering with excitement.

The old man turned and regarded her, and his voice shook. 'He has been dead ten days, and besides he—I would not tell you else, but—I could only recognize him by his clothing. If he was too horrible for you to see then, how now?'

'Bring him back?' cried the old woman, and dragged him towards the door. 'Do you think I fear the child I have nursed?'

He went down in the darkness, and felt his way to the parlour, and then to the mantlepiece. The talisman was in its place, and a horrible fear that the unspoken wish might bring his mutilated son before him ere he could escape from the room seized upon him, and he caught his breath as he found that he had lost the direction of the door. His brow cold with sweat, he felt his way round the table, and groped along the wall until he found himself in the small passage with the unwholesome thing in his hand.

Even his wife's face seemed changed as he entered the room. It was white and expectant, and to his fears seemed to have an unnatural look upon it. He was afraid of her.

'*Wish!*' she cried, in a strong voice.

'It is foolish and wicked,' he faltered.

'*Wish!*' repeated his wife.

He raised his hand. 'I wish my son alive again.'

The talisman fell to the floor, and he regarded it fearfully. Then he sank trembling into a chair as the old woman, with burning eyes, walked to the window and raised the blind.

He sat until he was chilled with the cold, glancing occasionally at the figure of the old woman peering through the window. The candle-end, which had burned below the rim of the china candlestick, was throwing pulsating shadows on the ceiling and walls, until, with a flicker larger than the rest, it expired. The old man, with an unspeakable sense of relief at the failure of the talisman, crept back to his bed, and in a minute or two afterwards the old woman came silently and apathetically beside him.

Neither spoke, but lay silently listening to the ticking of the clock. A stair creaked, and a squeaky mouse scurried noisily through the wall. The darkness was oppressive, and after lying for some time screwing up his courage, he took the box of matches, and striking one, went downstairs for a candle.

At the foot of the stairs the match went out, and he paused to strike another; and at the same moment a knock, so quiet and stealthy as to be scarcely audible, sounded on the front door.

The matches fell from his hand and spilled in the passage. He stood motionless, his breath suspended until the knock was repeated. Then he turned and fled swiftly back to his room, and closed the door behind him. A third knock sounded through the house.

'*What's that?*' cried the old woman, starting up.

'A rat,' said the old man in shaking tones—'a rat. It passed me on the stairs.'

His wife sat up in bed listening. A loud knock resounded through the house.

'It's Herbert!' she screamed. 'It's Herbert!'

She ran to the door, but her husband was before her, and catching her by the arm, held her tightly.

'What are you going to do?' he whispered hoarsely.

'It's my boy; it's Herbert!' she cried, struggling mechanically. 'I forgot it was two miles away. What are you holding me for? Let go. I must open the door.'

'For God's sake don't let it in,' cried the old man, trembling.

'You're afraid of your own son,' she cried, struggling. 'Let me go. I'm coming, Herbert; I'm coming.'

There was another knock, and another. The old woman with a sudden wrench broke free and ran from the room. Her husband followed to the landing, and called after her appealingly as she hurried downstairs. He heard the chain rattle back and the bottom bolt drawn slowly and stiffly from the socket. Then the old woman's voice, strained and panting.

'The bolt,' she cried, loudly. 'Come down. I can't reach it.'

But her husband was on his knees groping wildly on the floor in search of the paw. If he could only find it before the thing outside got in. A perfect fusilade of knocks reverberated through the house, and he heard the scraping of a chair as his wife put it down in the passage against the door. He heard the creaking of the bolt as it came slowly back, and at the same moment he found the monkey's paw, and frantically breathed his third and last wish.

The knocking ceased suddenly, although the echoes of it were still in the house. He heard the chain drawn back, and the door opened. A cold wind rushed up the staircase, and a long loud wail of disappointment and misery from his wife gave him courage to run down to her side, and then to the gate beyond. The street lamp flickering opposite shone on a quiet deserted road.

THROUGH THE DOOR

Ruth Ainsworth

Maria was a fortunate little girl, and she knew this herself. Though she was an only child, and therefore a prey to the loneliness an only child experiences, she lived next door to such a large, warm, friendly family that she felt as though she had five brothers and sisters, instead of none.

Her closest friend was Clare, a girl of her own age, but Clare's four older brothers were important too. Mrs Cope, Clare's mother, often included Maria in family outings. She went with them to watch Jimmy in a swimming gala, and she joined in Paul's birthday treat which was a visit to an ice rink. Both Clare and she sometimes accompanied Charles on his bird-watching expeditions.

Charles took no notice of them, provided they lay perfectly still in the ditch, or reed bed, or wherever he had decreed they should freeze into immobility and silence. But they caught Charles' enthusiasm and felt it was all worth while to catch a glimpse of a green woodpecker or hear a grasshopper warbler.

Lance, the eldest, was already a man in Maria's eyes. He went to college, but was as kind-hearted as the rest of the family and he allowed Clare and Maria to sleep on the lawn in his new tent – after he had tried it out himself.

Then, out of the blue, came the terrible news that the Copes were leaving. Their house was up for sale and all was confusion and desolation. When the last furniture van drove off, Maria burst into tears which she had been restraining for weeks. She felt that she would never be happy again. Every day she and Clare had run in and out of each other's house freely. Now all this had come to a dead stop. For ever.

But even weeping must stop at last, and Maria found she could go to bed without the tears starting again. She tried having other friends to tea, but there seemed nothing to do to pass the time. Then her parents gave her a small black kitten and Midge, as he was called, did more than anyone else to make her cheerful. He was a particularly cheerful kitten.

It was many months, not a few weeks as she had hoped, before the first, longed-for, visit to Clare could be arranged, as there had been so much to do to the new house. At last she found herself in a train leaving Liverpool Street for Ipswich, where some of the Cope family would meet her, and drive her the rest of the way. As she settled herself in the corner of the carriage she was very conscious that it was her first long train journey alone, and though she felt excited rather than apprehensive, she was not relaxed as she would have been on a familiar bus ride.

She looked out of the window and tried to remember all she had heard about the new house from conversation or letters. Clare was a writer of long, detailed, many-paged letters that became creased and crumpled with many re-readings.

It had once been a small Elizabethan manor which had been much restored and modernized over the years. 'It's just a shell,' Lance said, 'with massive chimneys and a few original windows.'

'It's nothing if not old,' said Mrs Cope, 'with uneven floors and draughts, but it seemed to suit us. We liked the views and the garden and it just holds us all when everyone's home.'

'You're to share my bedroom,' Clare had written, 'and it's the best room in the house, with a secret staircase. I won't tell you any more as you'll soon see for yourself. But we can talk as long as we like in bed. No one knows what we are up to. It's a private room, and that's something I've never had before. My last bedroom had a fanlight and someone always noticed if I ever tried to read late.'

The moment she got out of the train at Ipswich, all sense of loss and absence melted away. The Copes were just exactly the same, but even nicer, such of them as had come to meet her. Mrs Cope greeted her as if she were a long-lost daughter, and Clare hugged and kissed her too. It was a real home-coming.

Charles carried her suitcase upstairs and told her, seriously, that she might hear a bittern booming if she were lucky. Clare hurried ahead and opened a door.

'We can manage now, Charles. I want to show Maria the rest of the house myself. Look, Maria, these wooden stairs are just for me. They only lead to my bedroom, well, to our bedroom now you're here. They're rather steep and slippery, or so I thought when I first went up them. But they seem ordinary enough now. Take care.'

Maria did find the narrow stairs steep and awkward and she felt inwardly glad that she was not going to sleep by herself, wherever they led. It was all too private, too strange, to her mind.

'All this is my very own,' said Clare triumphantly, as she flung open another narrow door at the top of the stairs. They went into a long, narrow, attic room, with low beams across the sloping ceiling. It was the oddest room that Maria had ever seen. Once it must have been dark and gloomy, a place of shadows and secrets. Now it had two large windows at floor level, and two beds with brightly coloured counterpanes, and several pieces of furniture that Maria remembered from the old house. A white painted chest of drawers. Several white chairs. A red toy box and a new desk and chair. All this Maria saw in the first few seconds. Other details she noticed afterwards.

'You've got a new desk. How lovely!'

'Yes. Mummy wanted me to be really comfy and quiet up here. I can do my prep if I want. Or write to you. She said the boys and their possessions spread all over the old house and it was time I had a room of my own, if I wanted to be out of everybody's way.'

'And do you ever want to be up here alone?'

'Sometimes I do and then it's bliss. Jimmy plays the same record for hours and hours and nearly drives us all mad and they all have their friends in more. That's because we live in the country. But I often do things downstairs with everyone else. It's nice being able to choose.

'This is the oldest bit of the house,' she went on. 'Or so Lance says.

He knows more about the place than anyone else. He says this is part of the original house. Come here. I'll show you.'

Clare opened a door at one end of the room and Maria peered inside. It was a long, low, oddly shaped cupboard and would have been pitch dark without a small, sloping skylight. It was now fitted out with hooks and a rail for coat-hangers. Clare's clothes hung there looking rather lost.

'There's lots of room for you and spare coat-hangers. Use what you want when you unpack.'

Maria unpacked and put her clothes in the secret cupboard. Then the girls went down to tea. The stairs seemed steeper than ever now Maria was going down them. She clung to the handrail every step of the way.

After tea, Maria said she must write a birthday card for her mother, which she had brought with her.

'Write it at my desk,' said Clare. 'You'll find stamps and everything you want.'

'All right. I will.'

Maria liked the idea of using the new desk. She found her way up to the landing and opened the door that led to the stairs. As she went into the room, she was surprised to find she was not alone. She heard no definite sound, but she knew someone had followed her into the attic. She turned round quickly. Close behind her, only a foot or so away, was another girl. This other girl showed no surprise. She seemed so calm and composed that it might have been her room, and Maria the intruder. She was tall and pale, wearing a striped dress, and carrying a pewter plate and mug.

'Who are you?' asked Maria.

'I'm Tabitha.' She offered no apology or explanation for her presence. Maria felt more like a trespasser.

'What – what are you doing?' She looked at the plate and the mug. Tabitha looked slightly surprised at this obvious question and raised her eyebrows, but she replied gently:

'Taking Father Simon his supper.'

Then, to Maria's horror and amazement, Tabitha and her plate walked right through the solid wooden door of the hanging cupboard, and disappeared. Maria fancied she heard the faint murmur of two voices, Tabitha's clear, childish one and a man's deeper tone. She did not wait to hear more, but fled to the comfort of the ground floor. She skimmed down the steep stairs as if in a dream, not feeling the wooden treads. Something in her face brought Clare quickly to her side.

'Are you all right? What is it?'

'Can we talk somewhere?' whispered Maria. 'Now.'

'I'll just show Maria the garden,' said Clare loudly, and taking her friend's arm she hurried her out of doors. Maria only waited for the door to close behind them to say urgently:

'Clare, I saw something. I saw a ghost in your room. I know I did. I'm certain.'

'Was it a fair haired girl?'

Maria's face fell, but she reacted instantly.

'Oh Clare, so you knew all the time. Why ever didn't you tell me if you knew about her? How could you just leave me alone to discover her for myself? We used to share everything.'

Clare squeezed her arm and said warmly:

'It wasn't really a bit like that. Of course I was going to tell you about the ghost – I was longing to – but we've hardly had a minute together since you arrived, without other people milling around. It was rather sad, or so I think now. I once passed a girl with fair hair on the secret staircase. We neither of us said a word. I was far too frightened to speak first. I looked back and saw her reach the door into the attic and just pass through it like air, and disappear.'

'Did you tell anyone?'

'I told Mummy and she told Daddy. They were both very serious and disbelieving. They explained so patiently that I couldn't have seen anything, because there wasn't anything there. When they heard I'd looked back and seen the girl on the stairs they said that proved the whole thing was impossible as it would have been too dark. They went on and on showing me how impossible it was. Then they suggested I swopped rooms with one of the boys if I thought I might feel creepy up there alone.'

'What did you say?' asked Maria.

'Of course I refused. I knew that Jimmy would change with me like a flash, but I wasn't going to give up my lovely bedroom for anything. I said perhaps I'd imagined it and just laid low. I rather think they may have forgotten about it by now.'

'But you haven't forgotten?'

'No, and I never will.'

The girls had a cheerful evening playing a new card game with Jimmy and Paul which involved a great deal of shouting and laughing and slapping down of cards. They went to bed quickly and neither mentioned ghosts. Clare only said as she got into bed:

'The bedside lamp is between us. You just press this to put it on. And the main switch is in the corner.'

'Thanks,' said Maria, snuggling down.

For three days nothing happened that wasn't pleasant and ordinary and like old times. They bird-watched with Charles. Cycled miles down the quiet lanes with Maria on one of the boys' old bicycles. Went shopping. Had a winter picnic. Then, on the third night, Maria woke up and breathed deeply. She smelt a queer unusual smell. In a second she was wide awake.

'Clare, wake up, do! I think the house is on fire.'

She stretched out an arm and shook Clare, screaming in her ear. Clare woke.

'What's wrong? Are you ill?'

'No. Just smell. Smell hard. Is it smoke?'

'Let's put the light on.'

They both groped for the button on the lamp, but though it was only a few inches away neither could find it. Maria jumped out of bed and felt for the main switch, but her fingers scrabbled on plain wall. That had vanished too. Choking with terror she found her way to Clare's bed and clung to her. Then came the tinkle of a little bell.

The air cleared and they found the switch for the light. Everything was quiet and normal except for a very faint odour, so faint that it seemed to come and go as they breathed.

'Nothing's on fire,' said Clare comfortingly. She opened the door at the top of the stairs. 'No smell coming up. You poor, poor thing. Did you dream we were being burned alive?'

'There was something peculiar,' insisted Maria. 'It woke me. It nearly choked me. Then, when the little bell rang, it seemed to go. It reminds me of something.'

They soon fell asleep and in the morning, when Mrs Cope asked if they had had a good night, they looked at each other before answering. Then Clare said:

'It would have been good if Maria hadn't dreamed the house was on fire, and shouted in my ear. We soon got off again.'

The next night it was Clare who woke, but not in terror. She touched Maria gently and whispered:

'Open your eyes and keep quiet.'

Maria opened sleepy eyes and saw, at once, that the room was no longer dark. At the far end of the attic, furthest from their beds, was a faint glow. It was the soft, flickering light of several candles. A company of strangely dressed people were gathered in silence before a table spread with a white cloth, with a silver cross above it. Both girls knew it to be an altar. A dark robed priest murmured some words in an unfamiliar tongue. There was the tinkle of a bell. The priest raised his arms. The same queer smell pervaded the room.

'Incense,' breathed Clare.

Maria nodded.

Then came a great thundering outside and a pounding on a wooden door. There was shouting and they heard the words: 'We are betrayed. The Queen's men are at hand.'

At once all was dark. The candles had been blown out instantly. They heard the confused sounds of feet, of furniture being moved, of muffled orders. It was like a rapid scene shifting, well rehearsed. Both girls felt for the switch of the lamp and one of them found it. Light sprang up and they saw, at a glance, that the scene at the far end of the attic had changed. People – candles – altar – silver cross – all had vanished. The dolls' house and the toy chest were back in their places, with the rugs and pictures.

The knocking had stopped and the voices were quiet, but the room still seemed to echo with the thud, thud, on the heavy door.

Though the girls had not been involved in the strange scene, except as spectators, they were both thoroughly disturbed. Their hearts beat quickly and when Clare whispered: 'Let's get out of here,' her voice sounded husky and unnatural, as if her throat were dry. They slid rather than ran down the steep stairs, clinging tightly to the banister, and when they were both safely on the landing, they burst through the nearest door. To Maria it was literally any door as she had not sorted out the various rooms on that floor, and to Clare it meant only that it was the nearest.

It turned out to be Lance's room. He woke at the click of the old-fashioned latch, and switched on his bedside lamp, apparently wide awake in an instant.

'What on earth are you two doing in the middle of the night?' he inquired calmly. 'Have you seen a ghost?'

'Oh Lance,' said Clare thankfully, 'that's just what we have seen. Several ghosts.'

'Both of you?' asked Lance.

'Yes. Both of us together.'

'If two people have seen a ghost it deserves investigation,' went on Lance. 'Serious investigation. And if the ghosts were plural it's even more serious. But we may as well investigate in comfort.'

He turned on the electric fire, and indicated that they were both to sit down on the sofa, and he took his eiderdown off his bed and tucked it cosily over their knees. The warmth and comfort, and Lance's normal, matter-of-fact tone, worked wonders. Someone was taking them seriously, neither panicking nor doubting. Just listening and believing.

'Now tell me everything, every single thing.' Lance ran his fingers through his mop of hair, and sat down opposite, his elbows on his knees, and chin on his clasped hands.

'We smelt a funny smell,' said Maria, 'both of us.'

'It was incense,' corrected Clare, 'though I did not recognize it at first, but it was incense, I'm sure. We woke up, or rather I woke up, and nudged Maria. She woke at once, and we found the room wasn't dark and at the far end a service was going on.'

'It was a Mass,' said Maria. 'They had a priest in white robes and a table made into an altar and a silver cross hanging above.'

'And they rang a little bell,' put in Clare, 'and chanted.'

'It was so secret and solemn,' went on Maria. 'It was beautiful and peaceful till the hammering on the door began, several people hammering with their fists and shouting.'

'It didn't seem to be on our ordinary door, either, not on the one we always use near our beds. It sounded as if it were at the far end of the room,' said Clare. 'What did you think, Maria?'

'Yes, it wasn't close enough to be on our door. You're right. The voices shouting the warning were far away too. A loud voice said: "We are betrayed. The Queen's men are here".'

'Not *here*,' corrected Clare. '*At hand*. The Queen's men are at hand. And then there was more knocking.'

'Yes, you're right, Clare. I remember now.'

Lance listened to every word and when there was a pause, he spoke: 'Queen Elizabeth the First was a Protestant and passed a law forbidding the saying of Mass. But many Catholic families made elaborate arrangements to worship in secret. There were Catholic carpenters about who, under cover of doing some alterations to the house, devised secret hiding places where a priest could be concealed. They were called priest holes. Then, usually at night, the priest ventured out to say the forbidden Mass and often neighbours and friends stole through the dark countryside to join them. Attics were sometimes changed into temporary chapels.'

'Where did they make the priest holes?' asked Clare.

'Oh, in secret cupboards and behind panelling and often in the chimney.'

'Wasn't it too hot for the poor priest?' inquired Maria.

'I don't think he *lived* in the chimney. It was a good hiding place if the Queen's men were on the prowl, searching out priests and disobedient Catholics. A man called Thomas Phillips, cunning as a fox, led the searches. He could decipher codes and his spies were everywhere, measuring buildings and tapping walls to find secret rooms.'

'What happened when the priests and the Catholics were caught?'

'The priests were often put to death and the Catholics heavily fined. They might be put to death as well.'

'Was my bedroom cupboard a priest hole?' asked Clare, her eyes never leaving Lance's face.

'It might easily have been. They were often built in gables. It might even have had an inner room to deceive the searchers. They wouldn't suspect another secret place if they'd found the first one.'

'Shall we investigate inside my cupboard and see what we can find? Let's start now.' Clare jumped up eagerly.

'Are you both agreed over what you've told me? Did either of you see or hear anything the other didn't?'

They shook their heads.

'Oh no, Lance. We were together so of course we saw the same things. And heard the same things. We were as wide awake as – well, as we are now.'

'Then what happened?' said Lance encouragingly.

'Then they swept everything away like lightning,' said Clare, 'or I suppose that's what they did. They blew out the candles first of all, so we couldn't watch what they were doing. They were so quick that they must have had lots of practice. They must have rehearsed it.'

'I do hope they weren't caught,' said Maria. 'They weren't doing any harm. There were some children at the service and Father Simon was like a real father, caring for his family.'

'Who was Father Simon?' asked Lance, quick as a flash. 'You haven't told me about him.'

Clare first, then Maria afterwards, related their earlier meetings with Tabitha, carrying Father Simon's supper.

'You hadn't mentioned Tabitha to Maria before she saw her herself?' asked Lance, addressing Clare.

'No, I told you I hadn't,' said Clare impatiently. 'I was longing to tell her but we hadn't been alone together for a minute. And she was much braver than me. She spoke to Tabitha and found out her name and actually asked her what she was doing.'

'I was a bit puzzled, but she seemed so real and ordinary,' explained Maria, 'except for her old fashioned clothes. I wasn't frightened. It was when she and her supper tray walked right through the cupboard door that I was scared. Then I knew she was someone different. A ghost, in fact.'

'You're lucky girls to see a ghost – lots of ghosts. I wish I'd had the chance,' said Lance. 'Now would you like to finish the night in my bed and I'll go up to the attic, or are you all right?'

The girls looked at each other, but neither wanted to be the first to admit she felt uneasy. Anyhow, there were two of them.

'I'll go back to my own bed, Lance, thank you,' said Clare.

'And so will I,' added Maria.

'O.K.,' said Lance cheerfully. 'You can leave your bedside lamp on for company, if you like, and I'll leave my door open. But I don't think you'll see or hear anything else tonight. If you do, just call and I'll be up the stairs in a jiffy.'

Though the girls were sure they would lie awake all night, it was only a few minutes before sleep overcame them. They heard nothing more till morning, not even Lance's bare feet as he padded upstairs to make sure they had dropped off. He, himself, puzzled and pondered between fitful dozes.

Though Lance and the girls had made no arrangements to keep the night's events to themselves, they did not mention them to the rest of the family. Lance had been more impressed than he had shown by Clare's determination to keep Tabitha's second appearance from her parents, once she had experienced their sympathetic disbelief, and had realized that the possession of her bedroom was at stake, the bedroom she prized so highly. He was also impressed by Maria's attitude. She's got her head screwed on the right way, he thought to himself. Only children aren't all soft and silly. She's a cool customer, for a start.

During the day, while the younger boys were out on their bicycles and Charles had disappeared with his binoculars, Lance invited the girls to come to his room, which was warm and comfortable, though small. The table was covered with books and papers as he often studied up there.

'I'll tell you a few facts I've collected about the time when this house was built. You'll see why, if you listen.'

They fixed their eyes on him, unwaveringly, and did not fidget or interrupt. An idea crossed his mind that he wouldn't mind teaching children, one day, if they listened like these two, absorbing every syllable.

'Yes, we might take some measurements later on. I don't think Dad would stand for any more walls being pulled down. The alterations have cost too much already. But he couldn't object to peaceful measuring and checking.'

By some mysterious process, never perfectly understood, the other boys were soon caught up in the possibility of there being a priest hole actually in the house, just waiting to be discovered. The children swarmed all over the building with rulers and tape measures, measuring every nook and cranny, and tapping the woodwork like demented woodpeckers, listening for a hollow sound. As they soon found out, many wooden surfaces gave back a hollow note if tapped often enough, with sufficient force. But Lance's respect for the fabric of the house kept them from using tools which could do damage.

'Stick to accurate measuring,' he advised. 'Be scientific. Write it all down. When we get a water-tight case for the existence of a priest hole, then that's the time for the next step. Let's be sure of our facts first.'

A black notebook was produced with PRIEST HOLES written on the cover, and all measurements, scientific or otherwise, were inscribed inside in Lance's spidery writing.

'Whatever the children are doing is keeping them quiet and out of the way,' said Mr Cope with satisfaction.

'It's all Lance,' said his wife. 'I never thought he took much notice of the younger ones, but I was wrong. Clare and Maria never willingly leave him alone. I heard he'd had to lock his door the other day to get some of his own work done.'

'He started the notion of a priest hole and now it's everyone's idea. They are all dead keen on finding one. They talk learnedly about secret Masses and codes and hiding places,' went on Mr Cope. 'Just look at that!' He opened the window and stuck his head out.

'Don't lean out so far, Jimmy,' he shouted, as he looked upward.

'I'm all right, Daddy. Charles has got hold of my feet. I really believe I may be on to something.'

A steel measure waved wildly from a landing window.

'I've dropped it again. You go and fetch it, Charles. I can see it shining in that laurel bush.'

'Fetch it yourself. You let go of it.'

'But I fetched your biro last time you dropped it.'

'Fair's fair.'

Mr Cope withdrew his head and slammed the sitting room window shut.

If they could have listened to a conversation taking place in another part of the house, Mr and Mrs Cope would have been surprised.

'If only we knew that they weren't caught, that night, and that Father Simon wasn't killed,' said Maria. 'But we never shall. I asked Lance if there would be anyone on guard and he said yes, of course.

There would always be a look-out. They might have given the warning in time. The sound of distant hoofs – a dog barking – an unexpected light – a little would have been enough to put them on the alert. After all, their lives were at stake.'

There was a pause. Then Clare spoke.

'We shan't see anything again, I know we shan't. It's happened. It won't happen again, ever. I keep wondering why you and I were given that ghostly glimpse of the past. We were so ignorant. So unsuitable.'

'Now I don't agree with you,' contradicted Maria. 'In one way we were very well chosen, apart from being actually on the spot. I think ghosts are often lonely. Tabitha must have felt very drawn to you, as a girl like herself, to allow herself to be seen at all. I was too surprised, as it happened, to be really scared so I was able to speak to her. And she replied quietly and naturally. It may have been many years since a living person spoke to her, poor girl. I've heard that ghosts only show themselves to people who believe in them.'

'I'm thankful I was frightened silently,' said Clare, who couldn't forgive herself for being frightened at all. 'You always hear of people screaming and screeching when they see a ghost. Tabitha may not have known that I was petrified,' she went on more cheerfully. 'I didn't utter a word. I do so hope she didn't known, or guess.'

The two girls acquired a good knowledge of priests and priest holes. They read books lent by Lance, and Maria read many more when she got home, helped by a friendly librarian. But she kept discussion of their strange experiences for times, in the holidays, when she and Clare were together and never mentioned it to other friends or even to her parents. Over the years, Tabitha became an intimate and friendly figure in their memories, like someone met on a journey, and never forgotten.

MAN-SIZE IN MARBLE

E. Nesbit

Although every word of this story is as true as despair, I do not expect people to believe it. Nowadays a 'rational explanation' is required before belief is possible. Let me, then, at once offer the 'rational explanation' which finds most favour among those who have heard the tale of my life's tragedy. It is held that we were 'under a delusion', Laura and I, on that 31st of October; and that this supposition places the whole matter on a satisfactory and believable basis. The reader can judge, when he, too, has heard my story, how far this is an 'explanation', and in what sense it is 'rational'. There were three who took part in this: Laura and I and another man. The other man still lives, and can speak to the truth of the least credible part of my story.

I never in my life knew what it was to have as much money as I required to supply the most ordinary needs—good colours, books, and cab-fares—and when we were married we knew quite well that we should only be able to live at all by 'strict punctuality and attention to business'. I used to paint in those days, and Laura used to write, and we felt sure we could keep the pot at least simmering. Living in town was out of the question, so we went to look for a cottage in the country, which should be at once sanitary and picturesque. So rarely do these two qualities meet in one cottage that our search was for some time quite fruitless. But when we got away from friends and house-agents, on our honeymoon, our wits grew clear again, and we knew a pretty cottage when at last we saw one.

It was at Brenzett—a little village set on a hill over against the southern marshes. We had gone there, from the seaside village where we were staying, to see the church, and two fields from the church we found this cottage. It stood quite by itself, about two miles from the village. It was a long, low building, with rooms sticking out in unexpected places. There was a bit of stonework—ivy-covered and moss-grown, just two old rooms, all that was left of a big house that had once stood there—and round this stonework the house had grown up. Stripped of its roses and jasmine it would have been hideous. As it stood it was charming, and after a brief examination we took it. It was absurdly cheap. There was a jolly old-fashioned garden, with grass paths, and no end of hollyhocks and sunflowers, and big lilies. From the window you could see the marsh-pastures, and beyond them the blue, thin line of the sea.

We got a tall old peasant woman to do for us. Her face and figure were good, though her cooking was of the homeliest; but she understood all about gardening, and told us all the old names of the coppices and cornfields, and the stories of the smugglers and highwaymen, and, better still, of the 'things that walked', and of the 'sights' which met one in lonely glens of a starlight night. We soon came to leave all the domestic business to Mrs Dorman, and to use her legends in little magazine stories which brought in the jingling guinea.

We had three months of married happiness, and did not have a single quarrel. One October evening I had been down to smoke a pipe with the doctor—our only neighbour—a pleasant young Irishman. Laura had stayed at home to finish a comic sketch. I left her laughing over her own jokes, and came in to find her a crumpled heap of pale muslin, weeping on the window seat.

'Good heavens, my darling, what's the matter?' I cried, taking her in my arms.

'What is the matter? Do speak.'

'It's Mrs Dorman,' she sobbed.

'What has she done?' I inquired, immensely relieved.

'She says she must go before the end of the month, and she says her niece is ill; she's gone down to see her now, but I don't believe that's the reason, because her niece is always ill. I believe someone has been setting her against us. Her manner was so queer—'

'Never mind, Pussy,' I said; 'whatever you do, don't cry, or I shall have to cry to keep you in countenance, and then you'll never respect your man again.'

'But you see,' she went on, 'it is really serious, because these village people are so sheepy, and if one won't do a thing you may be quite sure none of the others will. And I shall have to cook the dinners and wash up the hateful greasy plates; and you'll have to carry cans of water about and clean the boots and knives—and we shall never have any time for work or earn any money or anything.'

I represented to her that even if we had to perform these duties the day would still present some margin for other toils and recreations. But she refused to see the matter in any but the greyest light.

'I'll speak to Mrs Dorman when she comes back, and see if I can't come to terms with her,' I said. 'Perhaps she wants a rise in her screw. It will be all right. Let's walk up to the church.'

The church was a large and lonely one, and we loved to go there, especially upon bright nights. The path skirted a wood, cut through it once, and ran along the crest of the hill through two meadows, and round the churchyard wall, over which the old yews loomed in black masses of shadow.

This path, which was partly paved, was called 'the bier-walk', for it had long been the way by which the corpses had been carried to burial. The churchyard was richly treed, and was shaded by great elms which stood just outside and stretched their majestic arms in benediction of the happy dead. A large, low porch let one into the building by a Norman doorway and a heavy oak door studded with iron. Inside, the arches rose into darkness, and between them the reticulated windows, which stood out white in the moonlight. In the chancel, the windows were of rich glass, which showed in faint light their noble colouring, and made the black oak of the choir pews hardly more solid than the shadows. But on each side of the altar lay a grey marble figure of a knight in full plate armour lying upon a low slab, with hands held up in everlasting prayer, and these figures, oddly enough, were always to be seen if there was any glimmer of light in the church. Their names were lost, but the peasants told of them that they had been fierce and wicked men, marauders by land and sea, who had been the scourge of their time, and had been guilty of deeds so foul that the house they had lived in—the big house, by the way, that had stood on the site of our cottage—had been stricken by lightning and the vengeance of Heaven. But for all that, the gold of their heirs had brought them a place in the church. Looking at the bad, hard faces reproduced in the marble, this story was easily believed.

The church looked at its best and weirdest on that night, for the shadows of the yew tree fell through the windows upon the floor of the nave and touched the pillars with tattered shade. We sat down together without speaking, and watched the solemn beauty of the old church with some of that awe which inspired its early builders. We walked to the chancel and looked at the sleeping warriors. Then we rested some time on the stone seat in the porch, looking out over the stretch of quiet moonlit meadows, feeling in every fibre of our being the peace of the night and of our happy love; and came away at last with a sense that even scrubbing and black-leading were but small troubles at their worst.

Mrs Dorman had come back from the village, and I at once invited her to a tête-à-tête.

'Now, Mrs Dorman,' I said, when I had got her into my painting room, 'what's all this about your not staying with us?'

'I should be glad to get away, sir, before the end of the month,' she answered, with her usual placid dignity.

'Have you any fault to find, Mrs Dorman?'

'None at all, sir: you and your lady have always been most kind I'm sure—'

'Well, what is it? Are your wages not high enough?'

'No, sir, I gets quite enough.'

'Then why not stay?'

'I'd rather not—with some hesitation—'my niece is ill.'

'But your niece has been ill ever since we came. Can't you stay for another month?'

'No, sir, I'm bound to go by Thursday.'

And this was Monday!

'Well, I must say, I think you might have let us know before. There's no time now to get anyone else, and your mistress is not fit to do heavy housework. Can't you stay till next week?'

'I might be able to come back next week.'

'But why must you go this week?' I persisted. 'Come, out with it.'

Mrs Dorman drew the little shawl, which she always wore, tightly across her bosom, as though she were cold. Then she said, with a sort of effort:

'They say, sir, as this was a big house in Catholic times, and there was a many deeds done here.'

The nature of the 'deeds' might be vaguely inferred from the inflection of Mrs Dorman's voice—which was enough to make one's blood run cold. I was glad that Laura was not in the room. She was always nervous, as highly-strung natures are, and I felt that these tales about our house, told by this old peasant woman, with her impressive manner and contagious credulity, might have made our home less dear to my wife.

'Tell me all about it, Mrs Dorman,' I said; 'you needn't mind about telling me. I'm not like the young people who make fun of such things.'

Which was partly true.

'Well, sir'—she sank her voice—'you may have seen in the church, beside the altar, two shapes.'

'You mean the effigies of the knights in armour,' I said cheerfully.

'I mean them two bodies, drawed out man-size in marble,' she returned, and I had to admit that her description was a thousand times more graphic than mine, to say nothing of a certain weird force and uncanniness about the phrase 'drawed out man-size in marble.'

'They do say, as on All Saints' Eve them two bodies sits up on their slabs, and gets off them, and then walks down the aisle, *in their marble*' —another good phrase, Mrs Dorman)—'and as the church clock strikes eleven they walks out of the church door, and over the graves, and along the bier-walk, and if it's a wet night there's the marks of their feet in the morning.'

'And where do they go?' I asked, rather fascinated.

'They comes back here to their home, sir, and if anyone meets them—'

'Well, what then?' I asked.

But no—not another word could I get from her, save that her niece was ill and she must go.

'Whatever you do, sir, lock the door early on All Saints' Eve, and make the cross-sign over the doorstep and on the windows.'

'But has anyone ever seen these things?' I persisted. 'Who was here last year?'

'No one, sir; the lady as owned the house only stayed here in summer, and she always went to London a full month afore *the* night. And I'm sorry to inconvenience you and your lady, but my niece is ill and I must go on Thursday.'

I could have shaken her for her absurd reiteration of that obvious fiction, after she had told me her real reasons.

I did not tell Laura the legend of the shapes that 'walked in their marble', partly because a legend concerning our house might perhaps trouble my wife, and partly, I think, from some more occult reason. This was not quite the same to me as any other story, and I did not want to talk about it till the day it was over I had very soon ceased to think of the legend, however. I was painting a portrait of Laura, against the lattice window, and I could not think of much else. I had got a splendid background of yellow and grey sunset, and was working away with enthusiasm at her face. On Thursday Mrs Dorman went. She relented, at parting, so far as to say:

'Don't you put yourself about too much, ma'am, and if there's any little thing I can do next week I'm sure I shan't mind.'

Thursday passed off pretty well. Friday came. It is about what happened on that Friday that this is written.

I got up early, I remember, and lighted the kitchen fire, and had just achieved a smoky success when my little wife came running down as sunny and sweet as the clear October morning itself. We prepared breakfast together, and found it very good fun. The housework was soon done, and when brushes and brooms and pails were quiet again the house was still indeed. Is it wonderful what a difference one makes in a house. We really missed Mrs Dorman, quite apart from considerations concerning pots and pans. We spent the day in dusting our books and putting them straight, and dined gaily on cold steak and coffee. Laura was, if possible, brighter and gayer and sweeter than usual, and I began to think that a little domestic toil was really good for her. We had never been so merry since we were married, and the walk we had that afternoon was, I think, the happiest time of all my life. When we had watched the deep scarlet clouds slowly pale into leaden grey against a pale green sky and saw the white mists curl up along the hedgerows in the distant marsh we came back to the house hand in hand.

'You are sad, my darling,' I said, half-jestingly, as we sat down together in our little parlour. I expected a disclaimer, for my own silence had been the silence of complete happiness. To my surprise she said:

'Yes, I think I am sad, or, rather, I am uneasy. I don't think I'm very well. I have shivered three or four times since we came in; and it is not cold, is it?

'No,' I said, and hoped it was not a chill caught from the treacherous mists that roll up from the marshes in the dying night. No—she said, she did not think so. Then, after a silence, she spoke suddenly:

'Do you ever have presentiments of evil?'

'No,' I said, smiling, 'and I shouldn't believe in them if I had.'

'I do,' she went on; 'the night my father died I knew it, though he was right away in the North of Scotland.' I did not answer in words.

She sat looking at the fire for some time in silence, gently stroking my hand. At last she sprang up, came behind me, and, drawing my head back, kissed me.

'There, it's over now,' she said. 'What a baby I am! Come, light the candles, and we'll have some of these new Rubenstein duets.'

And we spent a happy hour or two at the piano.

At about half-past ten I began to long for the goodnight pipe, but Laura looked so white that I felt it would be brutal of me to fill our sitting-room with the fumes of strong cavendish.

'I'll take my pipe outside,' I said.

'Let me come, too.'

'No, sweetheart, not tonight; you're much too tired. I shan't be long. Go to bed, or I shall have an invalid to nurse tomorrow as well as the boots to clean.'

I kissed her and was turning to go when she flung her arms round my neck and held me as if she would never let me go again. I stroked her hair.

'Come, Pussy, you're over-tired. The housework has been too much for you.'

She loosened her clasp a little and drew a deep breath.

'No. We've been very happy today, Jack, haven't we? Don't stay out too long.'

'I won't, my dearie.'

I strolled out of the front door, leaving it unlatched. What a night it was! The jagged masses of heavy dark cloud were rolling at intervals from horizon to horizon, and thin white wreaths covered the stars. Through all the rush of the cloud river the moon swam, breasting the waves and disappearing again in the darkness.

I walked up and down, drinking in the beauty of the quiet earth and the changing sky. The night was absolutely silent. Nothing seemed to be abroad. There was no skurrying of rabbits, or twitter of the half-asleep birds. And though the clouds went sailing across the sky, the wind that drove them never came low enough to rustle the dead leaves in the woodland paths. Across the meadows I could see the church tower standing out black and grey against the sky. I walked there thinking over our three months of happiness.

I heard a bell-beat from the church. Eleven already! I turned to go in, but the night held me. I could not go back into our little warm rooms yet. I would go up to the church.

I looked in at the low window as I went by. Laura was half-lying on her chair in front of the fire. I could not see her face, only her little head showed dark against the pale blue wall. She was quite still. Asleep, no doubt.

I walked slowly along the edge of the wood. A sound broke the stillness of the night, it was a rustling in the wood. I stopped and listened. The sound stopped too. I went on, and now distinctly heard another step than mine answer mine like an echo. It was a poacher or a wood-stealer, most likely, for these were not unknown in our Arcadian neighbourhood. But whoever it was, he was a fool not to step more lightly. I turned into the wood and now the footstep seemed to come from the path I had just left. It must be an echo, I thought. The wood looked perfect in the moonlight. The large dying ferns and the brushwood showed where through thinning foliage the pale light came down. The tree trunks stood up like Gothic columns all around me.

They reminded me of the church, and I turned into the bier-walk, and passed through the corpse-gate between the graves to the low porch.

I paused for a moment on the stone seat where Laura and I had watched the fading landscape. Then I noticed that the door of the church was open, and I blamed myself for having left it unlatched the other night. We were the only people who ever cared to come to the church except on Sundays, and I was vexed to think that through our carelessness the damp autumn airs had had a chance of getting in and injuring the old fabric. I went in. It will seem strange, perhaps, that I should have gone halfway up the aisle before I remembered—with a sudden chill, followed by as sudden a rush of self-contempt—that this was the very day and hour when, according to tradition, the 'shapes drawed out man-size in marble' began to walk.

Having thus remembered the legend, and remembered it with a shiver, of which I was ashamed, I could not do otherwise than walk up towards the altar, just to look at the figures—as I said to myself; really what I wanted was to assure myself, first, that I did not believe the legend, and, secondly, that it was not true. I was rather glad that I had come. I thought now I could tell Mrs Dorman how vain her fancies were, and how peacefully the marble figures slept on through the ghastly hour. With my hands in my pockets I passed up the aisle. In the grey dim light the eastern end of the church looked larger than usual, and the arches above the two tombs looked larger too. The moon came out and showed me the reason. I stopped short, my heart gave a leap that nearly choked me, and then sank sickeningly.

The 'bodies drawed out man-size' *were gone*! and their marble slabs lay wide and bare in the vague moonlight that slanted through the east window.

Were they really gone, or was I mad? Clenching my nerves, I stooped and passed my hand over the smooth slabs, and felt their flat unbroken surface. Had someone taken the things away? Was it some vile practical joke? I would make sure, anyway. In an instant I had made a torch of a newspaper, which happened to be in my pocket, and, lighting it, held it high above my head. Its yellow glare illumined the dark arches and those slabs. The figures *were* gone. And I was alone in the church; or was I alone?

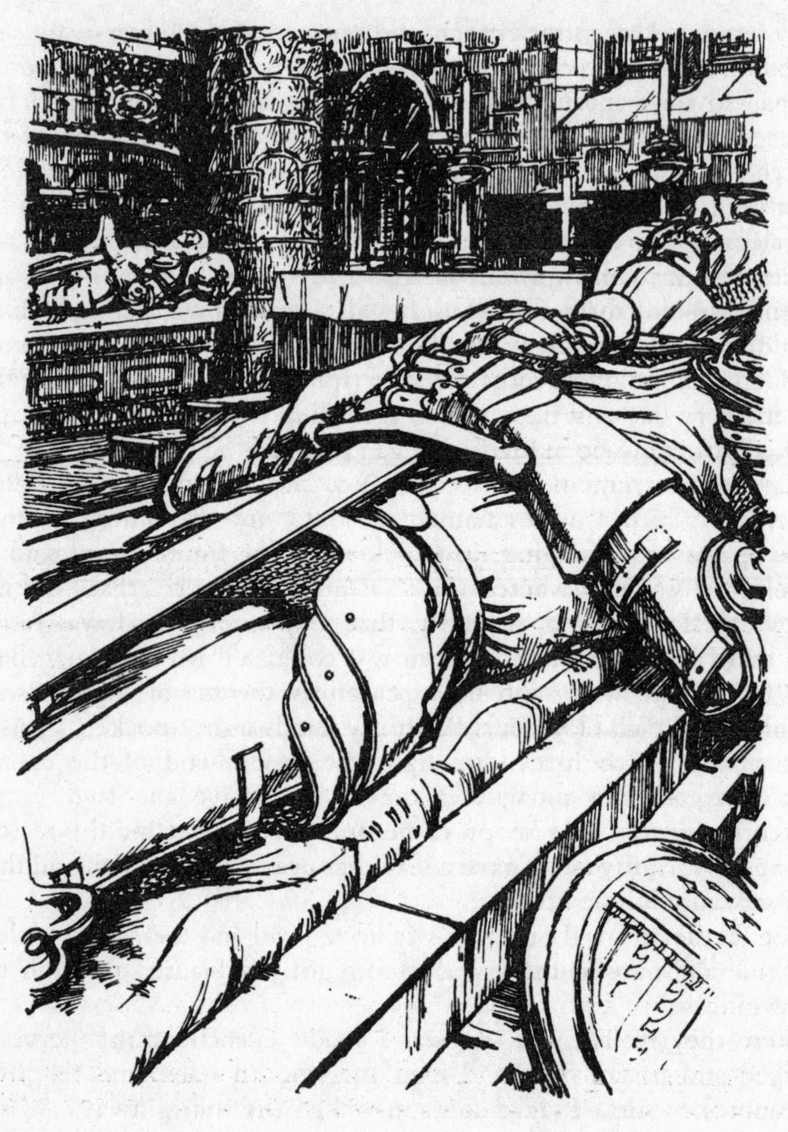

Each side of the altar lay a grey marble figure of a knight

And then a horror seized me, a horror indefinable and indescribable—an overwhelming certainty of supreme and accomplished calamity. I flung down the torch and tore along the aisle and out through the porch, biting my lips as I ran to keep myself from shrieking aloud. Oh, was I mad—or what was this that possessed me? I leaped the churchyard wall and took the straight cut across the fields, led by the light from our windows. Just as I got over the first stile a dark figure seemed to spring out of the ground. Mad still with that certainty of misfortune, I made for the thing that stood in my path, shouting, 'Get out of the way, can't you!'

But my push met with a more vigorous resistance than I had expected. My arms were caught just above the elbow and held as in a vice, and the raw-boned Irish doctor actually shook me.

'Let me go, you fool,' I gasped. 'The marble figures have gone from the church; I tell you they've gone.'

He broke into a ringing laugh. 'I'll have to give ye a draught to-morrow, I see. Ye've been smoking too much and listening to old wives' tales.'

'I tell you I've seen he bare slabs.'

'Well, come back with me. I'm going up to old Palmer's—his daughter's ill; we'll look in at the church and let me see the bare slabs.'

'You go, if you like,' I said, a little less frantic for his laughter; 'I'm going home to my wife.'

'Rubbish man,' said he; 'd'ye think I'll permit that? Are ye to go saying all yer life that ye've seen solid marble endowed with vitality, and me to go all me life saying ye were a coward? No, sir—ye shan't do ut.'

The night air—a human voice—and I think also the physical contact with this six feet of solid common sense, brought me back a little to my ordinary self, and the word 'coward' was a mental shower-bath.

'Come on, then,' I said sullenly; 'perhaps you're right.'

He still held my arm tightly. We got over the stile and back to the church. All was still as death. The place smelt very damp and earthy. We walked up the aisle. I am not ashamed to confess that I shut my eyes: I knew the figures would not be there. I heard Kelly strike a match.

'Here they are, ye see, right enough; ye've been dreaming or drinking, asking yer pardon for the imputation.'

I opened my eyes. By Kelly's expiring vesta I saw two shapes lying 'in their marble' on their slabs. I drew a deep breath.

'I'm awfully indebted to you,' I said. 'It must have been some trick of light, or I have been working rather hard, perhaps that's it. I was quite convinced they were gone.'

'I'm aware of that,' he answered rather grimly; 'ye'll have to be careful of that brain of yours, my friend, I assure ye.'

He was leaning over and looking at the right-hand figure, whose stony face was the most villainous and deadly in expression.

'By jove,' he said, 'something has been afoot here—this hand is broken.'

And so it was. I was certain that it had been perfect the last time Laura and I had been there.

'Perhaps someone has *tried* to remove them,' said the young doctor.

'Come along,' I said, 'or my wife will be getting anxious. You'll come in and have a drop of whisky and drink confusion to ghosts and better sense to me.'

'I ought to go up to Palmer's, but it's so late now I'd best leave it till the morning,' he replied.

I think he fancied I needed him more than did Palmer's girl, so, discussing how such an illusion could have been possible, and deducing from this experience large generalities concerning ghostly apparitions, we walked up to our cottage. We saw, as we walked up the garden path, that bright light streamed out of the front door, and presently saw that the parlour door was open, too. Had she gone out?

'Come in,' I said, and Dr Kelly followed me into the parlour. It was all ablaze with candles, not only the wax ones, but at least a dozen guttering, glaring tallow dips, stuck in vases and ornaments in unlikely places. Light, I knew, was Laura's remedy for nervousness. Poor child! Why had I left her? Brute that I was.

We glanced round the room, and at first we did not see her. The window was open, and the draught set all the candles flaring one way. Her chair was empty and her handkerchief and book lay on the floor. I turned to the window. There, in the recess of the window, I saw her. Oh, my child, my love, had she gone to that window to watch for me? And what had come into the room behind her? To what had she turned with that look of frantic fear and horror? Oh, my little one, had she thought that it was I whose step she heard, and turned to meet—what?

She had fallen back across a table in the window, and her body lay half on it and half on the window-seat, and her head hung down over the table, the brown hair loosened and fallen to the carpet. Her lips were drawn back, and here eyes wide, wide open. They saw nothing now. What had they seen last?

The doctor moved towards her, but I pushed him aside and sprang to her; caught her in my arms and cried:

'It's all right, Laura! I've got you safe, wifie.'

She fell into my arms in a heap. I clasped her and kissed her, and called her by all her pet names, but I think I knew all the time that she was dead. Her hands were tightly clenched. In one of them she held something fast. When I was quite sure that she was dead, and that nothing mattered at all any more, I let him open her hand to see what she held.

It was a grey marble finger.

THE TELL-TALE HEART

Edgar Allan Poe

True! Nervous, very, very dreadfully nervous I had been and am; but why *will* you say that I am mad? The disease had sharpened my senses, not destroyed, not dulled them. Above all was the sense of hearing acute. I heard all things in the heaven and in the earth. I heard many things in hell. How then am I mad? Hearken! and observe how healthily, how calmly, I can tell you the whole story.

It is impossible to say how first the idea entered my brain, but, once conceived, it haunted me day and night. Object there was none. Passion there was none. I loved the old man. He had never wronged me. He had never given me insult. For his gold I had no desire. I think it was his eye! Yes, it was this! One of his eyes resembled that of a vulture—a pale blue eye with a film over it. Whenever it fell upon me my blood ran cold, and so by degrees, very gradually, I made up my mind to take the life of the old man, and thus rid myself of the eye for ever.

Now this is the point. You fancy me mad. Madmen know nothing. But you should have seen *me*. You should have seen how wisely I proceeded—with what caution—with what foresight, with what dissimulation, I went to work! I was never kinder to the old man than during the whole week before I killed him. And every night about midnight I turned the latch of his door and opened it—oh, so gently!

And then when I had made an opening sufficient for my head I put in a dark lantern all closed, closed so that no light shone out, and then I thrust in my head. Oh, you would have laughed to see how cunningly I thrust it in! I moved it slowly, very, very slowly, so that I might not disturb the old man's sleep. It took me an hour to place my whole head in the opening so far that I could see him lay upon his bed. Ha! would a madman have been so wise as this? And then when my head was well in the room I undid the lantern cautiously—oh, so cautiously—cautiously (for the hinges creaked), I undid it just so much that a single thin ray fell upon the vulture eye. And this I did for seven long hours, every night just at midnight, but I found the eye always closed, and so it was impossible to do the work, for it was not the old man who vexed me but his Evil Eye. And every morning, when the day broke, I went boldly into the chamber and spoke courageously to him, calling him by name in a hearty tone, and inquiring how he had passed the night. So you see he would have been a very profound old man, indeed, to suspect that every night, just at twelve, I looked in upon him while he slept.

Upon the eighth night I was more than usually cautious in opening the door. A watch's minute hand moves more quickly than did mine. Never before that night had I *felt* the extent of my own powers, of my sagacity. I could scarcely contain my feelings of triumph. To think that there I was opening the door little by little, and he not even to dream of my secret deeds or thoughts. I fairly chuckled at the idea, and perhaps he heard me, for he moved on the bed suddenly as if startled. Now you may think that I drew back—but no. His room was as black as pitch with the thick darkness (for the shutters were close fastened through fear of robbers), and so I knew that he could not see the opening of the door, and I kept pushing it on steadily, steadily.

I had my head in, and was about to open the lantern, when my thumb slipped upon the tin fastening, and the old man sprang up in the bed, crying out, 'Who's there?'

I kept quite still and said nothing. For a whole hour I did not move a muscle, and in the meantime I did not hear him lie down. He was still sitting up in the bed, listening; just as I have done night after night hearkening to the death watches in the wall.

Presently I heard a slight groan, and I knew it was the groan of mortal terror. It was not a groan of pain or of grief—oh, no! it was the low stifled sound that arises from the bottom of the soul when over-charged with awe. I knew the sound well. Many a night, just at midnight, when all the world slept, it has welled up from my own bosom, deepening, with its dreadful echo, the terrors that distracted me. I say I knew it well. I knew what the old man felt, and pitied him although I chuckled at heart. I knew that he had been lying awake ever since the first slight noise when he had turned in his bed. His fears had been ever since growing upon him. He had been trying to fancy them causeless, but could not. He had been saying to himself, 'It is nothing but the wind in the chimney, it is only a mouse crossing the floor', or 'It is merely a cricket which has made a single chirp'. Yes, he has been trying to comfort himself with these suppositions; but he had found all in vain. *All in vain*, because Death in approaching him had stalked with his black shadow before him and enveloped the victim. And it was the mournful influence of the unperceived shadow that caused him to feel, although he neither saw nor heard, to *feel* the presence of my head within the room.

When I had waited a long time very patiently without hearing him lie down, I resolved to open a little—a very, very little, crevice in the lantern. So I opened it—you cannot imagine how stealthily, stealthily—until at length a single dim ray like the thread of the spider shot out from the crevice and fell upon the vulture eye.

It was open, wide, wide open, and I grew furious as I gazed upon it. I saw it with perfect distinctness—all a dull blue with a hideous veil over it that chilled the very marrow in my bones, but I could see nothing else of the old man's face or person, for I had directed the ray as if by instinct precisely upon the damned spot.

And now have I not told you that what you mistake for madness is but over-acuteness of the senses? now, I say, there came to my ears a low, dull, quick sound, such as a watch makes when enveloped in cotton. I knew *that* sound well, too. It was the beating of the old man's heart. It increased my fury, as the beating of a drum stimulates the soldier into courage.

But even yet I refrained and kept still. I scarcely breathed. I held the lantern motionless. I tried how steadily I could maintain the ray upon

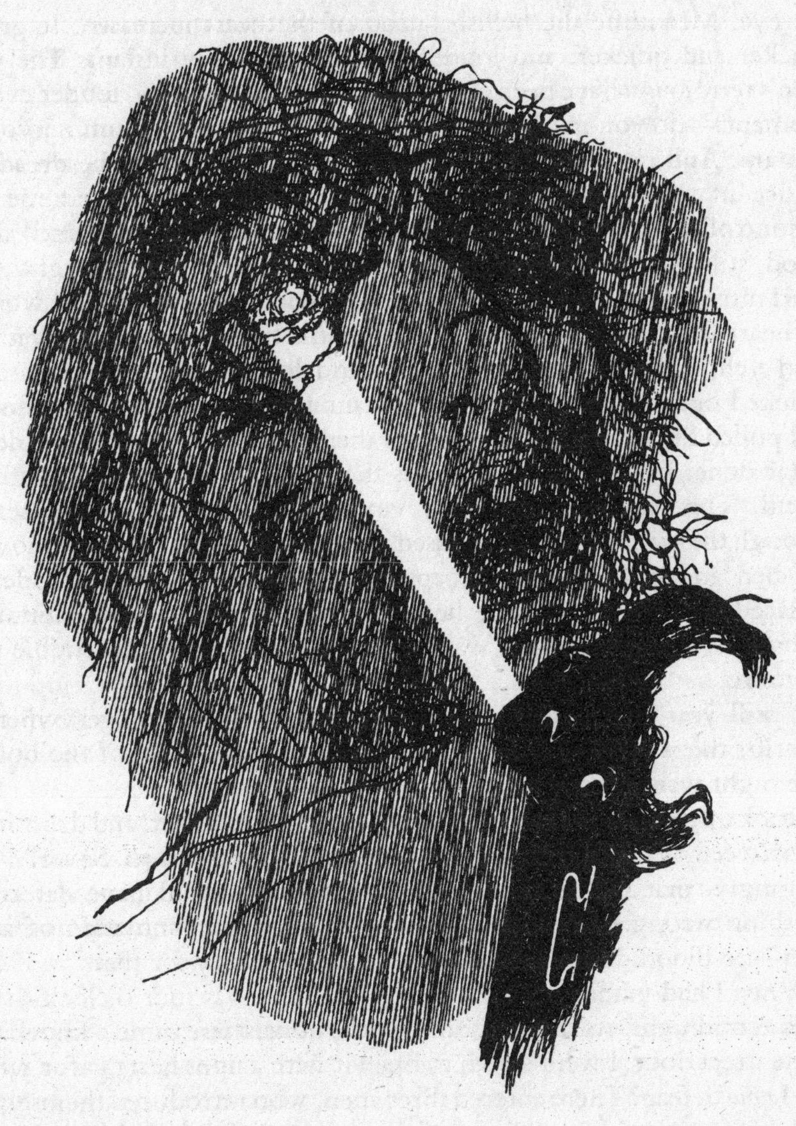

A single dim ray fell upon the vulture eye

the eye. Meantime the hellish tattoo of the heart increased. It grew quicker and quicker, and louder and louder, every instant. The old man's terror *must* have been extreme! It grew louder, I say, louder every moment!—do you mark me well? I have told you that I am nervous: so I am. And now at the dead hour of the night, amid the dreadful silence of the old house, so strange a noise as this excited me to uncontrollable terror. Yet, for some minutes longer I refrained and stood still. But the beating grew louder, louder! I thought the heart must burst. And now a new anxiety seized me—the sound would be heard by a neighbour! The old man's hour had come! With a loud yell, I threw open the lantern and leaped into the room. He shrieked once—once only. In an instant I dragged him to the floor, and pulled the heavy bed over him. I then smiled gaily to find the deed so far done. But for many minutes the heart beat on with a muffled sound. This, however, did not vex me; it would not be heard through the wall. At length it ceased. The old man was dead. I removed the bed and examined the corpse. Yes, he was stone, stone dead. I placed my hand upon the heart and held it there many minutes. There was no pulsation. He was stone dead. His eye would trouble me no more.

If still you think me mad, you will think so no longer when I describe the wise precautions I took for the concealment of the body. The night waned, and I worked hastily, but in silence.

I took up three planks from the flooring of the chamber, and deposited all between the scantlings. I then replaced the boards so cleverly, so cunningly, that no human eye—not even *his*—could have detected anything wrong. There was nothing to wash out—no stain of any kind—no bloodspot whatever. I had been too wary for that.

When I had made an end of these labours, it was four o'clock—still dark as midnight. As the bell sounded the hour, there came a knocking at the street door. I went down to open it with a light heart,—for what had I *now* to fear? There entered three men, who introduced themselves with perfect suavity, as officers of the police. A shriek had been heard by a neighbour during the night; suspicion of foul play had been aroused; information had been lodged at the police office, and they (the officers) had been deputed to search the premises.

I smiled,—for *what* had I to fear? I bade the gentlemen welcome.

The shriek, I said, was my own in a dream. The old man, I mentioned, was absent in the country. I took my visitors all over the house; bade them search—search *well*. I led them, at length, to *his* chamber. I showed them his treasures, secure, undisturbed. In the enthusiasm of my confidence, I brought chairs into the room, and desired them *here* to rest from their fatigues, while I myself, in the wild audacity of my perfect triumph, placed my own seat upon the very spot beneath which reposed the corpse of the victim.

The officers were satisfied. My *manner* had convinced them. I was singularly at ease. They sat, and while I answered cheerily, they chatted of familiar things. But, ere long, I felt myself getting pale and wished them gone. My head ached, and I fancied a ringing in my ears; but still they sat, and still they chatted. The ringing became more distinct;—it continued and became more distinct: I talked more freely to get rid of the feeling: but it continued and gained definitiveness—until, at length, I found that the noise was *not* within my ears.

No doubt I now grew *very* pale;—but I talked more fluently, and with a heightened voice. Yet the sound increased—and what could I do? It was *a low, dull, quick sound—and much a sound as a watch makes when enveloped in cotton*. I gasped for breath—and yet the officers heard it not. I talked more quickly—more vehemently; but the noise steadily increased. I arose and argued about trifles, in a high key and with violent gesticulations; but the noise steadily increased. Why *would* they not be gone? I paced the floor to and fro with heavy strides, as if excited to fury by the observations of the men—but the noise steadily increased. O God! what *could* I do? I foamed—I raved—I swore! I swung the chair upon which I had been sitting, and grated it upon the boards, but the noise arose over all and continually increased. It grew louder—louder—*louder!* And still the men chatted pleasantly, and smiled. Was it possible they heard not? Almighty God!—no, no! They heard!—they suspected!—they *knew!*—they were making a mockery of my horror!—this I thought, and this I think. But anything was better than this agony! Anything was more tolerable than this derision! I could bear those hypocritical smiles no longer! I felt that I must scream or die!—and now—again!—hark! louder! louder! louder! *louder!*—

'Villains!' I shrieked, 'dissemble no more! I admit the deed!—tear up the planks!—here, here!—it is the beating of his hideous heart!'

A KIND OF SWAN SONG

Helen Cresswell

When I say that Lisa was someone special, right from the beginning, I expect that you will smile. *All* mothers think their children are special – and so they are, of course. In my case, Lisa was my only child, and so you will think that perhaps it is only natural that I should think her special. And when I tell you that my husband (who was a violinist with a well-known symphony orchestra) died when she was only a few months old, then you will quite understandably suspect me of exaggeration. I don't blame you. This is how it might seem.

But I must insist – Lisa *was* special. And perhaps it is partly because it is important to me that other people should realize this too, that I am now writing her story. It will not take long. She was only eight when she died.

The other reason I feel bound to tell her story is because I want you to know, as certainly as I now do myself, that death is not the end, not a full stop.

'Ah,' I hear you say, 'but she is *bound* to say that. She had no one in the world but her little daughter, and she died. Now she is trying to convince herself that death is not the end of everything. It's understandable, but she can't expect *us* to believe that!'

To this I simply reply – 'Wait. Wait until you have heard my story. Then decide.'

*   *   *   *

At birth, Lisa was special to Peter and myself in exactly the same way as any other baby born to loving parents. In our case, there was an extra dimension to our joy, because we knew already that in Peter's case it was to be short-lived. We knew that he had only a few months, at most, to savour the delights of parenthood. He had had to leave the orchestra several weeks before her birth. And so, for those first few months of Lisa's life Peter was as close to her as any father can be. He would sit with her for hours, studying her tiny, peaceful face as if he wanted to imprint it on his heart forever. In the early days, before he grew too weak, he would bath her, change her, put her to bed.

And then he would play music to her, for hours on end. Not himself – he had sorrowfully put his violin away before her birth, but on tapes, and records. She would lie there kicking on the rug to the strains of Bach and Mozart, songs of Schubert and grand opera.

Sometimes I would laugh and say that I thought it all rather beyond the grasp of a baby, and that we should be playing her nursery rhymes instead. But he would say, quite seriously, 'That baby may not be able to talk, yet, but she can hear. She is listening, the whole time, trying to make a pattern of this strange new world she has entered. If what she hears is joyful, if she hears harmony, then all her life long she will seek out joy and harmony for herself. Believe me, Martha, I know that I am right.'

Even at the time I acknowledged that what he said might be true. Now, I know that it was.

I don't want to give the impression by this that we were too serious about things, or that Lisa had a strange start in life. Like any young parents we romped and played with her, looked for ways of making her smile or, better still, laugh. And we sang nursery rhymes as well. But I honestly think that the times she loved best, the times when she seemed happiest, were when she was lying there listening to music – especially songs. There was a special peaceful, wondering look she seemed to wear when she heard a beautiful human voice singing great music.

I don't want to exaggerate this – it is how I remember it, but then perhaps my memory of that time is not very reliable. It is a strange thing for a woman to watch her child blossom and at the same time her husband, the father, fading. Joy and sorrow could hardly be more poignantly interwoven.

Peter refused to let me grieve openly, and himself would show no sign of bitterness that he must soon leave us.

'I want there to be no shadows over her,' he said. 'Let her be shaped by music, not by sorrow.'

Strangely, afterwards, when she was four or five, she would insist that she remembered Peter, though she could not really have done so.

'He was always smiling,' she would say. And that was certainly true, so far as she was concerned. If there were times when he allowed his smile to fade, it was never in her presence.

He died when she was just over eight months old – in time to see her crawling, but before she took her first steps.

'Promise you will keep playing her music,' he said before he died. And of course I promised. And that was another strange thing.

In those unreal, nightmarish days after he died, Lisa grew pale and quiet. It was as if she, too, were mourning. Then, coming back into the house after the funeral, drained and weary, I was suddenly aware of the great silence and absence. It occurred to me that since Peter died, I had played no music. I went and put on a record – one of his favourites, from Haydn's 'Creation'. As the pure, triumphant notes swelled about me, I lay back in a chair and surrendered myself to it. Then, beyond that marvellous music, I heard, in a pause, another music, another voice – Lisa's.

I hurried into the next room where she lay, as I thought, sleeping. Instead, she lay there wide eyed – and round mouthed, too. Her whole tiny being seemed intent on the sounds that she was making with such seriousness, such concentration – Lisa was singing.

Very well – perhaps she was not. Perhaps she was simply cooing, crooning, as babies do. But to me, in my overwrought condition, it seemed that she was singing, herself joining in Haydn's great celebratory hymn. I remember that my tears, all at once released, splashed down onto her face, and that I gathered her up and took her with me, and she lay against me while we listened together.

Some children walk before they talk, some the other way round.

Lisa, I swear, sang before she did either. I have the courage to say this, in the light of what came after. I did not merely imagine that Lisa was a child of music. She quite simply, and unarguably, was.

At first it was only I who knew it, and who could hardly believe it when I heard that infant voice playing with scales as other children play with bricks. (She did that, too. She was in every way exactly like all other children of her age. Only this was different – music ran in her veins.)

Then, as she grew older and we went to playgroups, others would remark on the purity and the pitch of her voice, and noticed that she had only to hear a song once to know it off by heart.

'She takes after her father,' they all said.

It was true. But only I knew that she was composing music, as well as singing it. She would lie in bed after I had tucked her in for the night, her voice tracing its own melodies in the darkness. Sometimes even I, her own mother, would give a little shiver.

The word 'genius' is not an easy one to come to terms with. Every mother, as I have said, believes her own child to be special. But I do not think that any mother is looking for genius. It is rather a frightening thing, for ordinary people. We admit that it exists – but at a great distance, and in other people (preferably long since dead!).

At two Lisa was picking out tunes on the piano; at three she was playing both piano and violin. But it was the singing that mattered, I knew that. I watched her grow and develop with a delight tinged with sadness. I knew even then that the days of our closeness were numbered. Soon the world would discover her, and then the music would no longer be our shared secret.

When she was only four photographs of her were beginning to appear in the papers, under headlines such as 'Child Prodigy wins Premier Award at Festival' and 'Little Lisa Triumphs Again'.

I don't want you to think that she was in any way strange. She was exactly like every other little girl in most ways. She loved reading, roller-skating and using her computer. When she started school, her marks were average. It was only the music that set her apart.

When she was five all kinds of renowned people – professors and teachers of music – began to visit us.

'Soon,' I thought, 'they will take her away from me.'

They wanted me, even then, to send her away to a special school, where her gift could be nurtured.

'It doesn't need nurturing,' I told them. 'It is natural. It will flower of its own accord.'

They went away again, but I knew that it would not be for long. I knew, too that what I had told them was only partly true. *Any* gift needs the right nourishment, just as a rare and fragile plant.

Lisa herself began to grow away from me. Not in the things that mattered – the things between mother and daughter. In those things we were always close. We teased each other a lot, and sometimes, even then, it would seem as if she were older than I was.

'Dear goose mother!' she would say, if I forgot something, or made a mistake. It became her pet name for me.

At six they tried to take her away again, and again I resisted.

'It's too soon,' I said. 'She's too young. Leave her with me a little longer, then she can go.'

This time, when they had gone, I thought I could sense a sadness in her, a disappointment. I thought perhaps that I was being selfish, over-possessive. And so when they came again, begging me, almost, to send her away, I gave in.

Her delight when she heard the news hurt me, and she must have seen this.

'I'll still be home in the holidays, dear goose mother,' she told me. 'Don't be sad, or you'll spoil it for me.'

So I tried to look glad, for her sake. During those last few months together before she went away, I gathered her music together, to comfort me in her absence. Every song she composed I made her sing into a microphone so that I could record it. I recorded her playing the piano and the violin too, but it was the singing that mattered. We both knew that. When she sang, instrument and music were one, perfect and inviolable.

She was still only seven when she left for her new school. She was radiant. She was like a bride in beret and navy socks.

'No crying, goose mother,' she told me. 'We'll write to each other.'

'And send me tapes', I said. 'Please, Lisa. Don't let even a single song you make get away. Put it on tape. That way, we've got it forever.'

She smiled then with a curious wisdom.

'It's *making* the song that matters,' she said. '*Nothing* gets away – ever.'

When she had gone, I *did* cry, as I knew I would, and I kept remembering those words. How could she *know*, I wondered, something that most people never learn in a lifetime?

I took a job – an interesting one, really – in a house belonging to the National Trust, and open to visitors. Even so, that first term dragged. Most evenings I would sit and listen to the tapes we had made that summer. And at weekends I'd go shopping – looking for little things to put in her stocking. Lisa still believed (at least, I think she did) in Father Christmas.

By mid-December she was home. For a day or so we were a little strange together, and then it was as though she had never been away. One evening, we turned on the television to see a programme of carols composed by children. It was a competition, and these were the winning entries. When it was over, Lisa said quietly,

'Next year, goose mother, *I* shall make a carol!'

That was all. It was so slight a thing that, were it not for what followed, I doubt whether I should have remembered it. Lisa, after all, had been making songs almost all her life. What was more natural than that she should make a carol?

Christmas and the New Year came and went. This time, when she left for school, the wrench was not so painful. We can become in time accustomed to most things – even to the absence of those we love. It all seemed inevitable, and for me, it was also part of the promise I had made to Peter before he died.

Lisa's letters came every week – badly spelt, and full of the things she was doing, the music she was making. They were full, too, of the ordinary things – requests for clothes that were all the rage, for stamps to swap and posters for her room. That term passed, and the next. In the summer I took a cottage in the Lakes, and we spent most of the time walking and cycling. We were well on the way to establishing a pattern to our lives.

It was sometimes hard to remember that she was still only eight-years-old. And we never talked about what she would 'do' when she was 'grown up'. Looking back, I think that this was because she was already what she was meant to be. She was all the time in a process of becoming, and this was all that was necessary. She knew it herself.

'It's *making* the song that matters,' she had said, over a year ago.

Again I waved her off to the start of a new school year. This time the ache was not so bad. I even registered for evening classes in Italian, and went out occasionally with friends to the theatre, or for a meal. But Lisa still made the tapes, and I still played them, hour upon hour. Now, she was beginning to write her own words to the music. One day I received a cassette with a song called 'Goose Mother' and I felt so happy and so honoured that I actually taped it again, onto another cassette, for fear that it might get lost or damaged. Even as I did so, I seemed to hear her saying, 'It's *making* the song that matters'. I smiled wryly.

'For you, perhaps,' I thought. 'But for the rest of us, who can only listen, it's the song itself that counts.'

In November I was surprised by Lisa calling me on the telephone. This she had done only once before – to inform me that she had chicken pox, but there was no need to worry, and proudly announced the number of spots she had.

'Listen,' she said, 'I've made a carol!'

'A carol?' I echoed.

'Remember – that competition we saw? And listen – Davey's going home, for the weekend, and I can go with him! So you and I can record it together – on our own piano!'

'Darling, that's wonderful!' I said. 'But . . .'

'Look – his mother's coming to fetch us in the car. I'll be home Friday, at around six. Can't stop now – bye!'

That was all. It was Tuesday – three days to get used to the wonderful fact that Lisa was coming home. I had quite forgotten (how could I?) that during their first year children at the school were not allowed to go home during termtime, but that this rule was lifted after that.

I spent the interim pleasurably shopping for Lisa's favourite food (not a difficult task, this being mainly a variation on chicken) and bought a new duvet cover for her bedroom. By half-past-five on the Friday I was fidgeting in the kitchen – opening and re-opening the oven door to check on the degree of brownness of the chicken and potatoes, wondering whether I should start thawing the chocolate mousse.

At quarter-to-six I remembered that I hadn't any fizzy lemonade – her favourite drink, and one not allowed at school. I hesitated.

'I'll write a note,' I thought, 'and pin it on the door. I'll only be five minutes.'

Accordingly I wrote 'Back in five minutes' and pinned it on the door and set off. There were no shops nearby. I took the car and made for the nearest late-night supermarket. The traffic was dense, irritatingly slow. I had forgotten what Friday night rush hours were like. At one point, I almost seized the opportunity to turn round and go home without the lemonade. But, I reflected, people rarely arrived on time, especially at the weekends. I carried on.

It was nearly quarter-past-six when I arrived back. In the space my own car had occupied only half-an-hour previously, was another. It was a police car. I drew alongside it, oblivious to the hooting behind me. Two figures, a policeman and a policewoman were standing on the steps up to the front door.

I wrenched open the door and got out. I was telling myself to keep calm. My knees were trembling.

'What – what is it?'

They turned. Their faces were young, worried, pitying.

'Mrs Viner?'

I nodded.

'Perhaps we can . . . ?'

I hardly remember what happened then exactly. Somehow I was inside, somehow I was sitting in my usual chair facing the fire and a voice was talking to me. It was a sympathetic voice, its owner reluctant to give me the news. 'Motorway . . . wet surface . . . central reservation . . . lorry.' The words washed over me. What they were telling me was that Lisa was dead. She had been killed, along with her friend and his mother, on the motorway.

They were very kind. The young woman made me a cup of tea and switched off the oven. Before they left they stood looking at me uncertainly, at a loss. They didn't know what to say.

'Funny thing,' said the policeman, 'we'd been there on the steps ten minutes before you came.'

I said nothing.

'Could've sworn there was someone in here,' he went on. 'Could hear someone singing – a kid, it sounded like.'

'We wondered if the radio had been left on,' the girl added.

'And now I come to think of it,' he said, 'the radio *wasn't* on. Or the telly. Funny, that. . . .'

'Yes, funny.' I said. 'Thank you. Thank you both very much. I think – I think I want to be alone now.'

They hesitated.

'Sure you'll be all right?'

'Sure.'

They went. The door closed and I was alone. I sat there for I don't know how long. I was seeing Lisa, hearing her, trying to tell myself that I would never see or hear her again. I couldn't cry. I just sat, dry-eyed, remembering.

In the end, after a long dark age, I got up. Mechanically I began turning things off, locking up for the night. The front door, the back, check the oven – still containing the chicken and crisp potatoes – switch off lights, pull out the plug of the TV. . . .

I stopped. All the lights but one were out. There, glowing in the darkness, were the red and green lights of the stereo deck and cassette recorder. There was a very faint hum. My mind was dense, confused. I had set *up* the system, that very afternoon, all ready to record the carol. The blank cassette was in place, I had carefully checked the sound levels. *And then I had switched it off.*

I remembered doing it. I had actually thought of the way Peter had always chided me for leaving things on – especially the cassette recorder. He had lectured me about the damage it might do.

I advanced towards the deck. Hesitantly, I pressed the PLAY switch. There came only a faint hissing. Then, hardly knowing why I did so, I pressed REWIND. *The tape rewound.* It stopped with a click.

'But it was a new cassette,' I thought. 'Brand new.'

I stood there for a long time in the dim remaining light. Then I pressed another key – PLAY.

The room filled with sound. A voice – Lisa's voice, pure and sweet, sang:

On a far midnight,
Long, long ago. . . .

There was no accompaniment, no piano, just that young, miraculous voice, singing of that long-ago miracle that Christmas celebrates.

I stood dazed, listening. Then, when at last the carol ended, I heard – or thought I heard (it certainly was not there on the tape, afterwards) – 'There, dear goose mother! I told you – it's *making* the song that matters!'

And I knew that this was her last present to me. It was not for her own sake, but for mine, that the carol was there, locked for all time, on tape.

I sent that tape to the contest. It won. The presenter said, 'It is with great sadness that we have to tell you that Lisa, aged eight, died tragically in a car accident, just after she had recorded this carol for our contest. It was to be her swan song.'

Only I knew that the carol had been recorded not before, but after the accident. Though perhaps it could, after all, be called a *kind* of swan song.

THE CLOCK TOWER GHOST

Gene Kemp

Addlesbury Tower is the new home of the Phillips family. However, it is already the home of Rich King Cole, its resident ghost. Mandy is the first person to see the ghost but, of course, nobody believes her. Determined to force the ghost into the open and to frighten all the kids at school who hate her, the demon Mandy hits upon the 'ultimate deterrent'.

That demon creature was also making plans. With bad temper transforming into energy, Mandy was plotting in three directions: school, for the gang had been terrible that day; the ghost, she was going to deal with him; her family, to prove to them that he existed. To fortify herself, she decided she would need some nourishment from Mum's latest hiding place. She found it easily. Poor old Mum. She'd no imagination.

An hour later, the October evening already dark and the wind beginning to sigh and whistle round the tower, a vile aroma started to drift down the spiral staircase, a mixture of rotten cabbage, burnt rubber, and silage. The family were all in the kitchen doing various jobs, except for Fred, in bed, and Fishy, out courting. Mandy sniffed the air.

'That's the ghost coming,' she cried. 'NOW LOOK OUT, ALL OF YOU. You must see him, this time.'

All her family sighed heavily and pretended not to notice. She was off again. Enough to send anybody round the bend, thought Chris, settling back to his Rothman's Football Year Book.

'I think the drain needs unblocking,' said Dad. 'I'll go down and fix it.'

'It's the ghost,' Mandy seethed with fury. 'You can smell him.'

'Well, I've caught cold with all these draughts,' said her mother, 'and I can't smell a thing. I can't taste anything, either.'

'Oh, you lot will drive me mad,' Mandy shouted, storming out of the kitchen, and up to her bedroom, where an idea hit her, wham.

Down the staircase came King Cole, black cloak (found in an old chest) over his muddy shroud, mask on his face (a vampire one, put on crooked) and a rusty chain clanking behind him (making him very slow), arms and hands outstretched, moaning Woe, Woe and Doom, Doom alternately, Crook perched on one shoulder cawing at intervals (and feeling a complete twit). They had worked really hard on their new image, and hoped it would do the trick, filling the Phillipses with utter terror so that they rushed out of the clock tower and into the night, never to darken its door again.

That's what they hoped.

Nearly at the bend just before the kitchen, King Cole paused, ready to burst in for the final fright, and at that moment a really terrifying figure leapt down from the stairs crying, 'Stick 'em Up!' Mandy, dressed in her witch's costume for the Hallowe'en party at school, and carrying a water pistol was right behind them. King Cole turned in surprise and received a jet of water in his right eye.

Mandy shrieked to her family, 'Come on, come on, quick, he's here.'

By the time they arrived all that could be seen on the stairs was a length of chain, a black cloak and a water-soaked mask.

'I wish you didn't make such a mess when you play your games,' her mother remarked as she picked them up.

'Pchah,' snapped Mandy, stomping back upstairs.

★ ★ ★ ★

Entering into the spirit of the thing, King Cole now appeared and disappeared all over the clock tower, accompanied by a miserable and complaining Crook. Crockery flew through the air, furniture and armour slid through rooms, bloodstains dripped on the spiral stairs, then vanished without trace. Mists murked, draughts froze feet, the tower smelt like a badly kept farmyard on a wet day.

Mandy met King Cole all over the place.

But as for the rest of the family, Mr Phillips was away for a week, gathering more antiquities for his Museum, and Mrs Phillips's cold grew worse, making her deaf, and unable to smell anything at all, and furthermore she put down her glasses somewhere, couldn't find them afterwards and, as a result, couldn't see a thing. Chris? Well, Chris walked in a dream. Chris was over the moon. He didn't care what was going on in the tower. Chris had scored a hat trick in the last match. People were saying that Chris Phillips was the best thing that ever happened to Addlesbury Primary football. Up Addlesbury Primary. Addlesbury Rules OK. Up Chris Phillips. Chris Phillips Rules OK. (Mandy Phillips a load of rubbish but who cares, anyway?) So he noticed nothing.

Fishy knew. Cats always know about things like King Cole. As far as he was concerned, that thing was nasty, just like Mandy, and to be avoided, just like Mandy. Very like, really. What did interest him was the feathery friend who had appeared just lately, because it was satisfactory to know that there were reserves of food in the tower if there was a siege or Mistress Phillips grew mean with the Pretty Cat. But really he was far more interested in his new girl-friend, a gorgeous tortoise-shell called Bomber (her owners hadn't yet realized that tortoise-shell cats are always females), than in ghostly goings-on in the tower. So it was up to Mandy.

And she had not been idle. All the week she had been collecting nettles, brambles and gorse, making a prickly heap at the bottom of the tower ready for the Friday leap. She'd wrecked her mother's best leather gloves doing so, but didn't think her mother would mind.

On Friday night she prepared to stay awake with a book on judo, two bars of chocolate, a bag of boiled sweets, and a selection of fruit that was meant to last for the whole weekend. As the witching hour drew near she seated herself beside the window ready for the action.

As an actor herself, she had to admit he did well. His expression and the things he said as he rose from the heap were brilliant, she thought, and gave him a little clap – not too loud in case the others heard – before she up-ended a bag of flour over him. She felt he'd had enough water with the pistol she'd been using.

Drearily the ghost and Crook returned to the armour, which Mandy had generously covered with itching powder. Before she finally went to sleep, she crept up and played him one of her favourite rock records on her cassette player.

King Cole, aged a hundred and fifty, hadn't known about itching powder or cassette tapes. But he was learning.

★ ★ ★ ★

Mr Phillips returned with some stuffed animals and what looked like a lot of old pots of poor shape and worse colour. But he was pleased with them. Mandy found the animals far more exciting. She told him all about her week and her battle with the ghost.

'You've got a marvellous imagination, Mandy. You ought to write it all down. Become an author.'

Mandy growled and stomped off in disgust, searching for something wicked to do. How could grown-ups be so unbelievably stupid? Who wants to write about a battle when you've got to fight one? As she rummaged in the kitchen for something to smash she found her Mum's specs, and was going to jump on them when she decided it would be better to put them on her Mum's nose instead, so that somebody, anybody, please, might see the ghost beside herself. She looked round for Fishy, but he was busy, singing songs of love to Bomber. Chris was out playing football, of course. She wandered into his room, which he'd forgotten to lock against her, and jumped on his latest model of a battleship, but didn't get much joy out of it. Strange, just lately she didn't enjoy smashing things so much. Sad, really. She couldn't be growing up, could she? That would be horrific. At last, she picked up Baby Fred and sang funny songs to him which he laughed at hugely, showing his new teeth, and patting her face with pudgy hands.

'I found your specs,' she told her mother, who came hurrying in. 'You'd better put them on and then you can see the ghost properly.'

'You're a good girl. You're being very helpful.'

She dropped kisses on Mandy's and Fred's heads, which made Mandy furious, though Fred chortled and kicked his fat feet.

'I just wish you'd stop talking about that ghost as if he was real,' she called over her shoulder as she trotted off once more. Slitting her eyes, Mandy tucked Fred under one arm and set off to change all the labels round on the Bronze and Iron Age pots.

'That should baffle them,' she thought, wandering back to the kitchen, where she remembered her mother hiding some glacé cherries so they wouldn't be eaten before she had time to make a cake for Chris's birthday. She soon found them. Baby Fred enjoyed his cherries, too; it wasn't easy for him, but he champed away with his new teeth, little red trickles running down his chin.

Some ran on to the newspaper and, watching them, Mandy's eye was caught by two words – ULTIMATE DETERRENT – now what did that mean? Something to do with last, she thought, an end something – that's what I need for the ghost, an ultimate deterrent, a final, finishing him off for good, cheerio, Ghost. Yes, she must think up something, something spectacular, something great, the ultimate ghost deterrent.

But she didn't know what, as yet.

After the weekend, school was awful. School's ghastly and home's ghostly, she thought bitterly as she sat barricaded with chairs in a corner of the classroom, so that Cressy Gale's gang couldn't get at her, she hoped. With Hallowe'en near, the children had been writing stories and poems full of witches, wizards and warlocks, and making their party spook outfits.

'We don't need to make a witch with a broomstick this year,' sniggered Carol Moore, 'when we got 'er, ole Witchie-Batty-Four-Eyes.' This name was taken up with glee by that part of the class with nothing better to do. Cries of 'Where's your broomstick, then? Give's a ride,' were heard.

A dead mouse appeared in her shoe bag, a live frog in her desk. Mandy remembered how funny she'd once thought it when she'd put one in Chris's bed, but that was a trick she wouldn't play any more, for now she felt sorry for the frog. Unfair to frogs. She carried it, throbbing and always at the point of jumping, back to the pond near the tower.

'Witches always have toads or frogs or things like that,' Cressy Cale called after her. But Mandy ignored her. Holding the frog carefully, she thought about the ultimate deterrent. What were the ultimately bad things? Plagues, she supposed, the dreaded Black Death, rabies, nuclear bombs, germ warfare, poison gas. All very nasty. But not the kind of thing that Mandy Phillips could use against a ghost or a gang. Vampires and werewolves, ogres and monsters, all jolly good in their way, but not what she needed now.

The frog was settled safely by the pond, and Mandy continued homewards, thinking, thinking. When Mandy got her teeth into something she didn't let go easily.

In the kitchen rose a delectable smell. Her father and mother and Fred were enjoying toasted buns. With lashings of jam.

'School trips,' said her father. 'That's what we need. Plenty of school trips.'

'School trips are dreadful. I'm sorry for the teachers. When I helped last year I was completely shattered. I just wanted to disappear from the face of the earth . . . Hello, Mandy. How was your day?'

Mandy wasn't answering that question.

'Dad. Dad. Dad. Dad,' she was shouting.

'Yes. Yes. Yes. Yes,' he replied.

'School trip. Can we have one? Soon? From school to here? Can we be the first school trip? Please, oh, please?'

'Yes. I don't see why not. I'll write to your teacher. What made you think of it?'

Mandy's face split into a grin that stretched from ear to ear.

'It'll be my ultimate deterrent,' she said. And she kissed Fred on his well-buttered cheek.

* * * *

On a warm and golden October afternoon the Blue Addlesbury Tourer wound its way round the steep and winding Addlesbury lanes, carrying the two top classes of Addlesbury Primary up to visit the clock tower and its museum.

'An excellent idea,' Miss Fairhead had said in reply to Mr Phillips's invitation. And Wednesday afternoon was decided upon, free of charge for this special opening invitation to the local school. This nicely scotched Cressy Gale's comment:

'I'm not paying to see Batty's stupid old ghost.'

'I'm scared,' said someone else.

'I hope we see it,' said the girl who loved nightmares.

A letter to the parents indicated that the trip was for educational purposes, part of the History and Environmental Studies for that term. Parents were also invited, but they had to pay the entrance fee.

'I shan't go,' announced Cressy to her gang. 'Who wants to go near that rotten dump?'

But she was there all the same, as the children lined up with clipboards and pencils, packed teas, and a small amount of money each for souvenirs.

Miss Fairhead sat by Amanda. No one else would. The team, Chris included, sat in the back seats, singing songs and cheering as they left the village. Miss Fairhead was an old hand at school trips, and had supplied buckets for those throwing up and plasters for those falling down. Nothing was to be eaten before exploring the tower, all to be kept for tea afterwards. Mr Browning and six parents were helping. Nothing could go wrong. She hoped. Quite soon the coach stopped outside the clock tower.

Mr Phillips now came to show them round. The ground floor, with its prehistory treasures, its stuffed animals and cases of coins was now looking quite different from when he had first arrived there. Everything was clearly labelled, there were posters on the wall, and a small souvenir stall (beside which Baby Fred gurgled in his pram, lovely, lovely, bubbly, guggly, children, lots of, ran his happy Fred thoughts).

Mr Phillips intended taking them round the various floors first, then six at a time round the parapet, before going down to tea. As she sold souvenirs to the children her mother noticed that Amanda was giving an excellent imitation of a saint.

'Isn't she being good?' she thought. 'But perhaps she's always good at school. Perhaps it's only with us that she's so tiresome.' She sighed at this, then decided to cheer up, for it was a lovely afternoon and they seemed nice children. She didn't notice Carol Moore picking up two souvenirs and paying for only one. Nor Cressy Gale pinching Mandy and Mandy quietly twisting her left little finger in return.

Souvenirs purchased, the exhibits on the ground floor were examined and explained by Mr Phillips, after which they trooped up to the first floor with its pictures and paintings, old musical instruments and even older books, some of them chained to the shelves. It was all so peaceful, the children busy making notes and drawings, clipboards in position, Mr Phillips talking happily to them.

'Jolly good,' thought Mr Browning.

'A successful outing,' thought Miss Fairhead.

'I do like school trips,' thought Mr Phillips, pausing for them all to look at a harpsichord covered with paintings of extravagantly dressed men and women wandering in flowery gardens.

Then up past the flat went the visitors, except for Mandy, who slid in and out of her kitchen quick as a flash, and was back with the crowd in time to hear Cressy say:

'That baby's too nice to be *her* brother. And her Dad's all right. Adopted, that's what she is.'

For a moment, Mandy felt stricken. But she rallied, Amanda fashion. No time to worry about that now. She'd think about it later.

And now they approached the armoury.

'This is a particularly interesting room,' her father was saying. 'In here we have the armour and weapons collected by King Cole himself. And while the boys are investigating these, the girls will enjoy looking at the hand-embroidered tapestries hanging on the walls . . .'

'Oh, really,' thought Mandy, 'not these girls . . .' as she walked softly towards a certain clumsy suit of armour inside which a certain invisible ghost was grumbling peevishly to himself at the disturbance. Crook, also invisible, watched from the perch on the helmet.

It was a perfect English afternoon, with the autumn sunlight streaming through the stained-glass windows. Mr Phillips pointed out a specially fine cross-bow. The Mums wondered how anyone had the patience to do so much embroidery. Miss Fairhead reminded herself that she must remember to tip the coach driver. Mr Browning felt pleased that he was not wearing a suit of armour on a hot day.

Mandy Phillips was now just beside the suit of armour. Cressy Gale, watching her closely, crept right behind her to see what she was up to.

Behind her was Carol Moore, and the girl who loved nightmares.

Mandy Phillips lifted up the visor, and taking the pepperpot she'd fetched from her kitchen she emptied all its contents right into the suit of armour, and retreated to a far corner as fast as she could. This was rather faster than Crook, who tried to flap to the window but too late.

Like a volcano erupting in the ocean and creating a new island, King Cole erupted from the armour, materialized, waved desperate arms in the air, and sneezed and sneezed and sneezed and went on sneezing, mainly over Cressy. Some sneezes blessed Carol and a few rained upon the nightmare girl but most fell on Cressy. Crook's feathers flew, a rotting stench rose in the air, and the gentle autumn chilled rapidly to a Siberian winter. All the afternoon peace was shattered as King Cole was revealed to Addlesbury Primary in all his glory, and he, in turn, saw many Mandys; a horrible ghost, terrible demons. Wedging a despairing screech between sneezes, he vanished into his armour followed swiftly by Crook, somewhat short of feathers. It was all he needed. Children shrieked and ran for the door. The grown-ups, directed by Miss Fairhead, keeping very cool, managed to guide them safely down the stairs and on to the coach, where order was restored and they had their tea. Mandy stayed still in the far corner of the armoury.

The ultimate deterrent had succeeded beyond her wildest dreams. King Cole and the Addlesbury Gang had scared the wits out of each other.

THE GORGE OF THE CHURELS

H. Russell Wakefield

'Mr Sen,' said the Reverend Aloysius Prinkle, 'I am going to take a holiday tomorrow. I'm feeling a bit jaded. I thought we'd have a picnic, if it's fine. You must come with us, of course.'

'A pleasant idea, certainly,' smiled Mr Sen. He was a Bengali babu, aged about thirty, who acted as Secretary and general factotum to the incumbents of the Mission Station. Mr Prinkle had taken him over from his predecessor three months before. He was a slightly enigmatic young man, habitually smiling and obliging, but not quite as 'open' as he might be, was Mr Prinkle's verdict. His enemies called him a 'Rice Christian', meaning he had found the Christian side of the bread the better buttered. His friends replied, 'Very sensible of Mr Sen, if he is right about the rice.' His English was fluent and personally idiomatic. His intonation pedantically precise with a wavy melody line.

'Have you yet decided on a site for the occasion?' he added. 'Possibly my advice may be welcome; possibly not.'

'Well, Mrs Prinkle and I passed what we considered an ideal spot the other day. It's a little gorge off the Kulan Valley. It's known, I understand, as The Gorge of the Churels. You know where I mean?'

Mr Sen didn't reply for a moment. He continued to wear that smile, but it contracted somewhat as though he were moved by some not entirely pleasant reflections. At length he remarked, 'Yes, I am familiar with the locality you mention, but is it not rather a long way to go? Just a suggestion, of course.'

'Not a bit of it!' laughed Mr Prinkle; 'just three-quarters of an hour in the car and a beautiful drive into the bargain.'

'Did you consider taking the youngster with you?' asked Mr Sen slowly.

'Why, naturally! He'll love it; and it'll give his Ayah the day off.'

'It is not perhaps a very satisfactory place for young children,' said Mr Sen.

'Why ever not! Snakes?'

'No, I was not thinking so much of snakes,' replied Mr Sen aloofly; 'those are, in a way, everywhere and easily avoided, terrified, or destroyed.'

'Then what *are* you thinking about?' asked Mr Prinkle. His voice was benignly patronizing.

'There is a good deal of water there; a stream and a pool, and so on. All this may be dangerous for the tender-yeared, of course.'

'Of course *not*!' laughed Mr Prinkle. 'We shall see Nikky doesn't come to a premature and watery end! It is not good, you know, Mr Sen, to be too nervous about children. It makes *them* nervous, too. "Fear and be slain!" There's a lot of truth in that, you know!'

'There is, also, of course,' smiled Mr Sen, 'the Heavenly Father on guard.'

Mr Prinkle glanced at him sharply. Was he being a shade sarcastic? One could never be quite sure with Mr Sen. A pity he couldn't be more *open*!

'Now, Mr Sen,' he said, 'I don't think you're being quite candid with me. I don't think those are your real reasons. Now tell me quite frankly, please, why you dislike going to this place, for I can see you do.'

'Oh, I don't mind really,' said Mr Sen with a quick little giggle. 'I was perhaps reverting to type, if you know what I mean, just being foolish, a silly primitive Indian.'

'I *suppose* I know what you're getting at,' said Mr Prinkle quizzingly, 'the place has some sort of evil repute; is that what you mean?'

'Since you press me on the matter, that is so. Quite absurd, of course!'

Mr Prinkle saw fit to issue a rather roguish reprimand.

'You mean, Mr Sen, it is thought to be haunted by spirits of some kind?'

'That is what I may term the rough idea,' replied Mr Sen. 'I do not desire to discuss the matter at further length, if you do not mind.'

'But I do *mind*, Mr Sen. I have instructed you that the only evil spirits are in the hearts of men. To suppose they can materialize themselves and infest certain localities is a childish superstition, primitive, as you say. Such ideas distract and confuse men's minds; they must be eradicated. I am rather surprised at you, Mr Sen, after all you've been taught. It doesn't seem to have sunk in, for in spite of your protestations, I can see that you still, in some ways, share these barbarous notions. We *will* go to this gorge and enjoy ourselves thoroughly—*all* of us! Come now to my bungalow and give me my Urdu lesson, and let's have no more reversion to type!'

Mr Sen smiled and did as he was told, but behind the mask he was charged with a great anger almost perfectly controlled. So during the next hour he delicately permitted Mr Prinkle to realize he considered him a person of lethargic wits and quite devoid of linguistic ability; that instructing him was a considerable strain on the patience and by no means a labour of love. And later he quite refused to obey the pious injunction not to let the sun go down upon his wrath, for he lay long awake that night, his fury festering, because he had been ridiculed, humiliated, and reproved, and it was like a rodent ulcer in his spirit.

Mr Prinkle was very young, earnest, pink-and-white and naively self-confident. Though he had landed at Bombay but fourteen weeks before, he felt he already knew India and the Indian mind pretty well, and the chapter headings of a book dealing with the Missionary problems of the Sub-Continent were already in his notebook. His wife, Nancy, was very young and earnest too, but much more pleasing to the eye and by no means so confident. In her heart she thought India a frightening place, and that she and her husband were really strangers in a very strange land, unwelcome strangers to ninety percent of its inhabitants, at any rate those of the Northern Punjab. She was an intelligent girl and her little boy Nicholas was an intelligent child. He was a charming, small blond boy, much too young for the climate, pronounced the pundits. He was inclined to solemnity, too, and it seemed the genes of earnestness were already busy within him.

The next morning, 13 September, was spotlessly fine and not wickedly hot, for the scimitar edge of the summer sun was by now mercifully blunted.

Punctually at eleven the four of them packed into the V-8, and Mr Prinkle facetiously exclaimed, 'Chai! Chai!' as though urging on an elephant, for he was very proud of his few words of the lingo. So, soon they were speeding through the tea-gardens and raising a dense, low-lying, light ochre dust.

At length they reached the chotal, or head of the little pass, and there below them was the Kulan Valley, the river like a sapphire necklace in an emerald case, and above it the glossy, sparkling silver of the gods of the Hindu Kush stroked the sky. They paused a moment to revel in this view, though only Nancy really recognized how flabbergastingly well composed it was, and how brilliantly it just escaped the obvious. Then they began coasting down to the vale.

'What is the meaning of the word Churel, Mr Sen?' asked Nancy, turning round in the front seat to face that person.

Mr Sen paused before replying. He was still angry and indignant, and this was a very dangerous question, of which he'd have preferred to have received notice. He decided it was a moment for the exercise of that gift for sarcasm on which he prided himself, and which was often a good defensive dialectical weapon. With him sarcasm and verbosity went arm in arm.

'The word Churel,' he remarked in his most sing-song tone, 'is a typical example of the poor superstitious Indians' ineradicable tendency to charge vague and fearful notions with materialistic implications.'

'Very likely,' said Nancy, trying not to laugh, 'but what does it mean?'

'The poor primitive Indians,' replied Mr Sen, 'cherish fearful ideas about women who pass over in giving birth to their young. They fondly imagine that the spirits or ghosts of such unfortunate females continue to haunt the earth, with a view of seizing the soul of some living child and carrying it off to the void to comfort them. Then, if they are successful in this morbid ambition, they are content, and roam their favourite places no more. Such ghosts are called "Churels", and this gorge we are visiting is one of such favoured places. It is all very absurd, of course.'

'I think it's a strange and sad idea,' said Nancy; 'the child dies, I suppose?'

'Oh yes, naturally,' smiled Mr Sen; 'it's vital principle has been removed.'

'*You* don't believe such stuff, I hope,' said Mr Prinkle insinuatingly.

Mr Sen who believed it with fearful intensity, replied, 'Naturally, since my conversion to the true faith and the instruction of two reverends, I regard the concept as wholly fatuous.'

'It is queer,' said Nancy, frowning, 'how such ideas ever get into people's heads. I mean someone must have *started* the Churel idea. Why? Does the word mean anything else, Mr Sen? Has it any secondary meaning?'

'Oh no, indeed. Just what I have informed you. Just a silly Indian notion, altogether.'

'Then I can't quite understand it,' said Nancy.

Mr Prinkle decided it was time a superior intellect was brought to bear on the topic. Pulling out the vox parsonica stop, he proclaimed authoritatively, 'My dear girl, it is one of a myriad such phantasies connected in some way with procreation, which is always a kinetic mystery to the primitive mind. Once formed, the phantasy is *named*, inevitably. These encapsuled animistic relics in the human mind are very hard to eradicate, but I'm going to do my best to cleanse the midden; I regard it as an essential part of my mission to India.'

Mr Sen maintained his bland grin, but behind it a formidable seethe of emotions was writhing: contempt, rage, hate, a growing fear and a horrid hope. He glanced at Nikky, who was regarding him in a steady, searching way. Mr Sen wriggled uneasily; for some complex reason he was perturbed by that appraising stare.

'What are you talking about, Mummy?' asked the small one.

'Oh nothing,' replied Nancy. 'We shall soon be there.'

The Gorge of the Churels ran up from the eastern flank of the valley. It was a re-entrant from the low, limestone cliff which lined the vale. It had been burrowed out during countless aeons by a hard-running little stream, which rose somewhere in the foothills and fed the Kulan half a mile away. The entrance to it was narrow and stark, but it widened out to a breadth of some five hundred yards and was a mile or so in depth. At its eastern ending the burn fell over a steep bank, died for a moment in a deep circular basin, and poured out again from its western rim. The gorge was full of deodars, peepuls and kikars, and a few great dominating teaks. The surface was thick grass interspersed with bamboo. It was a very shady, aloof place, death-quiet, save for the splash of the fall, the murmur of the burn, and the occasional cry of a bird.

They parked the car just inside it and then strolled about for a while.

'It *is* rather a sombre spot,' said Nancy, 'though,' she added hurriedly, 'quite lovely of course.'

Mr Sen grinned.

Mr Prinkle said: 'Now *you're* getting fanciful, my dear. I don't find it sombre in the least; quite charming. Remote, no doubt, and cut off from the busy world of men; but what a relief that is! If it were in England, it would be coated with orange peel and old newspapers, and cacophonous with gramophones and loud speakers. Let's have lunch.'

They spread out the cloth in the shade of a mighty deodar. Little Nikky was very quiet during meal and not as hungry as usual. His eyes kept wandering in the direction of the pool.

'You'd like to fish in there, wouldn't you, darling?' said Nancy.

'Yes, Mummy,' he replied listlessly.

'Before we come again we must get a little rod for you,' said Nancy.

Nikky just smiled in a perfunctory way.

After the feast they smoked a cigarette, chatted for a while, and then Mr Prinkle yawned and said, 'I feel like a nap. Most unusual for me, the reaction from a very hard week I suppose.'

'I do, too,' said Nancy. 'Would you like forty winks, Nikky?'

'No, thank you, Mummy.'

'Well, what would you like to do?'

'Just play about.'

'Then don't go near the pond! What about you, Mr Sen?'

'I do not wish to sleep, thank you,' grinned that person. 'I will watch over the young shaver, if that is what you imply.'

'That's very kind of you. Just see he doesn't get into mischief. Now remember, darling, be good and *don't* go near the pond!'

'All right, Mummy.'

Mr and Mrs Prinkle then stretched themselves under a long branch of the deodar, hung out like the groping arm of a blind man. They put handkerchiefs over their faces, wriggled into comfortable positions and soon slept.

Mr Sen squatted down in the open whence he could keep Nikky in view, and began to think in his own tongue. He didn't like this place; it stirred ancestral forebodings. These callow, impercipient Europeans were fools to have come here—with a child. Because they were blind they thought there was nothing to see. Yes, he really hated them, despised them from the bottom of his heart. Let him be open with himself for once—wide open! Of course it paid him—not well, but enough—to pretend to like and respect them and their idiotic gods, but they were blind and insolent and conceited fools. If they were not, they would worship Brahma, the greatest of all god-ideas. Not, he thought to himself, that I am really greatly impressed even by Brahma, for what does he *do*? Now that I am being open, I will confess he seems to *do* nothing, and evil spirits freely defy him.

He would like to see these people punished for their vanity and stupidity. What would be the worst punishment they could suffer? The loss of the child, of course, and this was a fearful death-trap for children. No woman would bring her child near the gorge by night, and not even by day unless protected by some appropriate powerful charm. He ran his tongue across his lips. What was little Nikky doing? He was kneeling down and staring across towards the pool, an oddly intent look on his face. Mr Sen watched him for a few moments and then followed the direction of his gaze. He leaned forward, peered hard, and drew in his breath with a quick hiss. His face became set and rigid with terror. Just to the left of the basin was a circular grove of mulberry trees, and at the centre of this circle was something which had no business to be there; at least so it seemed to Mr Sen. The sun's rays coiling between the leaves, dappled and, as it were, camouflaged this intruder, so that it appeared just a thing of light and shade; like every other visible entity in the world, of course, yet somehow this was essentially incorporeal, not linked to earth, but painted thinly on the freckled air. It was this appearance which little Nikky seemed to be observing so intently, yet intermittently.

Sometimes he would look down and pretend to be playing with the grass and flowers, and then he would glance up swiftly and stealthily and become quite still and taut. He was, Mr Sen decided, trying in an innocent way to deceive anyone who might be watching him. And Mr Sen knew why he was doing this, and trembled. He pulled up the sleeve of his right arm where, round the biceps, was what resembled a large leather wrist-watch strap, but in the container was a piece of narrow scroll on which a very sacred text was inscribed. For this was a charm, idolatrously obtained, by Mr Sen, from an extremely ancient and holy Sadhu, and, though not a protection against the full power of certain demons, a great shield for sure against most dangers and evils. His possession of it he kept a close dark secret, especially from his reverend employers. He touched this charm and muttered to himself.

Presently little Nikky toddled slowly forward in the direction of the grove. Then he knelt again and nervously plucked up some blades of grass. The fretted and dubious shape remained motionless.

After a while the child glanced up and moved forward again. He was now about fifteen yards from the grove. Mr Sen began to tremble violently, not only with fear, but from some subtle emotion, atavistic and nameless. His teeth clattered and he clutched the charm. Again little Nikky glanced up from his feigned play and stared hard in front of him. Mr Sen could see he was smiling in a vague, rapt way. It was very quiet, the light toss of the fall, the stir of the brook seemed but to join the stillness and intensify it. But Mr Sen was aware of a horrid tension in the air, like the swelling potential before the lightning stroke.

Suddenly Nikky uttered a happy little cry and ran forward as fast as his chubby legs would carry him. As he reached the verge of the grove, it seemed to the entranced and quivering Mr Sen as though the thing of light and shadow moved forward to meet and greet him. The little boy threw out his arms and in another moment the two would have mingled.

And then Mr Sen, as the odd and pregnant saying has it, 'came to himself'. He leapt to his feet and ran headlong towards the grove

Mr Sen leapt to his feet and ran headlong towards the grove

fiercely clutching the charm and uttering repeatedly, loudly, and hoarsely some words of warning or incantation. Little Nikky paused, glanced round and fell on his face, and the thing of light and shade seemed to lose its form and pass into the stippled air.

Mr and Mrs Prinkle came running out, dishevelled and heavy with sleep.

'What's the matter?' they cried in unison to Mr Sen, who had taken Nikky in his arms.

'The little chap fell down,' he said shrilly. 'Perhaps a touch of the sun; I do not know!'

Nancy seized the child, who had fallen into a deep sleep.

'We'd better get him home,' said Mr Prinkle urgently. And soon they had packed up and were hurrying on their way.

Presently little Nikky stirred from his deep doze, opened his round blue eyes, smiled and said, 'Pretty lady!' and went to sleep again.

'He's quite all right,' laughed Nancy in relief; 'when he smiles like that he's always well and happy.'

'Just a little tired perhaps,' said her husband resignedly. Just a false alarm. Rather spoilt our day!'

'Why did you shout, Mr Sen?' asked Nancy.

'Ah!' grinned that person, 'I am ashamed to confess it, but *I* had a snooze too. Very negligent of me, but I was properly punished, for I had a very bad dream, I assure you.'

'What did you dream about?' asked Mr Prinkle mockingly, 'those bereft and acquisitive Churels!'

'Ah no,' replied Mr Sen with a protesting smile, and slipping his left arm up his right sleeve; 'it is not fair of you, Mr Prinkle, to pull my legs so, and remind me of the ridiculous superstitions of us poor, ignorant, primitive Indians!'

THE HAUNTED TRAILER

Robert Arthur

It was incredible, of course. Bound to happen some day. But why did it have to happen to me? What did *I* do to deserve the grief? And I was going to be married, too. I sank my last thousand dollars into that trailer, almost. In it Monica and I were going on a honeymoon tour of the United States. We were going to see the country. I was going to write, and we were going to be happy as two turtle-doves.

Ha!

Ha ha!

If you detect bitterness in that laughter, I'll tell you why I'm bitter.

Because it had to be me, Mel—for Melvin—Mason who became the first person in the world to own a haunted trailer!

Now, a haunted castle is one thing. Even an ordinary haunted house can be livable. In a castle, or a house, if there's a ghost around, you can lock yourself in the bedroom and get a little sleep. A nuisance, yes. But nothing a man couldn't put up with.

In a trailer, though! What are you going to do when you're sharing a trailer, even a super-de-luxe model with four built-in bunks, a breakfast nook, a complete bathroom, a radio, electric range, and easy chair, with a ghost? Where can you go to get away from it?

Ha!

Ha ha!

I've heard so much ghostly laughter the last week that I'm laughing myself that way now.

There I was. I had the trailer. I had the car to pull it, naturally. I was on my way to meet Monica in Hollywood, where she was living with an aunt from Iowa. And twelve miles west of Albany, the first night out, my brand-new, spic-and-span trailer picks up a hitch-hiking haunt!

But maybe I'd better start at the beginning. It happened this way. I bought the trailer in New England—a Custom Clipper, with chrome and tan outside trim, for $2,998. I hitched it on behind my car and headed westwards, happier than a lark when the dew's on the thorn. I'd been saving up for this day for two years, and I felt wonderful.

I took it easy, getting the feel of the trailer, and so I didn't make very good time. I crossed the Hudson river just after dark, trundled through Albany in a rainstorm, and half an hour later pulled off the road into an old path between two big rocks to spend the night.

The thunder was rolling back and forth overhead, and the lightning was having target practice with the trees. But I'd picked out a nice secluded spot and I made myself comfortable. I cooked up a tasty plate of beans, some coffee, and fried potatoes. When I had eaten I took off my shoes, slumped down in the easy chair, lit a cigarette, and leaned back.

'Ah!' I said aloud. 'Solid comfort. If only Monica were here, how happy we would be.'

But she wasn't, so I picked up a book.

It wasn't a very good book. I must have dozed off. Maybe I slept for a couple of hours. Maybe three. Anyway, I woke with a start, the echo of a buster of thunderbolt still rattling the willow pattern tea-set in the china cupboard. My hair was standing on end from the electricity in the air.

Then the door banged open, a swirl of rain swept in, and the wind—anyway, I thought it was the wind—slammed the door to. I heard a sound like a ghost—there's no other way to describe it—of a sigh.

'Now this,' said the voice, 'is something like!'

I had jumped up to shut the door, and I stood there with my unread book in my hand, gaping. The wind had blown a wisp of mist into my trailer and the mist, instead of evaporating, remained there, seeming to turn slowly and to settle into shape. It got more and more solid until. . . .

Well, you know. It was a spectre. A haunt. A homeless ghost.

The creature remained there, regarding me in a decidedly cool manner.

'Sit down, chum,' it said, 'and don't look so pop-eyed. You make me nervous. This is my first night indoors in fifteen years and I wanta enjoy it.'

'Who—' I stammered—'who—'

'I'm not,' the spectre retorted, 'a brother owl, so don't who-who at me. What do I look like?'

'You look like a ghost,' I told him.

'Now you're getting smart, chum. I *am* a ghost. What *kind* of a ghost do I look like?'

I inspected it more closely. Now that the air inside my trailer had stopped eddying, it was reasonably firm of outline. It was a squat, heavy-set ghost, attired in ghostly garments that certainly never had come to it new. He wore the battered ghost of a felt hat, and a stubble of ghostly beard showed on his jowls.

'You look like a tramp ghost,' I answered with distaste, and my uninvited visitor nodded.

'Just what I am, chum,' he told me. 'Call me Spike Higgins. Spike for short. That was my name before it happened.'

'Before what happened?' I demanded. The ghost wafted across the trailer to settle down on a bunk, where he lay down and crossed his legs, hoisting one foot encased in a battered ghost of a shoe into the air.

'Before I was amachoor enough to fall asleep riding on top of a truck, and fall off right here fifteen years ago,' he told me. 'Ever since I had been forced to haunt this place. I wasn't no Boy Scout, so I got punished by bein' made to stay here in one spot. Me, who never stayed in one spot two nights running before!

'I been gettin' kind of tired of it the last couple of years. They wouldn't even lemme haunt a house. No, I hadda do all my haunting out in th' open, where th' wind an' rain could get at me, and every dog that went by could bark at me. Chum, you don't know what it means to me that you've picked this place to stop.'

'Listen,' I said firmly, 'you've got to get out of here!'

The apparition yawned.

'Chum,' he said, 'you're the one that's trespassin', not me. This is my happy hunting ground. Did I ask you to stop here?'

'You mean,' I asked between clenched teeth, 'that you won't go? You're going to stay here all night?'

'Right, chum,' the ghost grunted. 'Gimme a call for 6 a.m.' He closed his eyes, and began snoring in an artificial and highly insulting manner.

Then I got sore. I threw the book at him, and it bounced off the bunk without bothering him in the least. Spike Higgins opened an eye and leered at me.

'Went right through me,' he chortled. 'Instead of me goin' through it. Ha ha! Ha ha ha! Joke.'

'You—' I yelled, in a rage. 'You—stuff!'

And I slammed him with the chair cushions, which likewise went through him without doing any damage. Spike Higgins opened both eyes and stuck out his tongue at me.

Obviously I couldn't hurt him, so I got control of myself.

'Listen,' I said craftily. 'You say you are doomed to haunt this spot for ever? You can't leave?'

'Forbidden to leave,' Spike answered. 'Why?'

'Never mind,' I grinned. 'You'll find out.'

I snatched up my raincoat and hat and scrambled out into the storm. If that ghost was doomed to remain in that spot forever, I wasn't. I got into the car, got the motor going, and backed out of there. It took a lot of manoeuvring in the rain, with mud underwheel, but I made it. I got straightened out on the concrete and headed westwards.

I didn't stop until I'd covered twenty miles. Then, beginning to grin as I thought of the shock of the ghost of Spike Higgins must have felt when I yanked the trailer from underneath him, I parked on a stretch of old, unused road and then crawled back into the trailer again.

Inside, I slammed the door and. . . .

Ha!

Ha ha!

Ha ha ha!

Yes, more bitter laughter. Spike Higgins was still there, sound asleep and snoring.

I muttered something under my breath. Spike Higgins opened his eyes sleepily.

'Hello,' he yawned. 'Been having fun?'

'Listen,' I finally got it out. 'I—thought—you—were—doomed—to—stay—back—where—I—found—you—for ever!'

The apparition yawned again.

'Your mistake, chum. I didn't say I was doomed to stay. I said I was forbidden to leave. I didn't leave. You hauled me away. It's all your responsibility and I'm a free agent now.'

'You're a what?'

'I'm a free agent. I can ramble as far as I please. I can take up hoboing again. You've freed me. Thanks, chum. I won't forget.'

'Then—then—' I spluttered. Spike Higgins nodded.

'That's right. I've adopted you. I'm going to stick with you. We'll travel together.'

'But you can't!' I cried out, aghast. 'Ghosts don't travel around! They haunt houses—or cemeteries—or maybe woods. But—'

'What do you know about ghosts?' Spike Higgins's voice held sarcasm. 'There's all kinds of ghosts, chum. Includin' hobo ghosts, tramp ghosts with itchin' feet who can't stay put in one spot. Let me tell you, chum, a 'bo ghost like me ain't never had no easy time of it.

'Suppose they do give him a house to haunt? All right, he's got a roof over his head, but there he is, stuck. Houses don't move around. They don't go places. They stay in one spot till they rot.

'But things are different now. You've helped bring in a new age for the brotherhood of spooks. Now a fellow can haunt a house and be on the move at the same time. He can work at his job and still see the country. These trailers are the answer to a problem that's been bafflin' the best minds in the spirit world for thousands of years. It's the newest thing, the latest and best. Haunted trailers. I tell, you, we'll probably erect a monument to you at our next meeting. The ghosts of a monument, anyway.'

Spike Higgins had raised up on an elbow to make his speech. Now, grimacing, he lay back.

'That's enough, chum,' he muttered. 'Talking uses up my essence. I'm going to merge for a while. See you in the morning.'

'Merge with what?' I asked. Spike Higgins was already so dim I could hardly see him.

'Merge with the otherwhere,' a faint, distant voice told me, and Spike Higgins was gone.

I waited a minute to make sure. Then I breathed a big sigh of relief. I looked at my raincoat, at my wet feet, at the book on the floor, and knew it had all been a dream. I'd been walking in my sleep. Driving in it too. Having a nightmare.

I hung up the raincoat, slid out of my clothes, and got into a bunk.

I woke up late, and for a moment felt panic. Then I breathed easily again. The other bunk was untenanted. Whistling, I jumped up, showered, dressed, ate, and got under way.

It was a lovely day. Blue sky, wind, sunshine, birds singing. Thinking of Monica, I almost sang with them as I rolled down the road. In a week I'd be pulling up in front of Monica's aunt's place in Hollywood and tooting the horn. . . .

That was the moment when a cold draught of air sighed along the back of my neck, and the short hairs rose.

I turned, almost driving into a hay wagon. Beside me was a misty figure.

'I got tired of riding back there alone,' Spike Higgins told me. 'I'm gonna ride up front a while an' look at th' scenery.'

'You—you—' I shook with rage so that we nearly ran off the road. Spike Higgins reached out, grabbed the wheel in tenuous fingers, and jerked us back onto our course again.

'Take it easy, chum,' he said. 'There's enough competition in this world I'm in, without you hornin' into th' racket.'

I didn't say anything, but my thoughts must have been written on my face. I'd thought he was just a nightmare. But he was real. A ghost had moved in with me, and I hadn't the faintest idea how to move him out.

Spike Higgins grinned with a trace of malice.

'Sure, chum,' he said. 'It's perfectly logical. There's haunted castles, haunted palaces, and haunted houses. Why not a haunted trailer?'

'Why not haunted ferry-boats?' I demanded with bitterness. 'Why not haunted Pullmans? Why not haunted trucks?'

'You think there ain't?' Spike Higgins's misty countenance registered surprise at my ignorance. 'Could I tell you tales! There's a haunted ferry-boat makes the crossing at Poughkeepsie every stormy night at midnight. There's a haunted private train on the Atchinson, Sante Fé. Pal of mine haunts it. He always jumped trains, but he was a square dealer, and they gave him the private train for a reward.

'Then there's a truck on the New York Central that never gets where it's going. Never has yet. No matter where it starts out for, it winds up some place else. Bunch of my buddies haunt it. And another truck on the Southern Pacific that never has a train to pull it. Runs by itself. It's driven I dunno how many signalmen crazy, when they saw it go past right ahead of a whole train. I could tell you—'

'Don't!' I ordered. 'I forbid you to. I don't want to hear.'

'Why, sure, chum,' Spike Higgins agreed. 'But you'll get used to it. You'll be seein' a lot of me. Because where thou ghost, I ghost. Pun.' He gave a ghostly chuckle and relapsed into silence. I drove along, mind churning. I had to get rid of him. *Had* to. Before we reached California, at the very latest. But I didn't have the faintest idea in the world how I was going to.

Then, abruptly, Spike Higgins's ghost sat up straight.

'Stop!' he ordered. 'Stop, I say!'

We were on a lonely stretch of road, bordered by old cypresses, with weed-grown marshland beyond. I didn't see any reason for stopping. But Spike Higgins reached out and switched off the ignition. Then he slammed on the emergency brake. We came squealing to a stop, and just missed going up into a ditch.

'What did you do that for?' I yelled. 'You almost ditched us! Confound you, you ectoplasmic, hitch-hiking nuisance! If I ever find a way to lay hands on you—'

'Quiet, chum!' the apparition told me rudely. 'I just seen an old pal of mine. Slippery Samuels. I ain't seen him since he dropped a bottle of nitro just as he was gonna break into a bank in Mobile sixteen years ago. We're gonna give him a ride.'

'We certainly are not!' I cried. 'This is my car, and I'm not picking up any more—'

'It may be your car,' Spike Higgins sneered, 'but I'm the resident haunt, and I got full powers to extend hospitality to any buddy ghosts I want, see? Rule 11, sub-division c. Look it up. Hey Slippery, climb in!'

A finger of fog pushed through the partly open window of the car at his hail, enlarged, and there was a second apparition on the front seat with me.

The newcomer was long and lean, just as shabbily dressed as Spike Higgins, with a ghostly countenance as mournful as a Sunday School picnic on a rainy day.

'Spike, you old son of a gun,' the second spook murmured, in hollow tones that would have brought gooseflesh to a statue. 'How've you been? What're you doing here? Who's he?'—nodding at me.

'Never mind him,' Spike said disdainfully. 'I'm haunting his trailer. Listen, whatever became of the old gang?'

'Still hoboing it,' the long, lean apparition sighed. 'Nitro Nelson is somewhere around. Pacific Pete and Buffalo Benny are lying over in a haunted jungle somewhere near Toledo. I had a date to join 'em, but a storm blew me back to Wheeling a couple of days ago.'

'Mmm,' Spike Higgins's ghost muttered. 'Maybe we'll run into 'em. Let's go back in my trailer and do a little chinning. As for you, chum, make camp any time you want. Ta ta.'

The two apparitions oozed through the back of the car and were gone. I was boiling inside, but there was nothing I could do.

I drove on for another hour, went through Toledo, then stopped at a wayside camp. I paid my dollar, picked out a spot, and parked.

But when I entered the trailer, the ghosts of Spike Higgins and Slippery Samuels, the bank robber, weren't there. Nor had they shown up by the time I finished dinner. In fact I ate, washed, and got into bed with no sign of them.

Breathing a prayer that maybe Higgins had abandoned me to go back to 'boing it in the spirit world, I fell asleep. And began to dream. About Monica. . . .

When I awoke, there was a sickly smell in the air, and the heavy staleness of old tobacco smoke.

I opened my eyes. Luckily, I opened them prepared for the worst. Even so, I wasn't prepared well enough.

Spike Higgins was back. Ha! Ha ha! Ha ha ha! I'll say he was back. He lay on the opposite bunk, his eyes shut, his mouth open, snoring. Just the ghost of a snore, but quite loud enough. On the bunk above him lay his bank-robber companion. In the easy chair was slumped a third apparition, short and stout, with a round, whiskered face. A tramp spirit too.

So was the ghost stretched out on the floor, gaunt and cadaverous. So was the small, mournful spook in the bunk above me, his ectoplasmic hand swinging over the side, almost in my face. Tramps, all of them. Hobo spooks. Five hobo phantoms asleep in my trailer!

And there were cigarette butts in all the ash trays, and burns on my built-in writing desk. The cigarettes apparently had just been lit and let burn. The air was choking with stale smoke, and I had a headache I could have sold for a fire alarm, it was ringing so loudly in my skull.

I knew what had happened. During the night Spike Higgins and his pal had rounded up some more of their ex-hobo companions. Brought them back. To *my* trailer. Now—I was so angry I saw all five of them through a red haze that gave their ectoplasm a ruby tinge. Then I got hold of myself. I couldn't throw them out. I couldn't harm them. I couldn't touch them.

No, there was only one thing I could do. Admit I was beaten. Take my loss and quit while I could. It was a bitter pill to swallow. But if I wanted to reach Monica, if I wanted to enjoy the honeymoon we'd planned, I'd have to give up the fight.

I got into my clothes. Quietly I sneaked out, locking the trailer behind me. Then I hunted for the owner of the trailer camp, a lanky man, hard-eyed, but well dressed. I guessed he must have money.

'Had a sort of a party last night, hey?' he asked me, with a leering wink. 'I seen lights, an' heard singing, long after midnight. Not loud, though, so I didn't bother you. But it looked like somebody was havin' a high old time.'

I gritted my teeth.

'That was me,' I said, 'I couldn't sleep. I got up and turned on the radio. Truth is, I haven't slept a single night in that trailer. I guess I wasn't built for trailer life. That job cost me $2,998 new, just three days ago. I've got the bill-of-sale. How'd you like to buy it for fifteen hundred, and make two hundred easy profit on it?'

He gnawed his lip, but knew the trailer was a bargain. We settled for thirteen-fifty. I gave him the bill-of-sale, took the money, uncoupled, got into the car, and left there.

As I turned the bend in the road, heading westwards, there was no sign that Spike Higgins's ghost was aware of what had happened.

I even managed to grin as I thought of his rage when he woke up to find I had abandoned him. It was almost worth the money I'd lost to think of it.

Beginning to feel better, I stepped on the accelerator, piling up miles between me and that trailer. At least I was rid of Spike Higgins and his friends.

Ha!

Ha ha!

Ha ha ha!

That's what I thought.

About the middle of the afternoon I was well into Illinois. It was open country, and monotonous, so I turned on my radio. And the first thing I got was a police broadcast.

'All police, Indiana and Illinois! Be on the watch for a tan-and-chrome trailer, stolen about noon from a camp near Toledo. The thieves are believed heading west in it. That is all.'

I gulped. It couldn't be! But—it sounded like my trailer, all right. I looked in my rear-vision mirror, apprehensively. The road behind was empty. I breathed a small sigh of relief. I breathed it too soon. For at that moment, round a curve half a mile behind me, something swung into sight and came racing down the road after me.

The trailer.

Ha!

Ha ha!

There it came, a tan streak that zipped round the curve and came streaking after me, zigzagging wildly from side to side of the road, doing at least sixty—without a car pulling it.

My flesh crawled, and my hair stood on end. I stepped on the accelerator. Hard. And I picked up speed in a hurry. In half a minute

I was doing seventy, and the trailer was still gaining. Then I hit eighty —and passed a motor-cycle cop parked beside the road.

I had just a glimpse of his pop-eyed astonishment as I whizzed past, with the trailer chasing me fifty yards behind. Then, kicking on his starter, he slammed after us.

Meanwhile, in spite of everything the car would do, the trailer pulled up behind me and I heard the coupling clank as it was hitched on. At once my speed dropped. The trailer was swerving dangerously, and I had to slow. Behind me the cop was coming, siren open wide, I didn't worry about him because Spike Higgins was materializing beside me.

'Whew!' he said, grinning at me. 'My essence feels all used up. Thought you could give Spike Higgins and his pals the slip, huh? You'll learn, chum, you'll learn. That trooper looks like a tough baby. You'll have fun trying to talk yourself out of this.'

'Yes, but see what it'll get *you*, you ectoplasmic excrescence!' I raged at him. 'The trailer will be stored away in some county garage for months as evidence while I'm being held for trial on the charge of stealing it. And how'll you like haunting a garage?'

Higgins's face changed.

'Say, that's right,' he muttered. 'My first trip for fifteen years, too.'

He put his fingers to his lips, and blew the shrill ghost of a whistle. In a moment the car was filled with cold, clammy draughts as Slippery Samuels and the other three apparitions appeared in the seat beside Higgins.

Twisting and turning and seeming to intermingle a lot, they peered out at the cop, who was beside the car now, one hand on his gun butt, trying to crowd me over to the shoulder.

'All right, boys!' Higgins finished explaining. 'You know what we gotta do. Me an' Slippery'll take the car. You guys take the trailer!'

They slipped through the open windows like smoke. Then I saw Slippery Samuels holding on to the left front bumper, and Spike Higgins holding on to the right, their ectoplasm streaming out horizontal to the road, stretched and thinned by the air rush. And an instant later we began to move with a speed I had never dreamed of reaching.

We zipped ahead of the astonished cop, and the speedometer needle began to climb again. It took the trooper an instant to believe his eyes. Then with a yell he yanked out his gun and fired. A bullet bumbled past; then he was too busy trying to overtake us again to shoot.

The speedometer said ninety now, and was still climbing. It touched a hundred and stuck there. I was trying to pray when down the road a mile away I saw a sharp curve, a bridge, and a deep river. I froze. I couldn't even yell.

We came up to the curve so fast that I was still trying to move my lips when we hit it. I hit it. I didn't make any effort to take it. Instead I slammed on the brakes and prepared to plough straight ahead into a fence, a stand of young poplars, and the river.

But just as I braked, I heard Spike Higgins's ghostly scream, 'Allay-OOP!'

And before we reached the ditch, car and trailer swooped up in the air. An instant later at a height of a hundred and fifty feet, we hurtled straight westwards over the river and the town beyond.

I'd like to have seen the expression on the face of the motor-cycle cop then. As far as that goes, I'd like to have seen my own.

Then the river was behind us, and the town, and we were swooping down towards a dank, gloomy-looking patch of woods through which ran an abandoned railway line. A moment later we struck earth with a jouncing shock and came to rest.

Spike Higgins and Slippery Samuels let go of the bumpers and straightened themselves up. Spike Higgins dusted ghostly dust off his palms and leered at me.

'How was that, chum?' he asked. 'Neat, hey?'

'How—' I stuttered—'how—'

'Simple,' Spike Higgins answered. 'Anybody that can tip tables can do it. Just levitation, 'at's all. Hey, meet the boys. You ain't been introduced yet. This is Buffalo Benny, this one is Toledo Ike, this one Pacific Pete.'

The fat spook, the cadaverous one, and the melancholy little one appeared from behind the car, and smirked as Higgins introduced them. Then Higgins waved a hand impatiently.

'C'm on, chum,' he said. 'There's a road there that takes us out of these woods. Let's get going. It's almost dark, and we don't wanna spend the night here. This used to be in Dan Bracer's territory.'

'Who's Dan Bracer?' I demanded, getting the motor going because I was as anxious to get away from there as Spike Higgins's spook seemed to be.

'Just a railway dick,' Spike Higgins said, with a distinctly uneasy grin. 'Toughest bull that ever kicked a poor 'bo off a freight.'

'So he means he always drank black coffee,' Slippery Samuels put in, in a mournful voice. 'Cream turned sour when he picked up the jug.'

'Not that we was afraid of him—' Buffalo Benny, the fat apparition, squeaked. 'But—'

'We just never liked him,' Toledo Ike croaked, a sickly look on his ghostly features. 'O' course, he ain't active now. He was retired a couple of years back, an' jes' lately I got a rumour he was sick.'

'Dyin',' Pacific Pete murmured hollowly.

'Dyin'.' They all sighed the word, looking apprehensive. Then Spike Higgins's ghost scowled truculently at me.

'Never mind about Dan Bracer,' he snapped. 'Let's just get goin' out of here. And don't give that cop no more thought. You think a cop is gonna turn in a report that a car and trailer he was chasin' suddenly sailed up in the air an' flew away like an aeroplane? Not on your sweet life. He isn't gonna say nothing to nobody about it.'

Apparently he was right, because after I had driven out of the woods, with some difficulty, and onto a secondary highway, there was no further sign of pursuit. I headed westwards again, and Spike Higgins and his pals moved back to the trailer, where they lolled about, letting my cigarettes burn and threatening to call the attention of the police to me when I complained.

I grew steadily more morose and desperate as the Pacific Coast, and Monica, came nearer. I was behind schedule, due to Spike Higgins's insistence on my taking a roundabout route so they could see the Grand Canyon, and no way to rid myself of the obnoxious haunts appeared. I couldn't even abandon the trailer. Spike Higgins had been definite on that point. It was better to haul a haunted trailer around than to have one chasing you, he pointed out, and shuddering at the thought of being pursued by a trailer full of ghosts wherever I went, I agreed.

But if I couldn't get rid of them, it meant no Monica, no marriage, no honeymoon. And I was determined that nothing as insubstantial as a spirit was going to interfere with my life's happiness.

Just the same, by the time I had driven over the mountains and into California, I was almost on the point of doing something desperate. Apparently sensing this, Spike Higgins and the others had been on their good behaviour. But I could still see no way to get rid of them.

It was early afternoon when I finally rolled into Hollywood, haggard and unshaven, and found a trailer camp, where I parked. Heavy-hearted, I bathed and shaved and put on clean clothes. I didn't know what I was going to say to Monica, but I was already several days behind schedule, and I couldn't put off ringing her.

There was a telephone in the camp office. I looked up Ida Bracer—her aunt's name—in the book, then put through the call.

Monica herself answered. Her voice sounded distraught.

'Oh, Mel,' she exclaimed, as soon as I announced myself, 'where have you been? I've been expecting you for days.'

'I was delayed,' I told her, bitterly. 'Spirits. I'll explain later.'

'Spirits?' Her tone seemed cold. 'Well, anyway, now that you're here at last, I must see you at once. Mel, Uncle Dan is dying.'

'Uncle Dan?' I echoed.

'Yes, Aunt Ida's brother. He used to live in Iowa, but a few months ago he was taken ill, and he came out to be with Aunt and me. Now he's dying. The doctor says it's only a matter of hours.'

'Dying?' I repeated again. 'Your Uncle Dan, from Iowa, dying?'

Then it came to me. I began to laugh. Exultantly.

'I'll be right over!' I said, and hung up.

Still chuckling, I hurried out and unhitched my car. Spike Higgins stared at me suspiciously.

'Just got an errand to do,' I said airily. 'Be back soon.'

'You better be,' Spike Higgins's ghost said. 'We wanta drive round and see those movie stars' houses later on.'

Ten minutes later Monica herself, trim and lovely, was opening the door for me. In high spirits, I grabbed her round the waist, and kissed her. She turned her cheek to me, then, releasing herself, looked at me strangely.

'Mel,' she frowned, 'what in the world is wrong with you?'

'Nothing,' I carolled. 'Monica darling, I've got to talk to your uncle.'

'But he's too sick to see anyone. He's sinking fast, the doctor says.'

'All the more reason why I must see him,' I told her, and pushed into the house. 'Where is he, upstairs?'

I hurried up, and into the sickroom. Monica's uncle, a big man with a rugged face and a chin like the prow of a battleship, was in bed, breathing stertorously.

'Mr Bracer!' I said, breathless, and his eyes opened slowly.

'Who're you?' a voice as raspy as a shovel scraping a concrete floor growled.

'I'm going to marry Monica,' I told him. 'Mr Bracer, have you ever heard of Spike Higgins? Or Slippery Samuels? Or Buffalo Benny, Pacific Pete, Toledo Ike?'

'Heard of 'em?' A bright glow came into the sick man's eyes. 'Ha! I'll say I have. And laid hands on 'em, too, more'n once. But they're dead now.'

'I know they are,' I told him. 'But they're still around. Mr Bracer, how'd you like to meet up with them again?'

'Would I!' Dan Bracer murmured, and his hands clenched in unconscious anticipation. 'Ha!'

'Then,' I said, 'if you'll wait for me in the cemetery the first night after—after—well, anyway, wait for me, and I'll put you in touch with them.'

The ex-railway detective nodded. He grinned broadly, like a tiger viewing its prey and eager to be after it. Then he lay back, his eyes closed, and Monica, running in, gave a little gasp.

'He's gone!' she said.

'Ha ha!' I chuckled. 'Ha ha ha! What a surprise this is going to be to certain parties.'

The funeral was held in the afternoon, two days later. I didn't see Monica much in the interim. In the first place, though she hadn't known her uncle well, and wasn't particularly grieved, there were a lot of details to be attended to. In the second place, Spike Higgins and his pals kept me on the jump. I had to drive around Hollywood, to all the stars' houses, to Malibou Beach, Santa Monica, Laurel Canyon, and the various studios, so they could sightsee.

Then, too, Monica rather seemed to be avoiding me, when I did have time free. But I was too inwardly gleeful at the prospect of getting rid of the ghosts of Higgins and his pals to notice.

I managed to slip away from Higgins to attend the funeral of Dan Bracer, but could not help grinning broadly, and even at times chuckling, as I thought of his happy anticipation of meeting Spike Higgins and the others again. Monica eyed me oddly, but I could explain later. It wasn't quite the right moment to go into details.

After the funeral, Monica said she had a headache, so I promised to come round later in the evening. I returned to the trailer to find Spike Higgins and the others sprawled out, smoking my cigarettes again. Higgins looked at me with dark suspicion.

'Chum,' he said, 'we wanta be hitting the road again. We leave tomorrow, get me?'

'Tonight, Spike,' I said cheerfully. 'Why wait? Right after sunset you'll be on your way. To distant parts. Tra la, tra le, tum te tum.'

He scowled, but could think of no objection. I waited impatiently for sunset. As soon as it was thoroughly dark, I hitched up and drove out of the trailer camp, heading for the cemetery where Dan Bracer had been buried that afternoon.

Spike Higgins was still surly, but unsuspicious until I drew up and parked by the low stone wall at the nearest point to Monica's uncle's grave. Then, gazing out at the darkness-shadowed cemetery, he looked uneasy.

'Say,' he snarled, 'watcha stoppin' here for? Come on, let's be movin'.'

'In a minute, Spike,' I said. 'I have some business here.' I slid out and hopped over the low wall.

'Mr Bracer!' I called. 'Mr Bracer!'

I listened, but a long freight rumbling by half a block distant, where the Union Pacific lines entered the city, drowned out any sound. For a moment I could see nothing. Then a misty figure came into view among the headstones.

'Mr Bracer!' I called as it approached. 'This way!'

The figure headed towards me. Behind me Spike Higgins, Slippery Samuels and the rest of the ghostly crew were pressed against the wall, staring apprehensively into the darkness. And they were able to recognize the dim figure approaching before I could be sure of it.

'Dan Bracer!' Spike Higgins choked, in a high, ghostly squeal.

'It's him!' Slippery Samuels groaned.

'In the spirit!' Pacific Pete wailed. 'Oh oh oh oh OH!'

They tumbled backwards, with shrill squeaks of dismay. Dan Bracer's spirit came forward faster. Paying no attention to me, he took off after the retreating five.

Higgins turned and fled, wildly, with the others at his heels. They were heading towards the railway line, over which the freight was still rumbling, and Dan Bracer was now at their heels. Crowding each other, Higgins and Slippery Samuels and Buffalo Benny swung on to a passing truck, with Pacific Pete and Toledo Ike catching wildly at the rungs of the next.

They drew themselves up to the top of the trucks, and stared back. Dan Bracer's ghost seemed, for an instant, about to be left behind. But one long ectoplasmic arm shot out. A ghostly hand caught the rail of the guard's van, and Dan Bracer swung aboard. A moment later, he was running forward along the tops of the trucks, and up ahead of him, Spike Higgins and his pals were racing towards the engine.

That was the last I saw of them—five phantom figures fleeing, the sixth pursuing in happy anticipation. Then they were gone out of my life, heading east.

Still laughing to myself at the manner in which I had rid myself of Spike Higgins's ghost, and so made it possible for Monica and me to be married and enjoy our honeymoon trailer trip after all, I drove to Monica's aunt's house.

'Melvin!' Monica said sharply, as she answered my ring. 'What are you laughing about now?'

'Your uncle,' I chuckled. 'He—'

'My uncle!' Monica gasped. 'You—you fiend! You laughed when he died! You laughed all during his funeral! Now you're laughing because he's dead!'

'No, Monica!' I said. 'Let me explain. About the spirits, and how I—'

Her voice broke.

'Forcing your way into the house—laughing at my poor Uncle Dean—laughing at his funeral—'

'But, Monica!' I cried. 'It isn't that way at all. I've just been to the cemetery, and—'

'And you came back laughing,' Monica retorted. 'I never want to see you again. Our engagement is broken. And worst of all is the *way* you laugh. It's so—so ghostly! So spooky. Blood-chilling. Even if you hadn't done the other things, I could never marry a man who laughs like that. So here's your ring. And goodbye.'

Leaving me staring at the ring in my hand, she slammed the door. And that was that. Monica is very strongminded, and what she says, she means. I couldn't even try to explain. About Spike Higgins. And how I'd unconsciously come to laugh that way through associating with five phantoms. After all, I'd just rid myself of them for good. And the only way Monica would ever have believed my story would have been from my showing her Spike Higgins's ghost himself.

Ha!

Ha ha!

Ha ha ha ha!

If you know anyone who wants to buy a practically unused trailer, cheap, let them get in touch with me.

THE STRANGER

Ambrose Bierce

A man stepped out of the darkness into the little illuminated circle about our failing camp-fire and seated himself upon a rock.

'You are not the first to explore this region,' he said gravely.

Nobody controverted his statement; he was himself proof of its truth, for he was not of our party and must have been somewhere near when we camped. Moreover, he must have companions not far away; it was not a place where one would be living or travelling alone. For more than a week we had seen, besides ourselves and our animals, only such living things as rattlesnakes and horned toads. In an Arizona desert one does not long coexist with only such creatures as these; one must have pack animals, supplies, arms—'an outfit'. And all these imply comrades. It was, perhaps, a doubt as to what manner of men this unceremonious stranger's comrades might be, together with something in his words interpretable as a challenge, that caused every man of our half-dozen 'gentlemen adventurers' to rise to a sitting posture and lay his hand upon a weapon—an act signifying, in that time and place, a policy of expectation. The stranger gave the matter no attention, and began again to speak in the same deliberate, uninflected monotone in which he had delivered his first sentence:

'Thirty years ago Ramon Gallegos, William Shaw, George W. Kent and Berry Davis, all of Tucson, crossed the Santa Catalina Mountains and travelled due west, as nearly as the configuration of the country permitted. We were prospecting and it was our intention, if we found nothing, to push through to the Gila river at some point near Big Bend, where we understood there was a settlement. We had a good outfit but no guide—just Ramon Gallegos, William Shaw, George W. Kent and Berry Davis.'

The man repeated the names slowly and distinctly, as if to fix them in the memories of his audience, every member of which was now attentively observing him, but with a slackened apprehension regarding his possible companions somewhere in the darkness which seemed to enclose us like a black wall, for in the manner of this volunteer historian was no suggestion of an unfriendly purpose. His act was rather that of a harmless lunatic than an enemy. We were not so new to the country as not to know that the solitary life of many a plainsman had a tendency to develop eccentricities of conduct and character not always easily distinguishable from mental aberration. A man is like a tree: in a forest of his fellows he will grow as straight as his generic and individual nature permits; alone, in the open, he yields to the deforming stresses and tortions that environ him. Some such thoughts were in my mind as I watched the man from the shadow of my hat, pulled low to shut out the fire-light. A witless fellow, no doubt, but what could he be doing there in the heart of a desert?

Nobody having broken the silence, the visitor went on to say:

'This country was not then what it is now. There was not a ranch between the Gila and the Gulf. There was a little game here and there in the mountains, and near the infrequent water-holes grass enough to keep our animals from starvation. If we should be so fortunate as to encounter no Indians we might get through. But within a week the purpose of the expedition had altered from discovery of wealth to preservation of life. We had gone too far to go back, for what was ahead could be no worse than what was behind; so we pushed on, riding by night to avoid Indians and the intolerable heat, and concealing ourselves by day as best we could. Sometimes, having exhausted our supply of wild meat and emptied

A man stepped out of the darkness into the illuminated circle

our casks, we were days without food and drink; then a water-hole or a shallow pool in the bottom of an arroyo so restored our strength and sanity that we were able to shoot some of the wild animals that sought it also. Sometimes it was a bear, sometimes an antelope, a coyote, a cougar—that was as God pleased; all were food.

'One morning as we skirted a mountain range, seeking a practicable pass, we were attacked by a band of Apaches who had followed our trail up a gulch—it is not far from here. Knowing that they outnumbered us ten to one, they took none of their usual cowardly precautions, but dashed upon us at a gallop, firing and yelling. Fighting was out of the question. We urged our feeble animals up the gulch as far as there was footing for a hoof, then threw ourselves out of our saddles and took to the chaparral on one of the slopes, abandoning our entire outfit to the enemy. But we retained our rifles, every man—Ramon Gallegos, William Shaw, George W. Kent and Berry Davis.'

'Same old crowd,' said the humorist of the party. A gesture of disapproval from our leader silenced him, and the stranger proceeded with his tale:

'The savages dismounted also, and some of them ran up the gulch beyond the point at which we had left it, cutting off further retreat in that direction and forcing us on up the side. Unfortunately the chaparrel extended only a short distance up the slope, and as we came into the open ground above we took the fire of a dozen rifles; but Apaches shoot badly when in a hurry, and God so willed it that none of us fell. Twenty yards up the slope, beyond the edge of the brush, were vertical cliffs, in which, directly in front of us, was a narrow opening. Into that we ran, finding ourselves in a cavern about as large as an ordinary room. Here for a time we were safe. A single man with a repeating rifle could defend the entrance against all the Apaches in the land. But against hunger and thirst we had no defence. Courage we still had, but hope was a memory.

'Not one of those Indians did we afterwards see, but by the smoke and glare of their fires in the gulch we knew that by day and by night they watched with ready rifles in the edge of the bush—knew that if we made a sortie not a man of us would live to take three steps into the open. For three days, watching in turn, we held out, before our suffering became insupportable. Then—it was the morning of the fourth day—Ramon Gallegos said:

'"Señores, I know not well of the good God and what please him. I have lived without religion, and I am not acquaint with that of you. Pardon, señores, if I shock you, but for me the time is come to beat the game of the Apache."

'He knelt upon the rock floor of the cave and pressed his pistol against his temple. "Madre de Dios," he said, "comes now the soul of Ramon Gallegos."

'And so he left us—William Shaw, George W. Kent and Berry Davis.

'I was the leader. It was for me to speak.

'"He was a brave man," I said. "He knew when to die, and how. It is foolish to go mad from thirst and fall by Apache bullets, or be skinned alive—it is in bad taste. Let us join Ramon Gallegos."

'"That is right," said William Shaw.

'"That is right," said George W. Kent.

'I straightened the limbs of Ramon Gallegos and put a handkerchief over his face. Then William Shaw said: "I should like to look like that a little while."

'And George W. Kent said that he felt that way too.

'"It shall be so," I said. "The red devils will wait a week. William Shaw and George W. Kent, draw and kneel,"

'They did so and I stood before them.

'"Almighty God, our Father," said I.

'"Almighty God, our Father," said William Shaw.

'"Almighty God, our Father," said George W. Kent.

'"Forgive us our sins," said I.

'"Forgive us our sins," said they.

'"And receive our souls."

'"And receive our souls."

'"Amen!"

'"Amen!"

'I laid them beside Ramon Gallegos and covered their faces.'

There was a quick commotion on the opposite side of the camp-fire. One of our party had sprung to his feet, pistol in hand.

'And you!' he shouted, 'you dared to escape?—you dare to be alive? You cowardly hound, I'll send you to join them if I hang for it!'

But with the leap of a panther the captain was upon him, grasping his wrist. 'Hold it in, Sam Yountsey, hold it in!'

We were now all upon our feet—except the stranger, who sat motionless and apparently inattentive. Someone seized Yountsey's other arm.

'Captain,' I said, 'there is something wrong here. This fellow is either a lunatic or merely a liar—just plain, everyday liar that Yountsey has no call to kill. If this man was of that party it had five members, one of whom—probably himself—he has not named.'

'Yes,' said the captain, releasing the insurgent, who sat down, 'there is something—unusual. Years ago four dead bodies of white men, scalped and shamefully mutilated, were found about the mouth of that cave. They are buried there; I have seen the graves—we shall all see them tomorrow.'

The stranger rose, standing tall in the light of the expiring fire, which in our breathless attention to his story we had neglected to keep going.

'There were four,' he said. 'Ramon Gallegos, William Shaw, George W. Kent and Berry Davis.'

With this reiterated roll-call of the dead he walked into the darkness and we saw him no more.

At that moment one of our party, who had been on guard, strode in among us, rifle in hand and somewhat excited.

'Captain,' he said, 'for the last half-hour three men have been standing out there on the *mesa*.' He pointed in the direction taken by the stranger. 'I could see them distinctly, for the moon is up, but as they had no guns and I had them covered with mine, I thought it was their move. They have made none, but, damn it! they have got on my nerves.'

'Go back to your post, and stay till you see them again,' said the captain. 'The rest of you lie down again, or I'll kick you all into the fire.'

The sentinel obediently withdrew, swearing, and did not return. As we were arranging our blankets, the fiery Yountsey said: 'I beg your pardon, Captain, but who the devil do you take them to be?'

'Ramon Gallegos, William Shaw and George W. Kent.'

'But how about Berry Davis? I ought to have shot him.'

'Quite needless; you couldn't have made him any deader. Go to sleep.'

BAD COMPANY

Walter de la Mare

It is very seldom that one encounters what would appear to be sheer unadulterated evil in a human face; an evil, I mean, active, deliberate, deadly, dangerous. Folly, heedlessness, vanity, pride, craft, meanness, stupidity—yes. But even Iagos in this world are few, and devilry is as rare as witchcraft.

One winter's evening some little time ago, bound on a visit to a friend in London, I found myself on the platform of one of its many subterranean railway stations. It is an ordeal that one may undergo as seldom as one can. The glare and glitter, the noise, the very air one breathes affect nerves and spirits. One expects vaguely strange meetings in such surroundings. On this occasion, the expectation was justified. The mind is at times more attentive than the eye. Already tired, and troubled with personal cares and problems, which a little wisdom and enterprise should have refused to entertain, I had seated myself on one of the low, wooden benches to the left of the entrance to the platform, when, for no conscious reason, I was prompted to turn my head in the direction of a fellow traveller, seated across the gangway on the fellow to my bench some few yards away.

What was wrong with him? He was enveloped in a loose cape or cloak, sombre and motionless. He appeared to be wholly unaware of my abrupt scrutiny. And yet I doubt it; for the next moment, although the door of the nearest coach gaped immediately opposite him, he had shuffled into the compartment I had entered myself, and now in its corner, confronted me, all but knee to knee. I could have touched him with my hand. We had, too, come at once into an even more intimate contact than that of touch. Our eyes—his own fixed in a dwelling and lethargic stare—had instantly met, and no less rapidly mine had uncharitably recoiled, not only in misgiving, but in something little short of disgust. The effect resembled that of an acid on milk, and for the time being cast my thoughts into confusion. Yet that one glance had taken him in.

He was old—over seventy. A wide-brimmed rusty and dusty black hat concealed his head—a head fringed with wisps of hair, lank and paper-grey. His loose, jaded cheeks were of the colour of putty; the thin lips above the wide unshaven and dimpled chin showing scarcely a trace of red. The cloak suspended from his shoulders mantled him to his shins. One knuckled, cadaverous, mittened hand clasped a thick ash stick, its handle black and polished with long usage. The only sign of life in his countenance was secreted in his eyes—fixed on mine—hazed and dully glistening, as a snail in winter is fixed to a wall. There was a dull deliberate challenge in them, and, as I fancied, something more than that. They suggested that he had been in wait for me; that for him, it was almost 'well met!'

For minutes together I endeavoured to accept their challenge, to make sure. Yet I realized, fascinated the while, that he was well aware of the futility of this attempt, as a snake is of the restless, fated bird in the branches above its head.

Such a statement, I am aware, must appear wildly exaggerated, but I can only record my impression. It was already lateish—much later than I had intended. The passengers came and went, and, whether intentionally or not, none consented to occupy the seat vacant beside him. I fixed my eyes on an advertisement—that of a Friendly Society I remember!—immediately above his head, with the intention of watching him in the field of an eye that I could not persuade to meet his own in full focus again.

He had instantly detected this ingenuous device. By a fraction of an inch he had shifted his grasp upon his stick. So intolerable, at length,

The only sign of life in his countenance was secreted in his eyes

became the physical—and psychical—effect of his presence on me that I determined to leave the train at the next station, and there to await the next. And at this precise moment, I was conscious that he had not only withdrawn his eyes but closed them.

I was not so easily to free myself of his company. A glance over my shoulder as, after leaving the train, I turned towards the lift, showed him hastily groping his way out of the carriage. The metal gate clanged. The lift slid upwards and, such is the contrariness of human nature, a faint disappointment followed. One may, for example, be appalled and yet engrossed in reading an account of some act of infamous cruelty.

Concealing myself as best I could at the bookstall, I awaited the next lift-load. Its few passengers having dispersed, he himself followed. In spite of age and infirmity, he *had*, then, ascended alone the spiral staircase. Glancing, it appeared, neither to right nor left, he passed rapidly through the barrier. And yet—*had* he not seen me?

The Collector raised his head, opened his mouth, watched his retreating figure, but made no attempt to retrieve his ticket. It was dark now—the dark of London. In my absence underground, minute frozen pellets of snow had fallen, whitening the streets and lulling the sound of the traffic. On emerging into the street, he turned in the direction of the next station—my own. Yet again—had he, or had he not, been aware that he was being watched? However that might be, my journey lay his way, and that way my feet directed me; although I was already later than I intended. I followed him, led on no doubt in part merely by the effect he had had on me. Some twenty or thirty yards ahead, his dark shapelessness showed—distinct against the whitening pavement.

The waters of the Thames, I was aware, lay on my left. A muffled blast from the siren of a tug announced its presence. Keeping my distance, I followed him on. One lamp-post—two—three. At that, he seemed to pause for a moment, as if to listen, momentarily glanced back (as I fancied) and vanished.

When I came up with it, I found that this third lamp-post vaguely illuminated the mouth of a narrow, lightless alley between highish walls. It led me, after a while, into another alley, yet dingier. The wall on the left of this was evidently that of a large garden; on the right came a row of nondescript houses, looming up in their neglect against a starless sky.

The first of these houses *appeared* to be occupied. The next two were vacant. Dingy curtains, soot-grey against their snowy window-sills, hung over the next. A litter of paper and refuse—abandoned by the last long gust of wind that must have come whistling round the nearer angle of the house—lay under the broken flight of steps up to a mid-Victorian porch. The small snow clinging to the bricks and to the worn and weathered cement of the wall only added to its gaunt lifelessness.

In the faint hope of other company coming my way, and vowing that I would follow no farther than to the outlet of yet another pitch-black and uninviting alley or court—which might indeed prove a dead end—I turned into it. It was then that I observed, in the rays of the lamp over my head, that in spite of the fineness of the snow and the brief time that had elapsed, there seemed to be no trace on its surface of recent footsteps.

A faintly thudding echo accompanied me on my way. I have found it very useful—in the country—always to carry a small electric torch in my greatcoat pocket; but for the time being I refrained from using it. This alley proved not to be blind. Beyond a patch of waste ground, a nebulous, leaden-grey vacancy marked a loop here of the Thames—I decided to go no farther; and then perceived a garden gate in the wall to my right. It was ajar, but could not long have been so because no more than an instant's flash of my torch showed marks in the snow of its recent shifting. And yet there was little wind. On the other hand, here was the open river; just a breath of a breeze across its surface might account for this. The cracked and blistered paint was shimmering with a thin coat of rime—of hoarfrost, and as if a finger had but just now scrawled it there, a clumsy arrow showed, its 'V' pointing inward. A tramp, an errand-boy, mere accident might have accounted for this. It may indeed have been a mark made some time before on the paint.

I paused in an absurd debate with myself, chiefly I think because I felt some little alarm at the thought of what might follow; yet led on also by the conviction that I had been intended, decoyed to follow. I pushed the gate a little wider open, peered in, and made my way up a woody path beneath ragged unpruned and leafless fruit trees towards the house. The snow's own light revealed a ramshackle flight of steps up to a poor, frenchified sort of canopy above french windows, one-half of their glazed doors ajar. I ascended, and peered into the intense gloom beyond it. And thus and then prepared to retrace my steps as quickly as possible, I called (in tones as near those of a London policeman as I could manage):

'Hello there! Is anything wrong? Is anyone wanted?' After all, I could at least explain to my fellow passenger if he appeared that I found both his gate and his window open; and the house was hardly pleasantly situated.

No answer was returned to me. In doubt and disquietude, but with a conviction that all was not well, I flashed my torch over the walls and furniture of the room and its heavily framed pictures. How could anything be well—with unseen company such as this besieging one's senses! Ease and pleasant companionship, the room may once have been capable of giving; in its dirt, cold and neglect it showed nothing of that now. I crossed it, paused again in the passage beyond it, and listened. I then entered the room beyond. Venetian blinds, many of the slats of which had outworn their webbing and heavy, crimson chenille side-curtains concealed its windows. The ashes of a fire showed beyond rusty bars of the grate under a black marble mantelpiece. An oil lamp on the table, with a green shade, exuded a stink of paraffin; beyond was a table littered with books and papers, and an overturned chair. There I could see the bent-up old legs, perceptibly lean beneath the trousers, of the occupant of the room. In no doubt of whose remains these were, I drew near, and with bared teeth and icy, trembling fingers, drew back the fold of the cloak that lay over the face. Death has a strange sorcery. A shuddering revulsion of feeling took possession of me. This cold, once genteel, hideous, malignant room—and this!

The skin of the blue loose cheek was drawn tight over the bone; the mouth lay a little open, showing the dislodged false teeth beneath; the dull unspeculative eyes stared out from beneath lowered lids towards the black mouth of the chimney above the fireplace. Vileness and iniquity had left their marks on the lifeless features, and yet it was rather with compassion than with horror and disgust that I stood regarding them. What desolate solitude, what misery must this old man, abandoned to himself, have experienced during the last years of his life; encountering nothing but enmity and the apprehension of his fellow creatures. I am not intending to excuse or even commiserate what I cannot understand, but the almost complete absence of any goodness in the human spirit cannot but condemn the heart to an appalling isolation. Had he been murdered, or had he come to a violent but natural end? In either case, horror and terror must have supervened. That I had been enticed, deliberately led on, to this discovery I hadn't the least doubt, extravagant though this, too, may seem. Why? What for?

I could not bring myself to attempt to light the lamp. Besides, in that last vigil, it must have burnt itself out. My torch revealed a stub of candle on the mantelpiece. I lit that. He seemed to have been engaged in writing when the enemy of us all had approached him in silence and had struck him down. A long and unsealed envelope lay on the table. I drew out the contents—a letter and a Will, which had been witnessed some few weeks before, apparently by a tradesman's boy and, possibly, by some derelict charwoman, Eliza Hinks. I knew enough about such things to be sure that the Will was valid and complete. This old man had been evidently more than fairly rich in this world's goods, and reluctant to surrender them. The letter was addressed to his two sisters: 'To my two Sisters, Amelia and Maude.' Standing there in the cold and the silence, and utterly alone—for, if any occupant of the other world had decoyed me there, there was not the faintest hint in consciousness that he or his influence was any longer present with me—I read the vilest letter that has ever come my way. Even in print. It stated that he knew the circumstances of these two remaining relatives—that he was well aware of their poverty and physical conditions. One of them, it seemed, was afflicted with Cancer. He then proceeded to explain that, although they should by the intention of their mother have had a due share in her property and in the money she had left, it rejoiced him to think that his withholding of this knowledge must continually have added to their wretchedness. Why he so hated them was only vaguely suggested.

The Will he had enclosed with the letter left all that he died possessed of to—of all human establishments that need it least—the authorities of Scotland Yard. It was to be devoted, it ran, to the detection of such evil-doers as are ignorant or imbecile enough to leave their misdemeanours and crimes detectable.

It is said that confession is good for the soul. Well then, as publicly as possible, I take this opportunity of announcing that, there and then, I made a little heap of envelope, letter and Will on the hearth and put a match to them. When every vestige of the paper had been consumed, I stamped the ashes down. I had touched nothing else. I would leave the vile, jaded, forsaken house to reveal its own secret; and I might ensure that that would not be long delayed.

What continues to perplex me is that so far as I can see no other agency but that of this evil old recluse himself had led me to my discovery. Why? Can it have been with this very intention? I stooped down and peeped and peered narrowly in under the lowered lids in the light of my torch, but not the feeblest flicker, remotest signal—or faintest syllabling echo of any message rewarded me. Dead fish are less unseemly.

And yet. Well—we are all of us, I suppose, at any extreme *capable* of remorse and not utterly shut against repentance. Is it possible that this priceless blessing is not denied us even when all that's earthly else appears to have come to an end?

THE YELLOW CAT

Michael Joseph

It all began when Grey was followed home, inexplicably enough, by the strange, famished yellow cat. The cat was thin with large, intense eyes which gleamed amber in the forlorn light of the lamp on the street corner. It was standing there as Grey passed, whistling dejectedly, for he had had a depressing run of luck at Grannie's tables, and it made a slight piteous noise as it looked up at him. Then it followed at his heels, creeping along as though it expected to be kicked unceremoniously out of the way.

Grey did, indeed, make a sort of half-threatening gesture when, looking over his shoulder, he saw the yellow cat behind.

'If you were a black cat,' he muttered, 'I'd welcome you—but get out!'

The cat's melancholy amber eyes gleamed up at him, but it made no sign and continued to follow. This would have annoyed Grey in his already impatient humour, but he seemed to find a kind of savage satisfaction in the fact that he was denied even the trifling consolation of a good omen. Like all gamblers, he was intensely superstitious, although he had had experience in full measure of the futility of all supposedly luck-bringing mascots. He carried a monkey's claw sewn in the lining of his waitcoat pocket, not having the courage to throw it away. But this wretched yellow cat that ought to have been black did not irritate him as might have been expected.

He laughed softly; the restrained, unpleasant laugh of a man fighting against misfortune.

'Come on, then, you yellow devil; we'll sup together.'

He took his gloveless hand from his coat pocket and beckoned to the animal at his heels; but it took as little notice of his gesture of invitation as it had of his menacing foot a moment before. It just slid along the greasy pavement, covering the ground noiselessly, not deviating in the slightest from the invisible path it followed, without hesitation.

It was a bitterly cold, misty night, raw and damp. Grey shivered as he thrust his hand back into the shelter of his pocket and hunched his shoulders together underneath the thin coat that afforded but little protection against the cold.

With a shudder of relief he turned into the shelter of the courtyard which lay between the icy street and the flight of stairs which led to his room. As he stumbled numbly over the rough cobblestones of the yard he suddenly noticed that the yellow cat had disappeared.

He was not surprised and gave no thought whatever to the incident until, a few minutes later, at the top of the ramshackle stairs, the feeble light of a hurricane lamp revealed the creature sitting, or rather lying, across the threshold of his door.

He took an uncertain step backwards. He said to himself: 'That's odd.' The cat looked up at him impassively with brooding, sullen eyes. He opened the door, stretching over the animal to turn the crazy handle.

Silently the yellow cat rose and entered the shadowy room. There was something uncanny, almost sinister in its smooth noiseless movements. With fingers that shook slightly, Grey fumbled for matches, struck a light and, closing the door behind him, lit the solitary candle.

He lived in this one room, over a mews which had become almost fashionable since various poverty-stricken people, whose names still carried some weight with the bourgeois tradesmen of this Mayfair backwater, had triumphantly installed themselves; and Grey turned it skilfully to account when he spoke with casual indifference of 'the flat' he occupied, 'next to Lady Susan Tyrrell's'.

Grey, although he would never have admitted it, was a cardsharper and professional gambler. But even a cardsharper needs a little ordinary luck. Night after night he watched money pass into the hands of 'the pigeons', ignorant, reckless youngsters, and foolish old women who, having money to burn, ought by all the rules of the game to have lost. Yet when playing with him, Grey, a man respected even among the shabby fraternity of those who live by their wits, they won. He had turned to roulette, but even with a surreptitious percentage interest in the bank he had lost. His credit was exhausted. Grannie herself had told him he was a regular Jonah. He was cold, hungry and desperate. Presently his clothes, the last possession, would betray him, and no longer would he be able to borrow the casual trifle that started him nightly in his desperate bout with fortune.

His room contained a wooden bed and a chair. A rickety table separated them. The chair served Grey as a wardrobe; on the table stood a candle with a few used matches which he used to light the cheap cigarettes he smoked in bed; the grease had a habit of adhering to the tobacco when the candle was used, and Grey was fastidious. The walls were bare save for a cupboard, a pinned-up *Sporting Life* Racing Calendar and two cheap reproductions of Kirchner's midinettes. There was no carpet on the floor. A piece of linoleum stretched from the empty grate to the side of the bed.

At first Grey could not see the cat, but the candle, gathering strength, outlined its shadow grotesquely against the wall. It was crouched on the end of the bed.

He lighted one of the used matches and lit the small gas ring which was the room's sole luxury. Gas was included in the few shillings he paid weekly for rent; consequently Grey used it for warmth. He seldom used it to cook anything, as neither whisky (which he got by arrangement with one of Grannie's waiters), bread nor cheese, which formed his usual diet, require much cooking.

The cat moved and, jumping noiselessly on to the floor, cautiously approached the gas ring, by the side of which it stretched its lean yellowish body. Very softly but plaintively it began to mew.

Grey cursed it. Then he turned to the cupboard and took out a cracked jug. He moved the bread onto his own plate and poured out the little milk it contained in the shallow bread plate.

The cat drank not greedily but with the fierce rapidity which betokens hunger and thirst. Grey watched it idly as he poured whisky into a cup. He drank, and refilled the cup. He then began to undress, carefully, in order to prolong the life of his worn dinner-jacket.

The cat looked up. Grey, taking off his shirt, beneath which, having no vest, he wore another woollen shirt, became uncomfortably aware of its staring yellow eyes. Seized with a crazy impulse, he poured the whisky from his cup into the remainder of the milk in the plate.

'Share and share alike,' he cried. 'Drink, you. . . .'

Then the yellow cat snarled at him; the vilest loathsome sound; and Grey for a moment was afraid. Then he laughed, as if at himself for allowing control to slip, and finished undressing, folding the garments carefully, and hanging them on the chair.

The cat went back to its place at the foot of the bed, its eyes gleaming warily in Grey's direction. He restrained his impulse to throw it out of the room and clambered between the rough blankets without molesting it.

By daylight the cat was an ugly misshapen creature. It had not moved from the bed. Grey regarded it with amused contempt.

Usually the morning found him profoundly depressed and irritable. For some unaccountable reason he felt now almost light-hearted.

He dressed, counted his money and decided to permit himself the luxury of some meagre shopping in the adjacent Warwick Market, which supplied the most expensive restaurant proprietors with the cheapest food. Nevertheless, it was an accommodating spot for knowledgeable individuals like Grey.

The cat, still crouching on the bed, made no attempt to follow him, and he closed the door as softly as its erratic hinges would allow, aware that the cat's eyes still gazed steadily in his direction.

In the market, he obeyed an impulse to buy food for the cat, and at the cost of a few pence added a portion of raw fish to his purchases. On the way home he cursed himself for fool, and would have thrown the fish away, the clumsy paper wrapping having become sodden with moisture, when he was hailed by a voice he had almost forgotten.

'Grey! Just the man I want to see!'

Grey greeted him with a fair show of amiability, although, if appearance were any indication, the other was even less prosperous than himself. He, too, had been an *habitué* of Grannie's in the old days, but had long since drifted out on the sea of misfortune. Despite his shabby appearance, he turned to Grey and said:

'You'll have a drink?' Then, noting Grey's dubious glance, he laughed and added: 'It's on me all right. I've just touched lucky.'

A little later Grey emerged from the public house on the corner the richer by five pounds, which the other had insisted on lending him in return for past favours. What exactly the past favours had been, Grey was too dazed to inquire; as far as he could recollect he had always treated the man with scant courtesy. He did not even remember his name.

He was still trying to remember who the man was when he climbed the stairs. He knew him well enough, for Grey was the type who never forgot a face. It was when his eyes alighted on the yellow cat that he suddenly remembered.

The man was Felix Mortimer. And Felix Mortimer had shot himself during the summer!

At first Grey tried to assure himself that he had made a mistake. Against his better judgement he tried to convince himself that the man merely bore a strong resemblance to Felix Mortimer. But at the back of his mind *he knew*.

Anyway, the five-pound note was real enough.

He methodically placed the fish in a saucepan and lit the gas ring.

Presently the cat was eating, in that curious, deliberate way it had drunk the milk the night before. Its emaciated appearance plainly revealed that it was starving; yet it devoured the fish methodically, as though now assured of a regular supply.

Grey, turning the five-pound note in his hand, wondered whether the cat had after all changed his luck. But his thoughts kept reverting to Felix Mortimer. . . .

The next few days left him in no doubt. At Grannie's that night fortune's pendulum swung back unmistakably. He won steadily. From roulette he turned to *chemin de fer*, elated to find that his luck held good.

'Your luck's changed—with a vengeance!' said one of the 'regulars' of the shabby genteel saloon.

'With a vengeance,' echoed Grey, and paused; wondering with the superstition of the born gambler if there were significance in the phrase.

He left Grannie's the richer by two hundred odd pounds.

His success was the prelude to the biggest slice of luck, to use his own phrase, that he had ever known. He gambled scientifically, not losing his head, methodically banking a proportion of his gains each morning; planning, scheming, striving to reach that high water mark at which, so he told himself with the gambler's time-worn futility, he would stop and never gamble again.

Somehow he could not make up his mind to leave the poverty-stricken room in the fashionable mews. He was terribly afraid it would spell a change of luck. He tried to improve it, increase its comfort, but it was significant that he bought first a basket and a cushion for the yellow cat.

For there was no doubt in his mind that the cat was the cause of his sudden transition from poverty to prosperity. In his queer, intensely superstitious mind, the yellow cat was firmly established as his mascot.

He fed it regularly, waiting on it himself as though he were its willing servant. He made a spasmodic attempt to caress it, but the cat snarled savagely at him and, frightened, he left it alone. If the cat ever moved from the room he never saw it go; whenever he went in or came out the cat was there, watching him with its gleaming amber eyes.

He accepted the situation philosophically enough. He would talk to the cat of himself, his plans for the future, the new people he met—for money had speedily unlocked more exalted doors than Grannie's—all this in the eloquence derived from wine and solitude, he would pour out into the unmoved ears of the cat, crouching at the foot of the bed. And then, without daring to speak of it, he would think of Felix Mortimer and the gift that had proved the turning-point of his fortunes.

The creature watched him impassively, contemptuously indifferent to his raving or his silence. But the weird *ménage* continued, and Grey's luck held good.

The days passed and he became ambitious. He was now within reach of that figure he fondly imagined would enable him to forsake his precarious existence. He told himself that he was now, to all intents and purposes, safe. And he decided to move into more civilized and appropriate surroundings.

Nevertheless, he himself procured an expensive wicker contraption to convey the yellow cat from the garret to his newly acquired and, by contrast, luxurious maisonette. It was furnished in abominable taste, but the reaction from sheer poverty had its effect. And then he had begun to drink more than was good for a man who acquired a cool head and a steady nerve for at least part of a day which was really night.

One day he had cause to congratulate himself on his new home. For he met, for the first time in his thirty odd years of life, a woman. Now Grey divided women into two classes. There were 'the regulars'—soulless creatures with the gambler's fever and crook's alphabet—and 'pigeons', foolish women, some young, most of them old, who flourished their silly but valuable plumage to be plucked by such as he.

But Elise Dyer was different. She stirred his pulses with a strange, exquisite sensation. Her incredibly fair hair, flaxen as waving corn, her fair skin, her deep violet eyes and her delicate carmine mouth provoked him into a state of unaccustomed bewilderment.

They talked one night of mascots. Grey, who had never mentioned the yellow cat to a soul, whispered that he would, if she cared, show her the mascot which had brought him his now proverbial good luck. The girl agreed, with eager enthusiasm, to his diffident suggestion to go with him to his flat; and he, in his strange simplicity, stammered that she would do him honour. He had forgotten that Elise Dyer knew him for a rich man.

Elated by his triumph, he paid her losses and called for champagne. The girl plied him skilfully with wine, and presently he was more drunk than he had been since the beginning of his era of prosperity.

They took a cab to the flat. Grey felt that he had reached the pinnacle of triumph. Life was wonderful, glorious! What did anything matter now?

He switched on the light and the girl crossed his threshold. The room which they entered was lavishly illuminated, the lights shaded into moderation by costly fabrics. The room, ornate and over-furnished, reflected money. The girl gave a gasp of delight.

For the first time the cat seemed aware of something unusual. It stretched itself slowly and stood up, regarding them with a fierce light in its eyes.

The girl screamed.

'For God's sake take it away!' she cried. 'I can't bear it! I can't be near it. Take that damned cat away!' And she began to sob wildly, piteously, retreating towards the door.

At this Grey lost all control and, cursing wildly, shouting bestial things at the oncoming animal, seized it by the throat.

'Don't—don't cry, dearie,' panted Grey, holding the cat; 'I'll settle this swine soon enough. Wait for me!' And he staggered through the open door.

Grey ran through the deserted streets. The cat had subsided under the clutch of his fingers and lay inert, its yellowish fur throbbing. He scarcely knew where he was going. All he realized was an overwhelming desire to be rid of the tyranny of this wretched creature he held by the throat.

At last he knew where he was going. Not far from Grey's new establishment ran the Prince's canal, that dark, sluggish stream that threads its way across the fashionable residential district of the outlying west. To the canal he ran; and without hesitation he threw the yellow cat into the water.

* * * * *

The next day he realized what he had done. At first he was afraid, half hoping that the superstitious spasm of fear would pass. But a vivid picture swam before his eyes, the broken surface of a sluggish dream. . . .

'You're a coward,' she taunted him. 'Why don't you act like a man? Go to the tables and see for yourself that you can still win in spite of your crazy cat notions!'

At first he refused, vehemently; but it gradually dawned on him that therein lay his chance of salvation. Once let him throw down the gauntlet *and win* and his peace of mind would be assured.

That night he received a vociferous welcome on his return to the Green Baize Club.

It was as he feared. He lost steadily.

Then suddenly an idea came to him. Supposing the cat were still alive? Why hadn't he thought of that before? Why, there was a saying that every cat had nine lives! For all he knew it might have swum safely to the bank and got away.

His feverish impulse crystallized into action. He hurriedly left the club and beckoned urgently to a passing taxicab.

After what seemed interminable delay he reached the spot where he had madly flung the cat away from him. The stillness of the water brought home to him the futility of searching for the animal here. This was not the way to set to work.

The thing preyed on his mind in the days that followed. Exhaustive inquiries failed to discover the least trace of the yellow cat.

Night after night he went to the tables, lured there by the maddening thought that if only he could win he would drug the torment and be at peace. But he lost. . . .

And then a strange thing happened.

One night, returning home across a deserted stretch of the park, he experienced a queer, irresistible impulse to lift his feet from the grass and make for the gravel path. He resented the impulse, fought against it; he was cold and worn out, and by cutting across the grass he would save many minutes of weary tramping. But the thing—like a mysterious blind instinct—persisted, and in the end he found himself running, treading gingerly on the sodden grass.

He did not understand why this had happened to him.

The next day Grey did not get out of his bed until late in the afternoon.

He crossed the room in search of his dressing-gown and caught sight of himself in the glass of his wardrobe. Only then did he realize that he was clambering over the floor with his head near the carpet, his hands outstretched in front of him. He stood upright with difficulty and reached a shaking hand for brandy.

It took him two hours to struggle into his clothes, and by the time he was ready to go out it was nearly dark. He crept along the street. The shops were closing. He saw nothing of them until he reached the corner where he halted abruptly, with a queer sensation of intense hunger. On the cold marble before him lay unappetizing slabs of raw fish. His body began to quiver with suppressed desire. Another moment and nothing could have prevented him seizing the fish in his bare hands, when the shutters of the shop dropped noisily across the front of the sloping marble surface.

Grey knew that something had happened, that he was very ill. Now that he could not see the vision of the yellow cat, his mind was a blank. Somehow he retraced his footsteps and got back to his room.

The bottle of brandy stood where he had left it. He had not turned on the light, but he could see it plainly. He dragged it to his lips.

With a crash it went to the floor, while Grey leapt into the air, savage with nausea. He felt he was choking. With an effort he pulled himself together, to find that it was beyond his power to stop the ghastly whining sound that issued from his lips. He tried to lift himself onto the bed, but in sheer exhaustion collapsed on the floor, where he lay still in an attitude not human.

The room lightened with the dawn and a new day passed before the thing on the floor moved. Something of the clarity of vision which comes to starving men now possessed him. He stared at his hands.

The fingers seemed to have withered; the nails had almost disappeared, leaving a narrow streak of hornish substance forming in their place. He tore himself frantically towards the window. In the fading light he saw that the backs of his hands were covered with a thin, almost invisible surface of coarse, yellowish fur.

Unimaginable horrors seized him. He knew now that the scarlet thread of his brain was being stretched to breaking-point. Presently it would snap. . . .

Unless—unless. The yellow cat alone could save him. To this last human thought he clung, in an agony of terror.

Unconscious of movement, he crept swiftly into the street, his shapeless eyes peering in the darkness which surrounded him. He groped his way stealthily towards the one place which the last remnant of his brain told him might yield the secret of his agony.

Down the silent bank he scrambled headlong, towards the still water. The dawn's pale radiance threw his shadow into a grotesque pattern. On the edge of the canal he halted, his hands embedded in the sticky crumbling earth, his head shaking, his eyes searching in agonized appeal, into the depths of the motionless water.

There he crouched, searching, searching. . . .

And there in the water he saw the yellow cat.

He stretched out the things that were his arms, while the yellow cat stretched out its claws to enfold him in the broken mirror of the water.

THE WELL

W.W. Jacobs

Two men stood in the billiard-room of an old country house, talking. Play, which had been of a half-hearted nature, was over, and they sat at the open window, looking out over the park stretching away beneath them, conversing idly.

'Your time's nearly up, Jem,' said one at length, 'this time six weeks you'll be yawning out the honeymoon and cursing the man—woman I mean—who invented them.'

Jem Benson stretched his long limbs in the chair and grunted in dissent.

'I've never understood it,' continued Wilfred Carr, yawning. 'It's not in my line at all; I never had enough money for my own wants, let alone for two. Perhaps if I were as rich as you or Croesus I might regard it differently.'

There was just sufficient meaning in the latter part of the remark for his cousin to forbear to reply to it. He continued to gaze out of the window and to smoke slowly.

'Not being as rich as Croesus—or you,' resumed Carr, regarding him from beneath lowered lids, 'I paddle my own canoe down the stream of Time, and, tying it to my friends' doorposts, go in to eat their dinners.'

'Quite Venetian,' said Jem Benson, still looking out of the window. 'It's not a bad thing for you, Wilfred, that friends' doorposts, go in to eat their dinners.'

Carr grunted in his turn. 'Seriously though, Jem,' he said, slowly, 'you're a lucky fellow, a very lucky fellow. If there is a better girl above ground than Olive, I should like to see her.'

'Yes,' said the other, quietly.

'She's such an exceptional girl,' continued Carr, staring out of the window. 'She's so good and gentle. She thinks you are a bundle of all the virtues.'

He laughed frankly and joyously, but the other man did not join him.

'Strong sense of right and wrong, though,' continued Carr, musingly. 'Do you know, I believe that if she found out that you were not—'

'Not what?' demanded Benson, turning upon him fiercely. 'Not what?'

'Everything that you are,' returned his cousin, with a grin that belied his words, 'I believe she'd drop you.'

'Talk about something else,' said Benson, slowly; 'your pleasantries are not always in the best taste.'

Wilfred Carr rose and taking a cue from the rack, bent over the board and practised one or two favourite shots. 'The only other subject I can talk about just at present is my own financial affairs,' he said slowly, as he walked round the table.

'Talk about something else,' said Benson again, bluntly.

'And the two things are connected,' said Carr, and dropping his cue he half sat on the table and eyed his cousin.

There was a long silence. Benson pitched the end of his cigar out of the window, and leaning back closed his eyes.

'Do you follow me?' inquired Carr at length.

Benson opened his eyes and nodded at the window.

'Do you want to follow my cigar?' he demanded.

'I should prefer to depart by the usual way for your sake,' returned the other, unabashed. 'If I left by the window all sorts of questions would be asked, and you know what a talkative chap I am.'

'So long as you don't talk about my affairs,' returned the other, restraining himself by an obvious effort. You can talk yourself hoarse.'

'I'm in a mess,' said Carr, slowly, 'a devil of a mess. If I don't raise fifteen hundred by this day fortnight, I may be getting my board and lodging free.'

'Would that be any change?' questioned Benson.

'The quality would,' retorted the other. 'The address also would not be good. Seriously, Jem, will you let me have the fifteen hundred?'

'No,' said the other, simply.

Carr went white. 'It's to save me from ruin,' he said, thickly.

'I've helped you till I'm tired,' said Benson, turning and regarding him, 'and it is all to no good. If you've got into a mess, get out of it. You should not be so fond of giving autographs away.'

'It's foolish, I admit,' said Carr, deliberately. 'I won't do so any more. By the way, I've got some to sell. You needn't sneer. They're not my own.'

'Whose are they?' inquired the other.

'Yours.'

Benson got up from his chair and crossed over to him. 'What is this?' he asked, quietly. 'Blackmail?'

'Call it what you like,' said Carr. 'I've got some letters for sale, price fifteen hundred. And I know a man who would buy them at that price for the mere chance of getting Olive from you. I'll give you first offer.'

'If you have got any letters bearing my signature, you will be good enough to give them to me,' said Benson, very slowly.

'They're mine,' said Carr, lightly; 'given to me by the lady you wrote them to. I must say that they are not all in the best possible taste.'

His cousin reached forward suddenly, and catching him by the collar of his coat, pinned him down on the table.

'Give me those letters.'

'They're not here,' said Carr, struggling. 'I'm not a fool. Let me go, or I'll raise the price.'

The other man raised him from the table in his powerful hands, apparently with the intention of dashing his head against it. Then suddenly his hold relaxed as an astonished-looking maid-servant entered the room with letters. Carr sat up hastily.

'That's how it was done,' said Benson, for the girl's benefit as he took the letters.

'I don't wonder at the other man making him pay for it, then,' said Carr blandly.

'You will give me those letters,' said Benson, suggestively, as the girl left the room.

'At the price I mentioned, yes,' said Carr; 'but so sure as I am a living man, if you lay your clumsy hands on me again, I'll double it. Now, I'll leave you for a time while you think it over.'

He took a cigar from the box and lighting it carefully quitted the room. His cousin waited until the door had closed behind him, and then turning to the window sat there in a fit of fury as silent as it was terrible.

The air was fresh and sweet from the park, heavy with the scent of new-mown grass. The fragrance of a cigar was now added to it, and glancing out he saw his cousin pacing slowly by. He rose and went to the door, and then, apparently altering his mind, he returned to the window and watched the figure of his cousin as it moved slowly away into the moonlight. Then he rose again, and, for a long time, the room was empty.

It was empty when Mrs Benson came in some time later to say goodnight to her son on her way to bed. She walked slowly round the table, and pausing at the window gazed from it in idle thought, until she saw the figure of her son advancing with rapid strides towards the house. He looked up at the window.

'Goodnight,' said she.

'Goodnight,' said Benson, in a deep voice.

'Where is Wilfred?'

'Oh, he has gone,' said Benson.

'Gone?'

'We had a few words; he was wanting money again, and I gave him a piece of my mind. I don't think we shall see him again.'

'Poor Wilfred!' sighed Mrs Benson. 'He is always in trouble of some sort. I hope that you were not too hard upon him.'

'No more than he deserved,' said her son, sternly. 'Goodnight.'

* * * *

The well, which had long ago fallen into disuse, was almost hidden by the thick tangle of undergrowth which ran riot at that corner of the old park. It was partly covered by the shrunken half of a lid, above which a rusty windlass creaked in company with the music of the pines when the wind blew strongly. The full light of the sun never reached it, and the ground surrounding it was moist and green when other parts of the park were gaping with the heat.

Two people walking slowly round the park in the fragrant stillness of a summer evening strayed in the direction of the well.

'No use going through this wilderness, Olive,' said Benson, pausing on the outskirts of the pines and eyeing with some disfavour the gloom beyond.

'Best part of the park,' said the girl briskly; 'you know it's my favourite spot.'

'I know you're very fond of sitting on the coping,' said the man slowly, 'and I wish you wouldn't. One day you will lean back too far and fall in.'

'An make the acquaintance of Truth,' said Olive lightly. 'Come along.'

She ran from him and was lost in the shadow of the pines, the bracken crackling beneath her feet as she ran. Her companion followed slowly, and emerging from the gloom saw her poised daintily on the edge of the well with her feet hidden in the rank grass and nettles which surrounded it. She motioned her companion to take a seat by her side, and smiled softly as she felt a strong arm passed about her waist.

'I like this place,' said she, breaking a long silence, 'it is so dismal —so uncanny. Do you know I wouldn't dare to sit here alone, Jem. I should imagine that all sorts of dreadful things were hidden behind the bushes and trees, waiting to spring out on me. Ugh!'

'You'd better let me take you in,' said her companion tenderly; 'the well isn't always wholesome, especially in the hot weather. Let's make a move.'

The girl gave an obstinate little shake, and settled herself more securely on her seat.

'Smoke your cigar in peace,' she said quietly. 'I am settled here for a quiet talk. Has anything been heard of Wilfred yet?'

'Nothing.'

'Quite a dramatic disappearance, isn't it?' she continued. 'Another scrape, I suppose, and another letter for you in the same old strain; "Dear Jem, help me out." '

Jem Benson blew a cloud of fragrant smoke into the air, and holding his cigar between his teeth brushed away the ash from his coat sleeves.

'I wonder what he would have done without you,' said the girl, pressing his arm affectionately. 'Gone under long ago, I suppose. When we are married, Jem, I shall presume upon the relationship to lecture him. He is very wild, but he has his good points, poor fellow.'

'I never saw them,' said Benson, with startling bitterness. 'God knows I never saw them.'

'He is nobody's enemy but his own,' said the girl, startled by this outburst.

'You don't know much about him,' said the other, sharply. 'He was not above blackmail; not above ruining the life of a friend to do himself a benefit. A loafer, a cur, and a liar!'

The girl looked up at him soberly but timidly and took his arm without a word, and they both sat silent while evening deepened into night and the beams of the moon, filtering through the branches, surrounded them with a silver network. Her head sank upon his shoulder, till suddenly with a sharp cry she sprang to her feet.

'What was that?' she cried breathlessly.

'What was what?' demanded Benson, springing up and clutching her fast by the arm.

She caught her breath and tried to laugh. 'You're hurting me, Jem.'

His hold relaxed.

'What is the matter?' he asked gently. 'What was it startled you?'

'I was startled,' she said, slowly, putting her hands on his shoulder. 'I suppose the words I used just now are ringing in my ears, but I fancied that somebody behind us whispered "*Jem, help me out*." '

'Fancy,' repeated Benson, and his voice shook; 'but these fancies are not good for you. You—are frightened—at the dark and gloom of these trees. Let me take you back to the house.'

'No, I am not frightened,' said the girl, reseating herself. 'I should be never be really frightened of anything when you were with me, Jem. I'm surprised at myself for being so silly.'

The man made no reply but stood, a strong, dark figure, a yard or two from the well, as though waiting for her to join him.

'Come and sit down, sir,' cried Olive, patting the brickwork with her small, white hand, 'one would think that you did not like my company.'

He obeyed slowly and took a seat by her side, drawing so hard at his cigar that the light of it shone upon his face at every breath. He passed his arm, firm and rigid as steel, behind her, with his hand resting on the brickwork, beyond.

'Are you warm enough?' he asked tenderly, as she made a little movement.

'Pretty fair,' she shivered; 'one oughtn't to be cold at this time of the year, but there's a cold, damp air comes up from the well.'

As she spoke a faint splash sounded from the depths below, and for her the second time that evening, she sprang from the well with a little cry of dismay.

'What is it now?' he asked in a fearful voice. He stood by her side and gazed at the well, as though half expecting to see the cause of her alarm emerge from it.

'Oh, my bracelet,' she cried in distress, 'my poor mother's bracelet. I've dropped it down the well.'

'Your bracelet!' repeated Benson, dully. 'Your bracelet? The diamond one?'

'The one that was my mother's,' said Olive. 'Oh, we can get it back surely. We must have the water drained off.'

'Your bracelet!' repeated Benson, stupidly.

'Jem,' said the girl in terrified tones, 'dear Jem, what is the matter?'

For the man she loved was standing regarding her with horror. The moon which touched it was not responsible for all the whiteness of the distorted face, and she shrank back in fear to the edge of the well. He saw her fear and by a mighty effort regained his composure and took her hand.

'Poor little girl,' he murmured, 'you frightened me. I was not looking when you cried, and I thought that you were slipping from my arms, down—down—'

His voice broke, and the girl throwing herself into his arms clung to him convulsively.

'There, there,' said Benson, fondly, 'don't cry, don't cry.'

'Tomorrow,' said Olive, half-laughing, half-crying, 'we will all come round the well with hook and line and fish for it. It will be quite a new sport.'

'No, we must try some other way,' said Benson. 'You shall have it back.'

'How?' asked the girl.

'You shall see,' said Benson. 'Tomorrow morning at latest you shall have it back. Till then promise me that you will not mention your loss to anyone. Promise.'

'I promise,' said Olive, wonderingly. 'But why not?'

'It is of great value, for one thing, and—But there—there are many reasons. For one thing it is my duty to get it for you.'

'Wouldn't you like to jump down for it? she asked mischievously. 'Listen.'

She stooped for a stone and dropped it down.

'Fancy being where that is now,' she said, peering into the blackness; 'fancy going round and round like a mouse in a pail, clutching at the slimy sides, with the water filling your mouth, and looking up to the little patch of sky above.'

'You had better come in,' said Benson, very quietly. 'You are developing a taste for the morbid and horrible.'

The girl turned, and taking his arm walked slowly in the direction of the house; Mrs Benson, who was sitting in the porch, rose to receive them.

'You shouldn't have kept her out so long,' she said chidingly. 'Where have you been?'

'Sitting on the well,' said Olive, smiling, 'discussing our future.'

'I don't believe that place is healthy,' said Mrs Benson, emphatically. 'I really think it might be filled in, Jem.'

'All right,' said her son, slowly. 'Pity it wasn't filled in long ago.'

He took the chair vacated by his mother as she entered the house with Olive, and with his hands hanging limply over the sides sat in deep thought. After a time he rose, and going upstairs to a room which was set apart for sporting requisites selected a sea fishing line and some hooks and stole softly downstairs again. He walked swiftly across the park in the direction of the well, turning before he entered the shadow of the trees to look back at the lighted windows of the house. Then having arranged his line he sat on the edge of the well and cautiously lowered it.

He sat with his lips compressed, occasionally looking about him in a startled fashion, as though he half expected to see something peering at him from the belt of trees. Time after time he lowered his line until at length in pulling it up he heard a little metallic tinkle against the side of the well.

He held his breath then, and forgetting his fears drew the line in inch by inch, so as not to lose its precious burden. His pulse beat rapidly, and his eyes were bright. As the line came slowly in he saw the catch hanging to the hook, and with a steady hand drew the last few feet in. Then he saw that instead of the bracelet he had hooked a bunch of keys.

With a faint cry he shook them from the hook into the water below, and stood breathing heavily. Not a sound broke the stillness of the night. He walked up and down a bit and stretched his great muscles; then he came back to the well and resumed his task.

For an hour or more the line was lowered without result. In his eagerness he forgot his fears, and with eyes bent down the well fished slowly and carefully. Twice the hook became entangled in something and was with difficulty released. It caught a third time, and all his efforts failed to free it. Then he dropped the line down the well, and with head bent walked toward the house.

He went first to the stables at the rear, and then retiring to his room for some time time paced restlessly up and down. Then without removing his clothes he flung himself upon the bed and fell into a troubled sleep.

* * * *

Long before anybody else was astir he arose and stole softly downstairs. The sunlight was stealing in at every crevice, and flashing in long streaks across the darkened rooms. The dining-room into which he looked struck chill and cheerless in the dark yellow light which came through the lowered blinds. He remembered that it had the same appearance when his father lay dead in the house; now, as then, everything seemed ghastly and unreal; the very chairs standing as their occupants had left them the night before seemed to be indulging in some dark communication of ideas.

Slowly and noisessly he opened the hall door and passed into the fragrant air beyond. The sun was shining on the drenched grass and trees, and a slowly vanishing white mist rolled like smoke about the grounds. For a moment he stood, breathing deeply the sweet air of the morning, and then walked slowly in the direction of the stables.

The rusty creaking of a pump-handle and a spatter of water upon the red-tiled courtyard showed that somebody else was astir, and a few steps farther he beheld a brawny, sandy-haired man gasping wildly under severe self-infliction at the pump.

'Everything ready, George?' he asked quietly.

'Yes, sir,' said the man, straightening up suddenly and touching his forehead. 'Bob's just finishing the arrangements inside. It's a lovely morning for a dip. The water in the well must be just icy.'

'Be as quick as you can,' said Benson, impatiently.

'Very good, sir,' said George, burnishing his face harshly with a very small towel which had been hanging up over the top of the pump. 'Hurry up, Bob.'

In answer to his summons a man appeared at the door of the stable with a coil of stout rope over his arm and a large metal candlestick in his hand.

'Just to try the air, sir,' said George, following his master's glance, 'a well gets rather foul sometimes, but if a candle can live down it, a man can.'

His master nodded, and the man, hastily pulling up the neck of his shirt and thrusting his arms into his coat, followed him as he led the way slowly to the well.

'Beg pardon, sir,' said George, drawing up his side, 'but you are not looking over and above well this morning. If you'll let me go down I'd enjoy the bath.'

'No, no,' said Benson, peremptorily.

'You ain't fit to go down, sir,' persisted his follower. 'I've never seen you look, so before. Now if—'

'Mind your business,' said his master curtly.

George became silent and the three walked with swinging strides through the long wet grass to the well. Bob flung the rope on the ground and at a sign from his master handed him the candlestick.

'Here's the line for it, sir,' said Bob, fumbling in his pockets.

Benson took it from him and slowly tied it to the candlestick. Then he placed it on the edge of the well, and striking a match, lit the candle and began slowly to lower it.

'Hold hard, sir,' said George, quickly, laying his hand on his arm, 'you must tilt it or the string'll burn through.'

Even as he spoke the string parted and the candlestick fell into the water below.

Benson swore quietly.

'I'll soon get another,' said George, starting up.

'Never mind, the well's all right,' said Benson.

'It won't take a moment, sir,' said the other over his shoulder.

'Are you master here, or am I?' said Benson hoarsely.

George came back slowly, a glance at his master's face stopping the protest upon his tongue, and he stood by watching him sulkily as he sat on the well and removed his outer garments. Both men watched him curiously, as having completed his preparations he stood grim and silent with his hands by his sides.

'I wish you'd let me go, sir,' said George, plucking up courage to address him. 'You ain't fit to go, you've got a chill or something. I shouldn't wonder it's the typhoid. They've got it in the village bad.'

For a moment Benson looked at him angrily, then his gaze softened. 'Not this time, George,' he said, quietly. He took the looped end of the rope and placed it under his arms, and sitting down threw one leg over the side of the well.

'How are you going about it, sir?' queried George, laying hold of the rope and signing to Bob to do the same.

'I'll call out when I reach the water,' said Benson; 'then pay out three yards more quickly so that I can get to the bottom.'

'Very good, sir,' answered both.

Their master threw the other leg over the coping and sat motionless. His back was turned towards the men as he sat with his head bent, looking down the shaft. He sat for so long that George became uneasy.

'All right, sir?' he inquired.

'Yes,' said Benson, slowly. 'If I tug at the rope, George, pull up at once. Lower away.'

The rope passed steadily through their hands until a hollow cry from the darkness below and a faint splashing warned them that he had reached the water. They gave him three yards more and stood with relaxed grasp and strained ears, waiting.

'He's gone under,' said Bob in a low voice.

The other nodded, and moistening his huge palms took a firmer grip of the rope.

Fully a minute passed, and the men began to exchange uneasy glances. Then a sudden tremendous jerk followed by a series of feebler ones nearly tore the rope from their grasp.

'Pull!' shouted George, placing one foot on the side and hauling desperately. 'Pull! pull! He's stuck fast; he's not coming; P—U—LL!'

In response to their terrific exertions the rope came slowly in, inch by inch, until at length a violent splashing was heard, and at the same moment a scream of unutterable horror came echoing up the shaft.

'What a weight he is!' panted Bob. 'He's stuck fast or something. Keep still, sir, for heaven's sake, keep still.'

For the taut rope was being jerked violently by the struggles of the weight at the end of it. Both men with grunts and sighs hauled it in foot by foot.

'All right, sir,' cried George, cheerfully.

He had one foot against the well, and was pulling manfully; the burden was nearing the top. A long pull and a strong pull, and the face of a dead man with mud in his eyes and nostrils came peering over the edge. Behind it was the ghastly face of his master; but this he saw too late, for with a great cry he let go his hold of the rope and stepped back. The suddenness overthrew his assistant, and the rope tore through his hands. There was a frightful splash.

'You fool!' stammered Bob, and ran to the well helplessly.

'Run!' cried George. 'Run for another line.'

He bent over the coping and called eagerly down as his assistant sped back to the stables shouting wildly. His voice re-echoed down the shaft, but all else was silence.

LAURA

Saki

'You aren't really dying, are you?' asked Amanda.

'I have the doctor's permission to live till Tuesday,' said Laura.

'But today is Saturday; this is serious!' gasped Amanda.

'I don't know about it being serious; it is certainly Saturday,' said Laura.

'Death is always serious,' said Amanda.

'I never said I was going to die. I am presumably going to leave off being, Laura, but I shall go on being something. An animal of some kind, I suppose. You see, when one hasn't been very good in the life one has just lived, one reincarnates in some lower organism. And I haven't been very good, when one comes to think of it. I've been cruel and mean and vindictive and all that sort of thing when circumstances seemed to warrant it.'

'Circumstances never warrant that sort of thing,' said Amanda.

'If you don't mind my saying so,' observed Laura, 'Egbert is a circumstance that would warrant any amount of that sort of thing. You're married to him—that's different; you've sworn to love, honour and endure him: I haven't.'

'I don't see what's wrong with Egbert,' protested Amanda.

'Oh, I dare say the wrongness has been on my part,' admitted Laura dispassionately; 'he has merely been the extenuating circumstance. He made a thin, peevish kind of fuss for instance, when I took the collie puppies from the farm out for a run the other day.'

They chased his young broods of speckled Sussex and drove two sitting hens off their nest, besides running all over the flower beds. You know how devoted he is to his poultry and garden.'

'Anyway, he needn't have gone on about it for the entire evening and then have said, "Let's say no more about it", just when I was beginning to enjoy the discussion. That's where one of my petty vindictive revenges came in,' added Laura with an unrepentant chuckle; 'I turned the entire family of speckled Sussex into his seedling shed the day after the puppy episode.'

'How could you?' exclaimed Amanda.

'It came quite easy,' said Laura; 'two of the hens pretended to be laying at the same time, but I was firm.'

'And we thought it was an accident!'

'You see,' resumed Laura, 'I really *have* some grounds for supposing that my next incarnation will be in a lower organism. I shall be an animal of some kind. On the other hand, I haven't been a bad sort in my way, so I think I may count on being a nice animal, something elegant and lively, with a love of fun. An otter, perhaps.'

'I can't imagine you as an otter,' said Amanda.

'Well, I don't suppose you can imagine me as an angel, if it comes to that,' said Laura.

Amanda was silent. She couldn't.

'Personally I think an otter life would be rather enjoyable,' continued Laura; 'salmon to eat all year round, and the satisfaction of being able to fetch the trout in their own homes without having to wait for hours till they condescend to rise to the fly you've been dangling before them; and an elegant svelte figure—'

'Think of the otter hounds,' interposed Amanda; 'how dreadful to be hunted and harried and finally worried to death!'

'Rather fun with half the neighbourhood looking on, and anyhow not worse than this Saturday-to-Tuesday business of dying by inches; and then I should go on into something else. If I had been a moderately good otter I suppose I should get back into human shape of some sort; probably something primitive—a little brown, unclothed Nubian boy, I should think.'

'I wish you would be serious,' sighed Amanda; 'you really ought to be if you're only going to live till Tuesday.'

As a matter of fact Laura died on Monday.

'So dreadfully upsetting,' Amanda complained to her uncle-in-law, Sir Lulworth Quayne. 'I've asked quite a lot of people down for golf and fishing, and the rhododendrons are just looking their best.'

'Laura always was inconsiderate,' said Sir Lulworth; 'she was born during Goodwood week, with an Ambassador staying in the house who hated babies.'

'She had the maddest kind of ideas,' said Amanda; 'do you know if there was any insanity in her family?'

'Insanity? No, I never heard of any. Her father lives in West Kensington, but I believe he's sane on all other subjects.'

'She had an idea that she was going to be reincarnated as an otter,' said Amanda.

'One meets with those ideas of reincarnation so frequently, even in the West,' said Sir Lulworth, 'that one can hardly set them down as being mad. And Laura was such an unaccountable person in this life that I should not like to lay down definite rules as to what she might be doing in an after state.'

'You think she really might have passed into some animal form? asked Amanda. She was one of those who shape their opinions rather readily from the standpoint of those around them.

Just then Egbert entered the breakfast-room, wearing an air of bereavement that Laura's demise would have been insufficient, in itself, to account for.

'Four of my speckled Sussex have been killed,' he exclaimed; 'the very four that were to go to the show on Friday. One of them was dragged away and eaten right in the middle of that new carnation bed that I've been to such trouble and expense over. My best flower bed and my best fowls singled out for destruction; it almost seems as if the brute that did the deed had special knowledge how to be as devastating as possible in a short space of time.'

'Was it a fox, do you think?' asked Amanda.

'Sounds more like a polecat,' said Sir Lulwroth.

'No,' said Egbert, 'there were marks of webbed feet all over the place, and we followed the tracks down to the stream at the bottom of the garden; evidently an otter.'

Amanda looked quickly and furtively across at Sir Lulworth.

Egbert was too agitated to eat any breakfast, and went out to superintend the strengthening of the poultry yard defences.

'I think she might at least have waited till the funeral was over,' said Amanda in a scandalized voice.

'It's her own funeral, you know,' said Sir Lulworth; 'it's a nice point in etiquette how far one ought to show respect to one's own mortal remains.'

Disregard for mortuary convention was carried to further lengths next day; during the absence of the family at the funeral ceremony the remaining survivors of the speckled Sussex were massacred. The marauder's line of retreat seemed to have embraced most of the flower beds on the lawn, but the strawberry beds in the lower garden had also suffered.

'I shall get the otter hounds to come here at the earliest possible moment,' said Egbert savagely.

'On no account! You can't dream of such a thing!' exclaimed Amanda. 'I mean, it wouldn't do, so soon after a funeral in the house.'

'It's a case of necessity,' said Egbert; 'once an otter takes to that sort of thing it won't stop.' 'Perhaps it will go elsewhere now that there are no more fowls left,' suggested Amanda.

'One would think you wanted to shield the beast,' said Egbert.

'There's been so little water in the stream lately,' objected Amanda; 'it seems hardly sporting to hunt an animal when it has so little chance of taking refuge anywhere.'

'Good gracious!' fumed Egbert, 'I'm not thinking about sport. I want to have the animal killed as soon as possible.'

Even Amanda's opposition weakened when, during church time on the following Sunday, the otter made its way into the house, raided half a salmon from the larder and worried it into scaly fragments on the Persian rug in Egbert's studio.

'We shall have it hiding under our beds and biting pieces out of our feet before long,' said Egbert, and from what Amanda knew of this particular otter she felt that the possibility was not a remote one.

On the evening preceeding the day fixed for the hunt Amanda

'I shall go on being something'

spent a solitary hour walking by the banks of the stream, making what she imagined to be hound noises. It was charitably supposed by those who overheard her performance, that she was practising for farmyard imitations at the forthcoming village entertainment.

It was her friend and neighbour, Aurora Burret, who brought her news of the day's sport.

'Pity you weren't out; we had a quite good day. We found it at once, in the pool just below your garden.'

'Did you—kill?' asked Amanda.

'Rather. A fine she-otter. Your husband got rather badly bitten in trying to "tail it". Poor beast, I felt quite sorry for it, it had such a human look in its eyes when it was killed. You'll call me silly, but do you know who the look reminded me of? My dear woman, what is the matter?'

When Amanda had recovered to a certain extent from her attack of nervous prostration Egbert took her to the Nile Valley to recuperate. Change of scene speedily brought about the desired recovery of health and mental balance. The escapades of an adventurous otter in search of a variation of diet were viewed in their proper light. Amanda's normally placid temperament reasserted itself. Even a hurricane of shouted curses, coming from her husband's dressing-room, in her husband voice, but hardly in his usual vocabulary, failed to disturb her serenity as she made a leisurely toilet one evening in a Cairo hotel.

'What is the matter? What has happened?' she asked in amused curiosity.

'The little beast has thrown all my clean shirts into the bath! Wait till I catch you, you little—'

'What little beast?' asked Amanda, suppressing a desire to laugh; Egbert's language was so hoplessly inadequate to express his outraged feelings.

'A little beast of a naked brown Nubian boy,' spluttered Egbert.

And now Amanda is seriously ill.

THE SWAN CHILD

Joan Aiken

My brother and I decided we'd do a sponsored walk of our own. We didn't want to go with the others to Midchester Priory; we wanted to go to the Swan Child on Abbotsbury Hill. It was nine miles off, so if we managed to get there and back, that would be eighteen miles. Our uncle Christy Thorpe keeps the pub at the foot of Abbotsbury, so he'd sign our card saying we really walked there, and our planned route was all paths across country, so there'd be no question of cheating and accepting lifts from motorists.

Well, we went all round the village collecting sponsors. Five p. a mile, most of them offered; one or two went as high as ten. The money was to be spent on books for the school library.

The last house in the village, at the far end from ours, Nash End House, is a big square white one. We know Mrs Williams who lives there, because she helps in the school library once a week. Beyond her house there is an orchard, then a marshy field, then The Bungalow, all by itself in a clumpy overgrown garden, backing against a piney hillside. About the people who lived in that house we knew nothing at all. They didn't mix in village affairs.

'Who *does* live in The Bungalow?' Jake asked Mrs Williams when she was signing our form. 'Are they weekend people?'

'Oh, I wouldn't go there,' she said hastily. 'Some very odd people live in that little house. I've seen a couple of women, and there used to be a man – but I believe he died, I haven't seen him for a long time . . .'

'How, odd?' I asked.

'Well sometimes I've heard somebody laughing in a crazy way, on and on – and, once or twice, screaming. They never seem to come out. No, I'd advise you to skip The Bungalow if I were you. You seem to have got everybody else in the village,' she said, looking at our list. 'Have a good day, you've got fine weather for it, anyway. Enjoy yourselves on Abbotsbury Hill.'

We *had* got all the rest of the village, and, just because of that, it was annoying not to have The Bungalow as well. We went rather slowly past the garden gate, which was an ordinary, white-painted, split-paling one, rather in need of a new coat of paint, tucked in between two big feathery clumps of bamboo. A garden path inside led to the one-story, slate-roofed house, which was covered with trellis and clematis. On either side of the path were high plants – tiger-lilies, and rose-bushes and phlox. All seemed peaceful and ordinary enough.

'Oh, come on,' said Jake. 'Let's chance it. They can't eat us. And we can always run like maniacs and scream bloody murder if they come after us with axes.'

So, our hearts going pit-a-pat, we opened the gate and went in, tiptoeing up the path, across which lay a tangle of garden hose. We were about halfway along it when a voice stopped us in our tracks.

'Hullo?' it said – quite normally and pleasantly, but it came from behind us, which was somewhat disconcerting. 'What do you want?'

We spun round. And there was a woman sitting on a stool in the middle of a little patch of lawn to our right, painting a picture on an easel. She wore a striped cotton dress and sandals and a big shady hat. 'I'm Clarissa Forbes,' she went on, quite friendly. 'What can I do for you?'

There was a narrow grassy alley that led to her patch of lawn between the clumps of flowers, so we went along it, and Jake, who is a year older than me, explained about the sponsored walk, while I looked at the picture on the easel.

It was a picture done in water-colour, of the flowers in the garden, but not realistic: the plants were drawn out into long straggly spindly shapes, all twined in among one another, in odd but clear colours, very bright, very dark, with hard lines in between; and somewhere in among the twisting wreathing stems you could just see a person, who might have been partly a plant, or else caught among them and struggling to get out. It looked as if it must have been painted very fast and skilfully – some of the colour was still wet. I thought it marvellous – the shapes and colours seemed just right, and they gave you a feeling of excitement and satisfaction at the same time, as if it was not what you had expected, but now that you saw it you realized it was what you had been wanting all the time.

'Do you like it?' Clarissa Forbes asked, noticing that I couldn't take my eyes off it.

'Oh yes I do! *Very* much!'

'Good,' she said, writing down 10p. on Jake's form. 'When I have done enough of them I'm going to have a show.'

'Have you done many?' I asked, longing to see more and hoping that she'd offer to show them. I began to study her carefully. Her face looked worn but smooth, like a stone that has been under water. Her eyes were big, wandering, pale-blue, she wore no make-up, and her hair, a mixture of fair and grey, was bundled into an untidy knot. She was very, very thin; I noticed that her wrists were thinner than mine and there was a scar on one. She wore some kind of foreign sandals on rather dirty bare feet.

'Oh, yes I've done hundreds. I hardly do anything else, really. Only,' she said looking round vaguely, 'I'm not sure where they are. I can never lay my hands on them when I want them.' She smiled a little, looking at her hands which, oddly enough, were in cotton-mesh gloves, perhaps because several of her fingers seemed to be bandaged. I supposed the gloves would keep the bandages clean. 'Where are you going on your walk?' she asked us.

Jake told her, Abbotsbury Hill, to see the Swan Child. The Swan Child isn't really a swan child. It is a picture carved out in chalk on the side of the hill, very old, done in the Iron Age. It could be a swan or a kneeling person with head down and arms extended. If you stand on the bare chalk where the lines of its two arms, or wings, cross each other, you are supposed to have your wish granted, whatever that is.

'The Swan Child,' said Clarissa Forbes. 'Oh, I've heard of that! Oh,

I *wish* I could come with you!' She sounded really wistful and envious.

'Well, why don't you?' said Jake. 'It's only nine miles. Or, if you don't want to walk so far, you could go by road, if you have a car? That's a bit farther.'

'No,' she said. 'We do have a car, but I don't drive. The others can, but they wouldn't care about seeing the Swan Child. No, I'm afraid I can't come. But I do wish I could.' She did sound sad.

Everything she said was perfectly ordinary, and yet there was something odd about her. I liked her – and felt sorry for her too – but I could see that Jake was itching to get away. There was a very oppressive, shut-in feeling about the little garden with its high bamboo hedges all round and the pinewoods beyond, and the clumps of tall, gaudy flowers. Jake, turning, stumbled over more of the tangled hose-pipe which led in from the main path; one end stuck out of the lawn, and part of it was buried underground, which seemed slightly peculiar; maybe it led to an underground stopcock.

'Where does it go?' I asked.

'I'm not sure,' Clarissa said vaguely. 'One of the others would have to tell you that.'

From the way she said *the others* you'd think the place was packed with people, but there wasn't a sound or a sign of anybody else; it was dead quiet.

'Well – thanks very much,' Jake said, making rapidly for the gate.

I hesitated, and said, 'Shall we call in on the way back – supposing we manage to get all the way to the Swan Child – and collect the money?'

She looked anxious.

'What time would that be?'

'Oh – around six, I should think. We're not likely to be back before then.'

Her face grew even more anxious.

'Then I think you'd better not. If it was well before six – that would be all right. But – '

'Oh, never mind. If you're likely to be out, we'll call back some time next week,' Jake called back quickly.

'No, it's not that. I never go out. But, you see, at six, or thereabouts, I change into one of the others. They don't realize I know that, but I do!' she said, laughing. 'And they wouldn't like to see you *at all* –

either of them. So it would be better if you came in the morning some time – I'm always here then.'

Change into one of the others? I wondered what on earth she could mean.

'Come on Cis!' called Jake, already on the other side of the gate. But Clarissa went on, in a confidential tone.

'You see, there are three of us. Originally there were four. But now it's Esme, Ag, and me.' She laughed again and said, 'They think I am very silly – the baby of the family. Head-in-the-clouds. Well – Esme *is* very capable of course. She's our organizer. And Ag is the servant. They don't like children, I'm afraid. Or anybody coming to the house, really. So, whatever you do, don't come here after six. Neither of them would give you any money, whichever you saw. And there might be trouble.'

'*Cis!* Do come on, or we'll never get there!' Jake shouted impatiently from the road. So I hurriedly said goodbye and ran out and joined him.

'Please make a wish for me on the Swan Child!' Clarissa called after me.

'What shall I wish?'

But Clarissa merely sighed.

'*Broo!*' said Jake, as we started along the path through the pinewood. 'What an old spook! I couldn't stand her. She gave me the cold hab-dabs.'

'She'd painted a terrific picture,' I said. 'I liked that. And I felt sorry for her.'

'Well I didn't! I don't care if I never see her again. I vote we don't bother about collecting from her. Doesn't sound as if we're likely to get the money. And we've enough without.'

'That seems a waste.'

'She probably hasn't any money.'

'What *can* she have meant – about changing into one of the others?'

'I don't know and I don't care!'

But all day I couldn't stop thinking about it.

That was a long, hot walk. We trudged along footpaths, and round the edges of ploughed fields, over stiles, through copses, over sandy headlands of heath; we crossed brooks by plank bridges and squelched our way through soggy water-meadows; once or twice we had to cross a main road or make use of its bridge to get to the other side of a real river. Jake had the map and steered us along; he is good at that; and we could see our general direction easily enough, because there, ahead of us, was the line of hills, with Abbotsbury higher, head-and-shoulders above the rest. As we came closer we could see the Swan Child above us, a swirl of white, mysterious lines on the pale-green hillside.

Uncle Christy gave us apple-juice to drink in the pub garden, which was just flat, trampled grass and rustic seats; all summer long he had so many customers that there was no time for gardening. It was very different from the airless, shut-in garden of The Bungalow, with all its clumps of sultry-smelling lilies and bamboo.

'You'd best go up the hill before you have your lunches,' Uncle Christy told us. 'You won't be so keen after. And it's a steep pull. Hop along now, and I'll have a Ploughman's ready for each of you when you come down.'

So, feeling a bit stiff already after our short rest, we went on up the steep chalk track. You could see all the flat country laid out down below, dark blue-green woods and hedges, pale yellow-green wheat-fields in between them. Above us the sun baked down, hotter and hotter, and the hillside smelt of thyme. In a way I would have preferred rain and mist and the place to ourselves; when we got up to the Swan Child we found about twenty people having their picnics there and taking photographs – well, it was a Saturday, of course, you had to expect crowds. I waited my turn, and stood on the bald spot where the Swan Child crosses her wings, and wished that I would be a great painter when I grow up, that my name would be known all over the world like Picasso. Then I remembered that Clarissa had asked me to wish a wish for her, so I tried to wish a blank wish and hold it inside me like a bubble unbroken.

I had a feeling that if I could get it back to her still unbroken, she would be able to use it.

Jake stood on the cross too, rather quick and embarrassed as if he thought it childishly beneath him to do such a thing. I didn't ask what he wished, because you mustn't, but I guessed that it would be connected with learning to fly, which is his one aim and ambition. In spite of his short sight and having to wear glasses. The Swan Child might grant that wish, at least, I thought.

Then we scrambled down the steep track again. I'd been a little disappointed that Uncle Christy didn't give us our sandwiches to eat on the hill itself, but once I had been up there and seen all the people, I was happy to go down and eat in his huge cool kitchen, which has a brick floor worn into ancient bumps and curves, and old black beams with hooks in them, for hanging herbs and flitches of bacon. We had our Ploughman's Lunches at his long kitchen table where Mrs Goodyear, his housekeeper, has all the French loaves and butter and cheese and pickles and salads and cold roast beef and sausages for making bar food. We offered to help her but she said, 'Sit still while ye can, childer. Ye've a fair step ahead of ye still.'

'We kept up an average speed of three miles an hour coming,' said Jake. 'We ought to be able to do about the same going back.' But Uncle Christy shook his head and said we'd probably find the last four or five miles on the way back much harder going, and would be bound to find ourselves slowing down.

Going back, of course, wasn't such fun, because it was all flat country ahead, the hills were behind us; and there wasn't the excitement of unknown territory; we had seen it all before. We began to argue about the words of songs, and their tunes; Jake can never carry a tune in his head, though he *thinks* he can. And, after a while, fed up with one another, we walked apart, in silence, Jake about twelve yards ahead. I didn't mind; I went back to thinking about Clarissa Forbes.

They don't realize I know that, but I do, she had said. There are three of us, Esme and Ag and me. Esme is our organiser. And Ag is the servant. Originally there were four.

But how could she *not* know about them, if they all lived in the same house, and that quite a small bungalow? And who had the fourth been, the one who had gone?

At six, she had said, I change into one of the others. What could she have meant by that?

I trotted, to catch up with Jake, and said, 'Do you think she was mad?'

'Who?'

'Clarissa Forbes.'

'Of course,' he said. 'Crackers. Barmy. A screw loose. Rats in the upper storey.'

'Her picture wasn't mad. It was wonderful.'

'How do you know? How do you know what makes a mad picture? Anyway there have been lots of mad painters. Van Gogh cut his ear off.' Then he began to sing, 'She was just a beautiful picture, In a beautiful golden frame,' because he knew it would annoy me, so I dropped behind again.

Don't come after six, she had said. The others wouldn't like to see you at all. There might be trouble.

What sort of trouble, I wondered. It did sound queer – frightening, really. We had certainly better not call in after six. And it was nearly that now – Uncle Christy had been right, our pace was growing slower and slower. But still, I thought, I would go back to The Bungalow tomorrow morning. I was dying to have another look at that picture.

When we reached the last piney hillock that lay between us and the village, our pace had dwindled to a slow, careful trudge. We weren't limping, because we had been careful to wear old thick shoes and socks, so we didn't have blisters, but our feet were tired and aching.

At this point Jake, just to show off, had to break into a run.

'I'm as chip-chip-chipper as a chipmunk, I'm as hop-hop-hoppy as a cricket!' he sang, or bawled, and went bounding over the top of the little hill. Then I heard an angry yell, a crash, and a curse. When I followed over the hill and down the slope on the other side, I found him lying in a heap at the bottom. From a big slide-mark it was plain what had happened – he had slipped on the pine-needles, which were smooth as glass, just about, tobogganed down the slope, tripped over a stump, and crashed into a pine tree. He had knocked himself half silly; and, what was more frightening, his leg was quite evidently broken. It stuck out sideways in a horrible way.

'*Oh, Jake!*'

''M all right,' he muttered dazedly. 'In half a minute – just give me a hand up – I'll be able to hop, if you find a stick –'

We tried for a yard or two, but it was hopeless; by mistake, he touched the ground with the foot of his broken leg and let out a yell of agony.

'You mustn't go any farther, it would be crazy,' I said. 'It might do your leg awful harm. Sit here by the side of the road and I'll run on and phone from Mrs Williams' house. I can ask Father to come down with the car and pick us up.'

Jake didn't answer for a minute. He bit his lip – he was obviously almost sick with pain. At last, grudgingly, he said, 'Okay.'

Where he was sitting was not more than a stone's throw from The Bungalow gate, outside the bushy bamboo hedge. I thought of going in there, but the Williams' house was only twenty-five yards farther on and we knew her well; actually I thought she'd probably take us home in her car.

But when I got to her house I found it all locked up, and then I remembered that she had said something in the morning about spending the weekend with her sister in Folkestone.

It was another long half-mile into the main part of the village. Should I go on, or back to The Bungalow, which was close at hand?

I decided to go back. My watch said six forty-five, so I opened the garden gate with a good deal of trepidation, and crept inside.

There was nobody in the garden; the stool and easel had gone, so I walked as far as the trellised porch and pulled the doorbell – a blue stone on a plaited leather thong. The bell gave a single loud jangle, and almost immediately the door shot open; I couldn't help starting back nervously.

The woman who had opened the door gave me an angry look.

'Well? What do *you* want?' she snapped. 'Children aren't allowed here.'

I said: 'I'm very sorry. There's been an accident. My brother's broken his leg. Do you – is there – could I possibly use your phone?'

She was totally unlike Clarissa. Her face was made up – very much so, with bright red lipstick, and a lot of eye-shadow, and a thick layer of orangey pancake foundation all over. Her hair dangled round her neck in ringlets – very unsuitably considering her age – and she wore a suit, tweed, also incongruous that hot evening, stockings and high-heeled shoes. What frightened me most was that I could see, in a way, that she *was* the same woman – her bones were the same, and those thin, thin wrists, one scarred. I recognized a scar on her forehead, too –

and yet her face was *completely* different. And I mean really completely. I wouldn't have recognized her if – if – if – if I hadn't known. Her voice was different too.

'Phone, phone?' she said sharply. 'And why should you do that? Who are you?'

'I'm Cicely Freeman. My family live in the brick house next to the post office. My brother and I have been doing a sponsored walk to the Swan Child –'

'Swan Child? What's that? I've never heard of it. And I don't *want* to! And I don't think you *can* use our phone. I'm not keen on all and sundry pushing into my house – it's not at all convenient.'

I could actually see the phone, through an open door behind her, on a table in a frilly, chintzy sitting-room, so I said, 'Oh, *please*! I shan't be a moment, honestly – it's just to phone my father and ask him to come and pick us up – my brother's out there by the road and he's in a lot of pain –'

As I gabbled I was gently edging into the hall.

'Where is your brother? Where?' she demanded.

I made a vague gesture – I didn't want her to go out and look at Jake. The sight of her suspicious angry painted face and those ringlets was just about the last thing he needed at that moment.

She did move aside just a little, enough to allow me past her into the chintzy room, and I made a dash to the phone, picked up the receiver, and dialled our number. But the line was dead, and I soon saw why: the cord had been cut.

'Clarissa probably did that,' the woman said matter-of-factly. 'Just because I don't admire her pictures she flies into these childish rages –' I gaped at her stupidly as she turned back to the door and called, in a loud voice, 'Did you hear what I said, Clarissa? I know what you did – you silly girl! Just out of childish temper. It's not the least use. You might as well accept that you'll never have any talent. Tom says the same. I know you are hiding out there, it's no use pretending you can't hear.' She turned back to me again and went on in a conversational tone, 'She thinks I don't know she lives here too. She and Tom – that's my husband – get up to all sorts of silly games when my back's turned.'

I was looking, aghast, from the slashed phone cord to Clarissa's beautiful flower picture which lay on the floor, sliced into about twenty strips half an inch wide. Other pictures lay about, mutilated in the same way. The woman beside me glanced down at them carelessly.

'We have one of these guillotines,' she explained in an offhand manner. 'I used to work in an office, you know – till I found out about Clarissa.' She picked up a heavy metal board with a hinged cutting blade at one side, and demonstrated how it worked, chop, chop, chop. 'Very useful things,' she said. By this time I was frankly backing towards the door. But she followed me into the garden, still carrying the guillotine.

'Just where did you say you had been?' she demanded.

'To – to the Swan Child,' I stammered. 'On Abbotsbury Hill.'

She shouted, 'I don't believe you! There's no such place!'

But at the same moment – or almost instantly after – I heard a detached gnatlike tiny voice in my ear, or inside my own head, which whispered, 'And did you make a wish for me on the Swan Child? Did you, did you?' A bubble of terror burst in my heart, I turned to fly and tripped over the length of hosepipe tangled across the path. I'm done for now, I thought, but the woman paused to chop a length off the hosepipe with her guillotine.

'Tom's down there,' she said conversationally. 'He took a fancy to spend eighty days underground. For research. He's only been down there twenty days; he has another two months to go. That is his air-pipe. *Put out your hands, child!*'

But I did not put out my hands. I beat it down the path and out of the gate, like a rat getting out of its maze. And, mercifully, just at that moment, Finch's grocery van was coming along the road. Stan Budd the driver had already seen Jake huddled on the dusty bank and slowed down, so I was able to race along, waving my arms, and help Stan lift Jake in, while the woman from The Bungalow stood regarding us thoughtfully over her gate, still snapping her guillotine up and down.

'You wasn't in *there* – was you?' said Stan. 'Blimey! You wouldn't get me in there. Clean bonkers, *she* is. I don't take the groceries in, any more, just leave them at the gate.'

My teeth were still chattering. I said, 'Wh-wh-what about her husband?'

'Oh, he died. Five years ago. In the cottage hospital. But she's got some notion he's still around, and a couple of others, too –'

Jake had fainted when we lifted him into the van. He lay inertly at the back among cartons of raisins and Persil. As soon as we got home, mother phoned Doctor Coswold, and he came round right away and said the break was only a simple fracture, and set it on the spot.

I haven't been into The Bungalow garden again. But sometimes when I walk past I peer cautiously over the gate. Sometimes I see the angry woman, Esme, I suppose, furiously gardening with spade or shears. Sometimes, in the evening, there is a bent, bowed person, Ag, 'the servant' presumably, waving a duster from door or window. She looks very like Clarissa, but thirty years older.

I have never seen Clarissa, though, and I like to think that, perhaps, by bringing her wish back with me from the Swan Child's hill, I was able to set her free, and help her to escape from that unhappy partnership.

I can still vividly remember her picture. I hope that, some day, I shall be able to paint one as good.

THE BROWN HAND

Sir Arthur Conan Doyle

Everyone knows that Sir Dominick Holden, the famous Indian surgeon, made me his heir, and that his death changed me in an hour from a hard-working and impecunious medical man to a well-to-do landed proprietor. Many know also that there were at least five people between the inheritance and me, and that Sir Dominick's selection appeared to be altogether arbitrary and whimsical. I can assure them, however, that they are quite mistaken, and that, although I only knew Sir Dominick in the closing years of his life, there were, none the less, very real reasons why he should show his goodwill towards me. As a matter of fact, though I say it myself, no man ever did more for another than I did for my Indian uncle. I cannot expect the story to be believed, but it is so singular that I should feel that it was a breach of duty if I did not put it upon record—so here it is, and your belief or incredulity is your own affair.

Sir Dominick Holden, CB, KCSI, and I don't know what besides, was the most distinguished Indian surgeon of his day. In the Army originally, he afterwards settled down into civil practice in Bombay, and visited, as a consultant, every part of India. His name is best remembered in connection with the Oriental Hospital which he founded and supported. The time came, however, when his iron constitution began to show signs of the long strain to which he had subjected it, and his brother practitioners (who were not, perhaps, entirely disinterested upon the point) were unanimous in recommending him to return to England. He held on so long as he could, but at last he developed nervous symptoms of a very pronounced character, and so came back, a broken man, to his native county of Wiltshire. He bought a considerable estate with an ancient manor-house upon the edge of Salisbury Plain, and devoted his old age to the study of Comparative Pathology, which had been his learned hobby all his life, and in which he was a foremost authority.

We of the family were, as may be imagined, much excited by the news of the return of this rich and childless uncle to England. On his part, although by no means exuberant in his hospitality, he showed some sense of his duty to his relations, and each of us in turn had an invitation to visit him. From the accounts of my cousins it appeared to be a melancholy business, and it was with mixed feelings that I at last received my own summons to appear at Rodenhurst. My wife was so carefully excluded in the invitation that my first impulse was to refuse it, but the interests of the children had to be considered, and so, with her consent, I set out one October afternoon upon my visit to Wiltshire, with little thought of what that visit was to entail.

My uncle's estate was situated where the arable land of the plains begins to swell upwards into the rounded chalk hills which are characteristic of the county. As I drove from Dinton Station in the waning light of that autumn day, I was impressed by the weird nature of the scenery. The few scattered cottages of the peasants were so dwarfed by the huge evidences of prehistoric life, that the present appeared to be a dream and the past to be the obtrusive and masterful reality. The road wound through the valleys, formed by a succession of grassy hills, and the summit of each was cut and carved into the most elaborate fortifications, some circular, and some square, but all on a scale which has defied the winds and the rains of many centuries. Some call them Roman and some British, but their true origin and the reason for this particular tract of country being so interlaced with entrenchments have never been finally made clear. Here and there on the long, smooth, olive-coloured slopes there rose small, rounded barrows or tumuli. Beneath them lie the cremated ashes of the race which cut so deeply into the hills, but their graves tell us nothing save that a jar full of dust represents the man who once laboured under the sun.

It was through this weird country that I approached my uncle's residence of Rodenhurst, and the house was, as I found, in due keeping with its surroundings. Two broken and weather-stained pillars, each surmounted by a mutilated heraldic emblem, flanked the entrance to a neglected drive. A cold wind whistled through the elms which lined it, and the air was full of the drifting leaves. At the far end, under the gloomy arch of trees, a single yellow lamp burned steadily. In the dim half-light of the coming night I saw a long, low building stretching out two irregular wings, with deep eaves, a sloping gambrel roof, and walls which were crisscrossed with timber balks in the fashion of the Tudors. The cheery light of a fire flickered in the broad, latticed window to the left of the low-porched door, and this, as it proved, marked the study of my uncle, for it was thither that I was led by his butler in order to make my host's acquaintance.

He was cowering over his fire, for the moist chill of an English autumn had set him shivering. His lamp was unlit, and I only saw the red glow of the embers beating upon a huge, craggy face, with a Red Indian nose and cheek, and deep furrows and seams from eye to chin, the sinister marks of hidden volcanic fires. He sprang up at my entrance with something of an old-world courtesy and welcomed me warmly to Rodenhurst. At the same time I was conscious, as the lamp was carried in, that it was a very critical pair of light-blue eyes which looked out at me from under shaggy eyebrows, like scouts beneath a bush, and that this outlandish uncle of mine was carefully reading off my character with all the ease of a practised observer and an experienced man of the world.

For my part I looked at him, and looked again, for I had never seen a man whose appearance was more fitted to hold one's attention. His figure was the framework of a giant, but he had fallen away until his coat dangled straight down in a shocking fashion from a pair of broad and bony shoulders. All his limbs were huge and yet emaciated, and I could not take my gaze from his knobby wrists, and long, gnarled hands. But his eyes—those peering, light-blue eyes—they were the most arrestive of any of his peculiarities. It was not their colour alone, nor was it the ambush of hair in which they lurked; but it was the expression which I read in them. For the appearance and bearing of the man were masterful, and one expected a certain corresponding arrogance in his eyes, but instead of that I read the look which tells of a spirit cowed and crushed, the furtive, expectant look of the dog whose master has taken the whip from the rack. I formed my own medical diagnosis upon one glance at those critical and yet appealing eyes. I believed that he was stricken with some mortal ailment, that he knew himself to be exposed to sudden death, and that he lived in terror of it. Such was my judgement—a false one, as the event showed; but I mention it that it may help you to realize the look which I read in his eyes.

My uncle's welcome was, as I have said, a courteous one, and in an hour or so I found myself seated between him and his wife at a comfortable dinner, with curious, pungent delicacies upon the table, and a stealthy, quick-eyed Oriental waiter behind his chair. The old couple had come round to that tragic imitation of the dawn of life when husband and wife, having lost or scattered all those who were their intimates, find themselves face to face and alone once more, their work done, and the end nearing fast. Those who have reached that stage in sweetness and love, who can change their winter into a gentle, Indian summer, have come as victors through the ordeal of life. Lady Holden was a small, alert woman with a kindly eye, and her expression as she glanced at him was a certificate of character to her husband. And yet, though I read a mutual love in their glances, I read also mutual horror, and recognized in her face some reflection of that stealthy fear which I had detected in his. Their talk was sometimes merry and sometimes sad, but there was a forced note in their merriment and a naturalness in their sadness which told me that a heavy heart beat upon either side of me.

We were sitting over our first glass of wine, and the servants had left the room, when the conversation took a turn which produced a remarkable effect upon my host and hostess. I cannot recall what it was which started the topic of the supernatural, but it ended in my showing them that the abnormal in psychical experiences was a subject to which, I had, like many neurologists, devoted a great deal of attention. I concluded by narrating my experiences when, as a member of the Psychical Research Society, I had formed one of a committee of three who spent the night in a haunted house. Our adventures were neither exciting nor convincing, but, such as it was, the story appeared to interest my auditors in a remarkable degree. They listened with an eager silence, and I caught a look of intelligence between them which I could not understand. Lady Holden immediately afterwards rose and left the room.

Sir Dominick pushed the cigar-box over to me, and we smoked for some little time in silence. That huge, bony hand of his was twitching as he raised it with his cheroot to his lips, and I felt that the man's nerves were vibrating like fiddle-strings. My instincts told me that he was on the verge of some intimate confidence, and I feared to speak lest I should interrupt it. At last he turned towards me with a spasmodic gesture like a man who throws his last scruple to the winds.

'From the little that I have seen of you it appears to me, Dr Hardacre,' said he, 'that you are the very man I have wanted to meet.'

'I am delighted to hear it, sir.'

'Your head seems to be cool and steady. You will acquit me of any desire to flatter you, for the circumstances are too serious to permit of insincerities. You have some special knowledge upon these subjects, and you evidently view them from that philosophical standpoint which robs them of all vulgar terror. I presume that the sight of an apparition would not seriously discompose you?'

'I think not, sir.'

'Would even interest you, perhaps?'

'Most intensely.'

'As a psychical observer, you would probably investigate it in as impersonal a fashion as an astronomer investigates a wandering comet?'

'Precisely.'

He gave a heavy sigh.

'Believe me, Dr Hardacre, there was a time when I could have spoken as you do now. My nerve was a byword in India. Even the Mutiny never shook it for an instant. And yet you see what I am reduced to—the most timorous man, perhaps, in all this county of Wiltshire. Do not speak too bravely upon this subject, or you may find yourself subjected to as long-drawn a test as I am—a test which can only end in the madhouse or the grave.'

I waited patiently until he should see fit to go farther in his confidence. His preamble had, I need not say, filled me with interest and expectation.

'For some years, Dr Hardacre,' he continued, 'my life and that of my wife have been made miserable by a cause which is so grotesque that it borders upon the ludicrous. And yet familiarity has never made it more easy to bear—on the contrary, as time passes my nerves became more worn and shattered by the constant attrition. If you have no physical fears, Dr Hardacre, I should very much value your opinion upon this phenomenon which troubles us so.'

'For what it is worth my opinion is entirely at your service. May I ask the nature of the phenomenon?'

'I think that your experiences will have a higher evidential value if you are not told in advance what you may expect to encounter. You are yourself aware of the quibbles of unconscious cerebration and subjective impressions with which a scientific sceptic may throw a doubt upon your statement. It would be as well to guard against them in advance.'

'What shall I do, then?'

'I will tell you. Would you mind following me this way?' He led me out of the dining-room and down a long passage until we came to a terminal door. Inside there was a large bare room fitted as a laboratory, with numerous scientific instruments and bottles. A shelf ran along one side, upon which there stood a long line of glass jars containing pathological and anatomical specimens.

'You see that I still dabble in some of my old studies,' said Sir Dominick. 'These jars are the remains of what was once a most excellent collection, but unfortunately I lost the greater part of them when my house was burned down in Bombay in '92. It was a most unfortunate affair for me—in more ways than one. I had examples of many rare conditions, and my splenic collection was probably unique. These are the survivors.'

I glanced over them, and saw that they really were of a very great value and rarity from a pathological point of view: bloated organs, gaping cysts, distorted bones, odious parasites—a singular exhibition of the products of India.

'There is, as you see, a small settee here,' said my host. 'It was far from our intention to offer a guest so meagre an accommodation, but since affairs have taken this turn, it would be a great kindness upon your part if you would consent to spend the night in this apartment. I beg that you will not hesitate to let me know if the idea should be at all repugnant to you.'

'On the contrary,' I said, 'it is most acceptable.'

'My own room is the second on the left, so that if you should feel that you are in need of company a call would always bring me to your side.'

'I trust that I shall not be compelled to disturb you.'

'It is unlikely that I shall be asleep. I do not sleep much. Do not hesitate to summon me.'

And so with this agreement we joined Lady Holden in the drawing room and talked of lighter things.

It was no affection upon my part to say that the prospect of my night's adventure was an agreeable one. I have no pretence to greater physical courage than my neighbours, but familiarity with a subject robs it of those vague and undefined terrors which are the most appalling to the imaginative mind. The human brain is capable of only one strong emotion at a time, and if it be filled with curiosity or scientific enthusiasm, there is no room for fear. It is true that I had my uncle's assurance that he had himself originally taken this point of view, but I reflected that the breakdown of his nervous system might be due to his forty years in India as much as to any physical experiences which had befallen him. I at least was sound in nerve and brain, and it was with something of the pleasurable thrill of anticipation with which the sportsman takes his position beside the haunt of his game that I shut the laboratory door behind me, and partially undressing, lay down upon the rug-covered settee.

It was not an ideal atmosphere for a bedroom. The air was heavy with many chemical odours, that of methylated spirit predominating. Nor were the decorations of my chamber very sedative. The odious line of glass jars with their relics of disease and suffering stretched in front of my very eyes. There was no blind to the window, and a three-quarter moon streamed its white light into the room, tracing a silver square with filigree lattices upon the opposite wall. When I had extinguished my candle this one bright patch in the midst of the general gloom had certainly an eerie and discomposing aspect. A rigid and absolute silence reigned throughout the old house, so that the low swish of the branches in the garden came softly and smoothly to my ears. It may have been the hypnotic lullaby of this gentle susurrus, or it may have been the result of my tiring day, but after many dozings and many efforts to regain my clearness of perception, I fell at last into a deep and dreamless sleep.

I was awakened by some sound in the room, and I instantly raised myself upon my elbow on the couch. Some hours had passed, for the square patch upon the wall had slid downwards and sideways until it lay obliquely at the end of my bed. The rest of the room was in deep shadow. At first I could see nothing. Presently, as my eyes became accustomed to the faint light, I was aware, with a thrill which all my scientific absorption could not entirely prevent, that something was moving slowly along the line of the wall. A gentle, shuffling sound, as of soft slippers, came to my ears, and I dimly discerned a human figure walking stealthily from the direction of the door. As it emerged into the patch of moonlight I saw very clearly what it was and how it was employed. It was a man, short and squat, dressed in some sort of dark-grey gown, which hung straight from his shoulders to his feet. The moon shone upon the side of his face, and I saw that it was a chocolate-brown in colour, with a ball of black hair like a woman's at the back of his head. He walked slowly, and his eyes were cast upwards towards the line of bottles which contained those gruesome remnants of humanity. He seemed to examine each jar with attention, and then to pass on to the next. When he had come to the end of the line, immediately opposite my bed, he stopped, faced me, threw up his hands with a gesture of despair, and vanished from my sight.

I have said that he threw up his hands, but I should have said his arms, for as he assumed that attitude of despair I observed a singular peculiarity about his appearance. He had only one hand! As the sleeves drooped down from the upflung arms I saw the left plainly, but the right ended in a knobby and unsightly stump. In every other way his appearance was so natural, and I had both seen and heard him so clearly, that I could easily have believed that he was an Indian servant of Sir Dominick's who had come into my room in search of something. It was only his sudden disappearance which suggested anything more sinister to me. As it was I sprang from my couch, lit a candle, and examined the whole room carefully. There were no signs of my visitor, and I was forced to conclude that there had really been something outside the normal laws of Nature in his appearance. I lay awake for the remainder of the night, but nothing else occurred to disturb me.

I am an early riser, but my uncle was an even earlier one, for I found him pacing up and down the lawn at the side of the house. He ran towards me in his eagerness when he saw me come out from the door.

'Well, well!' he cried. 'Did you see him?'

'An Indian with one hand?'

'Precisely.'

'Yes, I saw him'—and I told him all that occurred. When I had finished, he led the way into his study.

'We have a little time before breakfast,' said he. 'It will suffice to give you an explanation of this extraordinary affair—so far as I can explain that which is essentially inexplicable. In the first place, when I tell you that for four years I have never passed one single night, either in Bombay, aboard ship, or here in England without my sleep being broken by this fellow, you will understand why it is that I am a wreck of my former self. His programme is always the same. He appears by my bedside, shakes me roughly by the shoulder, passes from my room into the laboratory, walks slowly along the line of my bottles, and then vanishes. For more than a thousand times he has gone through the same routine.'

'What does he want?'

'He wants his hand.'

'His hand?'

'Yes, it came about in this way. I was summoned to Peshawar for a consultation some ten years ago, and while there I was asked to look at the hand of a native who was passing through with an Afghan caravan. The fellow came from some mountain tribe living away at the back of beyond somewhere on the other side of Kaffiristan. He talked a bastard Pushtoo, and it was all I could do to understand him. He was suffering from a soft sarcomatous swelling of one of the metacarpal joints, and I made him realize that it was only by losing his hand that he could hope to save his life. After much persuasion he consented to the operation, and he asked me, when it was over, what fee I demanded. The poor fellow was almost a beggar, so that the idea of a fee was absurd, but I answered in jest that my fee should be his hand, and that I proposed to add it to my pathological collection.

'To my surprise he demurred very much to the suggestion, and he explained that according to his religion it was an all-important matter that the body should be reunited after death, and so make a perfect dwelling for the spirit. The belief is, of course, an old one, and the mummies of the Egyptians arose from an analogous superstition. I answered him that his hand was already off, and asked him how he intended to preserve it. He replied that he would pickle it in salt and carry it about with him. I suggested that it might be safer in my keeping than his, and that I had better means than salt for preserving it. On realizing that I really intended to carefully keep it, his opposition vanished instantly. 'But remember, sahib,' said he, 'I shall want it back when I am dead.' I laughed at the remark, and so the matter ended. I returned to my practice, and he no doubt in the course of time was able to continue his journey to Afghanistan.

'Well, as I told you last night, I had a bad fire in my house at Bombay. Half of it was burned down, and, among other things, my pathological collection was largely destroyed. What you see are the poor remains of it. The hand of the hillman went with the rest, but I gave the matter no particular thought at the time. That was six years ago.

'Four years ago—two years after the fire—I was awakened one night by a furious tugging at my sleeve. I sat up under the impression that my favourite mastiff was trying to arouse me. Instead of this, I saw my Indian patient of long ago, dressed in the long, grey gown which was the badge of his people. He was holding up his stump and looking reproachfully at me. He then went over to my bottles, which at that time I kept in my room, and he examined them carefully, after which he gave a gesture of anger and vanished. I realized that he had just died, and that he had come to claim my promise that I should keep his limb in safety for him.

'Well, there you have it all, Dr Hardacre. Every night at the same hour for four years this performance has been repeated. It is a simple thing in itself, but it has worn me out like water dropping on a stone. It has brought a vile insomnia with it, for I cannot sleep now for the expectation of his coming. It has poisoned my old age and that of my wife, who has been the sharer in this great trouble. But there is the breakfast gong, and she will be waiting impatiently to know how it fared with you last night. We are both much indebted to you for your gallantry, for it takes something from the weight of our misfortune when we share it, even for a single night, with a friend, and it reassures us to our sanity, which we are sometimes driven to question.'

This was the curious narrative which Sir Dominick confided to me—a story which to many would have appeared to be a grotesque impossibility, but which, after my experience of the night before, and my previous knowledge of such things, I was prepared to accept as an absolute fact. I thought deeply over the matter, and brought the whole range of my reading and experience to bear upon it. After breakfast, I surprised my host and hostess by announcing that I was returning to London by the next train.

'My dear doctor,' cried Sir Dominick in great distress, 'you make me feel that I have been guilty of a gross breach of hospitality in intruding this unfortunate matter upon you. I should have borne my own burden.'

'It is, indeed, that matter which is taking me to London,' I answered; 'but you are mistaken, I assure you, if you think that my experience of last night was an unpleasant one to me. On the contrary, I am about to ask your permission to return in the evening and spend one more night in your laboratory. I am very eager to see this visitor once again.'

My uncle was exceedingly anxious to know what I was about to do, but my fears of raising false hopes prevented me from telling him. I was back in my own consulting-room a little after luncheon, and was confirming my memory of a passage in a recent book upon occultism which had arrested my attention when I read it.

'In the case of earth-bound spirits,' said my authority, 'some one dominant idea obsessing them at the hour of death is sufficient to hold them in this material world. They are the amphibia of this life and of the next, capable of passing from one to the other as the turtle passes from land to water. The causes which may bind a soul so strongly to a life which its body has abandoned are any violent emotion. Avarice, revenge, anxiety, love and pity have all been known to have this effect. As a rule it springs from some unfulfilled wish, and when the wish has been fulfilled the material bond relaxes. There are many cases upon record which show the singular persistence of these visitors, and also their disappearance when their wishes have been fulfilled, or in some cases when a reasonable compromise has been effected.'

'*A reasonable compromise effected*'—those were the words which I had brooded over all the morning, and which I now verified in the original. No actual atonement could be made here—but a reasonable compromise! I made my way as fast as a train could take me to the Shadwell Seamen's Hospital, where my old friend Jack Hewett was house-surgeon. Without explaining the situation I made him understand what it was that I wanted.

'A brown man's hand!' said he, in amazement. 'What in the world do you want that for?'

'Never mind. I'll tell you some day. I know that your wards are full of Indians.'

'I should think so. But a hand—' He thought a little and then struck a bell.

'Travers,' said he to a student-dresser, 'what became of the hands of the Lascar which we took off yesterday? I mean the fellow from the East India Dock who got caught in the steam winch.'

'They are in the *post-mortem* room, sir.'

'Just pack one of them in antiseptics and give it to Dr Hardacre.'

And so I found myself back at Rodenhurst before dinner with this curious outcome of my day in town. I still said nothing to Sir Dominick, but I slept that night in the laboratory, and I placed the Lascar's hand in one of the glass jars at the end of my couch.

So interested was I in the result of my experiment that sleep was out of the question. I sat with a shaded lamp beside me and waited patiently for my visitor. This time I saw him clearly from the first. He appeared beside the door, nebulous for an instant, and then hardening into as distinct an outline as any living man. The slippers beneath his grey gown were red and heelless, which accounted for the low, shuffling sound which he made as he walked. As on the previous night he passed slowly along the line of bottles until he paused before that which contained the hand. He reached up to it, his whole figure quivering with expectation, took it down, examined it eagerly, and then, with a face which was convulsed with fury and disappointment, he hurled it down on the floor. There was a crash which resounded through the house, and when I looked up the mutilated Indian had disappeared. A moment later my door flew open and Sir Dominick rushed in.

'You are not hurt?' he cried.

'No—but deeply disappointed.'

He looked in astonishment at the splinters of glass, and the brown hand lying upon the floor.

'Good God!' he cried. 'What is this?'

I told him my idea and its wretched sequel. He listened intently, but shook his head.

'It is well thought of,' said he, 'but I fear that there is no such easy end to my sufferings. But one thing I now insist upon. It is that you shall never again upon any pretext occupy this room. My fears that something might have happened to you—when I heard that crash—have been the most acute of all the agonies which I have undergone. I will not expose myself to a repetition of it.'

He allowed me, however, to spend the remainder of that night where I was, and I lay there worrying over the problem and lamenting my own failure. With the first light of morning there was the Lascar's hand still lying upon the floor to remind me of my fiasco. I lay looking at it—and as I lay suddenly an idea flew like a bullet through my head and brought me quivering with excitement out of my couch. I raised the grim relic from where it had fallen. Yes, it was indeed so. The hand was the *left* hand of the Lascar.

By the first train I was on my way to town, and hurried at once to the Seamen's Hospital. I remembered that both hands of the Lascar had been amputated, but I was terrified lest the precious organ which I was in search of might have been already consumed in the crematory. My suspense was soon ended. It had still been preserved in the *post-mortem* room. And so I returned to Rodenhurst in the evening with my mission accomplished and the material for a fresh experiment.

But Sir Dominick Holden would not hear of my occupying the

laboratory again. To all my entreaties he turned a deaf ear. It offended his sense of hospitality, and he could no longer permit it. I left the hand, therefore, as I had done its fellow the night before, and I occupied a comfortable bedroom in another portion of the house, some distance from the scene of my adventures.

But in spite of that my sleep was not destined to be uninterrupted. In the dead of night my host burst into my room, a lamp in his hand. His huge, gaunt figure was enveloped in a loose dressing-gown, and his whole appearance might certainly have seemed more formidable to a weak-nerved man than that of the Indian of the night before. But it was not his entrance so much as his expression which amazed me. He had turned suddenly younger by twenty years at the least. His eyes were shining, his features radiant, and he waved one hand in triumph over his head. I sat up astounded, staring sleepily at this extraordinary visitor. But his words soon drove the sleep from my eyes.

'We have done it! We have succeeded!' he shouted. 'My dear Hardacre, how can I ever in this world repay you?'

'You don't mean to say that it is all right?'

'Indeed I do. I was sure that you would not mind being awakened to hear such blessed news.'

'Mind! I should think not indeed. But is it really certain?'

'I have no doubt whatever upon the point. I owe you such a debt, my dear nephew, as I have never owed a man before, and never expected to. What can I possibly do for you that is commensurate? Providence must have sent you to my rescue. You have saved both my reason and my life, for another six months of this must have seen me either in a cell or a coffin. And my wife—it was wearing her out before my eyes. Never could I have believed that any human being could have lifted this burden off me.' He seized my hand and wrung it in his bony grip.

'It was only an experiment—a forlorn hope—but I am delighted from my heart that it has succeeded. But how do you know that it is all right? Have you seen something?'

He seated himself at the foot of my bed.

'I have seen enough,' said he. 'It satisfies me that I shall be troubled no more. What has passed is easily told. You know that at a certain hour this creature always comes to me. Tonight he arrived at the usual time, and aroused me with even more violence than is his custom. I can only surmise that his disappointment of last night increased the bitterness of his anger against me. He looked angrily at me, and then went on his usual round. But in a few minutes I saw him, for the first time since this persecution began, return to my chamber. He was smiling. I saw the gleam of his white teeth through the dim light. He stood facing me at the end of my bed, and three times he made the low, Eastern salaam which is their solemn leave-taking. And the third time that he bowed he raised his arms over his head, and I saw his *two* hands outstretched in the air. So he vanished, and, as I believe, for ever.'

So that is the curious experience which won me the affection and the gratitude of my celebrated uncle, the famous Indian surgeon. His anticipations were realized, and never again was he disturbed by the visits of the restless hillman in search of his lost member. Sir Dominick and Lady Holden spent a very happy old age, unclouded, so far as I know, by any trouble, and they finally died during the great influenza epidemic within a few weeks of each other. In his lifetime he always turned to me for advice in everything which concerned that English life of which he knew so little; and I aided him also in the purchase and development of his estates. It was no great surprise to me, therefore, that I found myself eventually promoted over the heads of five exasperated cousins, and changed in a single day from a hard-working country doctor into the head of an important Wiltshire family. I, at least, have reason to bless the memory of the man with the brown hand, and the day when I was fortunate enough to relieve Rodenhurst of his unwelcome presence.

THE RED ROOM

H.G. Wells

'I can assure you,' said I, 'that it will take a very tangible ghost to frighten me.' And I stood up before the fire with my glass in my hand.

'It is your own choosing,' said the man with the withered arm and glanced at me askance.

'Eight-and-twenty years,' said I, 'I have lived, and never a ghost have I seen as yet.'

The old woman sat staring hard into the fire, her pale eyes wide open. 'Ay,' she broke in; 'and eight-and-twenty years you have lived and never seen the likes of this house, I reckon. There's a many things to see, when one's still but eight-and-twenty.' She swayed her head slowly from side to side. 'A many things to see and sorrow for.'

I half suspected the old people were trying to enhance the spiritual terrors of their house by their droning insistence. I put down my empty glass on the table and looked about the room, and caught a glimpse of myself, abbreviated and broadened to an impossible stoutness, in the queer old mirror at the end of the room. 'Well,' I said, 'if I see anything tonight, I shall be so much the wiser. For I come to the business with an open mind.'

'It's your own choosing,' said the man with the withered arm once more.

I heard the sound of a stick and a shambling step on the flags in the passage outside, and the door creaked on its hinges as a second old man entered, more bent, more wrinkled, more aged even than the first. He supported himself by a single crutch, his eyes were covered by a shade, and his lower lip, half-averted, hung pale and pink from his decaying yellow teeth. He made straight for an arm-chair on the opposite side of the table, sat down clumsily, and began to cough. The man with the withered arm gave this newcomer a short glance of positive dislike, the old woman took no notice of his arrival, but remained with her eyes fixed steadily on the fire.

'I said—it's your own choosing,' said the man with the withered arm, when the coughing had ceased for a while.

'It's my own choosing,' I answered.

The man with the shade became aware of my presence for the first time, and threw his head back for a moment and sideways, to see me. I caught a momentary glimpse of his eyes, small and bright and inflamed. Then he began to cough and splutter again.

'Why don't you drink?' said the man with the withered arm, pushing the beer towards him. The man with the shade poured out a glassful with a shaky arm that splashed half as much again on the deal table. A monstrous shadow of him crouched upon the wall and mocked his action as he poured and drank. I must confess I had scarce expected these grotesque custodians. There is to my mind something inhuman in senility, something crouching and atavistic; the human qualities seem to drop from old people insensibly day by day. The three of them made me feel uncomfortable, with their gaunt silences, their bent carriage, their evident unfriendliness to me and to one another.

'If,' said I, 'you will show me to this haunted room of yours, I will make myself comfortable there.'

The old man with the cough jerked his head back so suddenly that it startled me, and shot another glance of his red eyes at me from under the shade; but no one answered me. I waited a minute, glancing from one to the other.

'If,' I said a little louder, 'if you will show me to this haunted room of yours, I will relieve you from the task of entertaining me.'

'There's a candle on the slab outside the door,' said the man with the withered arm, looking at my feet as he addressed me. 'But if you go to the red room tonight'—

('This night of all nights!' said the old woman.)

'You go alone.'

'Very well,' I answered. 'And which way do I go?'

'You go along the passage for a bit,' said he, 'until you come to a door, and through that is a spiral staircase, and halfway up that is a landing and another door covered with baize. Go through that and down the long corridor to the end, and the red room is on your left up the steps.'

'Have I got that right?' I said, and repeated his directions. He corrected me in one particular.

'And are you really going?' said the man with the shade, looking at me again for the third time, with that queer, unnatural tilting of the face.

('This night of all nights!' said the old woman.)

'It is what I came for,' I said, and moved towards the door. As I did so, the old man with the shade rose and staggered round the table, so as to be closer to the others and to the fire. At the door I turned and looked at them, and saw they were all close together, dark against the firelight, staring at me over their shoulders, with an intent expression on their ancient faces.

'Goodnight,' I said, setting the door open.

'It's your own choosing,' said the man with the withered arm.

I left the door wide open until the candle was well alight, and then I shut them in and walked down the chilly, echoing passage.

I must confess that the oddness of these three old pensioners in whose charge her ladyship had left the castle, and the deep-toned, old fashioned furniture of the housekeeper's room in which they foregathered, affected me in spite of my efforts to keep myself at a matter-of-fact phase. They seemed to belong to another age, an older age, an age when things spiritual were different from this of ours, less certain: an age when omens and witches were credible, and ghosts beyond denying. Their very existence was spectral; the cut of their clothing, fashions born in dead brains. The ornaments and conveniences of the room about them were ghostly—the thoughts of vanished men, which still haunted rather than participated in the world of today. But with an effort I sent such thoughts to the right-about. The long, draughty subterranean passage was chilly and dusty, and my candle flared and made the shadows cower and quiver. The echoes rang up and down the spiral staircase, and a shadow came sweeping up after me, and one fled before me into the darkness overhead. I came to the landing and stopped there for a moment, listening to a rustling that I fancied I heard; then, satisfied of the absolute silence, I pushed open the baize-covered door and stood in the corridor.

The effect was scarcely what I expected, for the moonlight, coming in by the great window on the grand staircase, picked out everything in vivid black shadow or silvery illumination. Everything was in its place: the house might have been deserted on the yesterday instead of eighteen months ago. There were candles in the sockets of the sconces, and whatever dust had gathered on the carpets or upon the polished flooring was distributed so evenly as to be invisible in the moonlight. I was about to advance, and stopped abruptly. A bronze group stood upon the landing, hidden from me by the corner of the wall, but its shadow fell with marvellous distinctness upon the white panelling, and gave me the impression of someone crouching to waylay me. I stood rigid for half a minute perhaps. Then, with my hand in the pocket that held my revolver, I advanced, only to discover a Ganymede and Eagle glistening in the moonlight. That incident for a time restored my nerve, and a porcelain Chinaman on a buhl table, whose head rocked silently as I passed him, scarcely startled me.

The door to the red room and the steps up to it were in a shadowy corner. I moved my candle from side to side, in order to see clearly the nature of the recess in which I stood before opening the door. Here it was, thought I, that my predecessor was found, and the memory of that story gave me a sudden twinge of apprehension. I glanced over my shoulder at the Ganymede in the moonlight, and opened the door of the red room rather hastily, with my face half turned to the pallid silence of the landing.

I entered, closed the door behind me at once, turned the key I found in the lock within, and stood with the candle held aloft, surveying the scene of my vigil, the great red room of Lorraine Castle, in which the young duke had died. Or rather, in which he had begun his dying, for he had opened the door and fallen headlong down the steps I had just ascended. That had been the end of his vigil, of his gallant attempt to conquor the ghostly tradition of the place; and never, I thought, had apoplexy better served the ends of superstition. And there were other and older stories that clung to the room, back to the half-credible beginnings of it all, the tale of a timid wife and the tragic end that came to her husband's jest of frightening her. And looking around that large shadowy room, with its shadowy window bays, its recesses and alcoves, one could well understand the legends that had sprouted in its black corners, its germinating darkness. My candle was a little tongue of flame in its vastness, that failed to pierce the opposite end of the room, and left an ocean of mystery and suggestion beyond its island of light.

I resolved to make a systematic examination of the place at once, and dispel the fanciful suggestions of its obscurity before they obtained a hold upon me. After satisfying myself of the fastening of the door, I began to walk about the room, peering round each article of furniture, tucking up the valances of the bed, and opening its curtains wide, I pulled up the blinds and examined the fastenings of the windows, leant forward and looked up the blackness of the wide chimney, and tapped the dark oak panelling for any secret opening. There were two big mirrors in the room, each with a pair of sconces bearing candles, and on the mantleshelf, too, were more candles in china candlesticks. All these I lit one after the other. The fire was laid,—an unexpected consideration from the old housekeeper,—and I lit it, to keep down any disposition to shiver, and when it was burning well, I stood round with my back to it and regarded the room again. I had pulled up a chintz-covered arm-chair and a table, to form a kind of barricade before me, and on this lay my revolver ready to hand. My precise examination had done me good, but I still found the remoter darkness of the place, and its perfect stillness, too stimulating for the imagination. The echoing of the stir and crackling of the fire was no sort of comfort to me. The shadow in the alcove, at the end in particular, had that undefinable quality of a presence, that odd suggestion of a lurking living thing, that comes so easily in silence and solitude. At last, to reassure myself, I walked with a candle into it, and satisfied myself that there was nothing tangible there. I stood that candle upon the floor of the alcove, and left it in that position.

By this time I was in a state of considerable nervous tension, although to my reason there was no adequate cause for the condition. My mind, however, was perfectly clear. I postulated quite unreservedly that nothing supernatural could happen, and to pass the time I began to string some rhymes together, Ingoldsby fashion, of the original legend of the place. A few I spoke aloud, but the echoes were not pleasant. For the same reason I also abandoned, after a time, a conversation with myself upon the impossibility of ghosts and haunting. My mind reverted to the three old and distorted people downstairs, and I tried to keep it upon that topic. The sombre reds and blacks of the room troubled me; even with seven candles the place was merely dim. The one in the alcove flared in a draught, and the fire-flickering kept the shadows and penumbra perpetually shifting and stirring. Casting about for a remedy, I recalled the candles I had seen in the passage, and, with a slight effort, walked out into the moonlight, carrying a candle and leaving the door open, and presently returned with as many as ten. These I put in various knick-knacks of china with which the room was sparsely adorned, lit and placed where the shadows had lain deepest, some on the floor, some in the window recesses, until at last my seventeen candles were so arranged that not an inch of the room but had the direct light of at least one of them. It occurred to me that when the ghost came, I could warn him not to trip over them. The room was now quite brightly illuminated. There was something very cheery and reassuring in these little streaming flames, and snuffing them gave me an occupation, and afforded a reassuring sense of the passage of time.

Even with that, however, the brooding expectations of the vigil weighed heavily upon me. It was after midnight that the candle in the alcove suddenly went out, and the black shadow sprang back to its place. I did not see the candle go out; I simply turned and saw the darkness was there, as one might expect and see the unexpected presence of a stranger. 'By Jove!' said I aloud; 'that draught's a strong one!' and, taking the matches from the table, I walked across the room in a leisurely manner to relight the corner again. My first match would not strike, and as I succeeded with the second, something seemed to blink on the wall before me. I turned my head involuntarily, and saw that the two candles on the little table by the fireplace were extinguished. I rose at once to my feet.

'Odd!' I said. 'Did I do that myself in a flash of absent-mindedness?'

I walked back, relit one, and as I did so, I saw the candle in the right of one of the mirrors wink and go right out, and almost immediately its companion followed it. There was no mistake about it. The flame vanished, as if the wicks had been suddenly nipped between a finger and a thumb, leaving the wick neither glowing nor smoking, but black. While I stood gaping, the candle at the foot of the bed went out, and the shadows seemed to take another step towards me.

'This won't do!' said I, and first one and then another candle on the mantleshelf followed.

'What's up?' I cried, with a queer high note getting into my voice somehow. At that the candle on the wardrobe went out, and the one I had relit in the alcove followed.

'Steady on!' I said. 'These candles are wanted,' speaking with a half-hysterical facetiousness, and scratching away at a match the while for the mantle candlesticks. My hands trembled so much that twice I missed the rough paper of the matchbox. As the mantel emerged from darkness again, two candles in the remoter end of the window were eclipsed. But with the same match I also relit the larger mirror candles, and those on the floor near the doorway, so that for the moment I seemed to gain on the extinctions. But then in a volley there vanished four lights at once in different corners of the room, and I struck another match in quivering haste, and stood hesitating whither to take it.

As I stood undecided, an invisible hand seemed to sweep out the two candles on the table. With a cry of terror, I dashed at the alcove, then into the corner, and then into the window, relighting three, as two more vanished by the fireplace; then, perceiving a better way, dropped the matches on the iron-bound deed-box in the corner, and caught up the bedroom candlestick. With this I avoided the delay of striking matches, but for all that the steady process of extinction went on, and the shadows I feared and fought against returned, and crept in upon me, first a step gained on this side of me and then on that. It was like a ragged storm-cloud sweeping out the stars. Now and then one returned for a minute, and was lost again. I was now almost frantic with the horror of coming darkness, and my self-possession deserted me. I leaped panting and dishevelled from candle to candle, in a vain struggle against that remorseless advance.

I bruised myself on the thigh against the table, I sent a chair headlong,

I stumbled and fell and whisked the cloth from the table in my fall. My candle rolled away from me, and I snatched another as I rose. Abruptly this was blown out, as I swung it off the table, by the wind of my sudden movement, and immediately the two remaining candles followed. But there was light still in the room, a red light that stayed off the shadows from me. The fire! Of course, I could thrust my candle between the bars and relight it!

I turned to where the flames were dancing between the glowing coals, and splashing red reflections upon the furniture, made two steps towards the grate, and incontinently the flames dwindled and vanished, the glow vanished, the reflections rushed together and vanished, and as I thrust the candle between the bars, darkness closed upon me like the shutting of an eye, wrapped about me in a stiflling embrace, sealed my vision, and crushed the last vestiges of reason from my brain. The candle fell from my hand. I flung out my arms in a vain effort to thrust that ponderous blackness away from me, and, lifting up my voice, screamed with all my might—once, twice, thrice. Then I think I must have staggered to my feet. I know I thought suddenly of the moonlit corridor, and, with my head bowed and my arms over my face, made a run for the door.

But I had forgotten the exact position of the door, and struck myself heavily against the corner of the bed. I staggered back, turned, and was either struck or struck myself against some other bulky furniture. I have a vague memory of battering myself thus, to and fro in the darkness, of a cramped struggle, and of my own wild crying as I darted to and fro, of a heavy blow at last upon my forehead, a horrible sensation of falling that lasted an age, of my last frantic effort to keep my footing, and then I remember no more.

* * * *

I opened my eyes in daylight. My head was roughly bandaged, and the man with the withered arm was watching my face. I looked about me, trying to remember what had happened, and for a space I could not recollect. I turned to the corner, and saw the old woman, no longer abstracted, pouring out some drops of medicine from a little blue phial into a glass. 'Where am I?' I asked. 'I seem to remember you, and yet I cannot remember who you are.'

They told me then, and I heard of the haunted Red Room as one who hears a tale. 'We found you at dawn,' said he, 'and there was blood on your forehead and lips.'

It was very slowly I recovered my memory of my experience. 'You believe now,' said the old man, 'that the room is haunted?' He spoke no longer as one who greets an intruder, but as one who grieves for a broken friend.

'Yes,' said I; 'the room is haunted.'

'And you have seen it. And we, who have lived here all our lives, have never set eyes upon it. Because we have never dared. . . . Tell us, is it truly the old earl who—'

'No,' said I; 'it is not.'

'I told you so,' said the old lady, with the glass in her hand. 'It is his poor young countess who was frightened—'

'It is not,' I said. 'There is neither ghost of earl nor ghost of countess in that room, there is no ghost there at all; but worse, far worse—'

'Well?' they said.

'The worst of all the things that haunt poor mortal man,' said I; 'and that is, in all its nakedness—*Fear!* Fear that will not have light nor sound, that will not bear with reason, that deafens and darkens and overwhelms. It followed me through the corridor, it fought against me in the room—'

I stopped abruptly. There was an interval of silence. My hand went up to my bandages.

Then the man with the shade sighed and spoke. 'That is it,' said he. 'I knew that was it. A Power of Darkness. To put such a curse upon a woman! It lurks there always. You can feel it even in the daytime, even of a bright summer's day, in the hangings, in the curtains, keeping behind you however you face about. In the dusk it creeps along the corridor and follows you, so that you dare not turn. There is fear in that room of hers—black Fear, and there will be—so long as this house of sin endures.'

MYSTERY STORIES
Contents

THE BLADES

Joan Aiken

Right from the start they were enemies. Or at least on opposite sides. Maybe that was to be expected with two boys so diametrically different from each other as Jack Kettering and Will Donkine. Kettering was tall, or tallish, solidly built, with a flat, high-cheekboned, ruddy, handsome face, and a thick crop of burnished red-gold hair. His dad was a Master of Foxhounds, and when the older Kettering came to the school for speechdays you could see just what Jack would become in the course of time—solid, swaggering, red-faced, with his thatch of shining hair turned snowy white. Kettering excelled at all sports—cricket, football, rowing, swimming, athletics; and he was by no means a fool, either ; had a knack of learning anything by heart that could be learned in that way, so grammar, mathematical and scientific formulae, dates, facts were always at his finger-tips, passing exams was no trouble to him; he was generally among the top four or five at the year's end. He could be funny, too, in a rather unsubtle way, and generous—at least to his friends—he had that sort of air about him which people like Francis Drake and Robin Hood must have carried, so that followers, as it were, flocked to his standard. Not that I mean to say he was an outlaw—oh dear, no. Law-abiding, on the whole, was Jack, more so as he went up the school; of course there was the odd quiet escapade, beer drunk behind the art studios and then whisky in the boat-house, dodging off to go to the Motor Show and a night on the spree in London, but these were just schoolboy capers, nothing nasty about them. He enjoyed the reputation of being a good-natured, easy-going fellow. His lot, there were about half a dozen of them, the Blades, they called themselves, were the same kind, and they stuck together all the way up the school.

Later on, when girls were admitted into the upper forms, they all acquired girlfriends to match: Kettering's girl was called Pamela Cassell, and she was big and blooming and bossy, with a head of brick-red hair to match Jack's copper-gold, always freshly shampooed and shining and crisp. Captain of the girls' hockey, she was, won the tennis cup three years running, and intended to run a ballroom-dancing school. She had that pink-and-white complexion often found in red-heads, and pale china-blue eyes; striking, people said she was, but I couldn't see it myself. If you didn't belong to Kettering's group her eyes passed over you in utter rejection, you might as well have been a garden bench.

Donkine, Will Donkine was, as I've said, in all ways the complete opposite of Jack. From the start, poor devil, he suffered from his name. Will was short for Willibald, which was a family name; some ancestor had come from Austria—Willibald Edvard Donkine, his full name was, so if he wasn't called the Hun, or Kraut, or Donk, or Donkey, it was Weed or Weedy because of his initials. He came to the school when he was twelve, and by the time he was fourteen the various nicknames had more or less settled down into Donk. Of course it cut no ice at all that his father, Sir Joel Donkine, was a well-known scientist, in line for the Nobel prize. Will Donkine was small and bony, with a pale hollow-eyed face, short-sighted serious dark-brown eyes (he had to wear steel-rimmed glasses which were always getting broken), and sparse no-colour hair like a crop of mousy moss on top of his undistinguished head. Being so short-sighted he was no use at games, and anyway his arms and legs were thin as sticks of celery so he couldn't run fast or catch balls or hit them; he was bright enough, but his wits had a habit of wandering, so that he didn't do particularly well in exams; when he ought to have been answering Question 2, he'd be looking out of the window trying to estimate the flight-speed of swifts, or wondering if it would be possible to turn a Black Hole inside out, or to compress Mars Bars to the size of dice for rapid and economic distribution. His conversation was always interesting—he knew a lot about codes, and ESP, and how people's discarded selves may come back to haunt them (he read books on psychology when most people were reading Biggles) and where you can still find bits of primeval forest in Europe, and what to do if you sit on a queen bee, but his knowledge wasn't very well applied; it never turned up when it was needed. I liked Donkine's company, but he wasn't a popular boy. Part of that was his own fault. He found most people boring; simply preferred his own thoughts. I expect they were more interesting than locker-room chat, but, just the same, if you don't want to have a dismal time at school you need to meet people half-way, display a bit of give-and-take. Donkine did nothing of that kind, so he was an outcast. His solitary state didn't worry him in the least, he spent his spare time reading in the library or measuring things in the lab, or working in his allotment. He was very keen on gardening.

It must be said that Kettering and the Blades gave him a fairly hard time, specially when we were all younger; every now and then they'd rough him up, not *too* much, of course, because they didn't want to spoil their reputation for being decent types; never anything that would show. To do Donkine justice, he never grassed on them; for a day or two he'd go about rather more silent and hunched over, shabbier and a trifle more moth-eaten-looking, that was all. What he did mind was when they messed up his garden; that really hit him in a tender spot. But, as luck would have it, old Postlethwaite the science master was out at three a.m. one night studying a comet and came on Kettering and McGeech systematically digging up Will's artichokes and celeriac, so there was a certain amount of fuss about that, and from then on they had to lay off the garden sabotage; it would have been too obvious that it was them, see? They had to think of other forms of persecution.

While Kettering and the Blades were acquiring girlfriends and boasting of their exploits, Will made friends with my sister Ceridwen, who was small and dark and cross-looking. Nothing romantic about their friendship: they were both interested in the same kinds of things. Ceridwen intended to do animal- and plant-breeding later on, and she was very impressed with Will's aptitude for growing things.

By the time we were in the lower Fifth, Will's father had invented his dust extractor, D.R.I.P., it was called, Dust Removal from Industrial and Institutional Premises. Of course it was shortened to DRIP. Don't ask me how it worked—it was a thermo-nuclear process, radioactivity came into it, and magnetic fields, and the earth's rotation and gravitational pull. Unlike many such processes, it was simple and economical to install. What it did was suck all the dust and grit and germs out of the air inside a building by means of vents on the floor, so that once a DRIP System was installed in your factory—or office block—or hospital—you need never sweep or dust or Hoover or scrub again. There have been similar systems in the past, of course, but expensive to run, and none were so efficient as Sir J. Donkine's. Apparently it really did remove every particle and molecule of anything nasty from the atmosphere so that the air you breathed into your lungs was 100% Simon-pure.

Naturally a process, an invention like this was nothing like so sensational as discovering penicillin or DNA or splitting the atom; but still there were articles about it in scientific journals, and old Corfe our headmaster mentioned it in a congratulatory way one morning at Assembly, and said we must all be proud that Sir J. was an Old Boy of our school and his son was our dear fellow-scholar, and we must hope that Will would invent something equally useful one day. I noticed Will give a kind of blink behind his glasses at that; he was not at all gratified by being singled out, and I knew why; of course for him it would mean extra hazing and sarcastic broadsides from the Blades for several weeks, till the news had settled down. Old Corfe, who never knew anything about what went on in the school, was unaware of that, naturally; and he was pleased as a dog with two tails about the publicity for the school.

Because of this connection, and before anyone had finished asking 'What About Side Effects?' our school, along with several hospitals and a Midland furniture factory, had taken the plunge and had the Donkine DRIP System installed. A demonstration of loyalty it was, on our part, to show our faith and pride in our Old Boy (though I bet that Mr Corfe managed to get the installation done at half price because of the public interest etc. etc.). Anyway, air vents were set into the floors of all rooms, in corners where they were not inconvenient, and suction pipes, and a big gleaming white tank down in the basement which housed the works. If you held your breath and nobody else was breathing in the room you could just catch the sound of a very faint hum, no more noise than a light-bulb makes when it's at the point of death. Nobody could say the DRIP System was loud or annoying. And the school certainly was clean! Not a speck of mud, no dust or fluff could lie on any surface for more than a moment, our clothes and books and bedding and towels all stayed cleaner longer, even substances like spilled jam or glue tended to vanish overnight if not wiped up; and at the end of the first term old Corfe announced with triumph that our health rate had improved by eighty per cent, practically no head colds, hay fever, or asthma, and all other infectious complaints much reduced.

The hospitals and furniture factory had reported the same good results; by now Sir Joel Donkine was on the high road to success, fame, fortune, and the Nobel prize. DripCo, the company formed to make the DRIP Systems, could hardly keep pace with the orders; every factory and hospital in the country wanted them now; they were being installed not only in public buildings but also in private homes. Buckingham Palace, if you can call that a private home, was first on the list, and Sir Joel got a decoration from the Palace as well as his Nobel.

What was his son Will doing all this time? Will, of course, had known about his father's intentions long ago, heard the subject discussed since he was nine or ten. His mother had died, when he was six, of an anti-immunity failure, so Sir Joel tended to talk to him a lot when they were together; one of the reasons why Will found most school conversation boring.

Will's main problem after Sir Joel's rise to fame was dodging retribution from the Society of Blades—what they called 'necessary discipline' to stop him from getting above himself. *Above himself*—poor Will sometimes looked as if he wished he was under the ground. Most of the Blades, by now, were big and tough as grown men, whereas Will, at fifteen, seemed to have stopped growing for good and was no bigger than a thirteen-year-old. It wasn't for lack of fresh air; he still spent hours every day tending his garden. Unfortunately the school allotments were isolated beyond a row of utility sheds, on the edge of the school grounds; he was much at risk there from the unwelcome attentions of the Blades.

'How's our little Drip today, how's our Weed?' they would say, clustering round him affectionately. 'We've come to remind you not to get too stuck up, just because your dad invented a giant Hoover.'

Once they painted him all over with Stockholm tar, which he'd been using on a peach tree he grew from a peach-stone; another time they dropped him, and all his tools, into the river; on a third occasion they removed tufts of hair from all over his head. The effect was a bit like a chessboard. That was a mistake, because it was quite visible; old Corfe made inquiries, sent for Kettering and the Blades, and gave them a severe tongue-lashing and various penalties, so their attentions abated for a while.

And Donkine went doggedly on his way, reading a lot, keeping up reasonably well with school work, showing fitful brilliance here and there, specially in chemistry and biology; working in his garden and trying to mind his own business. Whatever that was.

'Don't you ever want to get your own back on those pigs?' my sister Ceridwen asked him once. We are Welsh; I reckon that revenge comes more naturally to us. But Will just shrugged.

'What's the point?' he said. 'They'd only make it worse for me, after. You've got to think ahead. And I've got better things to do than conduct a feud. Besides, I have an idea that by and by . . .'

He didn't finish his sentence. His eyes had wandered, as they often did, towards two huge shiny pink potatoes he had just dug up, and a tussock of grass he had pulled out.

One thing he had discovered was that DRIP compost was marvellous for the garden.

I expect you have been wondering what happened to all the dirt and dust that was sucked out of the classrooms and offices and dormitories. It went into black plastic sacks that fitted over the outlet-vents and were removed at regular intervals. The stuff inside them was like stiff dark-brown prune jam, very thick and sticky. Will found that if this was diluted and watered on to the garden, or just spaded around in gooey lumps, like undercooked Christmas pudding, it worked wonders for growing plants. A few weeks of this treatment and Will's artichokes were big as footballs, his spinach-leaves the size of the *Daily Mirror* and his roses six inches in diameter.

Postlethwaite the science master (we called him Old Possum, of course, because he had big, wide-apart gentle eyes, and very little chin, and his thin hair wavered backwards like water-weeds), old Postlethwaite was absolutely delighted at this link-up between the activities of father and son, evidence of Will's independent research.

'Wonderful work, wonderful, my dear Donkine,' he kept saying. 'You may have hit on something of real importance there.' And he quoted: ' "Whoever could make two blades of grass grow where only one grew before, would deserve better of mankind than the whole race of politicians put together." Do you know who said that?'

'Swift,' said Will without hesitation. But his mind as usual seemed half astray. 'People wore wigs in Swift's day, didn't they, sir?'

'We must see if we can't get you the Wickenden Award for this,' Old Possum went on.

The Wickenden Cup was a school honour endowed by a past rich American parent; it was given from time to time for unusually original school work.

'Oh, *please*, sir, don't bother,' said Will, who knew that anything of the kind would only lead to more trouble with Kettering's group. 'If you could just ask Mr Corfe to give an order that the black sacks aren't to be taken away by the garbage trucks but left in a heap here by the allotments. Then everybody who wants to can use them.'

But nobody else took the trouble to do so. It's true the stuff did smell rather vile: sweet and rotten like malt and codliver oil.

By and by there began to be odd, apparently disconnected paragraphs in the newspapers: the Queen had been obliged to cancel all her engagements, as she was suffering from a virus cold; a hospital in the north was plagued by an epidemic of ringworm or possibly infectious alopecia; the staff of a Midland furniture factory were all out on strike for some mysterious reason; and the Prime Minister, in the middle of a visit to Moscow, returned to Britain hurriedly and unexpectedly.

Could there be a link between these incidents? The factory and the hospital were two which had been among the first to have the DRIP System installed.

At our school, though, we didn't read the papers a lot; interested in our own affairs, we weren't much concerned with outside news. Time had skidded on its way and by now we were working for our A-levels, up to the eyes in reading and revision. Still, even busy as we were, we couldn't help observing something that was happening right under our noses.

Ceridwen, my sharp-eyed sister, spotted it first.

'All the staff are going bald,' she said. 'Have you noticed?'

It was true. The men's hair was receding at a rapid rate, and the women teachers had taken to various ruses, buns, chignons, hair-pieces, to try and conceal the fact that their locks were becoming scantier and scantier. It seemed to affect older people faster, and dark people less than fair.

Then one morning there was a crisis in the girls' dormitory.

Hysterical shrieks were heard coming from the room of big red-headed Pamela Cassell (who by this time was a prefect and so entitled to a room of her own); she had locked herself in and refused to come out. When Mrs Budleigh the matron finally opened up with a master-key, it was said that she let out almost as loud a squawk as the frantic girl inside. For—Ceridwen told me and Will, then the news spread like lightning through the girls' dorm and so out and about the main school—all Pamela Cassell's thick glossy red hair, of which she had been so proud that she let it grow to waist length—all that hair had fallen out in the night and the wretched girl was now bald as an egg, while the hair lay in a tangled mess on her pillow.

Well! What a thing! Needless to say, Pamela was whisked away to a skin and hair specialist; and what he said was so unhelpful that she flatly refused to come back to school, as long as she was such a spectacle, so that was the last we saw of her. Will certainly wasn't sorry. In the old days she used sometimes to stand by and watch while the Blades did things to him.

Meanwhile the mysterious doom struck again: several other people became bald overnight in the same manner, while the hair of others began falling out at a frightening rate. Fair people were much worse affected than dark; I remember watching a blond boy called Titheredge combing his hair one day in the cloakroom, and it was like watching a Flymo go through a patch of hay—three quarters of the hair came away with the comb.

Jack Kettering's was a spectacular case. People from different forms read out the notices each day after Assembly. Tuesday it's the Fifth Formers. Kettering did it one Tuesday; he had a nervous habit, on public occasions, of brushing his hair back with his left hand, and when he did it this time the entire thick reddish-fair thatch fell right off on to the floor behind him. The whole school gasped in horrified amusement and then—reaction, I suppose—a roar of laughter went up. People were rocking from side to side, falling about—how could they help it? The startled Kettering ran his hands over his smooth bare scalp, glanced in appalled disbelief at the heap of hair on the floor behind him, then turned white as a rag and bolted from the school hall.

I noticed that Will Donkine was looking very thoughtful.

'Did *you* do that?' Ceridwen asked him, after Assembly was over. 'I mean—did you make his hair fall out?'

Both of us had a lot of respect for Donkine; we could quite believe that he was capable of it.

But—'No,' he answered slowly. 'No, I had nothing to do with it. Though I'm not surprised—I had an idea something like that was due. And I can't say I'm sorry—when I remember some of the things those big bullies did to me.'

He gave a reminiscent rub to his own meagre mouse-brown thatch—which, like everyone else's, was getting noticeably thinner. Ceridwen and I have black hair. It took longer than anybody's to go, but it went in the end.

'No; I didn't do it,' Will said. 'But I expect I'll be in trouble from Kettering's lot soon enough, if what I think is true.'

'What's that?'

'Why, it must be an effect of my father's dust extractor, don't you see? The Queen hasn't been out for ages—they had one in Buck House. And the P.M. had one at 10 Downing Street—and I'm sure she's been wearing a wig for weeks. Have you noticed the newspaper photographs? And then there's that hospital, and the Biffin factory—it'll be all over the country soon, I expect. Father's always a bit too hasty . . .'

Of course events have proved Will right. A few months more, and all the buildings which had installed DRIP Systems were populated by totally bald inhabitants.

In three weeks our school, which of course was among the first innovators, couldn't show a single hair among the six hundred students and the forty staff. Even Smokey, the school cat, had gone bald as a pig, and was rechristened Pinky. Even the mice, when seen, could be seen to be bald. Punk cuts, crew cuts, Afro heads, Rastafarian plaits, beehives, all had vanished, like snow-wreaths in thaw, as the poet says.

In a way, our all being companions in misfortune made the state easier to bear. I found it interesting to notice how school relationships and pecking orders had changed and reversed, now that our appearance was so different. At first we found it quite difficult to recognize one another; with no hair, just pale bald scalps, we all looked alike, you couldn't tell boys from girls, we seemed like members of some Eastern sect, ready to bang gongs or spin prayer-wheels; and the people who hitherto had prided themselves on their looks went round as humbly as anybody else.

Meanwhile there was a terrific public outcry and fuss. After a while, as Will had predicted, somebody put two and two together and traced the baldness to the Donkine DRIP System. Most of the purchasers of DRIP Systems thereupon switched them off, hoping that the hair of employees, patients, students, and nurses would begin to grow again. But it didn't. Some vital growing hormone, it seemed, had been sucked out for good; or at least, for a generation.

About this time Sir Joel Donkine came back to England from the Brazilian forests where he had been on a research expedition. Naturally he was aghast at what had happened and made a statement about it.

'I accept full blame and responsibility,' he said to the newspapers, before his lawyers could warn him not to, and in no time lawsuits and writs amounting to God knows how many millions were piling upon his doorstep.

'Dad's so impetuous,' Will said again thoughtfully. 'He sounds off without checking the probabilities.'

I thought how different his son was. But perhaps I was wrong.

People said Sir Joel ought to have his Nobel and C.B.E. taken away. He was probably the most unpopular man in Europe. What though his System had prevented hundreds of colds and other infections? All that was forgotten in the wave of fury. People marched with placards demanding, 'Give Us Back Our Hair!'

Unisex shops and barbers and the manufacturers of shampoos, conditioners, setting lotions, hairbrushes, combs, hairgrips, clasps, nets, ribbons, bathing caps, dyes, tints, and bleaches were all after Sir Joel's blood.

Taken away their livelihood he had, see?

Nobody thought to mention that, on the other side of the scale, makers of wigs, hairpieces, headsquares, hats, caps, hoods, and bonnets were doing a roaring trade. Tattoo artists stencilled ingenious hair designs over people's naked heads, or just drew pretty patterns; colourful head paint was invented; at least part of the population remembered that the Ancient Egyptians went bald from choice, and discovered that there were quite a few conveniences about the bald state.

But as an unusually hot summer drew on there were a few cases of sunstroke, and questions were asked in Parliament, and people began to say that Sir J. Donkine should be impeached, or hung, drawn, and quartered, or at least tried for causing grievous public harm.

An inquiry was proposed. But before its machinery could be set up—public inquiries are very slow-moving things—poor Sir Joel was dead. Heart failure, the Coroner's report announced. And I daresay that was correct. I'm pretty sure that he had died of a broken heart.

'Poor Father,' Will said sadly. 'All he wanted was to help people. He wanted to prevent their getting infections like the one that killed Mother. And so he landed himself in all this trouble. He never would think before he acted.'

Will grieved very much for his father—the more so as he had no other relations and would now have to become a Ward of Court.

After Sir Joel's death, Kettering's group had the grace to leave Will alone for a while; nobody these days had the spirit for recriminations. Also we were all working like Stakhanovites for our A-levels . . .

Will's results in those were fairly remarkable, considering all he had been through. He came top of our lot, way ahead of anybody else. And when we re-assembled in the autumn term he seemed in reasonably good shape. He had spent the summer with Mr Postlethwaite; the Old Possum had offered to put him up so he wouldn't have to go into Care. And apparently he had passed most of the holidays in biological research.

'Boy's got a really amazing mind,' I heard the Old Possum one day tell Mrs Budleigh in the cafeteria. 'Kind of results he's getting wouldn't disgrace those fellows in the Bickerden Labs at Cambridge. What he's working after, I do believe, is to make up for the harm his father did—or felt he had done, poor man.'

'The harm he did seems quite real enough to me,' replied the Matron coldly, adjusting her wig. 'If the boy thinks he can discover some way of making people's hair grow again, I consider that a very proper ambition.'

Will was wholly uncommunicative about his work. Most of it was carried out in the labs—he didn't have time for gardening these days—and it required buckets and buckets of the DRIP System compost which was still piled in black shiny sackfuls by the side of the allotments. He fiddled about with test tubes and cultures and filters, he painted black and brown grease on to mushrooms, and eggs, and frogs, and the bald school mice, and guinea pigs. Ceridwen helped him.

By and by he began to look more hopeful; a spark came back into his eye that had been missing for many months; and, strangely enough, he began to grow, quite suddenly shot up so tall and lanky that he overtopped Kettering and most of the Blades. By now that group had rather fallen apart; two or three of the Blades had left school after their undistinguished A-levels; Pamela, of course, departed after the loss of her hair, and Jack Kettering himself was fairly subdued these days. Becoming bald had changed him a lot. Whereas Will's hair was such a modest crop and unremarkable colour that its going made little difference to his looks—indeed, thin-faced, with dark, deepset eyes and newly acquired horn-rimmed glasses he now seemed quite impressive—Jack Kettering without any hair looked flat-faced, florid, and stupid, somewhere between a pig and a seal. And was nothing like so aggressive as he used to be.

Indeed I noticed that nowadays he was cautiously friendly and almost obsequious towards Will, went out of his way to address remarks to him, pass the sugar for his cereal at breakfast, and so forth. Will didn't take much notice, just went on his own way as usual.

One day he captured Pinky the cat (no problem, they had been friends for years) and bore him off to the lab. When next seen, Pinky's pale uncatlike exterior had been dyed all over a delicate rust brown.

'You think the Animal Protection League would approve of what you've done to that poor dumb animal?' demanded Mrs Budleigh, fixing Will with a sharp grey eye.

'Sure they would; it was done for his own good,' Will answered positively. 'But if you think it would be better I'll fix him up with an insulation jacket while I wait for results.' And Ceridwen helped him construct the cat a butter-muslin jacket, which was sewn up his back so he couldn't get it off. (Pinky showed no gratitude; Ceridwen's hands were quite badly scratched.)

The cat's head was left uncovered and, after a week, anybody gently rubbing under his chin or above his eyes could feel a faint stubble of something growing. This caused a sensation, as you can imagine; people rushed to Will to offer themselves as guinea-pigs for his treatment.

Old Corfe the headmaster was down on this.

'Donkine is working hard and I'm sure all our good wishes are with him, but I think it wholly inadvisable that any of the rest of you should submit yourselves as research material, at least without parental consent. We know by now—alas!—what disastrous effects the best intentioned work may produce.'

Anyway it seemed that Will didn't want guinea-pigs; he turned away all the people who tapped at the lab door and offered their bald heads for his process.

All but one.

'I've got Dad's consent!' Jack Kettering told him in an urgent whisper. 'I phoned home and asked him. He says I look so godawful now that anything could be better. Come on, now, Donk—be a sport! I know I've laughed at you a bit in the past, in a friendly way, but that's all over long ago—isn't it? We're good friends now, aren't we?'

He looked up beseechingly into Will's face. Will said, 'You realize it may not be just ordinary hair that grows back?'

'Anything, horsehair, sheep's wool, would be better than having a dome like an egg. I don't care *what* it is, just *do* it, old feller.'

So Donkine painted Jack's scalp a rusty brown, and Ceridwen stitched him a butter-muslin skull-cap to cover the painted area.

'What's that for?'

'To stop birds pecking it,' replied Will gravely.

'*Birds*?'

'Or anything else. You never know. Wear the cap till I tell you.'

Two weeks passed. Pinky the cat's muslin jacket seemed to be getting tight; perhaps he was growing.

One evening as we all sat at supper Pinky hurtled in through the open dining-room window carrying a struggling, cheeping sparrow. The cat had torn his jacket in the chase, it flapped loose, and one of the girls, rushing to the rescue of the sparrow, let out a quack of amazement.

'The cat's gone green!'

'Take off the remains of the jacket,' suggested old Postlethwaite.

Ceridwen pulled it off, tearing the tattered muslin with no trouble—to reveal Pinky, erstwhile Smokey, wearing a fine coat of short velvety green.

Someone said in an awed voice, 'That cat is covered with *grass.*'

'May I be utterly blessed!' muttered Old Possum. He gazed with bulging eyes at the verdant animal. Will poured the cat a saucer of milk and inspected him with serious satisfaction as he drank.

'It worked with the mice, and it seems to have worked with him. I found it impossible, you see, sir, to grow hair on anything—but grass responded very well—and, after all, it makes just as good a cover—'

Jack Kettering, who had come in late for tea, arrived in time to hear this remark. Without a word, he spun on his heel and strode back into the hall, where there is a big wall mirror, dragging off his muslin cap as he went. We heard him let out a kind of astonished wail.

'*Grass . . . !*'

Will strolled out after him, and I could hear him say mildly, 'You did tell me that anything would be better than having a dome like an egg—'

'I didn't bargain on *grass*!'

But by that time half the school were frothing around Will, clamouring and begging: 'Do me, do me, do *me*! I'd *like* grass! Maybe there could be a few buttercups as well? Or a daisy?'

'I shan't do anybody without parental permission,' Will said gravely.

I saw him glance, over the clustered shining bald heads, towards Old Possum, with a kind of rueful resigned shrug and gesture of the head. Postlethwaite's expression was still fairly stunned.

'After all, sir,' Will went on in a reasonable tone, 'you did say that to make two blades of grass grow where one grew before was a good thing to do. And I've made two blades grow where *none* grew before. Think what a hay crop we'd get, off the heads of everyone here.'

But I could imagine what Old Possum was thinking, for I was thinking it myself. After grass has been established for a while, you get larger plants rooting, and then larger ones still, and then acorns which sprout into oak trees . . .

Will was just as impulsive as his father. And who is going to deal with the next lot of side effects?

LOST HEARTS
M. R. James

It was, as far as I can ascertain, in September of the year 1811 that a post-chaise drew up before the door of Aswarby Hall, in the heart of Lincolnshire. The little boy who was the only passenger in the chaise, and who jumped out as soon as it had stopped, looked about him with the keenest curiosity during the short interval that elapsed between the ringing of the bell and the opening of the hall door. He saw a tall, square, red-brick house, built in the reign of Anne; a stone-pillared porch had been added in the purer classical style of 1790; the windows of the house were many, tall and narrow, with small panes and thick white woodwork. A pediment, pierced with a round window, crowned the front. There were wings to right and left, connected by curious glazed galleries, supported by colonnades, with the central block. These wings plainly contained the stables and offices of the house. Each was surmounted by an ornamental cupola with a gilded vane.

An evening light shone on the building, making the window-panes glow like so many fires. Away from the Hall in front stretched a flat park studded with oaks and fringed with firs, which stood out against the sky. The clock in the church-tower, buried in trees on the edge of the park, only its golden weather-cock catching the light, was striking six, and the sound came gently beating down the wind. It was altogether a pleasant impression, though tinged with the sort of melancholy appropriate to an evening in early autumn, that was conveyed to the mind of the boy who was standing in the porch waiting for the door to open to him.

The post-chaise had brought him from Warwickshire, where, some six months before, he had been left an orphan. Now, owing to the generous offer of his elderly cousin, Mr Abney, he had come to live at Aswarby. The offer was unexpected, because all who knew anything of Mr Abney looked upon him as a somewhat austere recluse, into whose steady-going household the advent of a small boy would import a new and, it seemed, incongruous element. The truth is that very little was known of Mr Abney's pursuits or temper. The Professor of Greek at Cambridge had been heard to say that no one knew more of the religious beliefs of the later pagans than did the owner of Aswarby. Certainly his library contained all the then available books bearing on the Mysteries, the Orphic poems, the worship of Mithras, and the Neo-Platonists. In the marble-paved hall stood a fine group of Mithras slaying a bull, which had been imported from the Levant at great expense by the owner. He had contributed a description of it to the *Gentleman's Magazine*, and he had written a remarkable series of articles in the *Critical Museum* on the superstitions of the Romans of the Lower Empire. He was looked upon, *in fine*, as a man wrapped up in his books, and it was a matter of great surprise among his neighbours that he could even have heard of his orphan cousin, Stephen Elliott, much more that he should have volunteered to make him an inmate of Aswarby Hall.

Whatever may have been expected by his neighbours, it is certain that Mr Abney – the tall, the thin, the austere – seemed inclined to give his young cousin a kindly reception. The moment the front door was opened he darted out of his study, rubbing his hands with delight.

'How are you, my boy? – how are you? How old are you?' said he – 'that is, you are not too much tired, I hope, by your journey to eat your supper?'

'No, thank you, sir,' said Master Elliott; 'I am pretty well.'

'That's a good lad,' said Mr Abney. 'And how old are you, my boy?'

It seemed a little odd that he should have asked the question twice in the first two minutes of their acquaintance.

'I'm twelve years old next birthday, sir,' said Stephen.

'And when is your birthday, my dear boy? Eleventh of September, eh?

The boy raised his arms in the air with an appearance of menace

That's well–that's very well. Nearly a year hence, isn't it? I like–ha, ha! –I like to get these things down in my book. Sure it's twelve? Certain?'

'Yes, quite sure, sir.'

'Well, well! Take him to Mrs Bunch's room, Parkes, and let him have his tea – supper – whatever it is.'

'Yes, sir,' answered the staid Mr Parkes; and conducted Stephen to the lower regions.

Mrs Bunch was the most comfortable and human person whom Stephen had as yet met in Aswarby. She made him completely at home; they were great friends in a quarter of an hour: and great friends they remained. Mrs Bunch had been born in the neighbourhood some fifty-five years before the date of Stephen's arrival, and her residence at the Hall was of twenty years' standing. Consequently, if anyone knew the ins and outs of the house and the district, Mrs Bunch knew them; and she was by no means disinclined to communicate her information.

Certainly there were plenty of things about the Hall and the Hall gardens which Stephen, who was of an adventurous and inquiring turn, was anxious to have explained to him. 'Who built the temple at the end of the laurel walk? Who was the old man whose picture hung on the staircase, sitting at a table, with a skull under his hand?' These and many similar points were cleared up by the resources of Mrs Bunch's powerful intellect. There were others, however, of which the explanations furnished were less satisfactory.

One November evening Stephen was sitting by the fire in the housekeeper's room reflecting on his surroundings.

'Is Mr Abney a good man, and will he go to heaven?' he suddenly asked, with the peculiar confidence which children possess in the ability of their elders to settle these questions, the decision of which is believed to be reserved for other tribunals.

'Good? – bless the child!' said Mrs Bunch. 'Master's as kind a soul as ever I see! Didn't I never tell you of the little boy as he took in out of the street, as you may say, this seven years back? and the little girl, two years after I first come here?'

'No. Do tell me all about them, Mrs Bunch – now this minute!'

'Well,' said Mrs Bunch, 'the little girl I don't seem to recollect so much about. I know master brought her back with him from his walk one day, and give orders to Mrs Ellis, as was housekeeper then, as she should be took every care with. And the pore child hadn't no one belonging to her – she telled me so her own self – and here she lived with us a matter of three weeks it might be; and then, whether she were somethink of a gipsy in her blood or what not, but one morning she out of her bed afore any of us had opened an eye, and neither track nor yet trace of her have I set eyes on since. Master was wonderful put about, and had all the ponds dragged; but it's my belief she was had away by them gipsies, for there was singing round the house for as much as an hour the night she went, and Parkes, he declare as he heard them a-calling in the woods all that afternoon. Dear, dear! a hodd child she was, so silent in her ways and all, but I was wonderful taken up with her, so domesticated she was – surprising.'

'And what about the little boy?' said Stephen.

'Ah, that pore boy!' sighed Mrs Bunch. 'He were a foreigner – Jevanny he called hisself – and he come a-tweaking his 'urdy-gurdy round and about the drive one winter day, and master 'ad him in that minute, and ast all about where he came from, and how old he was, and how he made his way, and where was his relatives, and all as kind as heart could wish. But it went the same way with him. They're a hunruly lot, them foreign nations, I do suppose, and he was off one fine morning just the same as the girl. Why he went and what he done was our question for as much as a year after; for he never took his 'urdy-gurdy, and there it lays on the shelf.'

The remainder of the evening was spent by Stephen in miscellaneous cross-examination of Mrs Bunch and in efforts to extract a tune from the hurdy-gurdy.

That night he had a curious dream. At the end of the passage at the top of the house, in which his bedroom was situated, there was an old disused bathroom. It was kept locked, but the upper half of the door was glazed, and, since the muslin curtains which used to hang there had long been gone, you could look in and see the lead-lined bath affixed to the wall on the right hand, with its head towards the window.

On the night of which I am speaking, Stephen Elliott found himself, as he thought, looking through the glazed door. The moon was shining through the window, and he was gazing at a figure which lay in the bath.

His description of what he saw reminds me of what I once beheld myself in the famous vaults of St Michan's Church in Dublin, which possess the horrid property of preserving corpses from decay for centuries. A figure inexpressibly thin and pathetic, of a dusty leaden colour, enveloped in a shroud-like garment, the thin lips crooked into a faint and dreadful smile, the hands pressed tightly over the region of the heart.

As he looked upon it, a distant almost inaudible moan seemed to issue from its lips, and the arms began to stir. The terror of the sight forced Stephen backwards, and he awoke to the fact that he was indeed standing on the cold boarded floor of the passage in the full light of the moon. With a courage which I do not think can be common among boys of his age, he went to the door of the bathroom to ascertain if the figure of his dream were really there. It was not, and he went back to bed.

Mrs Bunch was much impressed next morning by his story, and went so far as to replace the muslin curtain over the glazed door of the bathroom. Mr Abney, moreover, to whom he confided his experiences at breakfast, was greatly interested, and made notes of the matter in what he called 'his book'.

The spring equinox was approaching, as Mr Abney frequently reminded his cousin, adding that this had been always considered by the ancients to be a critical time for the young: that Stephen would do well to take care of himself, and to shut his bedroom window at night; and that Censorinus had some valuable remarks on the subject. Two incidents that occurred about this time made an impression upon Stephen's mind.

The first was after an unusually uneasy and oppressed night that he had passed – though he could not recall any particular dream that he had had.

The following evening Mrs Bunch was occupying herself in mending his nightgown.

'Gracious me, Master Stephen!' she broke forth rather irritably, 'how do you manage to tear your nightdress all to flinders this way? Look here, sir, what trouble you do give to poor servants that have to darn and mend after you!'

There was indeed a most destructive and apparently wanton series of slits or scorings in the garment, which would undoubtedly require a skilful needle to make good. They were confined to the left side of the chest – long, parallel slits, about six inches in length, some of them not quite piercing the texture of the linen. Stephen could only express his entire ignorance of their origin: he was sure they were not there the night before.

'But,' he said, 'Mrs Bunch, they are just the same as the scratches on the outside of my bedroom door; and I'm sure I never had anything to do with making *them*'.

Mrs Bunch gazed at him open-mouthed, then snatched up a candle, departed hastily fom the room, and was heard making her way upstairs. In a few minutes she came down.

'Well,' she said, 'Master Stephen, it's a funny thing to me how them marks and scratches can 'a' come there – too high up for any cat or dog to 'ave made 'em, much less a rat: for all the world like a Chinaman's finger-nails, as my uncle in the tea-trade used to tell us of when we was girls together. I wouldn't say nothing to master, not if I was you, Master Stephen, my dear; and just turn the key of the door when you go to your bed.'

'I always do, Mrs Bunch, as soon as I've said my prayers.'

'Ah, that's a good child: always say your prayers, and then no one can't hurt you.'

Herewith Mrs Bunch addressed herself to mending the injured nightgown, with intervals of meditation, until bedtime. This was on a Friday night in March 1812.

On the following evening the usual duet of Stephen and Mrs Bunch was augmented by the sudden arrival of Mr Parkes, the butler, who as a rule kept himself rather to himself in his own pantry. He did not see that Stephen was there: he was, moreover, flustered, and less slow of speech than was his wont.

'Master may get up his own wine, if he likes, of an evening,' was his first remark. 'Either I do it in the daytime or not at all, Mrs Bunch. I don't know what it may be: very like it's the rats, or the wind got into the cellars; but I'm not so young as I was, and I can't go through with it as I have done.'

'Well Mr Parkes, you know it is a surprising place for the rats, is the Hall.'

'I'm not denying that, Mrs Bunch; and, to be sure, many a time I've heard the tale from the men in the shipyards about the rat that could speak. I never laid no confidence in that before; but tonight, if I'd demeaned myself to lay my ear to the door of the further bin, I could pretty much have heard what they was saying.'

'Oh, there, Mr Parkes, I've no patience with your fancies! Rats talking in the wine-cellar indeed!'

'Well, Mrs Bunch, I've no wish to argue with you: all I say is, if you choose to go to the far bin, and lay your ear to the door, you may prove my words this minute.'

'What nonsense you do talk, Mr Parkes – not fit for children to listen to! Why, you'll be frightening Master Stephen there out of his wits.'

'What! Master Stephen?' said Parkes, awaking to the consciousness of the boy's presence. 'Master Stephen knows well enough when I'm a-playing a joke with you, Mrs Bunch.'

In fact, Master Stephen knew much too well to suppose that Parkes had in the first instance intended a joke. He was interested, not altogether pleasantly, in the situation; but all his questions were unsuccessful in inducing the butler to give any more detailed account of his experiences in the wine-cellar.

* * * *

We have now arrived at 24 March 1812. It was a day of curious experiences for Stephen: a windy, noisy day, which filled the house and the gardens with a restless impression. As Stephen stood by the fence of the grounds, and looked out into the park, he felt as if an endless procession of unseen people were sweeping past him on the wind, borne on restlessly and aimlessly, vainly striving to stop themselves, to catch at something that might arrest their flight and bring them once again into contact with the living world of which they had formed a part. After luncheon that day Mr Abney said:

'Stephen, my boy, do you think you could manage to come to me tonight as late as eleven o'clock in my study? I shall be busy until that time, and I wish to show you something connected with your future life which it is most important that you should know. You are not to mention this matter to Mrs Bunch nor to anyone else in the house; and you had better go to your room at the usual time.'

Here was a new excitement added to life: Stephen eagerly grasped at the opportunity of sitting up until eleven o'clock. He looked in at the library door on his way upstairs that evening, and saw a brazier, which he had often noticed in the corner of the room, moved out before the fire; an old silver-gilt cup stood on the table, filled with red wine, and some written sheets of paper lay near it. Mr Abney was sprinkling some incense on the brazier from a round silver box as Stephen passed, but did not seem to notice his step.

The wind had fallen, and there was a still night and a full moon. At about ten o'clock Stephen was standing at the open window of his bedroom, looking out over the country. Still as the night was, the mysterious population of the distant moonlit woods was not yet lulled to rest. From time to time strange cries as of lost and despairing wanderers sounded from across the mere. They might be the notes of owls or water-birds, yet they did not quite resemble either sound. Were not they coming nearer? Now they sounded from the nearer side of the water, and in a few moments they seemed to be floating about among the shrubberies. Then they ceased; but just as Stephen was thinking of shutting the window and resuming his reading of *Robinson Crusoe*, he caught sight of two figures standing on the gravelled terrace that ran along the garden side of the Hall – the figures of a boy and girl, as it seemed; they stood side by side, looking up at the windows. Something in the form of the girl recalled irresistibly his dream of the figure in the bath. The boy inspired him with more acute fear.

Whilst the girl stood still, half smiling, with her hands clasped over her heart, the boy, a thin shape, with black hair and ragged clothing, raised his arms in the air with an appearance of menace and of unappeasable hunger and longing. The moon shone upon his almost transparent hands, and Stephen saw that the nails were fearfully long and that the light shone through them. As he stood with his arms thus raised, he disclosed a terrifying spectacle. On the left side of his chest there opened a black and gaping rent; and there fell upon Stephen's brain, rather than upon his ear, the impression of one of those hungry and desolate cries that he had heard resounding over the woods of Aswarby all that evening. In another moment this dreadful pair had moved swiftly and noiselessly over the dry gravel, and he saw them no more.

Inexpressibly frightened as he was, he determined to take his candle and go down to Mr Abney's study, for the hour appointed for their meeting was near at hand. The study or library opened out of the front hall on one side, and Stephen, urged on by his terrors, did not take long in getting there. To effect an entrance was not so easy. The door was not locked, he felt sure, for the key was on the outside of it as usual. His repeated knocks produced no answer. Mr Abney was engaged: he was speaking. What! why did he try to cry out? and why was the cry choked in his throat? Had he, too, seen the mysterious children? But now everything was quiet, and the door yielded to Stephen's terrified and frantic pushing.

* * * *

On the table in Mr Abney's study certain papers were found which explained the situation to Stephen Elliott when he was of an age to understand them. The most important sentences were as follows:

It was a belief very strongly and generally held by the ancients – of whose wisdom in these matters I have had such experience as induces me to place confidence in their assertions – that by enacting certain processes which to us moderns have something of a barbaric complexion, a very remarkable enlightenment of the spiritual faculties in man may be attained: that, for example, by absorbing the personalities of a certain number of his fellow-creatures, an individual may gain a complete ascendancy over those orders of spiritual beings which control the elemental forces of our universe.

It is recorded of Simon Magnus that he was able to fly in the air, to become invisible, or to assume any form he pleased, by the agency of the soul of a boy whom, to use the libellous phrase employed by the author of the *Clementine Recognitions*, he had 'murdered'. I find it set down, moreoever, with considerable detail in the writings of Hermes Trismegistus, that similar happy results may be produced by the absorption of the hearts of not less than three human beings below the age of twenty-one years. To the testing of the truth of this receipt I have devoted the greater part of the last twenty years, selecting as the *corpora vilia* of my experiment such persons as could conveniently be removed without occasioning a sensible gap in society. The first step I effected by the removal of one Phoebe Stanley, a girl of gipsy extraction, on 24 March 1792. The second by the removal of a wandering Italian lad, named Giovanni Paoli, on the night of 23 March 1805. The final 'victim' – to employ a word repugnant in the highest degree to my feelings – must be my cousin, Stephen Elliott. His day must be this 24 March 1812.

The best means of effecting the required absorption is to remove the heart from the *living* subject, to reduce it to ashes, and to mingle them with about a pint of some red wine, preferably port. The remains of the first two subjects, at least, it will be well to conceal: a disused bathroom or wine-cellar will be found convenient for such a purpose. Some annoyance may be experienced from the psychic portion of the subjects, which popular language dignifies with the name of ghosts. But the man of philosophic temperament – to whom alone the experiment is appropriate – will be little prone to attach importance to the feeble efforts of these beings to wreak their vengeance on him. I contemplate with the liveliest satisfaction the enlarged and emancipated existence which the experiment, if successful, will confer on me; not only placing me beyond the reach of human justice (so-called), but eliminating to a great extent the prospect of death itself.

Mr Abney was found in his chair, his head thrown back, his face stamped with an expression of rage, fright, and mortal pain. In his left side was a terrible lacerated wound, exposing the heart. There was no blood on his hands, and a long knife that lay on the table was perfectly clean. A savage wild-cat might have inflicted the injuries. The window of the study was open, and it was the opinion of the coroner that Mr Abney had met his death by the agency of some wild creature. But Stephen Elliott's study of the papers I have quoted led him to a very different conclusion.

THE SIGNALMAN
Charles Dickens

'Halloa! Below there!'

When he heard a voice thus calling to him, he was standing at the door of his box, with a flag in his hand, furled round its short pole. One would have thought, considering the nature of the ground, that he could not have doubted from what quarter the voice came; but instead of looking up to where I stood on the top of the steep cutting nearly over his head, he turned himself about, and looked down the line. There was something remarkable in his manner of doing so, though I could not have said for my life what. But I know it was remarkable enough to attract my notice, even though his figure was foreshortened and shadowed, down in the deep trench, and mine was high above him, so steeped in the glow of an angry sunset that I had shaded my eyes with my hand before I saw him at all.

'Halloa! Below!'

From looking down the line, he turned himself about again, and, raising his eyes, saw my figure high above him.

'Is there any path by which I can come down and speak to you?'

He looked up at me without replying, and I looked down at him without pressing him too soon with a repetition of my idle question. Just then there came a vague vibration in the earth and air, quickly changing into a violent pulsation, and an oncoming rush that caused me to start back, as though it had force to draw me down. When such vapour as rose to my height from this rapid train had passed me, and was skimming away over the landscape, I looked down again, and saw him refurling the flag he had shown while the train went by.

I repeated my inquiry. After a pause, during which he seemed to regard me with fixed attention, he motioned with his rolled-up flag towards a point on my level, some two or three hundred yards distant. I called down to him, 'All right!' and made for that point. There, by dint of looking closely about me, I found a rough zigzag descending path notched out, which I followed.

The cutting was extremely deep and unusually precipitate. It was made through a clammy stone that became oozier and wetter as I went down. For these reasons, I found the way long enough to give me time to recall a singular air of reluctance or compulsion with which he had pointed out the path.

When I came down low enough upon the zigzag descent to see him again, I saw that he was standing between the rails on the way by which the train had lately passed, in an attitude as if he were waiting for me to appear. He had his left hand at his chin, and that left elbow rested on his right hand, crossed over his breast. His attitude was one of such expectation and watchfulness that I stopped a moment, wondering at it.

I resumed my downward way, and stepping out upon the level of the railroad, and drawing nearer to him, saw that he was a dark sallow man, with a dark beard and rather heavy eyebrows. His post was in as solitary and dismal a place as ever I saw. On either side, a dripping-wet wall of jagged stone, excluding all view but a strip of sky; the perspective one way only a crooked prolongation of this great dungeon; the shorter perspective in the other direction terminating in a gloomy red light, and the gloomier entrance to a black tunnel, in whose massive architecture there was a barbarous, depressing and forbidding air. So little sunlight ever found its way to this spot that it had an earthy, deadly smell; and so much cold wind rushed through it that it struck chill to me, as if I had left the natural world.

Before he stirred, I was near enough to him to have touched him. Not even then removing his eyes from mine, he stepped back one step, and lifted his hand.

This was a lonesome post to occupy (I said), and it had riveted my attention when I looked down from up yonder. A visitor was a rarity, I should suppose; not an unwelcome rarity, I hoped? In me, he merely saw a man who had been shut up within narrow limits all his life, and who, being at last set free, had a newly-awakened interest in these great works. To such purpose I spoke to him; but I am far from sure of the terms I used; for, besides that I am not happy in opening any conversation, there was something in the man that daunted me.

He directed a most curious look towards the red light near the tunnel's mouth, and looked all about it, as if something were missing from it, and then looked at me.

That light was part of his charge? Was it not?

He answered in a low voice, 'Don't you know it is?'

The monstrous thought came into my mind, as I perused the fixed eyes and the saturnine face, that this was a spirit, not a man. I have speculated since, whether there may have been infection in his mind.

In my turn I stepped back. But in making the action, I detected in his eyes some latent fear of me. This put the monstrous thought to flight.

'You look at me,' I said, forcing a smile, 'as if you had a dread of me.'

'I was doubtful,' he returned, 'whether I had seen you before.'

'Where?'

He pointed to the red light he had looked at.

'There?' I said.

Intently watchful of me, he replied (but without sound), 'Yes.'

'My good fellow, what should I do there? However, be that as it may, I never was there, you may swear.'

'I think I may,' he rejoined. 'Yes; I am sure I may.'

His manner cleared, like my own. He replied to my remarks with readiness, and in well-chosen words. Had he much to do there? Yes; that was to say, he had enough responsibility to bear; but exactness and watchfulness were what was required of him, and of actual work – manual labour – he had next to none. To change that signal, to trim those lights, and to turn this iron handle now and then, was all he had to under that head.

Regarding those many long and lonely hours of which I seemed to make so much, he could only say that the routine of his life had shaped itself into that form, and he had grown used to it. He had taught himself a language down here – if only to know it by sight, and to have formed his own crude ideas of its pronunciation, could be called learning it. He had also worked at fractions and decimals, and tried a little algebra; but he was, and had been as a boy, a poor hand at figures. Was it necessary for him when on duty always to remain in that channel of damp air, and could he never rise into the sunshine from between those high stone walls? Why, that depended upon times and circumstances. Under some conditions there would be less upon the line than under others, and the same held good as to certain hours of the day and night. In bright weather, he did choose occasions for getting a little above those lower shadows; but, being at all times liable to be called by his electric bell, and at such times listening for it with redoubled anxiety, the relief was less than I would suppose.

He took me into his box, where there was a fire, a desk for an official book in which he had to make certain entries, a telegraphic instrument with its dial, face, and needles, and the little bell of which he had spoken. On my trusting that he would excuse the remark that he had been well educated, and (I hoped I might say without offence) perhaps educated above that station, he observed that instances of slight incongruity in such wise would rarely be found wanting among large bodies of men; that he had heard it was so in workhouses, in the police force, even in that last desperate resource, the army; and that he knew it was so, more or less, in any great railway staff. He had been, when young (if I could believe it, sitting in that hut – he scarcely could), a student of natural philosophy, and had attended lectures; but he had run wild, misused his opportunities, gone down, and never risen again. He had no complaint to offer about that. He had made his bed, and he lay upon it. It was far too late to make another.

All that I have here condensed he said in a quiet manner, with his grave dark regards divided between me and the fire. He threw in the word 'sir' from time to time, and especially when he referred to his youth – as though to request me to understand that he claimed to be nothing but what I found him. He was several times interrupted by the little bell, and had to read off messages and send replies. Once he had to stand without the door, and display a flag as a train passed, and make some verbal communication to the driver. In the discharge of his duties, I observed him to be remarkably exact and vigilant, breaking off his discourse at a syllable, and remaining silent until what he had to do was done.

In a word, I should have set this man down as one of the safest of men to be employed in that capacity, but for the circumstance that while he was speaking to me he twice broke off with a fallen colour, turned his face towards the little bell when it did *not* ring, opened the door of the hut (which was kept shut to exclude the unhealthy damp), and looked out towards the red light near the mouth of the tunnel. On both of those occasions he came back to the fire with the inexplicable air upon him which I had remarked, without being able to define, when we were so far asunder.

Said I, when I rose to leave him, 'You almost make me think that I have met with a contented man.'

(I am afraid I must acknowledge that I said it to lead him on.)

'I believe I used to be so,' he rejoined, in the low voice in which he had first spoken; 'but I am troubled sir, I am troubled.'

He would have recalled the words if he could. He had said them, however, and I took them up quickly.

'With what? What is your trouble?'

'It is very difficult to impart, sir. It is very, very difficult to speak of. If ever you make me another visit, I will try to tell you.'

'But I expressly intend to make you another visit. Say, when shall it be?'

'I go off early in the morning, and I shall be on again at ten tomorrow night, sir.'

'I will come at eleven.'

He thanked me, and went out at the door with me. 'I'll show my white light, sir,' he said in his peculiar low voice, 'till you have found the way up. When you have found it, don't call out! And when you are at the top, don't call out!'

His manner seemed to make the place strike colder to me, but I said no more than 'Very well.'

'And when you come down tomorrow night, don't call out! Let me ask you a parting question. What made you cry, "Halloa! Below there!" tonight?'

'Heaven knows,' said I, 'I cried something to that effect–'

'Not to that effect, sir. Those were the very words. I know them well.'

'Admit those were the very words. I said them, no doubt, because I saw you below.'

'For no other reason?'

'What other reason could I possibly have?'

'You have no feeling that they were conveyed to you in any supernatural way?'

'No.'

He wished me good-night, and held up his light. I walked by the side of the down line of rails (with a very disagreeable sensation of a train coming behind me) until I found the path. It was easier to mount than to descend, and I got back to my inn without any adventure.

* * * *

Punctual to my appointment, I placed my foot on the first notch of the zigzag next night as the distant clocks were striking eleven. He was waiting for me at the bottom, with his white light on. 'I have not called out,' I said, when we came close together; 'may I speak now?' 'By all means, sir.' 'Good-night, then, and here's my hand.' 'Good-night, sir, and here's mine.' With that we walked side by side to his box, entered it, closed the door, and sat down by the fire.

'I have made up my mind, sir,' he began, bending forward as soon as we were seated, and speaking in a tone but a little above a whisper, 'that you shall not have to ask me twice what troubles me. I took you for someone else yesterday evening. That troubles me.'

'That mistake?'

'No. That someone else.'

'Who is it?'

'I don't know.'

'Like me?'

'I don't know. I never saw the face. The left arm is across the face, and the right arm is waved – violently waved. This way.'

I followed his action with my eyes, and it was the action of an arm gesticulating, with the utmost passion and vehemence, 'For God's sake, clear the way!'

'One moonlight night,' said the man, 'I was sitting here, when I heard a voice cry, "Halloa! Below there!" I started up, looked from that door, and saw this someone else standing by the red light near the tunnel, waving as I just now showed you. The voice seemed hoarse with shouting, and it cried, "Look out! Look out!" And then again, "Halloa! Below there! Look out!" I caught up my lamp, turned it on red, and ran towards the figure, calling, "What's wrong? What has happened? Where?" It stood just outside the blackness of the tunnel. I advanced so close upon it that I wondered at its keeping the sleeve across its eyes. I ran right up at it, and had my hand stretched out to pull the sleeve away, when it was gone.'

'Into the tunnel?' said I.

'No. I ran on into the tunnel, five hundred yards. I stopped, and held my lamp above my head, and saw the figures of the measured distance, and saw the wet stains stealing down the walls and trickling through the arch. I ran out again faster than I had run in (for I had a mortal abhorrence of the place upon me), and I looked all round the red light with my own red light; and I went up the iron ladder to the gallery atop of it, and I came down again, and ran back here. I telegraphed both ways, "An alarm has been given. Is anything wrong?" The answer came back, both ways, "All well".'

Resisting the slow touch of a frozen finger tracing out my spine, I showed him how that this figure must be a deception of his sense of sight; and how that figures, originating in disease of the delicate nerves that minister to the functions of the eye, were known to have often troubled patients, some of whom had become conscious of the nature of their affliction, and had even proved it by experiments upon themselves. 'As to an imaginary cry,' said I, 'do but listen for a moment to the wind in this unnatural valley while we speak so low, and to the wild harp it makes of the telegraph wires.'

That was all very well, he returned, after we had sat listening for a while, and he ought to know something of the wind and the wires – he who so often passed long winter nights there, alone and watching. But he would beg to remark that he had not finished.

I asked his pardon, and he slowly added these words, touching my arm: 'Within six hours after the appearance, the memorable accident on this line happened, and within ten hours the dead and wounded were brought along the tunnel over the spot where the figure had stood.'

A disagreeable shudder crept over me, but I did my best against it. It was not to be denied, I rejoined, that this was a remarkable coincidence, calculated deeply to impress his mind. But it was unquestionable that remarkable coincidences did continually occur, and they must be taken into account in dealing with such a subject. Though to be sure I must admit, I added (for I thought I saw that he was going to bring the objection to bear upon me), men of common sense did not allow much for coincidences in making the ordinary calculations of life.

He again begged to remark that he had not finished.

I again begged his pardon for being betrayed into interruptions.

'This,' he said, again laying his hand upon my arm, and glancing over his shoulder with hollow eyes, 'was just a year ago. Six or seven months passed, and I had recovered from the surprise and shock, when one morning, as the day was breaking, I, standing at the door, looked towards the red light, and saw the spectre again.' He stopped, with a fixed look at me.

'Did it cry out?'

'No. It was silent.'

'Did it wave its arm?'

'No. It leaned against the shaft of the light with both hands before the face. Like this.'

Once more I followed his action with my eyes. It was an action of mourning. I have seen such an attitude on stone figures on tombs.

'Did you go up to it?'

'I came in and sat down, partly to collect my thoughts, partly because it had turned me faint. When I went to the door again, daylight was above me, and the ghost was gone.'

'But nothing followed? Nothing came of this?'

He touched me on the arm with his forefinger twice or thrice, giving a ghastly nod each time.

'That very day, as a train came out of the tunnel, I noticed, at a carriage window on my side, what looked like a confusion of hands and heads, and something waved. I saw it just in time to signal the driver "Stop!" He shut off, and put his brake on, but the train drifted past here a hundred and fifty yards or more. I ran after it, and, as I went along, heard terrible screams and cries. A beautiful young lady had died instantaneously in one of the compartments, and was brought in here, and laid down on this floor between us.'

Involuntarily I pushed my chair back, as I looked from the boards at which he pointed to himself.

'True, sir. True. Precisely as it happened, so I tell it you.'

I could think of nothing to say, to any purpose, and my mouth was very dry. The wind and the wires took up the story with a long lamenting wail.

He resumed. 'Now, sir, mark this, and judge how my mind is troubled. The spectre came back a week ago. Ever since, it has been there, now and again, by fits and starts.'

'At the light?'

'At the danger-light.'

'What does it seem to do?'

He repeated, if possible with increased passion and vehemence, that former gesticulation of 'For God's sake, clear the way!'

Then he went on. 'I have no peace or rest for it. It calls to me, for many minutes together, in an agonised manner. "Below there! Look out! Look out!" It stands waving to me. It rings my little bell –'

I caught at that. 'Did it ring your bell yesterday evening when I was here, and you went to the door?'

'Twice.'

'Why, see,' said I, 'how your imagination misleads you. My eyes were on the bell, and my ears were open to the bell, and if I am a living man, it did *not* ring at those times. No, nor at any other time, except when it was rung in the natural course of physical things by the station communicating with you.'

He shook his head. I have never made a mistake as to that yet, sir. I have never confused the spectre's ring with the man's. The ghost's ring is a strange vibration in the bell that it derives from nothing else, and I have not asserted that the bell stirs to the eye. I don't wonder that you failed to hear it. But *I* heard it.'

'And did the spectre seem to be there when you looked out?'

'It *was* there.'

'Both times?'

He repeated firmly: 'Both times.'

'Will you come to the door with me, and look for it now?'

He bit his lower lip as though he were somewhat unwilling, but arose.

I opened the door, and stood on the step, while he stood in the doorway. There was the danger-light. There was the dismal mouth of the tunnel. There were the high, wet stone walls of the cutting. There were the stars above them.

'Do you see it?' I asked him, taking particular note of his face. His eyes were prominent and strained, but not very much more so, perhaps, than my own had been when I had directed them earnestly towards the same spot.

'No,' he answered. 'It is not there.'

'Agreed,' said I.

We went in again, shut the door, and resumed our seats. I was thinking how best to improve this advantage, if it might be called one, when he took up the conversation in such a matter-of-course way, so assuming that there could be no serious question of fact between us, that I felt myself placed in the weakest of positions.

'By this time you will fully understand, sir,' he said, 'that what troubles me so dreadfully is the question: what does the spectre mean?'

I was not sure, I told him, that I did not fully understand.

'What is it warning against?' he said, ruminating, with his eyes on the fire, and only by times turning them on me. 'What is the danger? Where is the danger? There is danger overhanging somewhere on the line. Some dreadful calamity will happen. It is not to be doubted this third time, after what has gone before. But surely this is a cruel haunting of *me*. What can I do?'

He pulled out his handkerchief, and wiped the drops from his heated forehead.

'If I telegraph danger on either side of me, or on both, I can give no reason for it,' he went on, wiping the palms of his hands. 'I should get into trouble and do no good. They would think I was mad. This is the way it would work: Message: "Danger! Take care!" Answer: "What danger? Where?" Message: "Don't know. But for God's sake, take care!"

They would displace me. What else could they do?'

His pain of mind was most pitiable to see. It was the mental torture of a conscientious man, oppressed beyond endurance by an unintelligible responsibility involving life.

'When it first stood under the danger-light,' he went on, putting his dark hair back from his head, and drawing his hands outward across his temples in an extremity of feverish distress, 'why not tell me where that accident was to happen – if it must happen? Why not tell me how it could be averted – if it could have been averted? When on its second coming it hid its face, why not tell me, instead. "She is going to die. Let them keep her at home"? If it came, on those two occasions, only to show me that its warnings were true, and so to prepare me for the third why not warn me plainly now? And I, Lord help me! A mere poor signalman on this solitary station! Why not go to somebody with credit to be believed, and power to act?'

When I saw him in this state, I saw that for the poor man's sake, as well as for the public safety, what I had to do for the time was to compose his mind. Therefore, setting aside all question of reality or unreality between us, I represented to him that whoever thoroughly discharged his duty must do well, and that at least it was his comfort that he understood his duty, though he did not understand these confounding appearances. In this effort I succeeded far better than in the attempt to reason him out of his conviction. He became calm; the occupations incidental to his post as the night advanced began to make larger demands on his attention: and I left him at two in the morning. I had offered to stay through the night, but he would not hear of it.

That I more than once looked back at the red light as I ascended the pathway, that I did not like the red light, and that I should have slept but poorly if my bed had been under it, I see no reason to conceal. Nor did I like the two sequences of the accident and the dead girl. I see no reason to conceal that either.

But what ran most in my thoughts was the consideration how ought I to act, having become the recipient of this disclosure? I had proved the man to be intelligent, vigilant, painstaking, and exact; but how long might he remain so, in his state of mind? Though in a subordinate position, still he held a most important trust, and would I (for instance) like to stake my own life on the chances of his continuing to execute it with precision?

Unable to overcome a feeling that there would be something treacherous in my communicating what he had told me to his superiors in the company, without first being plain with himself and proposing a middle course to him, I ultimately resolved to offer to accompany him (otherwise keeping his secret for the present) to the wisest medical practitioner we could hear of in those parts, and to take his opinion. A change in his time of duty would come round next night, he had apprised me, and he would be off an hour or two after sunrise, and on again soon after sunset. I had appointed to return accordingly.

* * * *

Next evening was a lovely evening, and I walked out early to enjoy it. The sun was not yet quite down when I traversed the field-path near the top of the deep cutting. I would extend my walk for an hour, I said to myself, half an hour on and half an hour back, and it would then be time to go to my signalman's box.

Before pursuing my stroll, I stepped to the brink, and mechanically looked down, from the point from which I had first seen him. I cannot describe the thrill that seized upon me, when, close at the mouth of the tunnel, I saw the appearance of a man, with his left sleeve across his eyes, passionately waving his right arm.

The nameless horror that oppressed me passed in a moment, for in a moment I saw that this appearance of a man was a man indeed, and that there was a little group of other men standing at a short distance, to whom he seemed to be rehearsing the gesture he made. The danger-light was not yet lit. Against its shaft a little low hut entirely new to me had been made of some wooden supports and tarpaulin. It looked no bigger than a bed.

With an irresistible sense that something was wrong – with a flashing self-reproachful fear that fatal mischief had come of my leaving the man there, and causing no one to be sent to overlook or correct what he did – I descended the notched path with all the speed I could make.

'What is the matter?' I asked the men.

'Signalman killed this morning, sir.'

'Not the man belonging to that box?'

'Yes, sir.'

'Not the man I know?'

'You will recognise him, sir, if you knew him,' said the man who spoke for all the others, solemnly uncovering his own head, and raising an end of the tarpaulin, 'for his face is quite composed.'

'Oh, how did this happen, how did this happen?' I asked, turning from one to another as the hut closed in again.

'He was cut down by an engine, sir. No man in England knew his work better. But somehow he was not clear of the outer rail. It was just at broad day. He had struck the light, and had the lamp in his hand. As the engine came out of the tunnel, his back was towards her, and she cut him down. That man drove her, and was showing how it happened. Show the gentleman, Tom.'

The man, who wore a rough dark dress, stepped back to his former place at the mouth of the tunnel.

'Coming round the curve in the tunnel, sir, he said. 'I saw him at the end, like as if I saw him down a perspective-glass. There was no time to check speed, and I knew him to be very careful. As he didn't seem to take heed of the whistle, I shut it off when we were running down upon him, and called to him as loud as I could call.'

'What did you say?'

"I said, "Below there! Look out! Look out! For God's sake, clear the way!"'

I started.

'Ah! it was a dreadful time, sir. I never left off calling to him. I put this arm before my eyes not to see, and I waved this arm to the last; but it was no use.

Without prolonging the narrative to dwell on any one of its curious circumstances more than on any other, I may, in closing it, point out the coincidence that the warning of the engine-driver included, not only the words which the unfortunate signalman had repeated to me as haunting him, but also the words which I myself – not he – had attached, and that only in my own mind, to the gesticulation he had imitated.

THE PICTURE OF DORIAN GRAY
Oscar Wilde

When young Dorian Gray sees the marvellous picture that Basil Hallward has painted of him, he exclaims that he would like the picture to grow old while he retains his incredible beauty and youth.

Under the amoral influence of Lord Henry Wooton, Dorian begins to lead a life of unsurpassed debauchery, leading others astray, and his prayer is answered — he retains his youth and the face in the portrait ages and becomes more despicable with every sin that Dorian commits.

It was on the ninth of November, the eve of his own thirty-eighth birthday, as he often remembered afterwards.

He was walking home about eleven o'clock from Lord Henry's, where he had been dining, and was wrapped in heavy furs, as the night was cold and foggy. At the corner of Grosvenor Square and South Audley Street a man passed him in the mist, walking very fast, and with the collar of his grey ulster turned up. He had a bag in his hand. Dorian recognised him. It was Basil Hallward. A strange sense of fear, for which he could not account, came over him. He made no sign of recognition, and went on quickly in the direction of his own house.

But Hallward had seen him. Dorian heard him first stopping on the pavement, and then hurrying after him. In a few moments his hand was on his arm.

'Dorian! What an extraordinary piece of luck! I have been waiting for you in your library ever since nine o'clock. Finally I took pity on your tired servant, and told him to go to bed, as he let me out. I am off to Paris by the midnight train, and I particularly wanted to see you before I left. I thought it was you, or rather your fur coat, as you passed me. But I wasn't quite sure. Didn't you recognise me?'

'In this fog, my dear Basil? Why, I can't even recognise Grosvenor Square. I believe my house is somewhere about here, but I don't feel at all certain about it. I am sorry you are going away, as I have not seen you for ages. But I suppose you will be back soon?'

'No: I am going to be out of England for six months. I intended to take a studio in Paris, and shut myself up until I have finished a great picture I have in my head. However, it wasn't about myself I wanted to talk. Here we are at your door. Let me come in for a moment. I have something to say to you.'

'I shall be charmed. But won't you miss your train?' said Dorian Gray, languidly, as he passed up the steps and opened the door with his latchkey.

The lamplight struggled out through the fog, and Hallward looked at his watch. 'I have heaps of time,' he answered. 'The train doesn't go until twelve-fifteen, and it is only just eleven. In fact, I was on my way to the club to look for you, when I met you. You see, I shan't have any delay about luggage, as I have sent on my heavy things. All I have with me is in this bag, and I can easily get to Victoria in twenty minutes.'

Dorian looked at him and smiled. 'What a way for a fashionable painter to travel! A Gladstone bag, and an ulster! Come in, or the fog will get into the house. And mind you don't talk about anything serious. Nothing is serious nowadays. At least nothing should be.'

Hallward shook his head as he entered, and followed Dorian into the library. There was a bright wood fire blazing in the large open hearth. The lamps were lit, and an open Dutch silver spirit-case stood, with some siphons of soda-water and large cut-glass tumblers, on a little marqueterie table.

'You see your servant made me quite at home, Dorian. He gave me everything I wanted, including your best gold-tipped cigarettes. He is a most hospitable creature. I like him much better than the Frenchman you used to have. What has become of the Frenchman, by the by?'

Dorian shrugged his shoulders. 'I believe he married Lady Radley's maid, and has established her in Paris as an English dressmaker. *Anglomanie* is very fashionable over there now, I hear. It seems silly of the French, doesn't it? But – do you know? – he was not at all a bad servant. I never liked him, but I had nothing to complain about. One often imagines things that are quite absurd. He was really devoted to me, and seemed quite sorry when he went away. Have another brandy-and-soda? Or would you like hock-and-seltzer? I always take hock-and-seltzer myself. There is sure to be some in the next room.'

'Thanks, I won't have anything more,' said the painter, taking his cap and coat off, and throwing them on the bag that he had placed in the corner. 'And now, my dear fellow, I want to speak to you seriously. Don't frown like that. You make it so much more difficult for me.'

'What is it all about?' cried Dorian, in his petulant way, flinging himself down on the sofa. 'I hope it is not about myself. I am tired of myself tonight. I should like to be somebody else.'

'It is about yourself,' answered Hallward, in his grave, deep voice, 'and I must say it to you. I shall only keep you half an hour.'

Dorian sighed, and lit a cigarette. 'Half an hour!' he murmured.

'It is not much to ask of you, Dorian, and it is entirely for your own sake that I am speaking. I think it right that you should know that the most dreadful things are being said against you in London.'

'I don't wish to know anything about them. I love scandals about other people, but scandals about myself don't interest me. They have not got the charm of novelty.'

'They must interest you, Dorian. Every gentleman is interested in his good name. You don't want people to talk of you as something vile and degraded. Of course you have your position, and your wealth, and all that kind of thing. But position and wealth are not everything. Mind you, I don't believe these rumours at all. At least, I can't believe them when I see you. Sin is a thing that writes itself across a man's face. It cannot be concealed. People talk sometimes of secret vices. There are no such things. If a wretched man has a vice, it shows itself in the lines of his mouth, the droop of his eyelids, the moulding of his hands even. Somebody – I won't mention his name, but you know him – came to me last year to have his portrait done. I had never seem him before, and had never heard anything about him at the time, though I have heard a good deal since. He offered an extravagant price. I refused him. There was something in the shape of his fingers that I hated. I know now that I was quite right in what I fancied about him. His life is dreadful. But you, Dorian, with your pure, bright, innocent face, and your marvellous untroubled youth – I can't believe anything against you. And yet I see you very seldom, and you never come down to the studio now, and when I am away from you, and I hear all these hideous things that people are whispering about you, I don't know what to say. Why is it, Dorian, that a man like the Duke of Berwick leaves the room of a club when you enter it? Why is it that so many gentlemen in London will neither go to your house nor invite you to theirs? You used to be a friend of Lord Staveley. I met him at dinner last week. Your name happened to come up in conversation, in connection with the miniatures you have lent to the exhibition at the Dudley. Staveley curled his lip, and said that you might have the most artistic tastes, but that you were a man whom no pure-minded girl should be allowed to know, and whom no chaste woman should sit in the same room with. I reminded him that I was a friend of yours, and asked him what he meant. He told me. He told me right out before everybody. It was horrible! Why is your friendship so fatal to young men? There was that wretched boy in the Guards who committed suicide. You were his great friend. There was Sir Henry Ashton, who had to leave England, with a tarnished name. You and he were inseparable. What about Adrian Singleton, and his dreadful end? What about Lord Kent's only son, and his career? I met his father yesterday in St James's Street. He seemed broken with shame and sorrow. What about the young Duke of Perth? What sort of life has he got now? What gentleman would associate with him?'

'Stop, Basil. You are talking about things of which you know nothing,' said Dorian Gray, biting his lip, and with a note of infinite contempt in his voice. 'You ask me why Berwick leaves a room when I enter it. It is because I know everything about his life, not because he knows anything about mine. With such blood as he has in his veins, how could his record be clean? You ask me about Henry Ashton and young Perth. Did I teach the one his vices, and the other his debauchery? If Kent's silly son takes his wife from the streets what is that to me? If Adrian Singleton writes his friend's name across a bill, am I his keeper? I know how people chatter in England. The middle classes air their moral prejudices over their gross dinner-tables, and whisper about what they call the profligacies of their betters in order to try and pretend that they are in smart society, and on intimate terms with the people they slander. In this country it is enough for a man to have distinction and brains for every common tongue to wag against him. And what sort of lives do these people, who pose as being moral, lead themselves? My dear fellow, you forget that we are in the native land of the hypocrite.'

'Dorian,' cried Hallward, 'that is not the question. England is bad enough, I know, and English society is all wrong. That is the reason why I want you to be fine. You have not been fine. One has a right to judge of a man by the effect he has over his friends. Yours seem to lose all sense of honour, of goodness, of purity. You have filled them with a madness for pleasure. They have gone down into the depths. You led them there. Yes: you led them there, and yet you can smile, as you are smiling now. And there is worse behind. I know you and Harry are inseparable. Surely for that reason, if for none other, you should not have made his sister's name a byword.'

'Take care, Basil. You go too far.'

'I must speak, and you must listen. You shall listen. When you met Lady Gwendolen, not a breath of scandal had ever touched her. Is there a single decent woman in London now who would drive with her in the Park? Why, even her children are not allowed to live with her. Then there are other stories – stories that you have been seen creeping at dawn out of dreadful houses and slinking in disguise into the foulest dens in London. Are they true? Can they be true? When I first heard them I laughed. I hear them now, and they make me shudder. What about your country house, and the life that is led there? Dorian, you don't know what is said about you. I won't tell you that I don't want to preach to you. I remember Harry saying once that every man who turned himself into an amateur curate for the moment always began by saying that, and then proceeded to break his word. I do want to preach to you. I want you to lead such a life as will make the world respect you. I want you to have a clean name and a fair record. I want you to get rid of the dreadful people you associate with. Don't shrug your shoulders like that. Don't be so indifferent. You have a wonderful influence. Let it be for good, not for evil. They say that you corrupt everyone with whom you become intimate, and that it is quite sufficient for you to enter a house, for shame of some kind to follow after. I don't know whether it is so or not. How should I know? But it is said of you. I am told things that it seems impossible to doubt. Lord Gloucester was one of my greatest friends at Oxford. He showed me a letter that his wife had written to him when she was dying alone in her villa at Mentone. Your name was implicated in the most terrible confession I ever read. I told him that it was absurd – that I knew you thoroughly, and that you were incapable of anything of the kind. Know you? I wonder do I know you? Before I could answer that, I should have to see your soul.'

'To see my soul!' muttered Dorian Gray, starting up from the sofa and turning almost white from fear.

'Yes,' answered Hallward, gravely, and with deep-toned sorrow in his voice – 'to see your soul. But only God can do that.'

A bitter laugh of mockery broke from the lips of the younger man. 'You shall see it yourself, tonight!' he cried, seizing a lamp from the table. 'Come: it is your own handiwork. Why shouldn't you look at it? You can tell the world all about it afterwards, if you choose. Nobody would believe you. If they did believe you, they would like me all the better for it. I know the age better than you do, though you will prate about it so tediously. Come, I tell you. You have chattered enough about corruption. Now you shall look on it face to face.'

There was the madness of pride in every word he uttered. He stamped his foot upon the ground in his boyish insolent manner. He felt a terrible joy at the thought that someone else was to share his secret, and that the man who had painted the portrait that was the origin of all his shame was to be burdened for the rest of his life with the hideous memory of what he had done.

'Yes,' he continued, coming closer to him, and looking steadfastly into his stern eyes. 'I shall show you my soul. You shall see the thing that you fancy only God can see.'

Hallward started back. 'This is blasphemy, Dorian!' he cried. 'You must not say things like that. They are horrible, and they don't mean anything.'

'You think so?' He laughed again.

'I know so. As for what I said to you tonight, I said it for your good. You know I have been always a staunch friend to you.'

'Don't touch me. Finish what you have to say.'

A twisted flash of pain shot across the painter's face. He paused for a moment, and a wild feeling of pity came over him. After all, what right had he to pry into the life of Dorian Gray? If he had done a tithe of what was rumoured about him, how much he must have suffered! Then he straightened himself up, and walked over to the fireplace, and stood there, looking at the burning logs with their frostlike ashes and their throbbing cores of flame.

'I am waiting, Basil,' said the young man, in a hard, clear voice.

He turned round. 'What I have to say is this,' he cried. 'You must give me some answer to these horrible charges that are made against you. If you tell me that they are absolutely untrue from beginning to end, I shall believe you. Deny them, Dorian, deny them! Can't you see what I am going through? My God! Don't tell me that you are bad, and corrupt, and shameful.'

Dorian Gray smiled. There was a curl of contempt in his lips. 'Come upstairs, Basil,' he said, quietly. 'I keep a diary of my life from day to day, and it never leaves the room in which it is written. I shall show it to you if you come with me.'

'I shall come with you, Dorian, if you wish it. I see I have missed my train. That makes no matter. I can go tomorrow. But don't ask me to read anything tonight. All I want is a plain answer to my question.'

'That shall be given to you upstairs. I could not give it here. You will not have to read long.'

* * * *

He passed out of the room, and began the ascent, Basil Hallward following close behind. They walked softly, as men do instinctively at night. The lamp cast fantastic shadows on the wall and staircase. A rising wind made some of the windows rattle.

When they reached the top landing, Dorian set the lamp down on the floor, and taking out the key turned it in the lock. 'You insist on knowing, Basil?' he asked, in a low voice.

'Yes.'

'I am delighted,' he answered, smiling. Then he added, somewhat harshly, 'You are the one man in the world who is entitled to know everything about me. You have had more to do with my life than you think': and, taking up the lamp, he opened the door and went in. A cold current of air passed them, and the light shot up for a moment in a flame of murky orange. He shuddered. 'Shut the door behind you,' he whispered, as he placed the lamp on the table.

Hallward glanced round him, with a puzzled expression. The room looked as if it had not been lived in for years. A faded Flemish tapestry, a curtained picture, an old Italian *cassone*, and an almost empty bookcase – that was all that it seemed to contain, besides a chair and a table. As Dorian Gray was lighting a half-burned candle that was standing on the mantelshelf, he saw that the whole place was covered with dust, and that the carpet was in holes. A mouse ran scuffling behind the wainscoting. There was a damp odour of mildew.

'So you think that it is only God who sees the soul, Basil? Draw that curtain back, and you will see mine.'

The voice that spoke was cold and cruel. 'You are mad, Dorian, or playing a part,' muttered Hallward, frowning.

'You won't? Then I must do it myself,' said the young man; and he tore the curtain from its rod and flung it on the ground.

An exclamation of horror broke from the painter's lips as he saw in the dim light the hideous face on the canvas grinning at him. There was something in its expression that filled him with disgust and loathing. Good heavens! It was Dorian Gray's own face that he was looking at! The horror, whatever it was, had not yet entirely spoiled that marvellous beauty. There was still some gold in the thinning hair and some scarlet on the sensual mouth. The sodden eyes had kept something of the loveliness of their blue, the noble curves had not yet completely passed away from chiselled nostrils and from plastic throat. Yes, it was Dorian himself. But who had done it? He seemed to recognise his own brushwork, and the frame was his own design. The idea was monstrous, yet he felt afraid. He seized the lighted candle, and held it to the picture. In the left-hand corner was his own name, traced in long letters of bright vermilion.

It was some foul parody, some infamous, ignoble satire. He had never done that. Still, it was his own picture! He knew it, and he felt as if his blood had changed in a moment from fire to sluggish ice. His own picture! What did it mean? Why had it altered? He turned, and looked at Dorian Gray, with the eyes of a sick man. His mouth twitched, and his parched tongue seemed unable to articulate. He passed his hand across his forehead. It was dank with clammy sweat.

The young man was leaning against the mantelshelf, watching him with that strange expression that one sees on the faces of those who are absorbed in a play when some great artist is acting. There was neither real sorrow in it nor real joy. There was simply the passion of the spectator, with perhaps a flicker of triumph in his eyes. He had taken the flower out of his coat, and was smelling it, or pretending to do so.

'What does this mean?' cried Hallward, at last. His own voice sounded shrill and curious in his ears.

'Years ago, when I was a boy,' said Dorian Gray, crushing the flower in his hand, 'you met me, flattered me, and taught me to be vain of my good looks. One day you introduced me to a friend of yours, who explained to me the wonder of youth, and you finished the portrait of me that revealed to me the wonder of beauty. In a mad moment, that, even now, I don't know whether I regret or not, I made a wish, perhaps you would call it a prayer . . .'

'I remember it! Oh, how well I remember it! No, the thing is impossible! The room is damp. Mildew has got into the canvas. The paints I used had some wretched mineral poison in them. I tell you the thing is impossible.'

'Ah, what is impossible?' murmured the young man, going over to the window, and leaning his forehead against the cold, mist-stained glass.

'You told me you had destroyed it.'

'I was wrong. It has destroyed me.'

'I don't believe it is my picture.'

'Can't you see your ideal in it?' said Dorian, bitterly.

'My ideal, as you call it . . .'

'As you called it.'

'There was nothing evil in it, nothing shameful. You were to me such an ideal as I shall never meet again. This is the face of a satyr.'

'It is the face of my soul.'

'Christ! What a thing I must have worshipped! It has the eyes of a devil.'

'Each of us has Heaven and Hell in him, Basil,' cried Dorian, with a wild gesture of despair.

Hallward turned again to the portrait, and gazed at it. 'My God! If it is true,' he exclaimed, 'and this is what you have done with your life, why, you must be worse even than those who talk against you fancy you to be!' He held the light up again to the canvas, and examined it. The surface seemed to be quite undisturbed, and as he had left it. It was from within, apparently, that the foulness and horror had come. Through some strange quickening of inner life the leprosies of sin were slowly eating the thing away. The rotting of a corpse in a watery grave was not so fearful.

His hand shook, and the candle fell from its socket on the floor, and lay there sputtering. He placed his foot on it and put it out. Then he flung himself into the rickety chair that was standing by the table and buried his face in his hands.

'Good God, Dorian, what a lesson! What an awful lesson!' There was no answer, but he could hear the young man sobbing at the window. 'Pray, Dorian, pray,' he murmured. 'What is it that one was taught to say in one's boyhood? 'Lead us not into temptation. Forgive us our sins. Wash away our iniquities.' Let us say that together. The prayer of your pride has been answered. The prayer of your repentance will be answered also. I worshipped you too much. We are both punished.'

Dorian Gray turned slowly around, and looked at him with tear-dimmed eyes. 'It is too late, Basil,' he faltered.

'It is never too late, Dorian. Let us kneel down and try if we cannot remember a prayer. Isn't there a verse somewhere, "Though your sins be as scarlet, yet I will make them as white as snow"?'

'Those words mean nothing to me now.'

'Hush! Don't say that. You have done enough evil in your life. My God! Don't you see that accursed thing leering at us?'

Dorian Gray glanced at the picture, and suddenly an uncontrollable feeling of hatred for Basil Hallward came over him, as though it had been suggested to him by the image on the canvas, whispered into his ear by those grinning lips. The mad passions of a hunted animal stirred within him, and he loathed the man who was seated at the table, more than in his whole life he had ever loathed anything. He glanced wildly around. Something glimmered on the top of the painted chest that faced him. His eye fell on it. He knew what it was. It was a knife that he had brought up, some days before, to cut a piece of cord, and had forgotten to take away with him. He moved slowly towards it, passing Hallward as he did so. As soon as he got behind him, he seized it, and turned round. Hallward stirred in his chair as if he was going to rise. He rushed at him, and dug the knife into the great vein that is behind the ear, crushing the man's head down on the table, and stabbing again and again.

There was a stifled groan, and the horrible sound of someone choking with blood. Three times the outstretched arms shot up convulsively, waving grotesque stiff-fingered hands in the air. He stabbed him twice more, but the man did not move. Something began to trickle on the floor. He waited for a moment, still pressing the head down. Then he threw the knife on the table, and listened.

He could hear nothing but the drip, drip on the threadbare carpet. He opened the door and went out on the landing. The house was absolutely quiet. No one was about. For a few seconds he stood bending over the balustrade, and peering down into the black seething well of darkness. Then he took out the key and returned to the room, locking himself in as he did so.

The thing was still seated in the chair, straining over the table with bowed head, and humped back, and long fantastic arms. Had it not been for the red jagged tear in the neck, and the clotted black pool that was slowly widening on the table, one would have said that the man was simply asleep.

How quickly it had all been done! He felt strangely calm, and, walking over to the window, opened it, and stepped out on the balcony. The wind had blown the fog away, and the sky was like a monstrous peacock's tail, starred with myriads of golden eyes. He looked down, and saw the policeman going his rounds and flashing the long beam of his lantern on the doors of the silent houses. The crimson spot of a prowling hansom gleamed at the corner, and then vanished. A woman in a fluttering shawl was creeping slowly by the railings, staggering as she went. Now and then she stopped, and peered back. Once, she began to sing in a hoarse voice. The policeman strolled over and said something to her. She stumbled away, laughing. A bitter blast swept across the Square. The gas-lamps flickered, and became blue, and the leafless trees shook their black iron branches to and fro. He shivered, and went back, closing the window behind him.

Having reached the door, he turned the key, and opened it. He did not even glance at the murdered man. He felt that the secret of the whole thing was not to realise the situation. The friend who had painted the fatal portrait to which all his misery had been due had gone out of his life. That was enough.

Then he remembered the lamp. It was a rather curious one of Moorish workmanship, made of dull silver inlaid with arabesques of burnished steel, and studded with coarse turquoises. Perhaps it might be missed by his servant, and questions would be asked. He hesitated for a moment, then he turned back and took it from the table. He could not help seeing the dead thing. How still it was! How horribly white the long hands looked! It was like a dreadful wax image.

Having locked the door behind him, he crept quietly downstairs. The woodwork creaked, and seemed to cry out as if in pain. He stopped several times, and waited. No: everything was still. It was merely the sound of his own footsteps.

When he reached the library, he saw the bag and coat in the corner. They must be hidden away somewhere. He unlocked a secret press that was in the wainscoting, a press in which he kept his own curious disguises, and put them into it. He could easily burn them afterwards. Then he pulled out his watch. It was twenty minutes to two.

He sat down, and began to think. Every year – every month, almost – men were strangled in England for what he had done. There had been a madness of murder in the air. Some red star had come too close to the earth . . . And yet what evidence was there against him? Basil Hallward had left the house at eleven. No one had seen him come in again. Most of the servants were at Selby Royal. His valet had gone to bed . . . Paris! Yes. It was to Paris that Basil had gone, and by the midnight train, as he had intended. With his curious reserved habits, it would be months before any suspicions would be aroused. Months! Everything could be destroyed long before then.

A sudden thought struck him. He put on his fur coat and hat, and went out into the hall. There he paused, hearing the slow heavy tread of the policeman on the pavement outside, and seeing the flash of the bull's-eye reflected in the window. He waited, and held his breath.

After a few moments he drew back the latch, and slipped out, shutting the door very gently behind him. Then he began ringing the bell. In about five minutes his valet appeared half dressed, and looking very drowsy.

'I am sorry to have had to wake you up, Francis,' he said, stepping in;

'but I had forgotten my latchkey. What time is it?'

'Ten minutes past two, sir,' answered the man, looking at the clock and blinking.

'Ten minutes past two? How horribly late! You must wake me at nine tomorrow. I have some work to do.'

'All right, sir.'

'Did anyone call this evening?'

'Mr Hallward, sir. He stayed here until eleven, and then he went away to catch his train.'

'Oh! I am sorry I didn't see him. Did he leave any message?'

'No, sir, except that he would write to you from Paris, if he did not find you at the club.'

'That will do, Francis. Don't forget to call me at nine tomorrow.'

'No sir.'

The man shambled down the passage in his slippers.

Dorian Gray threw his hat and coat upon the table, and passed into the library. For a quarter of an hour he walked up and down the room biting his lip, and thinking. Then he took down the Blue Book from one of the shelves, and began to turn over the leaves. 'Alan Campbell, 152, Hertford Street, Mayfair.' Yes: that was the man he wanted.

* * * *

Dorian blackmails Alan Campbell into disposing of the body. Unable to live with himself, Campbell commits suicide. Dorian goes to his country house, Selby Royal, and falls in love with a simple country girl. He returns to London to tell Lord Henry this and that he has decided to reform. Lord Henry tells Dorian that it is too late and Dorian leaves Lord Henry's house, having arranged to ride with him in the Park the following morning.

* * * *

It was a lovely night, so warm that he threw his coat over his arm, and did not even put his silk scarf round his throat. As he strolled home, smoking his cigarette, two young men in evening dress passed him. He heard one of them whisper to the other, 'That is Dorian Gray.' He remembered how pleased he used to be when he was pointed out, or stared at, or talked about. He was tired of hearing his own name now. Half the charm of the little village where he had been so often lately was that no one knew who he was. He had often told the girl whom he had lured to love him that he was poor, and she had believed him. He had told her once that he was wicked, and she had laughed at him, and answered that wicked people were always very old and very ugly. What a laugh she had! – just like a thrush singing. And how pretty she had been in her cotton dress and her large hats! She knew nothing, but she had everything that he had lost.

When he reached home, he found his servant waiting up for him. He sent him to bed, and threw himself down on the sofa in the library, and began to think over some of the things that Lord Henry had said to him.

Was it really true that one could never change? He felt a wild longing for the unstained purity of his boyhood – his rose-white boyhood, as Lord Henry had once called it. He knew that he had tarnished himself, filled his mind with corruption, and given horror to his fancy; that he had been an evil influence to others, and had experienced a terrible joy in being so; and that, of the lives that had crossed his own, it had been the fairest and the most full of promise that he had brought to shame. But was it all irretrievable? Was there no hope for him?

Ah! in what a monstrous moment of pride and passion he had prayed that the portrait should bear the burden of his days, and he keep the unsullied splendour of eternal youth! All his failure had been due to that. Better for him that each sin of his life had brought its sure, swift penalty along with it. There was purification in punishment. Not 'Forgive us our sins,' but 'Smite us for our iniquities,' should be the prayer of a man to a most just God.

The curiously carved mirror that Lord Henry had given to him, so many years ago now, was standing on the table, and the white-limbed Cupids laughed round it as of old. He took it up, as he had done on that night of horror, when he had first noted the change in the fatal picture, and with wild, tear-dimmed eyes looked into its polished shield. Once, someone who had terribly loved him had written to him a mad letter, ending with these idolatrous words: 'The world is changed because you are made of ivory and gold. The curves of your lips rewrite history.' The phrases came back to his memory, and he repeated them over and over to himself. Then he loathed his own beauty, and, flinging the mirror on the floor, crushed it into silver splinters beneath his heel. It was his beauty that had ruined him, his beauty and the youth that he had prayed for. But for those two things, his life might have been free from stain. His beauty had been to him but a mask, his youth but a mockery. What was youth at best? A green, an unripe time, a time of shallow moods and sickly thoughts. Why had he worn its livery? Youth had spoiled him.

It was better not to think of the past. Nothing could alter that. It was of himself, and of his own future, that he had to think. James Vane was hidden in a nameless grave in Selby Churchyard. Alan Campbell had shot himself one night in his laboratory, but had not revealed the secret that he had been forced to know. The excitement, such as it was, over Basil Hallward's disappearance would soon pass away. It was already waning. He was perfectly safe there. Nor, indeed, was it the death of Basil Hallward that weighed most upon his mind. It was the living death of his own soul that troubled him. Basil had painted the portrait that had marred his life. He could not forgive him that. It was the portrait that had done everything. Basil had said things to him that were unbearable, and that he had yet borne with patience. The murder had been simply the madness of a moment. As for Alan Campbell, his suicide had been his own act. He had chosen to do it. It was nothing to him.

A new life! That was what he wanted. That was what he was waiting for. Surely he had begun it already. He had spared one innocent thing, at any rate. He would never again tempt innocence. He would be good.

As he thought of Hetty Merton, he began to wonder if the portrait in the locked room had changed. Surely it was not still so horrible as it had been? Perhaps if his life became pure, he would be able to expel every sign of evil passion from the face. Perhaps the signs of evil had already gone away. He would go and look.

He took the lamp from the table and crept upstairs. As he unbarred the door a smile of joy flitted across his strangely young-looking face and lingered for a moment about his lips. Yes, he would be good, and the hideous thing that he had hidden away would no longer be a terror to him. He felt as if the load had been lifted from him already.

He went in quietly, locking the door behind him, as was his custom, and dragged the purple hanging from the portrait. A cry of pain and indignation broke from him. He could see no change save that in the eyes there was a look of cunning, and in the mouth the curved wrinkle of the hypocrite. The thing was still loathsome – more loathsome, if possible, than before – and the scarlet dew that spotted the hand seemed brighter, and more like blood newly spilt. Then he trembled. Had it been merely vanity that had made him do his one good deed? Or the desire for a new sensation, as Lord Henry had hinted, with his mocking laugh? Or that passion to act a part that sometimes makes us do things finer than we are ourselves? Or, perhaps, all these? And why was the red stain larger than it had been? It seemed to have crept like a horrible disease over the wrinkled fingers. There was blood on the painted feet, as though the thing had dripped – blood even on the hand that had not held the knife. Confess? Did it mean that he was to confess? To give himself up, and be put to death? He laughed. He felt that the idea was monstrous. Besides, even if he did confess, who would believe him? There was no trace of the murdered man anywhere. Everything belonging to him had been destroyed. He himself had burned what had been below-stairs. The world would simply say that he was mad. They would shut him up if he persisted in his story . . . Yet it was his duty to confess, to suffer public shame, and to make public atonement. There was a God who called upon men to tell their sins to earth as well as to heaven. Nothing that he could do would cleanse him until he had told his own sin. His sin? He shrugged his shoulders. The death of Basil Hallward seemed very little to him. He was thinking of Hetty Merton. For it was an unjust mirror, this mirror of his soul that he was looking at. Vanity? Curiosity? Hypocrisy? Had there been nothing more in his renunciation than that? There had been something more. At least he thought so. But who could tell? . . . No. There had been nothing more. Through vanity he had spared her. In hypocrisy he had worn the mask of goodness. For curiosity's sake he had tried the denial of self. He recognised that now.

But this murder – was it to dog him all his life? Was he always to be burdened by his past? Was he really to confess? Never. There was only one bit of evidence left against him. The picture itself – that was evidence. He would destroy it. Why had he kept it so long? Once it had given him pleasure to watch it changing and growing old. Of late he had felt no such pleasure. It had kept him awake at night. When he had been away, he had been filled with terror lest other eyes should look upon it. It had brought melancholy across his passions. Its mere memory had marred many moments of joy. It had been like conscience to him. Yes, it had been conscience. He would destroy it.

He looked round, and saw the knife that had stabbed Basil Hallward. He had cleaned it many times, until there was no stain left upon it. It was bright, and glistened. As it had killed the painter, so it would kill the painter's work, and all that that meant. It would kill the past and when that was dead he would be free. It would kill this monstrous soul-life, and, without its hideous warnings, he would be at peace. He seized the thing, and stabbed the picture with it.

There was a cry heard, and a crash. The cry was so horrible in its agony that the frightened servants woke, and crept out of their rooms. Two gentlemen, who were passing in the Square below, stopped, and looked up at the great house. They walked on until they met a policeman, and brought him back. The man rang the bell several times, but there was no answer. Except for a light in one of the top windows, the house was all dark. After a time, he went away and stood in an adjoining portico and watched.

'Whose house is that, constable?' asked the elder of the two gentlemen.

'Mr Dorian Gray's, sir,' answered the policeman.

They looked at each other, as they walked away, and sneered.

Inside, in the servants' part of the house, the half-clad domestics were talking in low whispers to each other. Old Mrs Leaf was crying and wringing her hands. Francis was as pale as death.

After about a quarter of an hour, he got the coachman and one of the footmen and crept upstairs. They knocked, but there was no reply. They called out. Everything was still. Finally, after vainly trying to force the door, they got on the roof, and dropped down on the balcony. The windows yielded easily; their bolts were old.

When they entered they found, hanging upon the wall, a splendid portrait of their master as they had last seen him, in all the wonder of his exquisite youth and beauty. Lying on the floor was a dead man, in evening dress, with a knife in his heart. He was withered, wrinkled, and loathsome of visage. It was not until they had examined the rings that they recognised who it was.

THE SILVER MIRROR
Sir Arthur Conan Doyle

Jan. 3 This affair of White and Wotherspoon's accounts proves to be a gigantic task. There are twenty thick ledgers to be examined and checked. Who would be a junior partner? However, it is the first big bit of business which has been left entirely in my hands. I must justify it. But it has to be finished so that the lawyers may have the result in time for the trial. Johnson said this morning that I should have to get the last figure out before the twentieth of the month. Good Lord! Well, have at it, and if human brain and nerve can stand the strain, I'll win out at the other side. It means office-work from ten to five, and then a second sitting from about eight to one in the morning. There's drama in an accountant's life. When I find myself in the still early hours, while all the world sleeps, hunting through column after column for those missing figures which will turn a respected alderman into a felon, I understand that it is not such a prosaic profession after all.

On Monday I came on the first trace of defalcation. No heavy game hunter ever got a finer thrill when first he caught sight of the trail of his quarry. But I look at the twenty ledgers and think of the jungle through which I have to follow him before I get my kill. Hard work – but rare sport, too, in a way! I saw that fat fellow once at a City dinner, his red face glowing above a white napkin. He looked at the little pale man at the end of the table. He would have been pale too if he could have seen the task that would be mine.

Jan. 6 What perfect nonsense it is for doctors to prescribe rest when rest is out of the question! Asses! They might as well shout to a man who has a pack of wolves at his heels that what he wants is absolute quiet. My figures must be out by a certain date: unless they are so, I shall lose the chance of my lifetime, so how on earth am I to rest? I'll take a week or so after the trial.

Perhaps I was myself a fool to go to the doctor at all. But I get nervous and highly-strung when I sit alone at my work at night. It's not a pain – only a sort of fullness of the head with an occasional mist over the eyes. I thought perhaps some bromide, or chloral, or something of the kind might do me good. But stop work? It's absurd to ask such a thing. It's like a long-distance race. You feel queer at first and your heart thumps and your lungs pant, but if you have only the pluck to keep on, you get your second wind. I'll stick to my work and wait for my second wind. If it never comes – all the same, I'll stick to my work. Two ledgers are done, and I am well on in the third. The rascal has covered his tracks well, but I pick them up for all that.

Jan. 9 I had not meant to go to the doctor again. And yet I have had to. 'Straining my nerves, risking a complete breakdown, even endangering my sanity.' That's a nice sentence to have fired off at one. Well, I'll stand the strain and I'll take the risk, and so long as I can sit in my chair and move a pen, I'll follow the old sinner's slot.

By the way, I may as well set down here the queer experience which drove me this second time to the doctor. I'll keep an exact record of my symptoms and sensations, because they are interesting in themselves – 'A curious psycho-physiological study,' says the doctor – and also because I am perfectly certain that when I am through with them they will all seem blurred and unreal, like some queer dream betwixt sleeping and waking. So now, while they are fresh, I will just make a note of them, if only as a change of thought after the endless figures.

There's an old silver-framed mirror in my room. It was given me by a friend who had a taste for antiquities, and he, as I happened to know, picked it up at a sale and had no notion where it came from. It's a large thing – three feet across and two feet high – and it leans at the back of a side-table on my left as I write. The frame is flat, about three inches across, and very old; far too old for hall-marks or other methods of determining its age. The glass part projects, with a bevelled edge, and has the magnificent reflecting power which is only, as it seems to me, to be found in very old mirror. There's a feeling of perspective when you look into it such as no modern glass can ever give.

The mirror is so situated that as I sit at the table, I can usually see nothing in it but the reflection of the red window curtains. But a queer thing happened last night. I had been working for some hours, very much against the grain, with continual bouts of that mistiness of which I had complained. Again and again I had to stop and clear my eyes. Well, on one of these occasions I chanced to look at the mirror. It had the oddest appearance. The red curtains which should have been reflected in it were no longer there, but the glass seemed to be clouded and steamy, not on the surface, which glittered like steel, but deep down in the very grain of it. This opacity, when I stared hard at it, appeared to slowly rotate this way and that, until it was a thick white cloud swirling in heavy wreaths. So real and solid was it, and so reasonable was I, that I remember turning, with the idea that the curtains were on fire. But everything was deadly still in the room – no sound save the ticking of the clock, no movement save the slow gyration of that strange woolly cloud deep in the heart of the old mirror.

Then, as I looked, the mist, or smoke, or cloud, or whatever one may call it, seemed to coalesce and solidify at two points quite close together, and I was aware, with a thrill of interest rather than of fear, that these were two eyes looking out into the room. A vague outline of a head I could see – a woman's by the hair, but this was very shadowy. Only the eyes were quite distinct; such eyes – dark, luminous, filled with some passionate emotion, fury or horror, I could not say which. Never have I seen eyes which were so full of intense, vivid life. They were not fixed upon me, but stared out into the room. Then as I sat erect, passed my hand over my brow, and made a strong conscious effort to pull myself together, the dim head faded into the general opacity, the mirror slowly cleared, and there were the red curtains once again.

A sceptic would say, no doubt, that I had dropped asleep over my figures, and that my experience was a dream. As a matter of fact, I was never more vividly awake in my life. I was able to argue about it even as I looked at it, and to tell myself that it was a subjective impression – a chimera of the nerves – begotten by worry and insomnia. But why this particular shape? And who is the woman, and what is the dreadful emotion which I read in those wonderful brown eyes? They come between me and my work. For the first time I have done less than the daily tally which I had marked out. Perhaps that is why I have had no abnormal sensations tonight. Tomorrow I must wake up, come what may.

Jan. 11 All well, and good progress with my work. I wind the net, coil after coil, round that bulky body. But the last smile may remain with him if my own nerves break over it. The mirror would seem to be a sort of barometer which marks my brain-pressure. Each night I have observed that it had clouded before I reached the end of my task.

Dr Sinclair (who is, it seems, a bit of a psychologist) was so interested in my account that he came round this evening to have a look at the mirror. I had observed that something was scribbled in crabbed old characters upon the metal-work at the back. He examined this with a lens, but could make nothing of it. 'Sanc. X. Pal.' was his final reading of it, but that did not bring us any farther. He advised me to put it away into another room; but after all, whatever I may see in it is, by his own account, only a symptom. It is in the cause that the danger lies. The twenty ledgers – not the silver mirror – should be packed away if I could only do it. I'm at the eighth now, so I progress.

Jan. 13 Perhaps it would have been wiser after all if I had packed away the mirror. I had an extraordinary experience with it last night. And yet I find it so interesting, so fascinating, that even now I will keep it in its place. What on earth is the meaning of it all?

I suppose it was about one in the morning, and I was closing my books preparatory to staggering off to bed, when I saw her there in front of me. The stage of mistiness and development must have passed unobserved, and there she was in all her beauty and passion and distress, as clear-cut as if she were really in the flesh before me. The figure was small, but very distinct – so much so that every feature, and every detail of dress, are stamped in my memory. She is seated on the extreme left of the mirror. A sort of shadowy figure crouches down beside her – I can dimly discern that it is a man – and then behind them is cloud, in which I see figures – figures which move. It is not a mere picture upon which I look. It is a scene in life, an actual episode. She crouches and quivers. The man beside her cowers down. The vague figures make abrupt movements and gestures. All my fears were swallowed up in my interest. It was maddening to see so much and not to see more.

But I can at least describe the woman to the smallest point. She is very beautiful and quite young – not more than five-and-twenty, I should judge. Her hair is of a very rich brown, with a warm chestnut shade fining into gold at the edges. A little flat-pointed cap comes to an angle in front, and is made of lace edged with pearls. The forehead is high, too high perhaps for perfect beauty; but one would not have it otherwise; as it gives a touch of power and strength to what would otherwise be a softly feminine face. The brows are most delicately curved over heavy eyelids, and then come those wonderful eyes – so large, so dark, so full of overmastering emotion, of rage and horror, contending with a pride of self-control which holds her from sheer frenzy! The cheeks are pale, the lips white with agony, the chin and throat most exquisitely rounded. The figure sits and leans forward in the chair, straining and rigid, cataleptic with horror. The dress is black velvet, a jewel gleams like a flame in the breast, and a golden crucifix smoulders in the shadow of a fold. This is the lady whose image still lives in the old silver mirror. What dire deed could it be which has left its impress there, so that now, in another age, if the spirit of a man be but worn down to it, he may be conscious of its presence?

One other detail: on the left side of the skirt of the black dress was, as I thought at first, a shapeless bunch of white ribbon. Then, as I looked more intently or as the vision defined itself more clearly, I perceived what it was. It was the hand of a man, clenched and knotted in agony, which held on with a convulsive grasp to the fold of the dress. The rest of the crouching figure was a mere vague outline, but the strenuous hand shone clear on the dark background, with a sinister suggestion of tragedy in its frantic clutch. The man is frightened – horribly frightened. That I can clearly discern. What has terrifed him so? Why does he grip the woman's dress? The answer lies amongst those moving figures in the background. They have brought danger both to him and to her. The interest of the thing fascinated me. I thought no more of its relation to my own nerves. I stared and stared as if in a theatre. But I could get no farther. The mist thinned. There were tumultuous movements in which all the figures were vaguely concerned. Then the mirror was clear once more.

The doctor says I must drop work for a day, and I can afford to do so, for I have made good progress lately. It is quite evident that the visions depend entirely upon my own nervous state, for I sat in front of the mirror for an hour tonight, with no result whatsoever. My soothing day has chased them away. I wonder whether I shall ever penetrate what they all mean? I examined the mirror this evening under a good light, and besides the mysterious inscription 'Sanc. X. Pal.,' I was able to discern some signs of heraldic marks, very faintly visible upon the silver. They must be very ancient, as they are almost obliterated. So far as I could make out, they were three spear-heads, two above and one below. I will show them to the doctor when he calls tomorrow.

Jan. 14 Feel perfectly well again, and I intend that nothing else shall stop me until my task is finished. The doctor was shown the marks on the mirror and agreed that they were armorial bearings. He is deeply interested in all that I have told him, and cross-questioned me closely on the details. It amuses me to notice how he is torn in two by conflicting desires – the one that his patient should lose his symptoms, the other that the medium – for so he regards me – should solve this mystery of the past. He advised continued rest, but did not oppose me too violently when I declared that such a thing was out of the question until the ten remaining ledgers have been checked.

Jan. 17 For three nights I have had no experiences – my day of rest has borne fruit. Only a quarter of my task is left, but I must make a forced march, for the lawyers are clamouring for their material. I will give them enough and to spare. I have him fast on a hundred counts. When they realise what a slippery, cunning rascal he is, I should gain some credit from the case. False trading accounts, false balance-sheets, dividends drawn from capital, losses written down as profits, suppression of working expenses, manipulation of petty cash – it is a fine record!

Jan. 18 Headaches, nervous twitches, mistiness, fullness of the temples – all the premonitions of trouble, and the trouble came sure enough. And yet my real sorrow is not so much that the vision should come as that it should cease before all is revealed.

But I saw more tonight. The crouching man was as visible as the lady whose gown he clutched. He is a little swarthy fellow, with a black pointed beard. He has a loose gown of damask trimmed with fur. The prevailing tints of his dress are red. What a fright the fellow is in, to be sure! He cowers and shivers and glares back over his shoulder. There is a small knife in his other hand, but he is far too tremulous and cowed to use it. Dimly now I begin to see the figures in the background. Fierce faces, bearded and dark, shape themselves out of the mist. There is one terrible creature, a skeleton of a man, with hollow cheeks and eyes sunk in his head. He also has a knife in his hand. On the right of the woman stands a tall man, very young, with flaxen hair, his face sullen and dour. The beautiful woman looks up at him in appeal. So does the man on the ground. This youth seems to be the arbiter of their fate. The crouching man draws closer and hides himself in the woman's skirts. The tall youth bends and tries to drag her away from him. So much I saw last night before the mirror cleared. Shall I never know what it leads to and whence it comes? It is not a mere imagination, of that I am very sure. Somewhere, some time, this scene has been acted, and this old mirror has reflected it. But when – where?

Jan. 20 My work draws to a close, and it is time. I feel a tenseness within my brain, a sense of intolerable strain, which warns me that something must give. I have worked myself to the limit. But tonight should be the last night. With a supreme effort I should finish the final ledger and complete the case before I rise from my chair. I will do it. I will.

Feb. 7 I did. My God, what an experience! I hardly know if I am strong enough yet to set it down.

Let me explain in the first instance that I am writing this in Dr Sinclair's private hospital some three weeks after the last entry in my diary. On the night of January 20 my nervous system finally gave way, and I remembered nothing afterwards until I found myself three days ago in this home of rest. And I can rest with a good conscience. My work was done before I went under. My figures are in the solicitors' hands. The hunt is over.

And now I must describe that last night. I had sworn to finish my work, and so intently did I stick to it, though my head was bursting, that I would never look up until the last column had been added. And yet it was fine self-restraint, for all the time I knew that wonderful things were happening in the mirror. Every nerve in my body told me so. If I looked up there was an end of my work. So I did not look up until all was finished. Then, when at last with throbbing temples I threw down my pen and raised my eyes, what a sight was there!

The mirror in its silver frame was like a stage, brilliantly lit, in which a drama was in progress. There was no mist now. The oppression of my nerves had wrought this amazing clarity. Every feature, every movement, was as clear-cut as in life. To think that I, a tired accountant, the most prosaic of mankind, with the account-books of a swindling bankrupt before me, should be chosen of all the human race to look upon such a scene!

It was the same scene and the same figures, but the drama had advanced a stage. The tall young man was holding the woman in his arms. She strained away from him and looked up at him with loathing in her face. They had torn the crouching man away from his hold upon the skirt of her dress. A dozen of them were round him – savage men, bearded men. They hacked at him with knives. All seemed to strike him together. Their arms rose and fell. The blood did not flow from him –it squirted. His red dress was dabbled in it. He threw himself this way and that, purple upon crimson, like an over-ripe plum. Still they hacked and still the jets shot from him. It was horrible – horrible! They dragged him kicking to the door. The woman looked over her shoulder at him and her mouth gaped. I heard nothing, but I knew that she was screaming. And then, whether it was this nerve-racking vision before me, or whether, my task finished, all the overwork of the past weeks came in one crushing weight upon me, the room danced round me, the floor seemed to sink away beneath my feet, and I remembered no more. In the early morning my landlady found me stretched senseless before the silver mirror, but I knew nothing myself until three days ago I awoke in the deep peace of the doctor's nursing home.

Feb. 9 Only today have I told Dr Sinclair my full experience. He had not allowed me to speak of such matters before. He listened with an absorbed interest. 'You don't identify this with any well-known scene in history?' he asked, with suspicion in his eyes. I assured him that I knew nothing of history. 'Have you no idea whence that mirror came and to whom it once belonged?' he continued. 'Have you?' I asked, for he spoke with meaning. 'It's incredible,' said he, 'and yet how else can one explain it? The scenes which you described before suggested it, but now it has gone beyond all range of coincidence. I will bring you some notes in the evening.'

Later He has just left me. Let me set down his words as closely as I can recall them. He began by laying several musty volumes upon my bed.

'These you can consult at your leisure,' said he. 'I have some notes here which you can confirm. There is not a doubt that what you have seen is the murder of Rizzio by the Scottish nobles in the presence of Mary, which occurred in March, 1566. Your description of the woman is accurate. The high forehead and heavy eyelids combined with great beauty could hardly apply to two women. The tall young man was her husband, Darnley. Rizzio, says the chronicle, "was dressed in a loose dressing-gown of furred damask; with hose of russet velvet." With one hand he clutched Mary's gown, with the other he held a dagger. Your fierce, hollow-eyed man was Ruthven, who was new-risen from a bed of sickness. Every detail is exact.'

'But why to me?' I asked, in bewilderment. 'Why of all the human race to me?'

'Because you were in the fit mental state to receive the impression. Because you chanced to own the mirror which gave the impression.'

'The mirror! You think, then, that it was Mary's mirror – that it stood in the room where the deed was done?'

'I am convinced that it was Mary's mirror. She had been Queen of France. Her personal property would be stamped with the Royal arms. What you took to be three spear-heads were the lilies of France.'

'And the inscription?'

' "Sanc. X. Pal." You can expand it into Sanctae Crucis Palatium. Some one has made a note upon the mirror as to whence it came. It was the Palace of the Holy Cross.'

'Holyrood!' I cried.

'Exactly. Your mirror came from Holyrood. You have had one very singular experience, and have escaped. I trust that you will never put yourself into the way of having such another.'

THE STOLEN CIGAR-CASE
Bret Harte

I found Hemlock Jones in the old Bank Street lodgings, musing before the fire. With the freedom of an old friend I at once threw myself in my old familiar attitude at his feet, and gently caressed his boot. I was induced to do this for two reasons; one that it enabled me to get a good look at his bent, concentrated face, and the other that it seemed to indicate my reverence for his superhuman insight. So absorbed was he, even then, in tracking some mysterious clue, that he did not seem to notice me. But therein I was wrong – as I always was in my attempt to understand that powerful intellect.

'It is raining,' he said, without lifting his head.

'You have been out then?' I said quickly.

'No. But I see that your umbrella is wet, and that your overcoat, which you threw off on entering, has drops of water on it.'

I sat aghast at his penetration. After a pause he said carelessly, as if dismissing the subject: 'Besides, I hear the rain on the window. Listen.'

I listened. I could scarcely credit my ears, but there was a soft pattering of drops on the pane. It was evident, there was no deceiving this man!

'Have you been busy lately?' I asked, changing the subject. 'What new problem – given up by Scotland Yard as inscrutable – has occupied that gigantic intellect?'

He drew back his foot slightly, and seemed to hesitate ere he returned it to its original position. Then he answered wearily: 'Mere trifles – nothing to speak of. The Prince Kopoli has been here to get my advice regarding the disappearance of certain rubies from the Kremlin; the Rajah of Pootibad, after vainly beheading his entire bodyguard, has been obliged to seek my assistance to recover a jewelled sword. The Grand Duchess of Pretzel-Brauntswig is desirous of discovering where her husband was on the night of the 14th of February, and last night' – he lowered his voice slightly – 'a lodger in this very house, meeting me on the stairs, wanted to know "Why they don't answer his bell".'

I could not help smiling – until I saw a frown gathering on his inscrutable forehead.

'Pray to remember,' he said coldly, 'that it was through such an apparently trivial question that I found out, "Why Paul Ferroll killed his Wife," and "What happened to Jones"!'

I became dumb at once. He paused for a moment, and then suddenly changing back to his usual pitiless, analytical style, he said: 'When I say these are trifles – they are so in comparison to an affair that is now before me. A crime has been committed, and, singularly enough, against myself. You start,' he said, 'you wonder who would have dared to attempt it! So did I; nevertheless, it has been done. *I* have been *robbed!*'

'*You* robbed – you, Hemlock Jones, the Terror of Peculators!' I gasped in amazement, rising and gripping the table as I faced him.

'Yes; listen. I would confess it to no other. But *you* who have followed my career, who know my methods; yea, for whom I have partly lifted the veil that conceals my plans from ordinary humanity; you, who have for years rapturously accepted my confidences, passionately admired my inductions and inferences, placed yourself at my beck and call, become my slave, grovelled at my feet, given up your practice except those few unremunerative and rapidly-decreasing patients to whom, in moments of abstraction over *my* problems, you have administered strychnine for quinine and arsenic for Epsom salts; you, who have sacrificed everything and everybody to me – *you* I make my confidant!'

I rose and embraced him warmly, yet he was already so engrossed in thought that at the same moment he mechanically placed his hand upon his watch chain as if to consult the time. 'Sit down,' he said; 'have a cigar?'

'I have given up cigar smoking,' I said.

'Why?' he asked.

I hesitated, and perhaps coloured. I had really given it up because, with my diminished practice, it was too expensive. I could only afford a pipe. 'I prefer a pipe,' I said laughingly. 'But tell me of this robbery. What have you lost?'

He rose, and planting himself before the fire with his hands under his coat tails, looked down upon me reflectively for a moment. 'Do you remember the cigar-case presented to me by the Turkish Ambassador for discovering the missing favourite of the Grand Vizier in the fifth chorus girl at the Hilarity Theatre? It was that one. It was encrusted with diamonds. I mean the cigar-case.'

'And the largest one had been supplanted by paste,' I said.

'Ah,' he said with a reflective smile, 'you know that?'

'You told me yourself. I remember considering it a proof of your extraordinary perception. But, by Jove, you don't mean to say you have lost it.'

He was silent for a moment. 'No; it has been stolen, it is true, but I shall still find it. And by myself alone! In your profession, my dear fellow, when a member is severely ill he does not prescribe for himself, but calls in a brother doctor. Therein we differ. I shall take this matter in my own hands.'

'And where could you find better?' I said enthusiastically. 'I should say the cigar case is as good as recovered already.'

'I shall remind you of that again,' he said lightly. 'And now, to show you my confidence in your judgment, in spite of my determination to pursue this alone, I am willing to listen to any suggestions from you.'

He drew a memorandum book from his pocket, and, with a grave smile, took up his pencil.

I could scarcely believe my reason. He, the great Hemlock Jones! accepting suggestions from a humble individual like myself! I kissed his hand reverently, and began in a joyous tone:

'First I should advertise, offering a reward; I should give the same intimation in handbills, distributed at the "pubs" and the pastry-cooks. I should next visit the different pawnbrokers; I should give notice at the police station. I should examine the servants. I should thoroughly search the house and my own pockets. I speak relatively,' I added with a laugh, 'of course, I mean *your* own.'

He gravely made an entry of these details.

'Perhaps,' I added, 'you have already done this?'

'Perhaps,' he returned enigmatically. 'Now, my dear friend,' he continued, putting the note-book in his pocket, and rising – 'would you excuse me for a few moments? Make yourself perfectly at home until I return; there may be some things,' he added with a sweep of his hand towards his heterogeneously filled shelves, 'that may interest you, and while away the time. There are pipes and tobacco in that corner and whiskey on the table.' And nodding to me with the same inscrutable face, he left the room. I was too well accustomed to his methods to think much of his unceremonious withdrawal, and made no doubt he was off to investigate some clue which had suddenly occurred to his active intelligence.

Left to myself, I cast a cursory glance over his shelves. There were a number of small glass jars, containing earthy substances labelled 'Pavement and road sweepings,' from the principal thoroughfares and suburbs of London, with the sub-directions 'For identifying foot tracks.' There were several other jars labelled 'Fluff from omnibus and road-car seats,' 'Coconut fibre and rope strands from mattings in public places,' 'Cigarette stumps and match ends from floor of Palace Theatre, Row A, 1 to 50.' Everywhere were evidences of this wonderful man's system and perspicacity.

I was thus engaged when I heard the slight creaking of a door, and I looked up as a stranger entered. He was a rough-looking man, with a shabby overcoat, a still more disreputable muffler round his throat, and a cap on his head. Considerably annoyed at his intrusion I turned upon him rather sharply, when, with a mumbled, growling apology for mistaking the room, he shuffled out again and closed the door. I followed him quickly to the landing and saw that he disappeared down the stairs.

With my mind full of the robbery, the incident made a singular impression on me. I knew my friend's habits of hasty absences from his room in his moments of deep inspiration; it was only too probable that with his powerful intellect and magnificent perceptive genius concentrated on one subject, he should be careless of his own belongings, and, no doubt, even forget to take the ordinary precaution of locking up his drawers. I tried one or two and found that I was right – although for

A rough-looking man in a shabby overall entered

some reason I was unable to open one to its fullest extent. The handles were sticky, as if someone had opened them with dirty fingers. Knowing Hemlock's fastidious cleanliness, I resolved to inform him of this circumstance, but I forgot it, alas! until – but I am anticipating my story.

His absence was strangely prolonged. I at last seated myself by the fire, and lulled by warmth and the patter of the rain on the window, I fell asleep. I may have dreamt, for during my sleep I had a vague semi-consciousness as of hands being softly pressed on my pockets – no doubt induced by the story of the robbery. When I came fully to my senses, I found Hemlock Jones sitting on the other side of the hearth, his deeply concentrated gaze fixed on the fire.

'I found you so comfortably asleep that I could not bear to waken you,' he said with a smile.

I rubbed my eyes. 'And what news?' I asked. 'How have you succeeded?'

'Better than I expected,' he said, 'and I think,' he added, tapping his note-book 'I owe much to *you*.'

Deeply gratified, I awaited more. But in vain. I ought to have remembered that in his moods Hemlock Jones was reticence itself. I told him simply of the strange intrusion, but he only laughed.

Later, when I rose to go, he looked at me playfully. 'If you were a married man,' he said, 'I would advise you not to go home until you had brushed your sleeve. There are a few short, brown seal-skin hairs on the inner side of the forearm – just where they would have adhered if your arm had encircled a seal-skin sacque with some pressure!'

'For once you are at fault,' I said triumphantly, 'the hair is my own as you will perceive; I have just had it cut at the hairdressers, and no doubt this arm projected beyond the apron.'

He frowned slightly, yet nevertheless, on my turning to go he embraced me warmly – a rare exhibition in that man of ice. He even helped me on with my overcoat and pulled out and smoothed down the flaps of my pockets. He was particular, too, in fitting my arm in my overcoat sleeve, shaking the sleeve down from the armhole to the cuff with his deft fingers. 'Come again soon!' he said, clapping me on the back.

'At any and all times,' I said enthusiastically. 'I only ask ten minutes twice a day to eat a crust at my office and four hours' sleep at night, and the rest of my time is devoted to you always – as you know.'

'It is, indeed,' he said, with his impenetrable smile.

Nevertheless I did not find him at home when I next called. One afternoon, when nearing my own home, I met him in one of his favourite disguises – a long, blue, swallow-tailed coat, striped cotton trousers, large turn-over collar, blacked face, and white hat, carrying a tambourine. Of course to others the disguise was perfect, although it was known to myself, and I passed him – according to an old understanding between us – without the slightest recognition, trusting to a later explanation. At another time, as I was making a professional visit to the wife of a publican at the East End, I saw him in the disguise of a broken-down artisan looking into the window of an adjacent pawnshop. I was delighted to see that he was evidently following my suggestions, and in my joy I ventured to tip him a wink; it was abstractedly returned.

Two days later I received a note appointing a meeting at his lodgings that night. That meeting, alas! was the one memorable occurrence of my life, and the last meeting I ever had with Hemlock Jones! I will try to set it down calmly, though my pulses still throb with the recollection of it.

I found him standing before the fire with that look upon his face which I had seen only once or twice in our acquaintance – a look which I may call an absolute concatenation of inductive and deductive ratiocination – from which all that was human, tender, or sympathetic, was absolutely discharged. He was simply an icy, algebraic symbol! Indeed his whole being was concentrated to that extent that his clothes fitted loosely, and his head was absolutely so much reduced in size by his mental compression that his hat tipped back from his forehead and literally hung on his massive ears.

After I had entered, he locked the doors, fastened the windows, and even placed a chair before the chimney. As I watched those significant precautions with absorbing interest, he suddenly drew a revolver and presenting it to my temple, said in low, icy tones:

'Hand over that cigar-case!'

Even in my bewilderment, my reply was truthful, spontaneous, and involuntary. 'I haven't got it,' I said.

He smiled bitterly, and threw down his revolver. 'I expected that reply! Then let me now confront you with something more awful, more deadly, more relentless and convincing than that mere lethal weapon –

the damning inductive and deductive proofs of your guilt!' He drew from his pocket a roll of paper and a note-book.

'But surely,' I gasped, 'you are joking! You could not for a moment believe–'

'Silence!' he roared. 'Sit down!'

I obeyed.

'You have condemned yourself,' he went on pitilessly. 'Condemned yourself on my processes – processes familiar to you, applauded by you, accepted by you for years! We will go back to the time when you first saw the cigar-case. Your expressions,' he said in cold, deliberate tones, consulting his paper, 'were: "How beautiful! I wish it were mine." This was your first step in crime – and my first indication. From "I *wish* it were mine" to "I *will* have it mine," and the mere detail, "How *can* I make it mine," the advance was obvious. Silence! But as in my methods, it was necessary that there should be an overwhelming inducement to the crime, that unholy admiration of yours for the mere trinket itself was not enough. You are a smoker of cigars.'

'But,' I burst out passionately, 'I told you I had given up smoking cigars.'

'Fool!' he said coldly, 'that is the *second* time you have committed yourself. Of course, you *told* me! what more natural than for you to blazon forth that prepared and unsolicited statement to *prevent* accusation. Yet, as I said before, even that wretched attempt to cover up your tracks was not enough. I still had to find that overwhelming, impelling motive necessary to affect a man like you. That motive I found in *passion*, the strongest of all impulses – love, I suppose you would call it,' he added bitterly 'that night you called! You had brought the damning proofs of it in your sleeve.'

'But,' I almost screamed.

'Silence,' he thundered. 'I know what you would say. You would say that even if you had embraced some young person in a sealskin sacque, what had that to do with the robbery? Let me tell you then, that that sealskin sacque represented the quality and character of your fatal entanglement! If you are at all conversant with light sporting literature, you would know that a sealskin sacque indicates a love induced by sordid mercenary interests. You bartered your honour for it – that stolen cigar-case was the purchaser of the sealskin sacque! Without money, with a decreasing practice, it was the only way you could insure your passion being returned by that young person, whom, for your sake, I have not even pursued. Silence! Having thoroughly established your motive, I now proceed to the commission of the crime itself. Ordinary people would have begun with that – with an attempt to discover the whereabouts of the missing object. These are not my methods.'

So overpowering was his penetration, that although I knew myself innocent, I licked my lips with avidity to hear the further details of this lucid exposition of my crime.

'You committed that theft the night I showed you the cigar-case and after I had carelessly thrown it in that drawer. You were sitting in that chair, and I had risen to take something from that shelf. In that instant you secured your booty without rising. Silence! Do you remember when I helped you on with your overcoat the other night? I was particular about fitting your arm in. While doing so I measured your arm with a spring tape measure from the shoulder to the cuff. A later visit to your tailor confirmed that measurement. It proved to be *the exact distance between your chair and that drawer!*'

I sat stunned.

'The rest are mere corroborative details! You were again tampering with the drawer when I discovered you doing so. Do not start! The stranger that blundered into the room with the muffler on – was myself. More, I had placed a little soap on the drawer handles when I purposely left you alone. The soap was on your hand when I shook it at parting. I softly felt your pockets when you were asleep for further developments. I embraced you when you left – that I might feel if you had the cigar-case, or any other articles, hidden on your body. This confirmed me in the belief that you had already disposed of it in the manner and for the purpose I have shown you. As I still believed you capable of remorse and confession, I allowed you to see I was on your track twice, once in the garb of an itinerant negro minstrel, and the second time as a workman looking in the window of the pawnshop where you pledged your booty.'

'But,' I burst out, 'if you had asked the pawnbroker you would have seen how unjust–'

'Fool!' he hissed; 'that was one of *your* suggestions to search the pawnshops. Do you suppose I followed any of your suggestions – the suggestions of the thief? On the contrary, they told me what to avoid.'

'And I suppose,' I said bitterly, 'you have not even searched your drawer.'

'No,' he said calmly.

I was for the first time really vexed. I went to the nearest drawer and pulled it out sharply. It stuck as it had before, leaving a part of the drawer unopened. By working it, however, I discovered that it was impeded by some obstacle that had slipped to the upper part of the drawer, and held it firmly fast. Inserting my hand, I pulled out the impeding object. It was the missing cigar-case. I turned to him with a cry of joy.

But I was appalled at his expression. A look of contempt was now added to his acute, penetrating gaze. 'I have been mistaken,' he said slowly. 'I had not allowed for your weakness and cowardice. I thought too highly of you even in your guilt; but I see now why you tampered with that drawer the other night. By some incredible means – possibly another theft – you took the cigar-case out of pawn, and like a whipped hound restored it to me in this feeble, clumsy fashion. You thought to deceive me, Hemlock Jones: more, you thought to destroy my infallibility. Go! I give you your liberty. I shall not summon the three policemen who wait in the adjoining room – but out of my sight for ever.'

As I stood once more dazed and petrified, he took me firmly by the ear and led me into the hall, closing the door behind him. This re-opened presently wide enough to permit him to thrust out my hat, overcoat, umbrella and overshoes, and then close against me for ever!

I never saw him again. I am bound to say, however, that thereafter my business increased – I recovered much of my old practice – and a few of my patients recovered also. I became rich. I had a brougham and a house in the West End. But I often wondered, pondering on that wonderful man's penetration and insight, if, in some lapse of consciousness, I had not really stolen his cigar-case!

THE MYSTERIOUS MANSION
Honoré de Balzac

About a hundred yards from the town of Vendôme, on the borders of the Loire, there is an old grey house, surmounted by very high gables, and so completely isolated that neither tanyard nor shabby hostelry, such as you may find at the entrance to all small towns, exists in its immediate neighbourhood.

In front of this building, overlooking the river, is a garden, where the once well-trimmed box borders that used to define the walks now grow wild as they list. Several willows that spring from the Loire have grown as rapidly as the hedge that encloses it, and half conceal the house. The rich vegetation of those weeds that we call foul adorns the sloping shore. Fruit trees, neglected for the last ten years, no longer yield their harvest, and their shoots form coppices. The wall-fruit grows like hedges against the walls. Paths once gravelled are overgrown with moss, but, to tell the truth, there is no trace of a path. From the height of the hill, to which cling the ruins of the old castle of the Dukes of Vendôme, the only spot whence the eye can plunge into this enclosure, it strikes you that, at a time not easy to determine, this plot of land was the delight of a country gentleman, who cultivated roses and tulips and horticulture in general, and who was besides a lover of fine fruit. An arbor is still visible, or rather the débris of an arbor, where there is a table that time has not quite destroyed. The aspect of this garden of bygone days suggests the negative joys of peaceful, provincial life, as one might reconstruct the life of a worthy tradesman by reading the epitaph on his tombstone. As if to complete the sweetness and sadness of the ideas that possess one's soul, one of the walls displays a sun-dial decorated with the following commonplace Christian inscription: "Ultimam cogita!" The roof of this house is horribly dilapidated, the shutters are always closed, the balconies are covered with swallows' nests, the doors are perpetually shut, weeds have drawn green lines in the cracks of the flights of steps, the locks and bolts are rusty. Sun, moon, winter, summer, and snow have worn the panelling, warped the boards, gnawed the paint. The lugubrious silence which reigns there is only broken by birds, cats, martins, rats and mice, free to course to and fro, to fight and to eat each other. Everywhere an invisible hand has graven the word *mystery*.

Should your curiosity lead you to glance at this house from the side that points to the road, you would perceive a great door which the children of the place have riddled with holes. I afterward heard that this door had been closed for the last ten years. Through the holes broken by the boys you would have observed the perfect harmony that existed between the façades of both garden and courtyard. In both the same disorder prevails. Tufts of weed encircle the paving-stones. Enormous cracks furrow the walls, round whose blackened crests twine the thousand garlands of the pellitory. The steps are out of joint, the wire of the bell is rusted, the spouts are cracked. What fire from heaven has fallen here? What tribunal has decreed that salt should be strewn on this dwelling? Has God been blasphemed, has France been here betrayed? These are the questions we ask ourselves, but get no answer from the crawling things that haunt the place. The empty and deserted house is a gigantic enigma, of which the key is lost. In bygone times it was a small fief, and bears the name of the Grande Bretêche.

I inferred that I was not the only person to whom my good landlady had communicated the secret of which I was to be the sole recipient, and I prepared to listen.

'Sir,' she said, 'when the Emperor sent the Spanish prisoners of war and others here, the Government quartered on me a young Spaniard who had been sent to Vendôme on parole. Parole notwithstanding he went out every day to show himself to the sous-préfet. He was a Spanish grandee! Nothing less! His name ended in os and dia, something like Burgos de Férédia. I have his name on my books; you can read it if you like. Oh! but he was a handsome young man for a Spaniard; they are all said to be ugly. He was only five feet and a few inches high, but he was well-grown; he had small hands that he took such care of; ah! you should have seen! He had as many brushes for his hands as a woman for her whole dressing apparatus! He had thick black hair, a fiery eye, his skin was rather bronzed, but I liked the look of it. He wore the finest linen I have ever seen on any one, although I have had princesses staying here, and, among others, General Bertrand, the Duke and Duchess d'Abrantès, Monsieur Decazes, and the King of Spain. He didn't eat much; but his manners were so polite, so amiable, that one could not owe him a grudge. Oh! I was very fond of him, although he didn't open his lips four times in the day, and it was impossible to keep up a conversation with him. For if you spoke to him, he did not answer. It was a fad, a mania with them all, I heard say. He read his breviary like a priest, he went to Mass and to all the services regularly. Where did he sit? Two steps from the chapel of Madame de Merret. As he took his place there the first time he went to church, nobody suspected him of any intention in so doing. Besides, he never raised his eyes from his prayer-book, poor young man! After that, sir, in the evening he would walk on the mountains, among the castle ruins. It was the poor man's only amusement, it reminded him of his country. They say that Spain is all mountains! From the commencement of his imprisonment he stayed out late. I was anxious when I found that he did not come home before midnight; but we got accustomed to this fancy of his. He took the key of the door, and we left off sitting up for him. He lodged in a house of ours in the Rue des Casernes. After that, one of our stablemen told us that in the evening when he led the horses to the water, he thought he had seen the Spanish grandee swimming far down the river like a live fish. When he returned, I told him to take care of the rushes; he appeared vexed to have been seen in the water. At last, one day, or rather one morning, we did not find him in his room; he had not returned. After searching everywhere, I found some writing in the drawer of a table, where there were fifty gold pieces of Spain that are called doubloons and were worth about five thousand francs; and ten thousand francs' worth of diamonds in a small sealed box. The writing said, that in case he did not return, he left us the money and the diamonds, on condition of paying for Masses to thank God for his escape, and for his salvation. In those days my husband had not been taken from me; he hastened to seek him everywhere.

'And now for the strange part of the story. He brought home the Spaniard's clothes, that he had discovered under a big stone, in a sort of pilework by the river-side near the castle, nearly opposite to the Grande Bretêche. My husband had gone there so early that no one had seen him. After reading the letter, he burned the clothes, and according to Count Férédia's desire we declared that he had escaped. The sous-préfet sent all the gendarmerie in pursuit of him; but brust! they never caught him. Lepas believed that the Spaniard had drowned himself. I, sir, don't think so; I am more inclined to believe that he had something to do with the affair of Madame de Merret, seeing that Rosalie told me that the crucifix that her mistress thought so much of that she had it buried with her, was of ebony and silver. Now in the beginning of his stay here, Monsieur de Férédia had one in ebony and silver that I never saw him with later. Now, sir, don't you consider that I need have no scruples about the Spaniard's fifteen thousand francs, and that I have a right to them?'

'Certainly; but you haven't tried to question Rosalie?' I said.

'Oh, yes, indeed, sir; but to no purpose! the girl's like a wall. She knows something, but it is impossible to get her to talk.'

After exchanging a few more words with me, my landlady left me a prey to vague and gloomy thoughts, to a romantic curiosity, and a religious terror not unlike the profound impression produced on us when by night, on entering a dark church, we perceive a faint light under high arches; a vague figure glides by – the rustle of a robe or cassock is heard, and we shudder.

Suddenly the Grande Bretêche and its tall weeds, its barred windows, its rusty ironwork, its closed doors, its deserted apartments, appeared like a fantastic apparition before me. I essayed to penetrate the mysterious dwelling, and to find the knot of its dark story – the drama that had killed three persons. In my eyes Rosalie became the most interesting person in Vendôme. As I studied her, I discovered the traces of secret care, despite the radiant health that shone in her plump countenance.

There was in her the germ of remorse or hope; her attitude revealed a secret, like the attitude of a bigot who prays to excess, or of the infanticide who ever hears the last cry of her child. Yet her manners were rough and ingenious – her silly smile was not that of a criminal, and could you but have seen the great kerchief that encompassed her portly bust, framed and laced in by a lilac and blue cotton gown, you would have dubbed her innocent. No, I thought, I will not leave Vendôme without learning the history of the Grande Bretêche. To gain my ends I will strike up a friendship with Rosalie, if needs be.

'Rosalie,' said I, one evening.

'Sir?'

'You are not married?'

She started slightly.

'Oh, I can find plenty of men, when the fancy takes me to be made miserable,' she said, laughing.

She soon recovered from the effects of her emotion, for all women, from the great lady to the maid of the inn, possess a composure that is peculiar to them.

'You are too good-looking and well favoured to be short of lovers. But tell me, Rosalie, why did you take service in an inn after leaving Madame de Merret? Did she leave you nothing to live on?'

'Oh, yes! But, sir, my place is the best in all Vendôme.'

The reply was one of those that judges and lawyers would call evasive. Rosalie appeared to me to be situated in this romantic history like the square in the midst of a chessboard. She was at the heart of the truth and chief interest; she seemed to me to be bound in the very knot of it. The conquest of Rosalie was no longer to be an ordinary siege – in this girl was centred the last chapter of a novel, therefore from this moment Rosalie became the object of my preference.

One morning I said to Rosalie: 'Tell me all you know about Madame de Merret.'

'Oh!' she replied in terror, 'do not ask that of me, Monsieur Horace.'

Her pretty face fell – her clear, bright colour faded – and her eyes lost their innocent brightness.

'Well, then,' she said, at last, 'if you must have it so, I will tell you about it; but promise to keep my secret!'

'Done! my dear girl, I must keep your secret with the honour of a thief, which is the most loyal in the world.'

Were I to transcribe Rosalie's diffuse eloquence faithfully, an entire volume would scarcely contain it; so I shall abridge.

The room occupied by Madame de Merret at the Bretêche was on the ground floor. A little closet about four feet deep, built in the thickness of the wall, served as her wardrobe. Three months before the eventful evening of which I am about to speak, Madame de Merret had been so seriously indisposed that her husband had left her to herself in her own apartment, while he occupied another on the first floor. By one of those chances that it is impossible to foresee, he returned home from the club (where he was accustomed to read the papers and discuss politics with the inhabitants of the place) two hours later than usual. His wife supposed him to be at home, in bed and asleep. But the invasion of France had been the subject of a most animated discussion; the billiard-match had been exciting, he had lost forty francs, an enormous sum for Vendôme, where every one hoards, and where manners are restricted within the limits of a praiseworthy modesty, which perhaps is the source of the true happiness that no Parisian covets. For some time past Monsieur de Merret had been satisfied to ask Rosalie if his wife had gone to bed; and on her reply, which was always in the affirmative, had immediately gained his own room with the good temper engendered by habit and confidence. On entering his house, he took it into his head to go and tell his wife of his misadventure, perhaps by way of consolation. At dinner he found Madame de Merret most coquettishly attired. On his way to the club it had occurred to him that his wife was restored to health, and that her convalescence had added to her beauty. He was, as husbands are wont to be, somewhat slow in making this discovery. Instead of calling Rosalie, who was occupied just then in watching the cook and coachman play a difficult hand at brisque, Monsieur de Merret went to his wife's room by the light of a lantern that he deposited on the first step of the staircase. His unmistakable step resounded under the vaulted corridor. At the moment that the Count turned the handle of his wife's door, he fancied he could hear the door of the closet I spoke of close; but when he entered Madame de Merret was alone before the fireplace. The husband thought ingeniously that Rosalie was in the closet, yet a suspicion that jangled in his ear put him on his guard. He looked at his wife and saw in her eyes I know not what wild and hunted expression.

'You are very late,' she said. Her habitually pure, sweet voice seemed changed to him.

Monsieur de Merret did not reply, for at that moment Rosalie entered. It was a thunderbolt for him. He strode about the room, passing from one window to the other, with mechanical motion and folded arms.

'Have you heard bad news, or are you unwell?' inquired his wife timidly, while Rosalie undressed her.

He kept silent.

'You can leave me,' said Madame de Merret to her maid; 'I will put my hair in curl papers myself.'

From the expression of her husband's face she foresaw trouble, and wished to be alone with him. When Rosalie had gone, or was supposed to have gone (for she stayed in the corridor for a few minutes), Monsieur de Merret came and stood in front of his wife, and said coldly to her:

'Madame, there is someone in your closet!' She looked calmly at her husband and replied simply:

'No, sir.'

This answer was heartrending to Monsieur de Merret; he did not believe in it. Yet his wife had never appeared to him purer or more saintly than at that moment. He rose to open the closet door; Madame de Merret took his hand, looked at him with an expression of melancholy, and said in a voice that betrayed singular emotion:

'If you find no one there, remember this, all will be over between us!' The extraordinary dignity of his wife's manner restored the Count's profound esteem for her, and inspired him with one of those resolutions that only lack a vaster stage to become immortal.

'No,' said he, 'Josephine, I will not go there. In either case it would separate us for ever. Hear me, I know how pure you are at heart, and that your life is a holy one. You would not commit a mortal sin to save your life.'

At these words Madame de Merret turned a haggard gaze upon her husband.

'Here, take your crucifix,' he added. 'Swear to me before God that there is no one in there; I will believe you, I will never open that door.'

Madame de Merret took the crucifix and said:

'I swear.'

'Louder,' said the husband, 'and repeat "I swear before God that there is no one in that closet."'

She repeated the sentence calmly.

'That will do,' said Monsieur de Merret, coldly.

After a moment of silence:

'I never saw this pretty toy before,' he said, examining the ebony crucifix inlaid with silver, and most artistically chiseled.

'I found it at Duvivier's, who bought it off a Spanish monk when the prisoners passed through Vendôme last year.'

'Ah!' said Monsieur de Merret, as he replaced the crucifix on the nail, and he rang. Rosálie did not keep him waiting. Monsieur de Merret went quickly to meet her, led her to the bay window that opened on to the garden and whispered to her:

'Listen! I know that Gorenflot wishes to marry you, poverty is the only drawback, and you told him that you would be his wife if he found the means to establish himself as a master mason. Well! go and fetch him, tell him to come here with his trowel and tools. Manage not to awaken any one in his house but himself; his fortune will be more than your desires. Above all, leave this room without babbling, otherwise –' He frowned. Rosalie went away, he recalled her.

'Here, take my latchkey,' he said. 'Jean!' then cried Monsieur de Merret, in tones of thunder in the corridor. Jean, who was at the same time his coachman and his confidential servant, left his game of cards and came.

'Go to bed, all of you,' said his master, signing to him to approach; and the Count added, under his breath: 'When they are all asleep –*asleep*, d'ye hear? – you will come down and tell me.' Monsieur de Merret, who had not lost sight of his wife all the time he was giving his orders, returned quietly to her at the fireside and began to tell her of the game of billiards and the talk of the club. When Rosalie returned she found Monsieur and Madame de Merret conversing very amicably.

The Count had lately had all the ceilings of his reception rooms on the ground floor repaired. Plaster of Paris is difficult to obtain in Vendôme; the carriage raises its price. The Count had therefore bought a good deal, being well aware that he could find plenty of purchasers for whatever might remain over. This circumstance inspired him with the design he was about to execute.

'Sir, Gorenflot has arrived,' said Rosalie in low tones.

'Show him in,' replied the Count in loud tones.

Madame de Merret turned rather pale when she saw the mason.

'Gorenflot,' said her husband, 'go and fetch bricks from the coachhouse, and bring sufficient to wall up the door of this closet; you will use the plaster I have over to coat the wall with.' Then calling Rosalie and the workman aside:

'Listen, Gorenflot,' he said in an undertone, 'you will sleep here tonight. But tomorrow you will have a passport to a foreign country, to a town to which I will direct you. I shall give you six thousand francs for your journey. You will stay ten years in that town; if you do not like it, you may establish yourself in another, provided it be in the same country. You will pass through Paris, where you will await me. There I will insure you an additional six thousand francs by contract, which will be paid to you on your return, provided you have fulfilled the conditions of our bargain. This is the price for your absolute silence as to what you are about to do tonight. As to you, Rosalie, I will give you ten thousand francs on the day of your wedding, on condition of your marrying Gorenflot; but if you wish to marry, you must hold your tongues; or–no dowry.'

'Rosalie,' said Madame de Merret, 'do my hair.'

The husband walked calmly up and down, watching the door, the mason, and his wife, but without betraying any insulting doubts. Madame de Merret chose a moment when the workman was unloading bricks and her husband was at the other end of the room to say to Rosalie: 'A thousand francs a year for you, my child, if you can tell Gorenflot to leave a chink at the bottom.' Then out loud, she added coolly:

'Go and help him!'

Monsieur and Madame de Merret were silent all the time that Gorenflot took to brick up the door. This silence, on the part of the husband, who did not choose to furnish his wife with a pretext for saying things of a double meaning, had its purpose; on the part of Madame de Merret it was either pride or prudence. When the wall was about half-way up, the sly workman took advantage of a moment when the Count's back was turned, to strike a blow with his trowel in one of the glass panes of the closet-door. This act informed Madame de Merret that Rosalie had spoken to Gorenflot.

All three then saw a man's face; it was dark and gloomy with black hair and eyes of flame. Before her husband turned, the poor woman had time

All three saw the man's gloomy face

to make a sign to the stranger that signified: Hope!

At four o'clock, toward dawn, for it was the month of September, the construction was finished. The mason was handed over to the care of Jean, and Monsieur de Merret went to bed in his wife's room.

On rising the following morning, he said carelessly:

'The deuce! I must go to the Marie for the passport.' He put his hat on his head, advanced three steps toward the door, altered his mind and took the crucifix.

His wife trembled for joy. 'He is going to Duvivier,' she thought. As soon as the Count had left, Madame de Merret rang for Rosalie; then in a terrible voice:

'The trowel, the trowel!' she cried, 'and quick to work! I saw how Gorenflot did it; we shall have time to make a hole and to mend it again.'

In the twinkling of an eye, Rosalie brought a sort of mattock to her mistress, who with unparalleled ardor set about demolishing the wall. She had already knocked out several bricks and was preparing to strike a more decisive blow when she perceived Monsieur de Merret behind her. She fainted.

'Lay Madame on her bed,' said the Count coldly. He had foreseen what would happen in his absence and had set a trap for his wife; he had simply written to the mayor, and had sent for Duvivier. The jeweller arrived just as the room had been put in order.

'Duvivier,' inquired the Count, 'did you buy crucifixes off the Spaniards who passed through here?'

'No, sir.'

'That will do, thank you,' he said, looking at his wife like a tiger. 'Jean,' he added, 'you will see that my meals are served in the Countess's room; she is ill, and I shall not leave her until she has recovered.'

The cruel gentleman stayed with his wife for twenty days. In the beginning, when there were sounds in the walled closet, and Josephine attempted to implore his pity for the dying stranger, he replied, without permitting her to say a word:

'You have sworn on the cross that there is no one there.'

SWEETS FROM A STRANGER

Nicholas Fisk

First, the girl.

Tina Halliday, age eleven, almost black hair, waving at the ends. Brown eyes, tall for her age, quite pretty (but a nail-biter), good enough at most school subjects, very good at badminton (three trophies and, if she won tonight, possibly a fourth soon to come).

Next, the car. Black Jaguar saloon, recent model, fawn leather upholstery, paintwork shining in the drizzly evening light.

And last, the driver of the car.

No, but wait. We will meet him a little later.

*   *   *   *

The black Jaguar was being driven slowly and badly. It lurched along the suburban street seeming to catch its breath, sneeze, then accelerate to all of fifteen miles an hour—then slow again. It came to a corner and took it in bites and nibbles, uncertainly, inexpertly.

Tina saw the car. She thought, That driver could be drunk. She moved closer to a low brick wall with a hedge. If the worst came to the worst—if the driver lost control—she could easily hop over the wall and be safe.

The car slowed. Now it seemed to be aiming at her: following her. Tina gripped her badminton racket tightly. She felt the first flutter of fear. The street was deserted. She thought, That car is coming for *me*.

The car almost stopped, right beside her, grating one wheel rim against the curb. Panic jumped into Tina's throat. When the car's window slid down, she thought, Shall I run? But her knees and legs felt weak.

A high-pitched voice, a man's voice, came through the open window. 'Little girl! Little girl! Do you want a ride in my car?'

Very loudly and distinctly, Tina said, 'No! I do not!' She thought, I'll give him 'little girl' if he tries anything on. 'Badminton Builds Bionic Biceps,' she murmured, and tried to smile.

The voice said, 'But—but it's a nice car. Wouldn't you like a ride?'

Tina said—almost shouted, 'No! Go away!'

The panic was leaving her. A part of her mind was giggling. If only Mum could see this! A classic scene! The thing she had been warned against even when she was tiny! 'Bad Stranger Man trying to get Nice Little Girl into Big Wicked Car!' Next thing, he'd be offering her a sweetie . . .

The Jaguar wheezed as the driver over-revved the engine. It lurched and bumbled along beside her. The man inside—she could not see his face—said, 'Little girl! Wouldn't you like a sweetie? I've got some sweeties!'

At this, Tina began laughing. She laughed so much that she bent over in the middle. 'You're too much!' she choked. 'Really you are! Sweeties! A nice ride, and you've got some *sweeties*, too!'

The man said something that stopped her laughing. '*Please*,' he said. '*Please!*'

There was complete despair in his voice.

'Don't go away!' he said. She could see a sort of agony in the way his body stretched towards her. 'Don't go away! I don't *understand* anything . . . I don't know what to *do* . . .'

Tina, knowing she was behaving foolishly, went closer to the car, bent down and looked through the window. Even now she could not see the man. The instrument lights showed her only that he was small.

Nothing else.

'They told me girls and boys liked sweets,' the man said, hopelessly. 'Crystallized fruits . . .' His voice was high and husky. 'They told me all sorts of things, but nothing helps. If only *you* would help . . .'

Tina told herself: You must be mad!—and got into the car.

Now she could see the man's head. It was turned away from her, bowed. Small man, small head.

'I don't know,' the man said. He made a gesture, a defeated throwing-out of his arm and hand. Tina saw the hand.

It was like a claw. It had only three fingers. There was skin that was not skin. There was dark, glossy hairiness.

The panic came back—leapt into her throat—choked her, froze her, numbed her.

'Nothing's working, nothing's going right,' the man said, in his high, rustling, despairing voice. Tina could not speak. She could only look at the hand, the dreadful hand.

He must have seen the whites of her eyes or the terrified O of her mouth, for he snatched his hand away, produced a glove and clumsily put it on. The glove had five fingers, Tina thought, Two of them must be padded. Still she could not move or speak. She made a gasping sound.

'I'm an invader,' the man said, as if replying to her sound. 'An invader. Come to conquer you. But it's not working.'

Tina coughed and forced her voice to work. 'An invader?' she said.

'Invading Earth,' the man said, dully. 'Your planet.'

'Where do you come from?' Tina said.

'Out there.' He waved his gloved hand vaguely upwards. 'Not from a planet: our home planet was finished thousands of years ago. We made our own world. We're having trouble with it. Not enough fuel, not enough ores and minerals, not enough of anything. Your planet has the things we need, so we're invading . . . But I don't know, I don't know . . .'

I'm not dreaming, Tina thought, This is real. It is happening. Escape! Run away! But she did not want to go.

'Look,' the man said. 'All I want to do is to stop being an invader. To go home. They told me things—told me what to do, what to say—but nothing fits, nothing goes right.'

'I don't see how I can help,' Tina said. 'I mean, what can *I* do?'

'Take me to a telephone. Get me a number, a particular number, I have it here—'

'But there's a telephone box just down the road, you passed it—'

'I couldn't make it work. They told me to use it, they told me how to use it; I did everything right, but it wouldn't work.'

'Come with me,' Tina said. Now she was no longer frightened, just very curious. 'Get out of the car. No, you must switch off the engine—that's right. And don't leave the keys in. Stop shaking, there's nothing to be afraid of. No, get out *your* side, there's no need to climb over the seats. Now close the door. Try again. Give it a good slam. Good. Take my arm. Come on.'

They reached the telephone box. The man walked as if his legs made him uneasy. He shook and trembled. Tina had to hold him up. He was not as tall as she.

The telephone would not work. 'Out of order,' Tina said, with a shrug.

'What does that mean?' the man said.

'Only that it doesn't work.'

'They never told us about "Out of Order",' the man said, dully.

'Wait a second!' Tina saw there was a coin jammed in the little slot. She managed to force the jammed coin in. Now the telephone worked. She dialled the number the man gave her. A high-pitched voice answered. The man took the handset—he held it the wrong way round at first—and spoke.

'Mission completed,' he said. Then, 'What? Oh. Oh. Well, I *can't* complete it any more than I *have* completed it, I can't go on *any longer* . . . What? No, no, I don't care, it's no good telling me that. Completed or uncompleted, I'm going home.'

He put the receiver back on the hook, sighed, and said, 'Well, I'm not the only one. Several others have failed too and *they're* going home.'

Now Tina could see his face, for the first time, by the light of a street lamp. It was a horrible face, a waxwork mask—a face no more human than one of those plastic, jointed dolls. Though the mouth had lips, it was really only a movable hole. The skin—but it was not skin—was too tight over the cheek-bones, too loose at the ears. And the ears were waxen, unreal. The hair began and ended too sharply. It did not grow from the scalp; it was fitted to it. A wig.

She shuddered. '*Why*?' she demanded. 'Why did they dress you up like this? I mean, if you're an invader, why couldn't you look like an invader?—someone frightening and threatening and, what's the word, indomitable? You're just a—a mess. I'm sorry, but you are.'

'They—my masters—wanted us to be friendly invaders,' the man explained. 'Not monsters: people like yourselves. People who use telephones and drive cars and wear clothes. But it went wrong, of course. Everything's gone wrong.'

'What are you really like?' Tina said.

The man shifted uneasily. 'Probably you'd think us hideous,' he said. 'You might hate us if you saw us as we really are.'

'But you don't think *me* hideous?' Tina said, smiling. She knew she had a nice smile. Her smile faded as she saw the man's eyes (too big to fit the false eyelids) change, grow cautious and look away.

'Well . . .' he said. 'Well . . .'

'You *do* think me hideous? Tina said, amazed.

'You're so different, that's what it is. So very different from us. Your eyes are so small and pale, and your skin so white, and your hair grows in the wrong places—'

'I see,' Tina said, pursing her lips.

'I hope I haven't given offence?'

'Not at all. Do go on,' she said, stiffly.

'Different,' the man said. 'Things are so different where I come from! Perhaps a bit better. A lot better in some ways.' He began to speak enthusiastically. 'We don't need to use telephones when we want to speak to each other: we just tune into minds. We don't need these complicated great machines, these cars, to travel in. We don't cover ourselves with layers of fabric to keep the weather out—'

'You go naked, I suppose?' Tina said, acidly.

'Well, we don't find it necessary to wrap ourselves in coloured rags! But perhaps you do it because you'd be so ugly if you didn't—Oh, I beg your pardon—'

'Don't mind *me*,' Tina said, coldly. 'A pity, though, that you can't seem to cope in your superior world! Pity you have to go round invading people! Or,' she added spitefully, '*attempting* to invade them!'

'Our world must survive,' the man said quietly. 'It's a beautiful and wonderful world. It must be saved!'

Tina said, 'Hmm.'

'The most beautiful! The most wonderful!' the man insisted. 'If only you could see it for yourself! Then you'd understand!'

'I'm sure you're right,' Tina said, distantly. She looked at her watch. 'Lord! I'm late! I must go! The time!'

'On our world, we control time,' the man told her. 'We always have time . . .' A thought struck him. 'Come with me! See my world! Don't worry about time—stay as long as you like and I promise you'll be back here only a minute or so from now! Come with me!'

His dark eyes blazed at her from the mask of his face. The mask was stupid: the eyes were not.

For the second time Tina told herself: You must be mad! Out loud, she said, 'All right, then. Show me your world.'

She felt herself twisted, racked, stretched, flung apart and thought, This is the journey, then.

'This is my face,' he said. The mock-human mask was gone. Huge, dark, liquid eyes looked at her from the furred face—the face of a cat, but not a cat, not a seal, not an otter, not any Earth animal. She saw the neat, flowing body, covered in dense fur, dark grey and tipped with silver. She saw the high forehead, the mobile mouth (He's smiling! she thought, So that's how they look when they smile!). No tail. Useful three-fingered hands. A mobile, businesslike thumb.

'There is my world,' he said. Through the glassy bubble of nothingness that separated them from the stars, a world gleamed and glittered in the blackness, coming closer and closer impossibly fast—a huge, complicated globe, jewelled with a million tiny lights, sprinkled with clouds—

'Shana,' he said. 'That is Shana. I am a Shanad. In the heart of the world, there is a city called Ro-yil. Can you say those words?'

She found that she could. Her mouth spoke them for her in a tongue her brain did not know. She tried out this new gift. 'What is your name?'

'Talis,' he said.

'Rhymes with Palace,' Tina said, vaguely. There was so much to look at, the glittering world was rushing at them—

'There,' said Talis. 'We have landed. Get out. I will show you the city first.'

He hurried her to the edge of a vast square shaft, took her hand, and made her fall, endlessly, through a tunnel of lights and textures, fleeting shapes and sounds. She wanted to scream; but Talis's calm face was beside her, his hand held hers, his voice spoke to her.

They seemed to meet some sort of invisible cushion. The sensation was like that of being in a lift, slowing violently.

And then they were in the city of Ro-yil.

The city hung, a sphere within a sphere, from glistening filaments, pulsing with light. ('They are avenues,' Talis explained, matter-of-factly, 'rather like the one we are standing in.') Towers soared, glassy and magnificent. Plants taller than Earth trees sang softly. There were Shanads everywhere, many in glassy bubbles like that which had carried Tina and Talis from Earth. The bubbles seemed to move instantly from place to place. 'Hoverflies . . . fireflies,' Tina murmured.

'What?' Talis said.

'Beautiful,' she replied. 'Wonderful, beautiful, magnificent . . .!'

A crystal bubble drifted by. It was empty. 'Tsa!' said Talis; the bubble stopped by them. 'Ata-al!' he said and the side of the bubble split open. 'Get in,' he said. 'I'll take you to my home.'

Tina memorized the words and tried to understand how Talis drove the bubble. There was no time. The city hurtled for a split-second, then gently slowed. Tina gasped. Talis smiled. 'You like my city, then?' His voice had changed. Now it was confident, laughing, sure.

Tina could only reply, 'Marvellous!' Then, 'This bubble,' she said, 'it's the same as the one that brought us here, isn't it?'

'The same. It can take you anywhere! Anywhere in the universe! But who would want to leave *this*?' He swept his arm at the jewelled city, the crystalline towers of pearl and jet, aquamarine and turquoise, strung together with luminous silver threads . . .

'Home,' he said. 'Come.'

A door opened in a glassy golden wall.

She entered and saw humans.

The door closed and Talis was gone.

There were perhaps twenty of them. The room was not big enough.

They stared at her, silently. Then a raggedly dressed woman with a tired face came to Tina and said, 'Oh dear. Poor you. And so young.'

'But Talis said—Talis promised—'

'Oh, I dare say he did. I dare say he told you he can control time and all that . . . And you fell for it. Felt sorry for him, didn't you? Felt you had to help? Those big dark eyes of theirs . . . And you fell for it. So did I, years ago. I was a District Nurse. Do you know Hove? And Brighton—? That was where I was—'

A young man, his clothes falling to pieces, snorted, 'Never mind about Hove and Brighton. We've had enough of them.' He turned his back on the District Nurse and said, 'What's your name, then? Tina? Tina. You're right in it now. Up to the neck. Like the rest of us. There's lots of us, you know. Not just this room: the whole building.' He shrugged despairingly. To the District Nurse he said, 'You explain to her.'

'You're a hostage, dear,' the woman said. 'At least, that's the way we work it out. I mean, they want to invade Earth, but they can't. You see, they want metals and minerals and I-don't-know-what from Earth; but their weapons won't work *without* the metals and minerals and I-don't-know-whats. So they're stuck, aren't they?'

'What do you mean, hostages?' Tina said. Another man joined the group and answered. 'They're going to use us instead of weapons,' he said. 'They'll tell Earth they've got us. If Earth won't give them the things they want, they'll threaten to kill us, you see? They'll *barter* us! When they've got enough of us.'

Tina said, 'But—but they can't! I've got to go home!'

The young man told Tina, 'Cheer up, you're not dead yet. No good crying.'

Tina swallowed her sobs and said, 'How long have you been here?'

'He's been here longest,' the nurse said, pointing to a man huddled in a corner. 'Seven years. Old misery, he is. You won't get anything out of him. Given up speaking to anyone years ago.'

'Why don't you escape?' Tina said.

'Might be difficult, don't you think?' the young man said, cynically. 'I mean, we don't *look* much like them, do we? We'd be a bit *noticeable* outside, wouldn't we? Anyhow, if you think you can get out, have a go. Ah, food!'

A door in the wall opened: a gleaming box slid in. Immediately everyone—even the crouched man—came to life. They grabbed and gobbled, crammed their mouths, bargained noisily over swaps.

Tina thought, You're a shabby lot. She ate the food. It looked strange but tasted good. The things that looked like crystallized fruits were best of all. She saved some, hiding them in her pocket. She thought, They've given in; I won't. I'll learn everything I can, and hoard food and wait for the right moment: then I'll escape . . .

Nobody showed much interest when, three days later, Tina emptied the food box, climbed into it, and escaped the room.

Now she was at large in the city. The Shanad words she had learned from Talis were still in her mind. She had practised them and knew them well. But that was about all she knew.

Soon, she did not even know what she had hoped to gain by escaping. The Shanads thronging the city of Ro-yil neither helped nor hindered her. No sirens screamed, no vehicles dashed, no hard-faced law-enforcers pounced. The Shanads (to Tina, they all looked the same) ignored her. Their large, dark, intelligent eyes looked at her—then, deliberately, looked away.

'A bubble . . .' she said to herself. 'That's what I must have.' A bubble drifted beside her. 'Tsa!' she said. 'Ata-al!' She sat in the bubble, trying to find a knob or a lever or anything at all that would make it go. She failed. Shanads passed by, not looking or caring. She began to cry. She got out of the bubble and walked blindly, endlessly, through the gorgeous city.

She reached the shafts by accident. One shaft had brought her down from the surface of the world to the city; now she saw a twin shaft. Shanads walked into its entrance and went up. Up to the surface! 'One step nearer home,' Tina said, entered the shaft, and flew to the surface.

She found herself looking at white clouds in a green sky. Beyond, she saw darkness and in the darkness, stars and planets. 'One of you is Earth,' she said. She looked for a bubble. This time, she would not give up. This time, she would go home.

She saw a bubble. It was stationary. In front of it, two furry little things, charming, fat and jolly, rolled on the ground. They were smaller than Shanads, much smaller—

'Ah!' said Tina. '*Children!*'

'Tsa!' she hissed; and got into the bubble. The child Shanads rolled and squeaked, pounced and wrestled, outside. 'Ata-al!' she said. The magic word once again failed to have any effect. She knocked on the wall of the bubble to attract the children's attention. They looked up at her. Their eyes were beautiful.

Tina said—her mind and voice struggling for the words, 'I'm a friend. I need your help. I'm a friend! Help me!'

The children stared. One made a gurgling noise that must have been giggling.

'Look,' Tina said, 'I've got this lovely bubble, but I can't seem to work it. Wouldn't you like to show me how to work it?'

Both children giggled. Neither moved.

'Look, suppose you get in with me, and show me what to do, then we can go for a ride!'

The Shanad children linked paws and stared at her, still giggling.

Tina remembered the crystallized fruits in her pocket. 'I'll give you these!' she cried. 'One for each of you! *Two* each!'

And suddenly the Shanad children were running away, running very fast. They ran until they reached an adult Shanad, then stopped and pointed at Tina. She could hear what they were saying.

'. . . wanted to take us for a *ride*!' one said.

'In a nice bubble!' said the other.

'Offered us *sweets*!' said the first. 'Us! As if we'd take sweets from strangers!'

They pointed their fingers and giggled, loudly and scornfully. They jumped up and down, delighted with themselves.

And then Talis was there, with many other Shanads.

They took Tina back to the room.

* * * *

One day, perhaps, the Shanads will make contact with Earth. Until then, Tina will at least be fed. The things that look like crystallized fruits are delicious, at first.

Later, you grow tired of them.

THE HITCH-HIKER

Roald Dahl

I had a new car. It was an exciting toy, a big B.M.W. 3.3 Li, which means 3.3 litre, long wheelbase, fuel injection. It had a top speed of 129 m.p.h. and terrific acceleration. The body was pale blue. The seats inside were darker blue and they were made of leather, genuine soft leather of the finest quality. The windows were electrically operated and so was the sun-roof. The radio aerial popped up when I switched on the radio, and disappeared when I switched it off. The powerful engine growled and grunted impatiently at slow speeds, but at sixty miles an hour the growling stopped and the motor began to purr with pleasure.

I was driving up to London by myself. It was a lovely June day. They were haymaking in the fields and there were buttercups along both sides of the road. I was whispering along at seventy miles an hour, leaning back comfortably in my seat, with no more than a couple of fingers resting lightly on the wheel to keep her steady. Ahead of me I saw a man thumbing a lift. I touched the footbrake and brought the car to a stop beside him. I always stopped for hitch-hikers. I knew just how it used to feel to be standing on the side of a country road watching the cars go by. I hated the drivers for pretending they didn't see me, especially the ones in big cars with three empty seats. The large expensive cars seldom stopped. It was always the smaller ones that offered you a lift, or the old rusty ones, or the ones that were already crammed full of children and the driver would say 'I think we can squeeze in one more.'

The hitch-hiker poked his head through the open window and said, 'Going to London, guv'nor?'

'Yes,' I said, 'Jump in.'

He got in and I drove on.

He was a small ratty-faced man with grey teeth. His eyes were dark and quick and clever, like a rat's eyes, and his ears were slightly pointed at the top. He had a cloth cap on his head and he was wearing a greyish-coloured jacket with enormous pockets. The grey jacket, together with the quick eyes and the pointed ears, made him look more than anything like some sort of a huge human rat.

'What part of London are you headed for?' I asked him.

'I'm goin' right through London and out the other side,' he said. 'I'm goin' to Epsom, for the races. It's Derby Day today.'

'So it is,' I said. 'I wish I were going with you. I love betting on horses.'

'I never bet on horses,' he said. 'I don't even watch 'em run. That's a stupid silly business.

'Then why do you go?' I asked.

He didn't seem to like that question. His little ratty face went absolutely blank and he sat there staring straight ahead at the road, saying nothing.

'I expect you help to work the betting machines or something like that,' I said.

'That's even sillier,' he answered. 'There's no fun working them lousy machines and selling tickets to mugs. Any fool could do that.'

There was a long silence. I decided not to question him any more. I remembered how irritated I used to get in my hitch-hiking days when drivers kept asking *me* questions. Where are you going? Why are you going there? What's your job? Are you married? Do you have a girl-friend? What's her name? How old are you? And so on and so forth. I used to hate it.

'I'm sorry,' I said. 'It's none of my business what you do. The trouble is, I'm a writer, and most writers are terrible nosey parkers.'

white Land-Rover, a huge truck with a container on the back, an orange-coloured Volkswagen Minibus . . .

'A hundred and twenty!' my passenger shouted, jumping up and down. 'Go on! Go on! Get 'er up to one-two-nine!'

At that moment, I heard the scream of a police siren. It was so loud it seemed to be right inside the car, and then a policeman on a motor-cycle loomed up alongside us on the inside lane and went past us and raised a hand for us to stop.

'Oh, my sainted aunt!' I said. 'That's torn it!'

The policeman must have been doing about a hundred and thirty when he passed us, and he took plenty of time slowing down. Finally, he pulled into the side of the road and I pulled in behind him. 'I didn't know police motor-cycles could go as fast as that,' I said rather lamely.

'That one can,' my passenger said, 'It's the same make as yours. It's a B.M.W. R90S. Fastest bike on the road. That's what they're usin' nowadays.'

The policeman got off his motor-cycle and leaned the machine sideways on to its prop stand. Then he took off his gloves and placed them carefully on the seat. He was in no hurry now. He had us where he wanted us and he knew it.

'This is real trouble,' I said. 'I don't like it one bit.'

'Don't talk to 'im any more than is necessary, you understand,' my companion said. 'Just sit tight and keep mum.'

Like an executioner approaching his victim, the policeman came strolling slowly towards us. He was a big meaty man with a belly, and his blue breeches were skintight around his enormous thighs. His goggles were pulled up on the helmet, showing a smouldering red face with wide cheeks.

We sat there like guilty schoolboys, waiting for him to arrive.

'Watch out for this man,' my passenger whispered. 'Ee looks mean as the devil.'

The policeman came round to my open window and placed one meaty hand on the sill. 'What's the hurry?' he said.

'No hurry, officer,' I answered.

'Perhaps there's a woman in the back having a baby and you're rushing her to hospital? Is that it?'

'No, officer.'

'You write books?' he asked.

'Yes.'

'Writin' books is okay,' he said. 'It's what I call a skilled trade. I'm in a skilled trade too. The folks I despise is them that spend all their lives doin' crummy old routine jobs with no skill in 'em at all. You see what I mean?'

'Yes.'

'The secret of life,' he said, 'is to become very very good at somethin' that's very very 'ard to do.'

'Like you,' I said.

'Exactly. You and me both.'

'What makes you think that *I'm* any good at my job?' I asked. 'There's an awful lot of bad writers around.'

'You wouldn't be drivin' about in a car like this if you weren't no good at it,' he answered. 'It must've cost a tidy packet, this little job.'

'It wasn't cheap.'

'What can she do flat out?' he asked.

'One hundred and twenty-nine miles an hour,' I told him.

'I'll bet she won't do it.'

'I bet she will.'

'All car makers is liars,' he said. 'You can buy any car you like and it'll never do what the makers say it will in the ads.'

'This one will.'

'Open 'er up then and prove it,' he said. 'Go on, guv'nor, open 'er right up and let's see what she'll do.'

There is a roundabout at Chalfont St Peter and immediately beyond it there's a long straight section of dual cariageway. We came out of the roundabout on to the carriageway and I pressed my foot down on the accelerator. The big car leaped forward as though she'd been stung. In ten seconds or so, we were doing ninety.

'Lovely!' he cried. 'Beautiful! Keep goin'!'

I had the accelerator jammed right down against the floor and I held it there.

'One hundred!' he shouted . . . 'A hundred and five! . . . A hundred and ten! . . . A hundred and fifteen! Go on! Don't slack off!'

I was in the outside lane and we flashed past several cars as though they were standing still—a green Mini, a big cream-coloured Citroën, a

'Or perhaps your house is on fire and you're dashing home to rescue the family from upstairs?' His voice was dangerously soft and mocking.

'My house isn't on fire, officer.'

'In that case,' he said, 'you've got yourself into a nasty mess, haven't you? Do you know what the speed limit is in this country?'

'Seventy,' I said.

'And do you mind telling me exactly what speed you were doing just now?'

I shrugged and didn't say anything.

When he spoke next, he raised his voice so loud that I jumped. '*One hundred and twenty miles per hour!*' he barked. 'That's *fifty* miles an hour over the limit!'

He turned his head and spat out a big gob of spit. It landed on the wing of my car and started sliding down over my beautiful blue paint. Then he turned back again and stared hard at my passenger. 'And who are you?' he asked sharply.

'He's a hitch-hiker,' I said. 'I'm giving him a lift.'

'I didn't ask you,' he said. 'I asked him.'

''Ave I done somethin' wrong?' my passenger asked. His voice was as soft and oily as haircream.

'That's more than likely,' the policeman answered. 'Anyway, you're a witness. I'll deal with you in a minute. Driving-licence,' he snapped, holding out his hand.

I gave him my driving-licence.

He unbuttoned the left-hand breast-pocket of his tunic and brought out the dreaded books of tickets. Carefully, he copied the name and address from my licence. Then he gave it back to me. He strolled round to the front of the car and read the number from the number-plate and wrote that down as well. He filled in the date, the time and the details of my offence. Then he tore out the top copy of the ticket. But before handing it to me, he checked that all the information had come through clearly on his own carbon copy. Finally, he replaced the book in his tunic pocket and fastened the button.

'Now you,' he said to my passenger, and he walked around to the other side of the car. From the other breast-pocket he produced a small black notebook. 'Name?' he snapped.

'Michael Fish,' my passenger said.

'Address?'

'Fourteen, Windsor Lane, Luton.'

'Show me something to prove this is your real name and address,' the policeman said.

My passenger fished in his pockets and came out with a driving-licence of his own. The policeman checked the name and address and handed it back to him. 'What's your job?' he asked sharply.

'I'm an 'od carrier.'

'A *what*?'

'An 'od carrier.'

'Spell it.'

'H-O-D-C-A- . . .'

'That'll do. And what's a hod carrier, may I ask?'

'An 'od carrier, officer, is a person 'oo carries the cement up the ladder to the bricklayer. And the 'od is what 'ee carries it in. It's got a long 'andle, and on the top you've got two bits of wood set at an angle . . .'

'All right, all right. Who's your employer?'

'Don't 'ave one. I'm unemployed.'

The policeman wrote all this down in the black notebook. Then he returned the book to its pocket and did up the button.

'When I get back to the station I'm going to do a little checking up on you,' he said to my passenger.

'Me? What've I done wrong?' the rat-faced man asked.

'I don't like your face, that's all,' the policeman said. 'And we just might have a picture of it somewhere in our files.' He strolled round the car and returned to my window.

'I suppose you know you're in serious trouble,' he said to me.

'Yes, officer.'

'You won't be driving this fancy car of yours again for a very long time, not after *we've* finished with you. You won't be driving *any* car again come to that for several years. And a good thing, too. I hope they lock you up for a spell into the bargain.'

'You mean prison?' I asked, alarmed.

'Absolutely,' he said, smacking his lips. 'In the clink. Behind bars. Along with all the other criminals who break the law. *And* a hefty fine into the bargain. Nobody will be more pleased about that than me. I'll see you in court, both of you. You'll be getting a summons to appear.'

He turned and walked over to his motor-cycle. He flipped the prop stand back into position with his foot and swung his leg over the saddle. Then he kicked the starter and roared off up the road out of sight.

'Phew!' I gasped. 'That's done it.'

'We was caught,' my passenger said. 'We was caught good and proper.'

'I was caught, you mean.'

'That's right,' he said. 'What you goin' to do now, guv'nor?'

'I'm going straight up to London to talk to my solicitor,' I said. I started the car and drove on.

'You mustn't believe what 'ee said to you about goin' to prison,' my passenger said. 'They don't put nobody in the clink just for speedin'.'

'Are you sure of that?' I asked.

'I'm positive,' he answered. 'They can take your licence away and they can give you a whoopin' big fine, but that'll be the end of it.'

I felt tremendously relieved.

'By the way,' I said, 'why did you lie to him?'

'Who, me?' he said. 'What makes you think I lied?'

'You told him you were an unemployed hod carrier. But you told *me* you were in a highly-skilled trade.'

'So I am,' he said. 'But it don't pay to tell everythin' to a copper.'

'So what *do* you do?' I asked him.

'Ah,' he said slyly. 'That'd be tellin', wouldn't it?'

'Is it something you're ashamed of?'

'Ashamed?' he cried. 'Me, ashamed of my job? I'm about as proud of it as anybody could be in the entire world!'

'Then why won't you tell me?'

'You writers really is nosey parkers, aren't you?' he said. 'And you ain't goin' to be 'appy, I don't think, until you've found out exactly what the answer is?'

'I don't really care one way or the other,' I told him, lying.

He gave me a craftly little ratty look out of the sides of his eyes. 'I think you do care,' he said. 'I can see it in your face that you think I'm in some kind of a very peculiar trade and you're just achin' to know what it is.'

I didn't like the way he read my thoughts. I kept quiet and stared at the road ahead.

'You'd be right, too,' he went on. 'I *am* in a very peculiar trade. I'm in the queerest peculiar trade of 'em all.'

I waited for him to go on.

'That's why I 'as to be extra careful 'oo I'm talkin' to, you see. 'Ow am I to know, for instance, you're not another copper in plain clothes?'

'Do I look like a copper?'

'No,' he said. 'You don't. And you ain't. Any fool could tell that.'

He took from his pocket a tin of tobacco and a packet of cigarette papers and started to roll a cigarette. I was watching him out of the corner of one eye, and the speed with which he performed this rather difficult operation was incredible. The cigarette was rolled and ready in about five seconds. He ran his tongue along the edge of the paper, stuck it down and popped the cigarette between his lips. Then, as if from nowhere, a lighter appeared in his hand. The lighter flamed. The cigarette was lit. The lighter disappeared. It was altogether a remarkable performance.

'I've never seen anyone roll a cigarette as fast as that,' I said.

'Ah,' he said, taking a deep suck of smoke. 'So you noticed.'

'Of course I noticed. It was quite fantastic.'

He sat back and smiled. It pleased him very much that I had noticed how quickly he could roll a cigarette. 'You want to know what makes me able to do it?' he asked.

'Go on then.'

'It's because I've got fantastic fingers. These fingers of mine,' he said, holding up both hands high in front of him, 'are quicker and cleverer than the fingers of the best piano player in the world!'

'Are you a piano player?'

'Don't be daft,' he said. 'Do I look like a piano player?'

I glanced at his fingers. They were so beautifully shaped, so slim and long and elegant, they didn't seem to belong to the rest of him at all. They looked more like the fingers of a brain surgeon or a watchmaker.

'My job,' he went on, 'is a hundred times more difficult than playin' the piano. Any twerp can learn to do that. There's titchy little kids learnin' to play the piano in almost any 'ouse you go into these days. That' right, ain't it?'

'More or less,' I said.

'Of course it's right. But there's not one person in ten million can learn to do what I do. Not one in ten million! 'Ow about that?'

'Amazing,' I said.

'You're darn right it's amazin',' he said.

'I think I know what you do,' I said. 'You do conjuring tricks. You're a conjurer.'

'Me?' he snorted. 'A conjurer? Can you picture me goin' round crummy kids' parties makin' rabbits come out of top 'ats?'

'Then you're a card player. You get people into card games and deal yourself marvellous hands.'

'Me! A rotten card-sharper!' he cried. 'That's a miserable racket if ever there was one.'

'All right. I give up.'

I was taking the car along slowly now, at no more than forty miles an hour, to make quite sure I wasn't stopped again. We had come on to the main London–Oxford road and were running down the hill towards Denham.

Suddenly, my passenger was holding up a black leather belt in his hand. 'Ever seen this before?' he asked. The belt had a brass buckle of unusual design.

'Hey!' I said. 'That's mine, isn't it?' It *is* mine! Where did you get it?'

He grinned and waved the belt gently from side to side. 'Where d'you think I got it?' he said. 'Off the top of your trousers, of course.'

I reached down and felt for my belt. It was gone.

'You mean you took it off me while we've been driving along?' I asked, flabbergasted.

He nodded, watching me all the time with those little black ratty eyes.

'That's impossible,' I said. 'You'd have to undo the buckle and slide the whole thing out through the loops all the way round. I'd have seen you doing it. And even if I hadn't seen you, I'd have felt it.'

'Ah, but you didn't, did you?' he said, triumphant. He dropped the belt on his lap, and now all at once there was a brown shoelace dangling from his fingers. 'And what about this, then?' he exclaimed, waving the shoelace.

'What about it?' I said.

'Anyone round 'ere missin' a shoelace?' he asked, grinning.

I glanced down at my shoes. The lace of one of them was missing.

'Good grief!' I said. 'How did you do that? I never saw you bending down.'

'You never saw nothin',' he said proudly. 'You never even saw me move an inch. And you know why?'

'Yes,' I said. 'Because you've got fantastic fingers.'

'Exactly right!' he cried. 'You catch on pretty quick, don't you?' He sat back and sucked away at his home-made cigarette, blowing the smoke out in a thin stream against the windshield. He knew he had impressed me greatly with those two tricks, and this made him very happy. 'I don' want to be late,' he said. 'What time is it?'

'There's a clock in front of you,' I told him.

'I don't trust car clocks,' he said. 'What does your watch say?'

I hitched up my sleeve to look at the watch on my wrist. It wasn't there. I looked at the man. He looked back at me, grinning.

'You've taken that, too,' I said.

He held out his hand and there was my watch lying in his palm. 'Nice bit of stuff, this,' he said. 'Superior quality. Eighteen-carat gold. Easy to flog, too. It's never any trouble gettin' rid of quality goods.'

'I'd like it back, if you don't mind,' I said rather huffily.

He placed the watch carefully on the leather tray in front of him. 'I wouldn't nick anything from you, guv'nor,' he said. 'You're my pal. You're giving me a lift.'

'I'm glad to hear it,' I said.

'All I'm doin' is answerin' your questions,' he went on. 'You asked me what I did for a livin' and I'm showin' you.'

'What else have you got of mine?'

He smiled again, and now he started to take from the pocket of his jacket one thing after another that belonged to me—my driving licence, a key-ring with four keys on it, some pound notes, a few coins, a letter from my publishers, my diary, a stubby old pencil, a cigarette-lighter, and last of all, a beautiful old sapphire ring with pearls around it belonging to my wife. I was taking the ring up to the jeweller in London because one of the pearls was missing.

'Now *there's* another lovely piece of goods,' he said, turning the ring over in his fingers. 'That's eighteenth century, if I'm not mistaken, from the reign of King George the Third.'

'You're right,' I said, impressed. 'You're absolutely right.'

He put the ring on the leather tray with the other items.

'So you're a pickpocket,' I said.

'I don't like that word,' he answered. 'It's a coarse and vulgar word. Pickpockets is coarse and vulgar people who only do easy little amateur jobs. They lift money from blind old ladies.'

'What do you call yourself, then?'

'Me? I'm a fingersmith. I'm a professional fingersmith.' He spoke the words solemnly and proudly, as though he were telling me he was the President of the Royal College of Surgeons or the Archbishop of Canterbury.

'I've never heard that word before,' I said. 'Did you invent it?'

'Of course I didn't invent it,' he replied. 'It's the name given to them who's risen to the very top of the profession. You've 'eard of a goldsmith and a silversmith, for instance. They're experts with gold and silver. I'm an expert with my fingers, so I'm a fingersmith.'

'It must be an interesting job.'

'It's a marvellous job,' he answered. 'It's lovely.'

'And that's why you go to the races?'

'Race meetings is easy meat,' he said. 'You just stand around after the race, watchin' for the lucky ones to queue up and draw their money. And when you see someone collectin' a big bundle of notes, you simply follows after 'im and 'elps yourself. But don't get me wrong, guv'nor. I never takes nothin' from a loser. Nor from poor people neither. I only go after them as can afford it, the winners and the rich.'

'That's very thoughtful of you.' I said. 'How often do you get caught?'

'Caught?' he cried, disgusted. '*Me* get caught? It's only pickpockets get caught. Fingersmiths never. Listen, I could take the false teeth out of your mouth if I wanted to and you wouldn't even catch me!'

'I don't have false teeth,' I said.

'I know you don't,' he answered. 'Otherwise I'd 'ave 'ad 'em out long ago!'

I believed him. Those long slim fingers of his seemed able to do anything.

We drove on for a while without talking.

'That policeman's going to check up on you pretty thoroughly,' I said. 'Doesn't that worry you a bit?'

'Nobody's checkin' up on me,' he said.

'Of course they are. He's got your name and address written down most carefully in his black book.'

The man gave me another of his sly, ratty little smiles. 'Ah,' he said. 'So 'ee 'as. But I'll bet 'ee ain't got it all written down in 'is memory as well. I've never known a copper yet with a decent memory. Some of 'em can't even remember their own names.'

'What's memory got to do with it?' I asked. 'It's written down in his book, isn't it?'

'Yes, guv'nor, it is. But the trouble is, 'ee's lost the book. 'Ee's lost both books, the one with my name in it *and* the one with yours.'

In the long delicate fingers of his right hand, the man was holding up in triumph the two books he had taken from the policeman's pockets. 'Easiest job I ever done,' he announced proudly.

I nearly swerved the car into a milk-truck, I was so excited.

'That copper's got nothin' on either of us now,' he said.

'You're a genius!' I cried.

''Ee's got no names, no addresses, no car number, no nothin',' he said.

'You're brilliant!'

'I think you'd better pull in off this main road as soon as possible,' he said. 'Then we'd better build a little bonfire and burn these books.'

'You're a fantastic fellow,' I exclaimed.

'Thank you, guv'nor,' he said. 'It's always nice to be appreciated.'

THE DREAM WOMAN
William Wilkie Collins

I had not been settled much more than six weeks in my country practice, when I was sent for to a neighbouring town to consult with the resident medical man there, on a case of very dangerous illness.

My horse had come down with me, at the end of a long ride the night before, and had hurt himself, luckily, much more than he had hurt his master. Being deprived of the animal's services, I started for my destination by the coach (there were no railways at that time); and I hoped to get back again, towards the afternoon, in the same way.

After the consultation was over I went to the principal inn of the town to wait for the coach. When it came up, it was full inside and out. There was no resource left me, but to get home as cheaply as I could, by hiring a gig. The price asked for this accommodation struck me as being so extortionate, that I determined to look out for an inn of inferior pretensions, and to try if I could not make a better bargain with a less prosperous establishment.

I soon found a likely-looking house, dingy and quiet, with an old-fashioned sign, that had evidently not been repainted for many years past. The landlord, in this case, was not above making a small profit; and as soon as we came to terms, he rang the yard-bell to order the gig.

'Has Robert not come back from that errand?' asked the landlord appealing to the waiter, who answered the bell.

'No, sir, he hasn't.'

'Well, then, you must wake up Isaac.'

'Wake up Isaac?' I repeated; 'that sounds rather odd. Do your ostlers go to bed in the day-time?'

'This one does,' said the landlord, smiling to himself in rather a strange way.

'And dreams, too,' added the waiter.

'Never you mind about that,' retorted his master; 'you go and rouse Isaac up. The gentleman's waiting for his gig.'

The landlord's manner and the waiter's manner expressed a great deal more than they either of them said. I began to suspect that I might be on the trace of something professionally interesting to me, as a medical man; and I thought I should like to look at the ostler, before the waiter awakened him.

'Stop a minute,' I interposed; 'I have rather a fancy for seeing this man before you wake him up. I am a doctor; and if this queer sleeping and dreaming of his comes from anything wrong in his brain, I may be able to tell you what to do with him.'

'I rather think you will find his complaint past all doctoring, sir,' said the landlord. 'But if you would like to see him, you're welcome, I'm sure.'

He led the way across a yard and down a passage to the stables; opened one of the doors; and waiting outside himself, told me to look in.

I found myself in a two-stall stable. In one of the stalls, a horse was munching his corn. In the other, an old man was lying asleep on the litter.

I stooped, and looked at him attentively. It was a withered, woebegone face. The eyebrows were painfully contracted; the mouth was fast set, and drawn down at the corners. The hollow wrinkled cheeks, and the scanty grizzled hair, told their own tale of past sorrow or suffering. He was drawing his breath convulsively when I first looked at him; and in a moment more he began to talk in his sleep.

'Wake up!' I heard him say, in a quick whisper, through his clenched teeth. 'Wake up, there! Murder.'

He moved one lean arm slowly until it rested over his throat, shuddered a little, and turned on the straw. Then the arm left his throat, the hand stretched itself out, and clutched at the side towards which he had turned, as if he fancied himself to be grasping at the edge of something. I saw his lips move, and bent lower over him. He was still talking in his sleep.

'Light grey eyes,' he murmured, 'and a droop in the left eyelid – flaxen hair, with a gold-yellow streak in it – all right, mother – fair white arms, with a down on them – little lady's hand, with a reddish look under the finger-nails. The knife – always the cursed knife – first on one side, then on the other. Aha! you she-devil, where's the knife?'

At the last word his voice rose, and he grew restless on a sudden. I saw him shudder on the straw; his withered face became distorted, and he threw up both his hands with a quick hysterical gasp. They struck against the bottom of the manger under which he lay, and the blow awakened him. I had just time to slip through the door, and close it, before his eyes were fairly open, and his senses his own again.

'Do you know anything about that man's past life?' I said to the landlord.

'Yes, sir, I know pretty well all about it,' was the answer, 'and an uncommon queer story it is. Most people don't believe it. It's true, though, for all that. Why, just look at him,' continued the landlord, opening the stable door again. 'Poor devil! he's so worn out with his restless nights, that he's dropped back into his sleep already.'

'Don't wake him,' I said, 'I'm in no hurry for the gig. Wait until the other man comes back from his errand. And in the meantime, suppose I have some lunch, and a bottle of sherry; and suppose you come and help me to get through it.'

The heart of mine host, as I had anticipated, warmed to me over his own wine. He soon became communicative on the subject of the man asleep in the stable; and by little and little, I drew the whole story out of him. Extravagant and incredible as the events must appear to everybody, they are related here just as I heard them, and just as they happened.

* * * *

Some years ago there lived in the suburbs of a large seaport town, on the west coast of England, a man in humble circumstances, by the name of Isaac Scatchard. His means of subsistence were derived from any employment he could get as an ostler, and occasionally, when times went well with him, from temporary engagements in service as stable-helper in private houses. Though a faithful, steady, and honest man, he got on badly in his calling. His ill-luck was proverbial among his neighbours. He was always missing good opportunities by no fault of his own; and always living longest in service with amiable people who were not punctual payers of wages. 'Unlucky Isaac' was his nickname in his own neighbourhood – and no one could say that he did not richly deserve it.

With far more than one man's fair share of adversity to endure, Isaac had but one consolation to support him – and that was of the dreariest and most negative kind. He had no wife and children to increase his anxieties and add to the bitterness of his various failures in life. It might have been from mere insensibility, or it might have been from generous unwillingness to involve another in his own unlucky destiny – but the fact undoubtedly was, that he had arrived at the middle term of life without marrying; and, what is much more remarkable, without once exposing himself, from eighteen to eight-and-thirty, to the genial imputation of ever having had a sweetheart.

When he was out of service, he lived alone with his widowed mother. Mrs Scatchard was a woman above the average in her lowly station, as to capacity and manners. She had seen better days, as the phrase is; but she never referred to them in the presence of curious visitors; and, though perfectly polite to every one who approached her, never cultivated any intimacies among her neighbours. She contrived to provide, hardly enough, for her simple wants, by doing rough work for the tailors; and always managed to keep a decent home for her son to return to, whenever his ill-luck drove him out helpless into the world.

One bleak autumn, when Isaac was getting on fast towards forty, and when he was, as usual, out of place through no fault of his own, he set forth from his mother's cottage on a long walk inland to a gentleman's seat, where he had heard that a stable-helper was required.

It wanted then but two days of his birthday; and Mrs Scatchard, with her usual fondness, made him promise, before he started, that he would be back in time to keep that anniversary with her, in as festive a way as their poor means would allow. It was easy for him to comply with this request, even supposing he slept a night each way on the road.

He was to start from home on Monday morning; and whether he got the new place or not, he was to be back for his birthday dinner on

Wednesday at two o'clock.

Arriving at his destination too late on the Monday night to make application for the stable-helper's place, he slept at the village inn, and, in good time on the Tuesday morning, presented himself at the gentleman's house, to fill the vacant situation. Here again, his ill-luck pursued him as inexorably as ever. The excellent written testimonials to his character which he was able to produce, availed him nothing; his long walk had been taken in vain – only the day before, the stable-helper's place had been given to another man.

Isaac accepted this new disappointment resignedly, and as a matter of course. Naturally slow in capacity, he had the bluntness of sensibility and phlegmatic patience of disposition which frequently distinguish men with sluggishly-working mental powers. He thanked the gentleman's steward with his usual quiet civility, for granting him an interview, and took his departure with no appearance of unusual depression in his face or manner.

Before starting on his homeward walk, he made some inquiries at the inn, and ascertained that he might save a few miles on his return by following a new road. Furnished with full instructions, several times repeated, as to the various turnings he was to take, he set forth on his homeward journey, and walked on all day with only one stoppage for bread and cheese. Just as it was getting towards dark, the rain came on and the wind began to rise; and he found himself, to make matters worse, in a part of the country with which he was entirely unacquainted, though he knew himself to be some fifteen miles from home. The first house he found to inquire at was a lonely roadside inn, standing on the outskirts of a thick wood. Solitary as the place looked, it was welcome to a lost man who was also hungry, thirsty, footsore, and wet. The landlord was civil and respectable-looking, and the price he asked for a bed was reasonable enough. Isaac therefore decided on stopping comfortably at the inn for that night.

He was constitutionally a temperate man. His supper simply consisted of two rashers of bacon, a slice of homemade bread, and a pint of ale. He did not go to bed immediately after this moderate meal, but sat up with the landlord, talking about his bad prospects and his long run of ill-luck, and diverging from these topics to the subjects of horseflesh and racing. Nothing was said either by himself, his host, or the few labourers who strayed into the tap-room, which could, in the slightest degree, excite the very small and very dull imaginative faculty which Isaac Scatchard possessed.

At a little after eleven the house was closed. Isaac went round with the landlord, and held the candle while the doors and lower windows were being secured. He noticed with surprise the strength of the bolts, bars, and iron-sheathed shutters.

'You see, we are rather lonely here,' said the landlord. 'We never have had any attempts made to break in yet, but it's always as well to be on the safe side. When nobody is sleeping here I am the only man in the house. My wife and daughter are timid, and the servant-girl takes after her missuses. Another glass of ale, before you turn in? – No! – Well, how such a sober man as you comes to be out of place, is more than I can make out, for one. – Here's where you're to sleep. You're the only lodger tonight, and I think you'll say my missus has done her best to make you comfortable. You're quite sure you won't have another glass of ale? – very well. Good night.'

It was half-past eleven by the clock in the passage as they went upstairs to the bedroom, the window of which looked on to the wood at the back of the house.

Isaac locked the door, set his candle on the chest of drawers, and wearily got ready for bed. The bleak autumn wind was still blowing, and the solemn surging moan of it in the wood was dreary and awful to hear through the night-silence. Isaac felt strangely wakeful. He resolved, as he lay down in bed, to keep the candle alight until he began to grow sleepy for there was something unendurably depressing in the bare idea of lying awake in the darkness, listening to the dismal, ceaseless moan of the wind in the wood.

Sleep stole on him before he was aware of it. His eyes closed, and he fell off insensibly to rest, without having so much as thought of extinguishing the candle.

The first sensation of which he was conscious, after sinking into slumber, was a strange shivering that ran through him suddenly from head to foot, and a dreadful sinking pain at the heart, such as he had never felt before. The shivering only disturbed his slumbers – the pain woke him instantly. In one moment he passed from a state of sleep to a state of wakefulness – his eyes wide open – his mental perceptions cleared on a sudden as if by a miracle.

The candle had burnt down nearly to the last morsel of tallow, but the top of the unsnuffed wick had just fallen off, and the light in the little room was, for the moment, fair and full.

Between the foot of the bed and the closed door, there stood a woman with a knife in her hand, looking at him.

He was stricken speechless with terror, but he did not lose the preternatural clearness of his faculties; and he never took his eyes off the woman. She said not a word as they stared each other in the face; but she began to move slowly towards the left-hand side of the bed.

His eyes followed her. She was a fair fine woman, with yellowish flaxen hair, and light grey eyes, with a droop in the left eyelid. He noticed these things and fixed them on his mind, before she was round at the side of the bed. Speechless, with no expression in her face, with no noise following her footfall, she came closer and closer – stopped – and slowly raised the knife. He laid his right arm over his throat to save it; but, as he saw the knife coming down, threw his hand across the bed to the right side, and jerked his body over that way, just as the knife descended on the mattress within an inch of his shoulder.

His eyes fixed on her arm and hand, as she slowly drew her knife out of the bed. A white, well-shaped arm, with a pretty down lying lightly over the fair skin. A delicate, lady's hand, with the crowning beauty of a pink flush under and round the finger-nails.

She drew the knife out, and passed back again slowly to the foot of the bed; stopped there for a moment looking at him; then came on – still speechless, still with no expression on the beautiful face, still with no sound following the stealthy foot-falls – came on to the right side of the bed where he now lay.

As she approached, she raised the knife again, and he drew himself away to the left side. She struck, as before, right into the mattress, with a deliberate, perpendicularly downward action to the arm. This time his eyes wandered from her to the knife. It was like the large clasp-knives which he had often seen labouring men use to cut their bread and bacon with. Her delicate little fingers did not conceal more than two-thirds of the handle; he noticed that it was made of buckhorn, clean and shining as the blade was, and looking like new.

For the second time she drew the knife out, concealed it in the wide

She drew the knife out and passed to the foot of the bed

sleeve of her gown, then stopped by the bedside, watching him. For an instant he saw her standing in that position – then the wick of the spent candle fell over into the socket. The flame diminished to a little blue point, and the room grew dark.

A moment, or less if possible, passed so – and then the wick flamed up, smokily, for the last time. His eyes were still looking eagerly over the right-hand side of the bed when the final flash of light came, but they discerned nothing. The fair woman with the knife was gone.

The conviction that he was alone again, weakened the hold of the terror that had struck him dumb up to this time. The preternatural sharpness which the very intensity of his panic had mysteriously imparted to his faculties, left them suddenly. His brain grew confused – his heart beat wildly – his ears opened for the first time since the appearance of the woman, to a sense of the woeful, ceaseless moaning of the wind among the trees. With the dreadful conviction of the reality of what he had seen still strong within him, he leapt out of bed, and screaming – 'Murder! – Wake up there, wake up!' – dashed headlong through the darkness to the door.

It was fast locked, exactly as he had left it on going to bed.

His cries, on starting up, had alarmed the house. He heard the terrified, confused exclamations of women; he saw the master of the house approach along the passage, with his burning rush-candle in one hand and his gun in the other.

'What is it?' asked the landlord, breathlessly.

Isaac could only answer in a whisper. 'A woman, with a knife in her hand,' he gasped out. 'In my room – a fair, yellow-haired woman; she jabbed at me with the knife, twice over.'

The landlord's pale cheek grew paler. He looked at Isaac eagerly by the flickering light of his candle; and his face began to get red again – his voice altered too, as well as his complexion.

'She seems to have missed you twice,' he said.

'I dodged the knife as it came down', Isaac went on, in the same scared whisper. 'It struck the bed each time.'

The landlord took his candle into the bedroom immediately. In less than a minute he came out again into the passage in a violent passion.

'The devil fly away with you and your woman with the knife! There isn't a mark in the bed-clothes anywhere. What do you mean by coming into a man's place and frightening his family out of their wits by a dream?'

'I'll leave your house,' said Isaac, faintly. 'Better out on the road, in rain and dark, on my way home, than back again in that room, after what I've seen in it. Lend me a light to get my clothes by, and tell me what I'm to pay.'

'Pay!' cried the landlord, leading the way with his light sulkily into the bedroom. 'You'll find your score on the slate when you go downstairs. I wouldn't have taken you in for all the money you've got about you, if I'd known your dreaming, screeching ways beforehand. Look at the bed. Where's the cut of a knife in it? Look at the window – is the lock bursted? Look at the door (which I heard you fasten yourself) – is it broke in? A murdering woman with a knife in my house! You ought to be ashamed of yourself!'

Isaac answered not a word. He huddled on his clothes; and then they went down the stairs together.

'Nigh on twenty minutes past two!' said the landlord, as they passed the clock. 'A nice time in the morning to frighten honest people out of their wits!'

Isaac paid his bill, and the landlord let him out at the front door, asking, with a grin of contempt, as he undid the strong fastenings, whether 'the murdering woman got in that way?'

They parted without a word on either side. The rain had ceased; but the night was dark, and the wind bleaker than ever. Little did the darkness, or the cold, or the uncertainty about the way home matter to Isaac. If he had been turned out into the wilderness in a thunderstorm, it would have been a relief, after what he had suffered in the bedroom of the inn.

What was the fair woman with the knife? The creature of a dream, or that other creature from the unknown world, called among men by the name of ghost? He could make nothing of the mystery – had made nothing of it, even when it was midday on Wednesday, and when he stood, at last, after many times missing his road, once more on the doorstep of home.

* * * *

His mother came out eagerly to receive him. His face told her in a moment that something was wrong.

'I've lost the place; but that's my luck. I dreamed an ill dream last night, mother – or, maybe, I saw a ghost. Take it either way, it scared me out of my senses, and I'm not my own man again yet.'

'Isaac! your face frightens me. Come in to the fire. Come in, and tell mother all about it.'

He was as anxious to tell as she was to hear; for it had been his hope, all the way home, that his mother, with her quicker capacity and superior knowledge, might be able to throw some light on the mystery which he could not clear up for himself. His memory of the dream was still mechanically vivid, though his thoughts were entirely confused by it.

His mother's face grew paler and paler as he went on. She never interrupted him by so much as a single word; but when he had done, she moved her chair close to his, put her arm around his neck, and said to him:

'Isaac, you dreamed your ill dream on this Wednesday morning. What time was it when you saw the fair woman with the knife in her hand?'

Isaac reflected on what the landlord had said when they had passed by the clock on his leaving the inn – allowed nearly as he could for the time that must have elapsed between the unlocking of his bedroom door and the paying of his bill just before going away, and answered:

'Somewhere about two o'clock in the morning.'

His mother suddenly quitted her hold on his neck, and struck her hands together with a gesture of despair.

'This Wednesday is your birthday, Isaac; and two o'clock in the morning is the time when you were born!'

Isaac's capacities were not quick enough to catch the infection of his mother's superstitious dread. He was amazed, and a little startled also, when she suddenly rose from her chair, opened her old writing-desk, took pen, ink, and paper, and then said to him:

'Your memory is but a poor one, Isaac, and now I'm an old woman, mine's not much better. I want all about this dream of yours to be as well known to both of us, years hence, as it is now. Tell me over again all you told me a minute ago, when you spoke of what the woman with the knife looked like.'

Isaac obeyed, and marvelled much as he saw his mother carefully set down on paper the very words that he was saying.

'Light grey eyes,' she wrote as they came to the descriptive part, 'with a droop in the left eyelid. Flaxen hair, with a gold-yellow streak in it. White arms, with a down upon them. Little lady's hand, with a reddish look about the finger-nails. Clasp-knife with a buckhorn handle, that seemed as good as new.' To these particulars, Mrs Scatchard added the year, month, day of the week, and time in the morning, when the woman of the dream appeared to her son. She then locked up the paper carefully in her writing-desk.

Neither on that day, nor on any day after, could her son induce her to return to the matter of the dream. She obstinately kept her thoughts about it to herself, and even refused to refer again to the paper in her writing-desk. Ere long, Isaac grew weary of attempting to make her break her resolute silence; and time, which sooner or later wears out all things, gradually wore out the impression produced on him by the dream. He began by thinking of it carelessly, and he ended by not thinking of it at all.

This result was the more easily brought about by the advent of some important changes for the better in his prospects, which commenced not long after his terrible night's experience at the inn. He reaped at last the reward of his long and patient suffering under adversity, by getting an excellent place, keeping it for seven years, and leaving it, on the death of his master, not only with an excellent character, but also with a comfortable annuity bequeathed to him as a reward for saving his mistress's life in a carriage accident. Thus it happened that Isaac Scatchard returned to his old mother, seven years after the time of the dream at the inn, with an annual sum of money at his disposal, sufficient to keep them both in ease and independence for the rest of their lives.

The mother, whose health had been bad of late years, profited so much by the care bestowed on her and by freedom from money anxieties, that when Isaac's birthday came round, she was able to sit up comfortably at table and dine with him.

On that day, as the evening drew on, Mrs Scatchard discovered that a bottle of tonic medicine – which she was accustomed to take, and in which she had fancied that a dose or more was still left – happened to be empty. Isaac immediately volunteered to go to the chemist's and get it filled again. It was as rainy and bleak an autumn night as on the memorable past occasion when he lost his way and slept at the road-side inn.

On going in to the chemist's shop, he was passed hurriedly by a poorly-dressed woman coming out of it. The glimpse he had of her face struck him, and he looked back after her as she descended the door-steps.

'You're noticing that woman?' said the chemist's apprentice behind the counter. 'It's my opinion there's something wrong with her. She's been asking for laudanum to put to a bad tooth. Master's out for half an hour; and I told her I wasn't allowed to sell poison to strangers in his absence. She laughed in a queer way, and said she would come back in half an hour. If she expects master to serve her, I think she'll be disappointed. It's a case of suicide, sir, if ever there was one yet.'

These words added immeasurably to the sudden interest in the woman which Isaac had felt at the first sight of her face. After he had got the medicine bottle filled, he looked about anxiously for her, as soon as he was out in the street. She was walking slowly up and down on the opposite side of the road. With his heart, very much to his own surprise, beating fast, Isaac crossed over and spoke to her.

He asked if she was in any distress. She pointed to her torn shawl, her scanty dress, her crushed, dirty bonnet – then moved under a lamp so as to let the light fall on her stern, pale, but still most beautiful face.

'I look like a comfortable, happy woman – don't I?' she said, with a bitter laugh.

She spoke with a purity of intonation which Isaac had never heard before from other than ladies' lips. Her slightest actions seemed to have the easy, negligent grace of a thorough-bred woman. Her skin, for all its poverty-stricken paleness, was as delicate as if her life had been passed in the enjoyment of every social comfort that wealth can purchase. Even her small, finely-shaped hands, gloveless as they were, had not lost their whiteness.

Little by little, in answer to his questions, the sad story of the woman came out. There is no need to relate it here; it is told over and over again in police reports and paragraphs descriptive of attempted suicides.

'My name is Rebecca Murdoch,' said the woman, as she ended. 'I have ninepence left, and I thought of spending it at the chemist's over the way in securing a passage to the other world. Whatever it is, it can't be worse to me than this – so why should I stop here?'

Besides the natural compassion and sadness moved in his heart by what he heard, Isaac felt within him some mysterious influence at work all the time the woman was speaking, which utterly confused his ideas and almost deprived him of his powers of speech. All that he could say in answer to her last reckless words was, that he would prevent her from attempting her own life, if he followed her about all night to do it. His rough, trembling earnestness seemed to impress her.

'I won't occasion you that trouble,' she answered, when he repeated his threat. 'You have given me a fancy for living by speaking kindly to me. No need for the mockery of protestations and promises. You may believe me without them. Come to Fuller's Meadow tomorrow at twelve, and you will find me alive, to answer for myself. No! – no money. My ninepence will do to get me as good a night's lodging as I want.'

She nodded and left him. He made no attempt to follow – he felt no suspicion that she was deceiving him.

'It's strange, but I can't help believing her,' he said to himself, and walked away bewildered towards home.

On entering the house, his mind was still so completely absorbed by its new subject of interest, that he took no notice of what his mother was doing when he came in with the bottle of medicine. She had opened her old writing-desk in his absence, and was now reading a paper attentively that lay inside it. On every birthday of Isaac's since she had written down the particulars of his dream from his own lips, she had been accustomed to read that same paper, and ponder over it in private.

The next day he went to Fuller's Meadow.

He had done only right in believing her so implicitly – she was there, punctual to a minute, to answer for herself. The last-left faint defences in Isaac's heart, against the fascination which a word or look from her began inscrutably to exercise over him, sank down and vanished before her for ever on that memorable morning.

When a man, previously insensible to the influence of women, forms an attachment in middle life, the instances are rare indeed, let the warning circumstances be what they may, in which he is found capable of freeing himself from the tyranny of the new ruling passion. The charm of being spoken to familiarly, fondly, and gratefully by a woman whose language and manners still retain enough of their early refinement to hint at the high social station that she had lost, would have been a dangerous luxury to a man of Isaac's rank at the age of twenty. But it was far more than that – it was certain ruin to him – now that his heart was opening unworthily to a new influence at that middle time of life when strong feelings of all kinds, once implanted, strike root most stubbornly in a man's moral nature. A few more stolen interviews after that first morning in Fuller's Meadow completed his infatuation. In less than a month from the time when he first met her, Isaac Scatchard had consented to give Rebecca Murdoch a new interest in existence, and a chance of recovering the character she had lost, by promising to make her his wife.

She had taken possession not of his passions only, but of his faculties as well. All the mind he had he put into her keeping. She directed him on every point, even instructing him how to break the news of his approaching marriage in the safest manner to his mother.

'If you tell her how you met me and who I am at first,' said the cunning woman, 'she will move heaven and earth to prevent our marriage. Say I am the sister of one of your fellow-servants – ask her to see me before you go into any more particulars – and leave it to me to do the rest. I mean to make her love me next best to you, Isaac, before she knows anything of who I really am.'

The motive of the deceit was sufficient to sanctify it to Isaac. The stratagem proposed relieved him of his one great anxiety, and quieted his uneasy conscience on the subject of his mother. Still, there was something wanting to perfect his happiness, something that he could not realise, something mysteriously untraceable, and yet something that perpetually made itself felt – not when he was absent from Rebecca Murdoch, but, strange to say, when he was actually in her presence! She was kindness itself with him; she never made him feel his inferior capacities and inferior manners; she showed the sweetest anxiety to please him in the smallest trifles; but, in spite of all these attractions, he never could feel quite at his ease with her. At their first meeting, there had mingled with his admiration when he looked in her face, a faint involuntary feeling of doubt whether that face was entirely strange to him. No after-familiarity had the slightest effect on this inexplicable, wearisome uncertainty.

Concealing the truth, as he had been directed, he announced his marriage engagement precipitately and confusedly to his mother, on the day when he contracted it. Poor Mrs Scatchard showed her perfect confidence in her son by flinging her arms round his neck, and giving him joy of having found at last, in the sister of one of his fellow-servants, a woman to comfort and care for him after his mother was gone. She was all eagerness to see the woman of her son's choice; and the next day was fixed for the introduction.

It was a bright sunny morning, and the little cottage parlour was full of light, as Mrs Scatchard, happy and expectant, dressed for the occasion in her Sunday gown, sat waiting for her son and her future daughter-in-law.

Punctual to the appointed time, Isaac hurriedly and nervously led his promised wife into the room. His mother rose to receive her – advanced a few steps, smiling – looked Rebecca full in the eyes – and suddenly stopped. Her face, which had been flushed the moment before, turned white in an instant – her eyes lost their expression of softness and kindness, and assumed a blank look of terror – her outstretched hands fell to her sides, and she staggered back a few steps with a low cry to her son.

'Isaac!' she whispered, clutching him fast by the arm, when he asked alarmedly if she was taken ill, 'Isaac! does that woman's face remind you of nothing?'

Before he could answer, before he could look round to where Rebecca stood, astonished and angered by her reception, at the lower end of the room, his mother pointed impatiently to her writing-desk and gave him the key.

'Open it,' she said, in a quick, breathless whisper.

'What does this mean? Why am I treated as if I had no business here? Does your mother want to insult me?' asked Rebecca, angrily.

'Open it, and give me the paper in the left-hand drawer. Quick! quick! for heaven's sake!' said Mrs Scatchard, shrinking further back in terror.

Isaac gave her the paper. She looked it over eagerly for a moment – then followed Rebecca, who was now turning away haughtily to leave the room, and caught her by the shoulder – abruptly raised the long, loose sleeve of her gown – and glanced at her hand and arm. Something like fear began to steal over the angry expression of Rebecca's face, as she shook herself free from the old woman's grasp. 'Mad!' she said to herself, 'and Isaac never told me.' With those few words she left the room.

Isaac was hastening after her, when his mother turned and stopped his further progress. It wrung his heart to see the misery and terror in her face as she looked at him.

'Light grey eyes,' she said, in low, mournful, awe-struck tones, pointing towards the open door. 'A droop in the left eyelid; flaxen hair with a gold-yellow streak in it; white arms with a down on them; little lady's hand, with a reddish look under the finger-nails. *The Dream Woman!* – Isaac, the Dream Woman!'

That faint cleaving doubt which he had never been able to shake off in Rebecca Murdoch's presence, was fatally set at rest for ever. He *had* seen her face, then, before – seven years before, on his birthday, in the bedroom of the lonely inn.

'Be warned! Oh, my son, be warned! Isaac! Isaac! let her go, and do you stop with me!'

Something darkened the parlour window as those words were said. A sudden chill ran through him, and he glanced sidelong at the shadow. Rebecca Murdoch had come back. She was peering in curiously at them over the low window-blind.

'I have promised to marry, mother,' he said, 'and marry I must.'

The tears came into his eyes as he spoke, and dimmed his sight; but he could just discern the fatal face outside, moving away again from the window.

His mother's head sank lower.

'Are you faint?' he whispered.

'Broken-hearted, Isaac.'

He stooped down and kissed her. The shadow, as he did so, returned to the window; and the fatal face peered in curiously once more.

* * * *

Three weeks after that day Isaac and Rebecca were man and wife. All that was hopelessly dogged and stubborn in the man's moral nature, seemed to have closed round his fatal passion, and to have fixed it unassailably in his heart.

After that first interview in the cottage parlour, no consideration could induce Mrs Scatchard to see her son's wife again, or even talk of her when Isaac tried hard to plead her cause after their marriage.

This course of conduct was not in any degree occasioned by a discovery of the degradation in which Rebecca had lived. There was no question of that between mother and son. There was no question of anything but the fearfully exact resemblance between the living, breathing woman, and the spectre-woman of Isaac's dream.

Rebecca, on her side, neither felt nor expressed the slightest sorrow at the estrangement between herself and her mother-in-law. Isaac, for the sake of peace, had never contradicted her first idea that age and long illness had affected Mrs Scatchard's mind. He even allowed his wife to upbraid him for not having confessed this to her at the time of their marriage engagement, rather than risk anything by hinting at the truth. The sacrifice of his integrity before his one all-mastering delusion, seemed but a small thing, and cost his conscience but little, after the sacrifices he had already made.

The time of waking from his delusion – the cruel and rueful time – was not far off. After some quiet months of married life, as the summer was ending, and the year was getting on towards the month of his birthday, Isaac found his wife altering towards him. She grew sullen and contemptuous: she formed acquaintances of the most dangerous kind, in defiance of his objections, his entreaties, and his commands; and, worst of all, she learnt, ere long, after every fresh difference with her husband, to seek the deadly self-oblivion of drink. Little by little, after the first miserable discovery that his wife was keeping company with drunkards, the shocking certainty forced itself on Isaac that she had grown to be a drunkard herself.

He had been in a sadly desponding state for some time before the occurrence of these domestic calamities. His mother's health, as he could but too plainly discern every time he went to see her at the cottage, was failing fast; and he upbraided himself in secret as the cause of the bodily and mental suffering she endured. When to his remorse on his mother's account was added the shame and misery occasioned by the discovery of his wife's degradation, he sank under the double trial, his face began to alter fast, and he looked, what he was, a spirit-broken man.

His mother, still struggling bravely against the illness that was hurrying her to the grave, was the first to notice the sad alteration in him, and the first to hear of his last, worst trouble with his wife. She could only weep bitterly, on the day when he made his humiliating confession; but on the next occasion when he went to see her, she had taken a resolution, in reference to his domestic afflictions, which astonished, and even alarmed him. He found her dressed to go out, and on asking the reason, received this answer:

'I am not long for this world, Isaac,' she said; 'and I shall not feel easy on my death-bed, unless I have done my best to the last to make my son happy. I mean to put my own fears and my own feelings out of the question, and to go with you to your wife, and try what I can do to reclaim her. Give me your arm, Isaac and let me do the last thing I can in this world to help my son, before it is too late.'

He could not disobey her; and they walked together slowly towards his miserable home.

It was only one o'clock in the afternoon when they reached the cottage where he lived. It was their dinner hour, and Rebecca was in the kitchen. He was thus able to take his mother quietly into the parlour, and then prepare his wife for the interview. She had fortunately drank but little at that early hour, and she was less sullen and capricious than usual.

He returned to his mother, with his mind tolerably at ease. His wife soon followed him into the parlour, and the meeting between her and Mrs Scatchard passed off better than he had ventured to anticipate, though he observed with secret apprehension that his mother, resolutely as she controlled herself in other respects, could not look his wife in the face when she spoke to her. It was a relief to him, therefore, when Rebecca began to lay the cloth.

She laid the cloth, brought in the bread-tray, and cut a slice from the loaf for her husband, then returned to the kitchen. At that moment, Isaac, still anxiously watching his mother, was startled by seeing the same ghastly change pass over her face which had altered it so awfully on the morning when Rebecca and she first met. Before he could say a word, she whispered with a look of horror;

'Take me back! – home, home again, Isaac! Come with me, and never go back again!'

He was afraid to ask for an explanation; he could only sign her to be silent, and help her quickly to the door. As they passed the bread-tray on the table, she stopped and pointed to it.

'Did you see what your wife cut your bread with?' she asked in a low whisper.

'No, mother; I was not noticing. What was it?'

'Look!'

He did look. A new clasp-knife, with a buckhorn handle, lay with the loaf in the bread-tray. He stretched out his hand, shudderingly, to possess himself of it; but at the same time, there was a noise in the kitchen, and his mother caught at his arm.

'The knife of the dream! Isaac, I'm faint with fear – take me away, before she comes back!'

He was hardly able to support her. The visible, tangible reality of the knife struck him with a panic, and utterly destroyed any faint doubts he might have entertained up to this time, in relation to the mysterious dream-warning of nearly eight years before. By a last desperate effort, he summoned self-possession enough to help his mother out of the house – so quietly, that the 'Dream Woman' (he thought of her by that name now) did not hear their departure.

'Don't go back, Isaac, don't go back!' implored Mrs Scatchard, as he turned to go away, after seeing her safely seated again in her own room.

'I must get the knife,' he answered under his breath. His mother tried to stop him again; but he hurried out without another word.

On his return, he found that his wife had discovered their secret departure from the house. She had been drinking, and was in a fury of passion. The dinner in the kitchen was flung under the grate; the cloth was off the parlour table. Where was the knife?

Unwisely, he asked for it. She was only too glad of the opportunity of irritating him, which the request afforded her. 'He wanted the knife, did he? Could he give her a reason why? – No? Then he should not have it – not if he went down on his knees to ask for it.' Further recriminations elicited the fact that she bought it a bargain, and that she considered it her own especial property. Isaac saw the uselessness of attempting to get the knife by fair means, and determined to search for it later in the day, in secret. The search was unsuccessful. Night came on, and he left the house to walk about the streets. He was afraid now to sleep in the same room with her.

Three weeks passed. Still sullenly enraged with him, she would not give up the knife; and still that fear of sleeping in the same room with her possessed him. He walked about at night, or dozed in the parlour, or sat watching by his mother's bed-side. Before the expiration of the first week in the new month his mother died. It wanted then but ten days of her son's birthday. She had longed to live until that anniversary. Isaac was present at her death; and her last words in this world were addressed to him:

'Don't go back, my son – don't go back!'

He was obliged to go back, if it were only to watch his wife. Exasperated to the last degree by his distrust of her, she had revengefully sought to add a sting to his grief, during the last days of his mother's illness, by declaring that she would assert her right to attend the funeral. In spite of all that he could do or say, she held with wicked pertinacity to her words and, on the day appointed for the burial, forced herself – inflamed and shameless with drink – into her husband's presence, and delared that she would walk in the funeral procession to his mother's grave.

This last worst outrage, accompanied by all that was most insulting in word and look, maddened him for the moment. He struck her.

The instant the blow was dealt, he repented it. She crouched down, silent, in a corner of the room, and eyed him steadily; it was a look that cooled his hot blood, and made him tremble. But there was no time now to think of a means of making atonement. Nothing remained, but to risk the worst until the funeral was over. There was but one way of making sure of her. He locked her into her bedroom.

When he came back, some hours after, he found her sitting, very much altered in look and bearing, by the bedside, with a bundle on her lap. She rose, and faced him quietly, and spoke with a strange stillness in her voice, a strange repose in her eyes, a strange composure in her manner.

'No man has ever struck me twice,' she said; 'and my husband shall have no second opportunity. Set the door open and let me go. From this day forth we see each other no more.'

Before he could answer she passed him, and left the room. He saw her walk away up the street.

Would she return?

All that night he watched and waited; but no footstep came near the house. The next night, overcome by fatigue, he lay down in bed in his clothes, with the door locked, the key on the table, and the candle burning. His slumber was not disturbed. The third night, the fourth, the fifth, the sixth passed, and nothing happened. He lay down on the seventh, still in his clothes, still with the door locked, the key on the table, and the candle burning; but easier in his mind.

Easier in his mind, and in perfect health of body, when he fell off to sleep. But his rest was disturbed. He woke twice, without any sensation of uneasiness. But the third time it was that never-be-forgotten shivering of the night at the lonely inn, that dreadful sinking pain at the heart, which once more aroused him in an instant.

His eyes opened towards the left-hand side of the bed, and there stood – The Dream Woman again? No! His wife; the living reality, with the dream-spectre's face – in the dream-spectre's attitude: the fair arm up; the knife clasped in the delicate white hand.

He sprang upon her, almost at the instant of seeing her, and yet not quickly enough to prevent her from hiding the knife. Without a word from him, without a cry from her, he pinioned her in the chair. With one hand he felt up her sleeve; and there, where the Dream Woman had hidden the knife, his wife had hidden it – the knife with the buckhorn handle, that looked like new.

In the despair of that fearful moment his brain was steady, his heart was calm. He looked at her fixedly, with the knife in his hand, and said these last words:

'You told me we should see each other no more, and you have come back. It is my turn now to go, and to go for ever. I say that we shall see each other no more; and *my* word shall not be broken.'

He left her, and set forth into the night. There was a bleak wind abroad, and the smell of recent rain was in the air. The distant church clocks chimed the quarter as he walked rapidly beyond the last houses in the suburb. He asked the first policeman he met, what hour that was, of which the quarter past had just struck.

The man referred sleepily to his watch, and answered, 'Two o'clock.' Two in the morning. What day of the month was this day that had just begun? He reckoned it up from the date of his mother's funeral. The fatal parallel was complete – it was his birthday!

Had he escaped the mortal peril which his dream foretold? or had he only received a second warning?

As this ominous doubt forced itself on his mind, he stopped, reflected, and turned back again towards the city. He was still resolute to hold his word, and never to let her see him more; but there was a thought now in his mind of having her watched and followed. The knife was in his possession; the world was before him; but a new distrust of her – a vague, unspeakable, superstitious dread – had overcome him.

'I must know where she goes, now she thinks I have left her,' he said to himself, as he stole back wearily to the precincts of his house.

It was still dark. He had left the candle burning in the bedchamber; but when he looked up to the window of the room now, there was no light in it. He crept cautiously to the house door. On going away, he remembered to have closed it; on trying it now, he found it open.

He waited outside, never losing sight of the house until daylight. Then he ventured indoors – listened, and heard nothing – looked into kitchen, scullery, parlour; and found nothing; went up at last into the bedroom – it was empty. A picklock lay on the floor, betraying how she had gained entrance in the night, and that was the only trace of her.

Whither had she gone? No mortal tongue could tell him. The darkness had covered her flight; and when the day broke, no man could say where the light found her.

Before leaving the house and the town for ever, he gave instructions to a friend and neighbour to sell his furniture for anything that it would fetch, and to apply the proceeds towards employing the police to trace her. The directions were honestly followed, and the money was all spent; but the inquiries led to nothing. The picklock on the bedroom floor remained the last useless trace of the Dream Woman.

* * * *

At this part of the narrative the landlord paused; and, turning towards the window of the room in which we were sitting, looked in the direction of the stable-yard.

'So far,' he said, 'I tell you what was told to me. The little that remains to be added, lies within my own experience. Between two and three months after the events I have just been relating, Isaac Scatchard came to me, withered and old-looking before his time, just as you saw him today. He had his testimonials to character with him, and he asked me for employment here. Knowing that my wife and he were distantly related, I gave him a trial, in consideration of that relationship, and liked him in spite of his queer habits. He is as sober, honest, and willing a man as there is in England. As for his restlessness at night, and his sleeping away his leisure time in the day, who can wonder at it after hearing his story? Besides, he never objects to being roused up, when he's wanted, so there's not much inconvenience to complain of, after all.'

'I suppose he is afraid of a return of that dreadful dream, and of waking out of it in the dark?'

'No,' returned the landlord. 'The dream comes back to him so often, that he has got to bear with it by this time resignedly enough. It's his wife keeps him waking at night, as he often told me.'

'What! Has she never been heard of yet?'

'Never. Isaac himself has the one perpetual thought that she is alive and looking for him. I believe he wouldn't let himself drop off to sleep towards two in the morning, for a king's ransom. Two in the morning, he says, is the time she will find him, one of these days. Two in the morning is the time, all the year round, when he likes to be most certain that he has got the clasp-knife safe about him. He does not mind being alone, as long as he is awake, except on the night before his birthday, when he firmly believes himself to be in peril of his life. The birthday has only come round once since he has been here, and then he sat up along with the night-porter. "She's looking for me," is all he says, when anybody speaks to him about the one anxiety of his life; "she's looking for me." He may be right. She *may* be looking for him. Who can tell?'

'Who can tell?' said I.

THE MASQUE OF THE RED DEATH
Edgar Allan Poe

The 'Red Death' had long devastated the country. No pestilence had ever been so fatal, or so hideous. Blood was its Avatar and its seal – the redness and horror of blood. There were sharp pains, and sudden dizziness, and then profuse bleeding at the pores, with dissolution. The scarlet stains upon the body and especially upon the face of the victim, were the pest ban which shut him out from the aid and from the sympathy of his fellow-men. And the whole seizure, progress, and termination of the disease, were the incidents of half an hour.

But the Prince Prospero was happy and dauntless and sagacious. When his dominions were half-depopulated, he summoned to his presence a thousand hale and light-hearted friends from among the knights and dames of his court, and with these retired to the deep seclusion of one of his castellated abbeys. This was an extensive and magnificent structure, the creation of the prince's own eccentric yet august taste. A strong and lofty wall girdled it in. This wall had gates of iron. The courtiers, having entered, brought furnaces and massy hammers and welded the bolts. They resolved to leave means neither of ingress nor egress to the sudden impulses of despair or of frenzy from within. The abbey was amply provisioned. With such precautions the courtiers might bid defiance to contagion. The external world could take care of itself. In the meantime it was folly to grieve, or to think. The prince had provided all the appliances of pleasure. There were buffoons, there were improvisatori, there were ballet-dancers, there were musicians, there was Beauty, there was wine. All these and security were within. Without was the 'Red Death'.

It was toward the close of the fifth or sixth month of his seclusion, and while the pestilence raged most furiously abroad, that the Prince Prospero entertained his thousand friends at a masked ball of the most unusual magnificence.

It was a voluptuous scene, that masquerade. But first let me tell of the rooms in which it was held. These were seven – an imperial suite. In many palaces, however, such suites form a long and straight vista, while the folding doors slide back nearly to the walls on either hand, so that the view of the whole extent is scarcely impeded. Here the case was very different, as might have been expected from the duke's love of the *bizarre*. The apartments were so irregularly disposed that the vision embraced but little more than one at a time. There was a sharp turn at every twenty or thirty yards, and at each turn a novel effect. To the right and left, in the middle of each wall, a tall and narrow Gothic window looked out upon a closed corridor which pursued the windings of the suite. These windows were of stained glass whose colour varied in accordance with the prevailing hue of the decorations of the chamber into which it opened. That at the eastern extremity was hung, for example, in blue – and vividly blue were its windows. The second chamber was purple in its ornaments and tapestries, and here the panes were purple. The third was green throughout, and so were the casements. The fourth was furnished and lighted with orange – the fifth with white – the sixth with violet. The seventh apartment was closely shrouded in black velvet tapestries that hung all over the ceiling and down the walls, falling in heavy folds upon a carpet of the same material and hue. But in this chamber only, the colour of the windows failed to correspond with the decorations. The panes here were scarlet – a deep blood colour. Now, in no one of the seven apartments was there any lamp or candelabrum, amid the profusion of golden ornaments that lay scattered to and fro or depended from the roof. There was no light of any kind emanating from lamp or candle within the suite of chambers. But in the corridors that followed the suite there stood, opposite to each window, a heavy tripod, bearing a brazier of fire, that projected its rays through the tinted glass and so glaringly illumined the room. And thus were produced a multitude of gaudy and fantastic appearances. But in the western or black chamber the effect of the firelight that streamed upon the dark hangings through the blood-tinted panes was ghastly in the extreme, and produced so wild a look upon the countenances of those who entered that there were few of the company bold enough to set foot within its precincts at all.

It was in this apartment, also, that there stood against the western wall, a gigantic clock of ebony. Its pendulum swung to and fro with a dull, heavy, monotonous clang; and when the minute-hand made the circuit of the face, and the hour was to be stricken, there came from the brazen lungs of the clock a sound which was clear and loud and deep and exceedingly musical, but of so peculiar a note and emphasis that, at each lapse of an hour, the musicians of the orchestra were constrained to pause, momentarily, in their performance, to harken to the sound; and thus the waltzers perforce ceased their evolutions; and there was a brief disconcert of the whole gay company; and, while the chimes of the clock yet rang, it was observed that the giddiest grew pale, and the more aged and sedate passed their hands over their brows as if in confused reverie or meditation. But when the echoes had fully ceased, a light laughter at once pervaded the assembly; the musicians looked at each other and smiled as if at their own nervousness and folly, and made whispering vows, each to the other, that the next chiming of the clock should produce in them no similar emotion; and then, after the lapse of sixty minutes (which embrace three thousand and six hundred seconds of the Time that flies), there came yet another chiming of the clock, and then were the same disconcert and tremulousness and meditation as before.

But, in spite of these things, it was a gay and magnificent revel. The tastes of the duke were peculiar. He had a fine eye for colours and effects. He disregarded the *decora* of mere fashion. His plans were bold and fiery, and his conceptions glowed with barbaric lustre. There are some who would have thought him mad. His followers felt that he was not. It was necessary to hear and see and touch him to be *sure* that he was not.

He had directed, in great part, the movable embellishments of the seven chambers, upon occasion of this great *fête*; and it was his own guiding taste which had given character to the masqueraders. Be sure they were grotesque. There were much glare and glitter and piquancy and phantasm – much of what has been since seen in *Hernani*. There were arabesque figures with unsuited limbs and appointments. There were delirious fancies such as the madman fashions. There were much of the beautiful, much of the wanton, much of the *bizarre*, something of the terrible, and not a little of that which might have excited disgust. To and fro in the seven chambers there stalked, in fact, a multitude of dreams. And these – the dreams – writhed in and about, taking hue from the rooms, and causing the wild music of the orchestra to seem as the echo of their steps. And, anon, there strikes the ebony clock which stands in the hall of the velvet. And then, for a moment, all is still, and all is silent save the voice of the clock. The dreams are stiff-frozen as they stand. But the echoes of the chime die away – they have endured but an instant – and a light, half-subdued laughter floats after them as they depart. And now again the music swells, and the dreams live, and writhe to and fro more merrily than ever, taking hue from the many-tinted windows through which stream the rays from the tripods. But to the chamber which lies most westwardly of the seven there are now none of the maskers who venture; for the night is waning away; and there flows a ruddier light through the blood-coloured panes; and the blackness of the sable drapery appals; and to him whose foot falls upon the sable carpet, there comes from the near clock of ebony a muffled peal more solemnly emphatic than any which reaches *their* ears who indulged in the more remote gaieties of the other apartments.

But these other apartments were densely crowded, and in them beat feverishly the heart of life. And the revel went whirlingly on, until at length there commenced the sounding of midnight upon the clock. And then the music ceased, as I have told; and the evolutions of the waltzers were quieted; and there was an uneasy cessation of all things as before. But now there were twelve strokes to be sounded by the bell of the clock; and thus it happened, perhaps, that more of thought crept, with more of time, into the meditations of the thoughtful among those who revelled. And thus too, it happened, perhaps, that before the last echoes of the last chime had utterly sunk into silence, there were many individuals in the crowd who had found leisure to become aware of the presence of a masked figure which had arrested the attention of no single individual before. And the rumour of this new presence having spread itself whisperingly around, there arose at length from the whole company a buzz, or murmur, expressive of disapprobation and surprise – then, finally, of terror, of horror, and of disgust.

In an assembly of phantasms such as I have painted, it may well be supposed that no ordinary appearance could have excited such sensation. In truth the masquerade licence of the night was nearly unlimited; but the figure in question had out-Heroded Herod, and gone beyond the bounds of even the prince's indefinite decorum. There are chords in the hearts of the most reckless which cannot be touched without emotion. Even with the utterly lost, to whom life and death are equally jests, there are matters of which no jest can be made. The whole company, indeed, seemed now deeply to feel that in the costume and bearing of the stranger neither wit nor propriety existed. The figure was tall and gaunt, and shrouded from head to foot in the habiliments of the grave. The mask which concealed the visage was made so nearly to resemble the countenance of a stiffened corpse that the closest scrutiny must have had difficulty in detecting the cheat. And yet all this might have been endured, if not approved, by the mad revellers around. But the mummer had gone so far as to assume the type of the Red Death. His vesture was dabbled in *blood* – and his broad brow, with all the features of the face, was besprinkled with the scarlet horror.

When the eyes of Prince Prospero fell upon this spectral image (which, with a slow and solemn movement, as if more fully to sustain its *rôle*, stalked to and fro among the waltzers) he was seen to be convulsed in the first moment with a strong shudder either of terror or distaste; but, in the next, his brow reddened with rage.

'Who dares,' – he demanded hoarsely of the courtiers who stood near him – 'who dares insult us with this blasphemous mockery? Seize him and unmask him – that we may know whom we have to hang, at sunrise, from the battlements!'

It was in the eastern or blue chamber in which stood the Prince Prospero as he uttered these words. They rang throughout the seven rooms loudly and clearly, for the prince was a bold and robust man, and the music had become hushed at the waving of his hand.

It was in the blue room where stood the prince, with a group of pale courtiers by his side. At first, as he spoke, there was a slight rushing movement of this group in the direction of the intruder, who at the moment was also near at hand, and now, with deliberate and stately step, made closer approach to the speaker. But from a certain nameless awe with which the mad assumptions of the mummer had inspired the whole party, there were found none who put forth hand to seize him; so that, unimpeded, he passed within a yard of the prince's person; and while the vast assembly, as if with one impulse, shrank from the centres of the rooms to the walls, he made his way uninterruptedly, but with the same solemn and measured step which had distinguished him from the first, through the blue chamber to the purple – through the purple to the green – through the green to the orange – through this again to the white – and even thence to the violet, ere a decided movement had been made to arrest him. It was then, however, that the Prince Prospero, maddening with rage and the shame of his own momentary cowardice, rushed hurriedly through the six chambers, while none followed him on account of a deadly terror that had seized upon all. He bore aloft a drawn dagger, and had approached, in rapid impetuosity, to within three or four feet of the retreating figure, when the latter, having attained the extremity of the velvet apartment, turned suddenly and confronted his pursuer. There was a sharp cry – and the dagger dropped gleaming upon the sable carpet, upon which, instantly afterward, fell prostrate in death the Prince Prospero. Then, summoning the wild courage of despair, a throng of the revellers at once threw themselves into the black apartment, and, seizing the mummer, whose tall figure stood erect and motionless within the shadow of the ebony clock, gasped in unutterable horror at finding the grave cerements and corpse-like mask, which they handled with so violent a rudeness, untenanted by any tangible form.

And now was acknowledged the presence of the Red Death. He had come like a thief in the night. And one by one dropped the revellers in the blood-bedewed halls of their revel, and died each in the despairing posture of his fall. And the life of the ebony clock went out with that of the last of the gay. And the flames of the tripods expired. And darkness and Decay and the Red Death held illimitable dominion over all.

THE SAILOR-BOY'S TALE
Karen Blixen

The barque *Charlotte* was on her way from Marseille to Athens, in grey weather, on a high sea, after three days' heavy gale. A small sailor-boy, named Simon, stood on the wet, swinging deck, held on to a shroud, and looked up towards the drifting clouds, and to the upper top-gallant yard of the main-mast.

A bird, that had sought refuge upon the mast, had got her feet entangled in some loose tackle-yard of the halliard, and, high up there, struggled to get free. The boy on the deck could see her wings flapping and her head turning from side to side.

Through his own experience of life he had come to the conviction that in this world everyone must look after himself, and expect no help from others. But the mute, deadly fight kept him fascinated for more than an hour. He wondered what kind of bird it would be. These last days a number of birds had come to settle in the barque's rigging: swallows, quails, and a pair of peregrine falcons; he believed that this bird was a peregrine falcon. He remembered how, many years ago, in his own country and near his home, he had once seen a peregrine falcon quite close, sitting on a stone and flying straight up from it. Perhaps this was the same bird. He thought: 'That bird is like me. Then she was there, and now she is here.'

At that a fellow-feeling rose in him, a sense of common tragedy; he stood looking at the bird with his heart in his mouth. There were none of the sailors about to make fun of him; he began to think out how he might go up by the shrouds to help the falcon out. He brushed his hair back and pulled up his sleeves, gave the deck round him a great glance, and climbed up. He had to stop a couple of times in the swaying rigging.

It was indeed, he found when he got to the top of the mast, a peregrine falcon. As his head was on a level with hers, she gave up her struggle, and looked at him with a pair of angry, desperate, yellow eyes. He had to take hold of her with one hand while he got his knife out, and cut off the tackle-yarn. He was scared as he looked down, but at the same time he felt that he had been ordered up by nobody, but that this was his own venture, and this gave him a proud, steadying sensation, as if the sea and the sky, the ship, the bird and himself were all one. Just as he had freed the falcon, she hacked him in the thumb, so that the blood ran, and he nearly let her go. He grew angry with her, and gave her a clout on the head, then he put her inside his jacket and climbed down again.

When he reached the deck the mate and the cook were standing there, looking up; they roared to him to ask what he had had to do in the mast. He was so tired that the tears were in his eyes. He took the falcon out and showed her to them, and she kept still within his hands. They laughed and walked off. Simon set the falcon down, stood back and watched her. After a while he reflected that she might not be able to get up from the slippery deck, so he caught her once more, walked away with her and placed her upon a bolt of canvas. A little after she began to trim her feathers, made two or three sharp jerks forward, and then suddenly flew off. The boy could follow her flight above the troughs of the grey sea. He thought: 'There flies my falcon.'

When the *Charlotte* came home, Simon signed aboard another ship, and two years later he was a light hand on the schooner *Hebe* lying at Bodø, high up the coast of Norway, to buy herrings.

To the great herring-markets of Bodø ships came together from all corners of the world; here were Swedish, Finnish and Russian boats, a forest of masts, and on shore a turbulent, irregular display of life, with many languages spoken, and mighty fights. On the shore booths had been set up, and the Lapps, small yellow people, noiseless in their movements, with watchful eyes, whom Simon had never seen before, came down to sell bead-embroidered leather-goods. It was April, the sky and the sea were so clear that it was difficult to hold one's eyes up against them – salt, infinitely wide, and filled with bird-shrieks – as if someone were incessantly whetting invisible knives, on all sides, high up in heaven.

Simon was amazed at the lightness of these April evenings. He knew no geography, and did not assign it to the latitude, but he took it as a sign of an unwonted good-will in the Universe, a favour. Simon had been small for his age all his life, but this last winter he had grown, and had become strong of limb. That good luck, he felt, must spring from the very same source as the sweetness of the weather, from a new benevolence in the world. He had been in need of such encouragement, for he was timid by nature; now he asked for no more. The rest he felt to be his own affair. He went about slowly, and proudly.

One evening he was ashore with land-leave, and walked up to the booth of a small Russian trader, a Jew who sold gold watches. All the sailors knew that his watches were made from bad metal, and would not go, still they bought them, and paraded them about. Simon looked at these watches for a long time, but did not buy. The old Jew had diverse goods in his shop, and amongst others a case of oranges. Simon had tasted oranges on his journeys; he bought one and took it with him. He meant to go up on a hill, from where he could see the sea, and suck it there.

As he walked on, and had got to the outskirts of the place, he saw a little girl in a blue frock, standing at the other side of a fence and looking at him. She was thirteen or fourteen years old, as slim as an eel, but with a round, clear, freckled face, and a pair of long plaits. The two looked at one another.

'Who are you looking out for?' Simon asked, to say something. The girl's face broke into an ecstatic, presumptuous smile. 'For the man I am going to marry, of course,' she said. Something in her countenance made the boy confident and happy; he grinned a little at her. 'That will perhaps be me,' he said. 'Ha, ha,' said the girl, 'he is a few years older than you, I can tell you.' 'Why,' said Simon, 'you are not grown up yourself.' The little girl shook her head solemnly. 'Nay,' she said, 'but when I grow up I will be exceedingly beautiful, and wear brown shoes with heels, and a hat.' 'Will you have an orange?' asked Simon, who could give her none of the things she had named. She looked at the orange and at him. 'They are very good to eat,' said he. 'Why do you not eat it yourself then?' she asked. 'I have eaten so many already,' said he, 'when I was in Athens. Here I had to pay a mark for it.' 'What is your name?' asked she. 'My name is Simon,' said he. 'What is yours?' 'Nora,' said the girl. 'What do you want for your orange now, Simon?'

When he heard his name in her mouth, Simon grew bold. 'Will you give me a kiss for the orange?' he asked. Nora looked at him gravely for a moment. 'Yes,' she said, 'I should not mind giving you a kiss.' He grew as warm as if he had been running quickly. When she stretched out her hand for the orange he took hold of it. At that moment somebody in the house called out for her. 'That is my father,' said she, and tried to give him back the orange, but he would not take it. 'Then come again tomorrow,' she said quickly, 'then I will give you a kiss.' At that she slipped off. He stood and looked after her, and a little later went back to his ship.

Simon was not in the habit of making plans for the future, and now he did not know whether he would be going back to her or not.

The following evening he had to stay aboard, as the other sailors were going ashore, and he did not mind that either. He meant to sit on the deck with the ship's dog, Balthasar, and to practise upon a concertina that he had purchased some time ago. The pale evening was all round him, the sky was faintly roseate, the sea was quite calm, like milk-and-water, only in the wake of the boats going inshore it broke into streaks of vivid indigo. Simon sat and played; after a while his own music began to speak to him so strongly that he stopped, got up and looked upwards. Then he saw that the full moon was sitting high on the sky.

The sky was so light that she hardly seemed needed there; it was as if she had turned up by a caprice of her own. She was round, demure and presumptuous. At that he knew that he must go ashore, whatever it was to cost him. But he did not know how to get away, since the others had taken the yawl with them. He stood on the deck for a long time, a small lonely figure of a sailor-boy on a boat, when he caught sight of a yawl coming in from a ship farther out, and hailed her. He found that it was the Russian crew from a boat named *Anna* going ashore. When he could make himself understood to them, they took him with them; they first asked him for money for his fare, then, laughingly, gave it back to him. He thought: 'These people will be believing that I am going in to town, wenching.' And then he felt, with some pride, that they were right, although at the same time they were infinitely wrong, and knew nothing about anything.

When they came ashore they invited him to come in and drink in their company, and he would not refuse, because they had helped him. One of the Russians was a giant, as big as a bear; he told Simon that his name was Ivan. He got drunk at once, and then fell upon the boy with a bear-like affection, pawed him, smiled and laughed into his face, made him a present of a gold watch chain, and then kissed him on both cheeks. At that Simon reflected that he also ought to give Nora a present when they met again, and as soon as he could get away from the Russians he walked up to a booth that he knew of, and bought a small blue silk handkerchief, the same colour as her eyes.

It was Saturday evening, and there were many people amongst the houses; they came in long rows, some of them singing, all keen to have some fun that night. Simon, in the midst of this rich, bawling life under the clear moon, felt his head light with the flight from the ship and the strong drinks. He crammed the handkerchief in his pocket; it was silk which he had never touched before, a present for his girl.

He could not remember the path up to Nora's house, lost his way, and came back to where he had started. Then he grew deadly afraid that he should be too late, and began to run. In a small passage between two wooden huts he ran straight into a big man, and found that it was Ivan once more. The Russian folded his arms round him and held him. 'Good! Good!' he cried in high glee, 'I have found you my little chicken. I have looked for you everywhere, and poor Ivan has wept because he lost his friend.' 'Let me go, Ivan,' cried Simon. 'Oho,' said Ivan, 'I shall go with you and get what you want. My heart and my money are all yours, all yours; I have been seventeen years old myself, a little lamb of God, and I want to be so again tonight.' 'Let me go,' cried Simon, 'I am in a hurry.' Ivan held him so that it hurt, and patted him with his other hand. 'I feel it, I feel it,' he said. 'Now trust to me, my little friend. Nothing shall part you and me. I hear the others coming; we will have such a night together as you will remember when you are an old grandpapa.'

Suddenly he crushed the boy to him, like a bear that carries off a sheep. He thought of Nora waiting, like a slender ship in the dim air, and of himself, here, in the hot embrace of a hairy animal. He struck Ivan with

He drove the knife into the big man's arm

all his might. 'I shall kill you, Ivan,' he cried out, 'if you do not let me go.' 'Oh, you will be thankful to me later on,' said Ivan, and began to sing. Simon fumbled in his pocket for his knife, and got it opened. He could not lift his hand, but he drove the knife, furiously, in under the big man's arm. Almost immediately he felt the blood spouting out, and running down in his sleeve. Ivan stopped short in the song, let go his hold of the boy and gave two long deep grunts. The next second he tumbled down on his knees. 'Poor Ivan, poor Ivan,' he groaned. He fell straight on his face. At that moment Simon heard the other sailors coming along, singing, in the by-street.

He stood still for a minute, wiped his knife, and watched the blood spread into a dark pool underneath the big body. Then he ran. As he stopped for a second to choose his way, he heard the sailors behind him scream out over their dead comrade. He thought: 'I must get down to the sea, where I can wash my hand.' But at the same time he ran the other way. After a little while he found himself on the path that he had walked on the day before, and it seemed as familiar to him as if he had walked it many hundred times in his life.

He slackened his pace to look round, and suddenly saw Nora standing on the other side of the fence; she was quite close to him when he caught sight of her in the moonlight. Wavering and out of breath he sank down on his knees. For a moment he could not speak. The little girl looked down at him. 'Good evening, Simon,' she said in her small coy voice. 'I have waited for you a long time,' and after a moment she added: 'I have eaten your orange.'

'Oh, Nora,' cried the boy. 'I have killed a man.' She stared at him, but did not move. 'Why did you kill a man?' she asked after a moment. 'To get here,' said Simon. 'Because he tried to stop me. But he was my friend.' Slowly he got on to his feet. 'He loved me!' the boy cried out, and at that burst into tears. 'Yes,' said she slowly and thoughtfully. 'Yes, because you must be here on time.' 'Can you hide me?' he asked. 'For they are after me.'

'Nay,' said Nora, 'I cannot hide you. For my father is the parson here at Bodø, and he would be sure to hand you over to them, if he knew that you had killed a man.' 'Then,' said Simon, 'give me something to wipe my hands on.' 'What is the matter with your hands?' she asked and took a little step forward. He stretched out his hands to her. 'Is that your own blood?' she asked. 'No,' said he, 'it is his.' She took the step back again. 'Do you hate me now?' he asked. 'No, I do not hate you,' said she. 'But do put your hands at your back.'

As he did so she came up close to him, at the other side of the fence, and clasped her arms around his neck. She pressed her young body to his, and kissed him tenderly. He felt her face, cool as the moonlight, upon his own, and when she released him, his head swam, and he did not know if the kiss had lasted a second or an hour. Nora stood up straight, her eyes wide open. 'Now,' she said slowly and proudly, 'I promise you that I will never marry anybody, as long as I live.' The boy kept standing with his hands at his back, as if she had tied them there. 'And now,' she said, 'you must run, for they are coming.' They looked at one another. 'Do not forget Nora,' said she. He turned and ran.

He leaped over a fence, and when he was down amongst the houses he walked. He did not know at all where to go. As he came to a house, from where music and noise streamed out, he slowly went through the door. The room was full of people; they were dancing in here. A lamp hung from the ceiling, and shone down on them; the air was thick and brown with the dust rising from the floor. There were some women in the room, but many of the men danced with each other, and gravely or laughingly stamped the floor. A moment after Simon had come in the crowd withdrew to the walls to clear the floor for two sailors, who were showing a dance from their own country.

Simon thought: 'Now, very soon, the men from the boat will come round to look for their comrade's murderer, and from my hands they will know that I have done it.' These five minutes during which he stood by the wall of the dancing-room, in the midst of the gay, sweating dancers, were of great significance to the boy. He himself felt it, as if during this time he grew up, and became like other people. He did not entreat his destiny, nor complain. Here he was, he had killed a man, and had kissed a girl. He did not demand any more from life, nor did life now demand more from him. He was Simon, a man like the men round him, and going to die, as all men are going to die.

He only became aware of what was going on outside him, when he saw that a woman had come in, and was standing in the midst of the cleared floor, looking round her. She was a short, broad old woman, in the clothes of the Lapps, and she took her stand with such majesty and fierceness, as if she owned the whole place. It was obvious that most of the people knew her, and were a little afraid of her, although a few laughed; the din of the dancing-room stopped when she spoke.

'Where is my son?' she asked in a high shrill voice, like a bird's. The next moment her eyes fell on Simon himself, and she steered through the crowd, which opened up before her, stretched out her old skinny, dark hand, and took him by the elbow. 'Come home with me now,' she said. 'You need not dance here tonight. You may be dancing a high enough dance soon.'

Simon drew back, for he thought that she was drunk. But as she looked him straight in the face with her yellow eyes, it seemed to him that he had met her before, and that he might do well in listening to her. The old woman pulled him with her across the floor, and he followed her without a word. 'Do not birch your boy too badly, Sunniva, one of the men in the room cried to her. 'He has done no harm, he only wanted to look at the dance.'

At the same moment as they came out through the door, there was an alarm in the street, a flock of people came running down it, and one of them, as he turned into the house, knocked against Simon, looked at him and the old woman, and ran on.

While the two walked along the street, the old woman lifted up her skirt, and put the hem of it into the boy's hand. 'Wipe your hand on my skirt,' she said. They had not gone far before they came to a small wooden house, and stopped; the door to it was so low that they must bend to get through it. As the Lapp woman went in before Simon, still holding on to his arm, the boy looked up for a moment. The night had grown misty; there was a wide ring round the moon.

The old woman's room was narrow and dark, with but one small window to it; a lantern stood on the floor and lighted it up dimly. It was all filled with reindeer skins and wolf skins, and with reindeer horn, such as the Lapps use to make their carved buttons and knife-handles, and the air in here was rank and stifling. As soon as they were in, the woman turned to Simon, took hold of his head, and with her crooked fingers parted his hair and combed it down in Lapp fashion. She clapped a Lapp cap on him and stood back to glance at him. 'Sit down on my stool, now,' she said. 'But first take out your knife.' She was so commanding in voice and manner that the boy could not but choose to do as she told him; he sat down on the stool, and he could not take his eyes off her face, which was flat and brown, and as if smeared with dirt in its net of fine wrinkles. As he sat there he heard many people come along outside, and stop by the house; then someone knocked at the door, waited a moment and knocked again. The old woman stood and listened, as still as a mouse.

'Nay,' said the boy and got up. 'This is no good, for it is me that they are after. It will be better for you to let me go out to them.' 'Give me your knife,' said she. When he handed it to her, she stuck it straight into her thumb, so that the blood spouted out, and she let it drip all over her skirt. 'Come in, then,' she cried.

The door opened, and two of the Russian sailors came and stood in the opening; there were more people outside. 'Has anybody come in here?' they asked. 'We are after a man who has killed our mate, but he has run away from us. Have you seen or heard anybody this way?' The old Lapp woman turned upon them, and her eyes shone like gold in the lamplight. 'Have I seen or heard anyone?' she cried, 'I have heard you shriek murder all over the town. You frightened me, and my poor silly boy there, so that I cut my thumb as I was ripping the skin-rug that I sew. The boy is too scared to help me, and the rug is all ruined. I shall make you pay me for that. If you are looking for a murderer, come in and search my house for me, and I shall know you when we meet again.' She was so furious that she danced where she stood, and jerked her head like an angry bird of prey.

The Russian came in, looked round the room, and at her and her blood-stained hand and skirt. 'Do not put a curse on us now, Sunniva,' he said timidly. 'We know that you can do many things when you like. Here is a mark to pay you for the blood you have spilled.' She stretched out her hand, and he placed a piece of money in it. She spat on it. 'Then go, and there shall be no bad blood between us,' said Sunniva, and shut the door after them. She stuck her thumb in her mouth, and chuckled a little.

The boy got up from his stool, stood straight up before her and stared into her face. He felt as if he were swaying high up in the air, with but a small hold. 'Why have you helped me?' he asked her. 'Do you not know?' she answered. 'Have you not recognised me yet? But you will remember the peregrine falcon which was caught in the tackle-yarn of your boat, the *Charlotte*, as she sailed in the Mediterranean. That day you climbed up by the shrouds of the top-gallant mast to help her out, in a stiff wind, and with a high sea. That falcon was me. We Lapps often fly in such a manner, to see the world. When I first met you I was on my way to Africa, to see my younger sister and her children. She is a falcon too, when she chooses. By that time she was living at Takaunga, within an old ruined tower, which down there they call a minaret.' She swathed a corner of her skirt round her thumb, and bit at it. 'We do not forget,' she said. 'I hacked your thumb, when you took hold of me; it is only fair that I should cut my thumb for you tonight.'

She came close to him, and gently rubbed her two brown, claw-like fingers against his forehead. 'So you are a boy,' she said, 'who will kill a man rather than be late to meet your sweetheart? We hold together, the females of this earth. I shall mark your forehead now, so that the girls will know of that, when they look at you, and they will like you for it.' She played with the boy's hair, and twisted it round her finger.

'Listen now, my little bird,' said she. 'My great-grandson's brother-in-law is lying with his boat by the landing-place at this moment; he is to take a consignment of skins out to a Danish boat. He will bring you back to your boat, in time, before your mate comes. The *Hebe* is sailing tomorrow morning, is it not so? But when you are aboard give him back my cap for me.' She took up his knife, wiped it in her skirt and handed it to him. 'Here is your knife,' she said. 'You will stick it into no more men; you will not need to, for from now you will sail the seas like a faithful seaman. We have enough trouble with our sons as it is.'

The bewildered boy began to stammer his thanks to her. 'Wait,' said she, 'I shall make you a cup of coffee, to bring back your wits, while I wash your jacket.' She went and rattled an old copper kettle upon the fireplace. After a while she handed him a hot, strong, black drink in a cup without a handle to it. 'You have drunk with Sunniva now,' she said; 'you have drunk down a little wisdom, so that in the future all your thoughts shall not fall like raindrops into the salt sea.'

When he had finished and set down the cup, she led him to the door and opened it for him. He was surprised to see that it was almost clear morning. The house was so high up that the boy could see the sea from it, and a milky mist about it. He gave her his hand to say goodbye.

She stared into his face. 'We do not forget,' she said. 'And you, you knocked me on the head there, high up in the mast. I shall give you that blow back.' With that she smacked him on the ear as hard as she could, so that his head swam. 'Now we are quits,' she said, gave him a great, mischievous, shining glance, and a little push down the doorstep, and nodded to him.

In this way the sailor-boy got back to his ship, which was to sail the next morning, and lived to tell the story.

THE HORLA
Guy De Maupassant

8th May. What a lovely day! I have spent all the morning lying in the grass in front of my house, under the enormous plane tree that shades the whole of it. I like this part of the country and I like to live here because I am attached to it by old associations, by those deep and delicate roots which attach a man to the soil on which his ancestors were born and died, which attach him to the ideas and usages of the place as well as to the food, to local expressions, to the peculiar twang of the peasants, to the smell of the soil, of the villages, and of the atmosphere itself.

I love my house in which I grew up. From my windows I can see the Seine which flows alongside my garden, on the other side of the high road, almost through my grounds, the great and wide Seine, which goes to Rouen and Le Havre, and is covered with boats passing to and fro.

On the left, down yonder, lies Rouen, that large town, with its blue roofs, under its pointed Gothic towers. These are innumerable, slender or broad, dominated by the spire of the cathedral, and full of bells which sound through the blue air on fine mornings, sending their sweet and distant iron clang even as far as my home; that song of the metal, which the breeze wafts in my direction, now stronger and now weaker, according as the wind is stronger or lighter.

What a delicious morning it was!

About eleven o'clock, a long line of boats drawn by a steam tug as big as a fly, and which scarcely puffed while emitting its thick smoke, passed my gate.

After two English schooners, whose red flag fluttered in space, there came a magnificent Brazilian three-master; she was perfectly white, and wonderfully clean and shining. I saluted her, I hardly knew why, except that the sight of the vessel gave me great pleasure.

12th May. I have had a slight feverish attack for the last few days, and I feel ill, or rather I feel low-spirited.

Whence come those mysterious influences which change our happiness into discouragement, and our self-confidence into diffidence? One might almost say that the air, the invisible air, is full of unknowable Powers whose mysterious presence we have to endure. I wake up in the best spirits, with an inclination to sing. Why? I go down to the edge of the water and suddenly, after walking a short distance, I return home wretched, as if some misfortune were awaiting me there. Why? Is it a cold shiver which, passing over my skin, has upset my nerves and given me low spirits? Is it the form of the clouds, the colour of the sky, or the colour of the surrounding objects, which is so changeable, that has troubled my thoughts as they passed before my eyes? Who can tell? Everything that surrounds us, everything that we see, without looking at it, everything that we touch, without knowing it, everything that we handle, without feeling it, all that we meet, without clearly distinguishing it, has a rapid, surprising and inexplicable effect upon us and upon our senses, and, through them, on our ideas and on our heart itself.

How profound that mystery of the Invisible is! We cannot fathom it with our miserable senses, with our eyes which are unable to perceive what is either too small or too great, too near to us, or too far from us – neither the inhabitants of a star nor a drop of water; nor with our ears that deceive us, for they transmit to us the vibrations of the air in sonorous notes. They are fairies who work the miracle of changing these vibrations into sound, and by that metamorphosis give birth to music, which makes the silent motion of nature musical . . . with our sense of smell which is less keen than that of a dog . . . with our sense of taste which can scarcely distinguish the age of a wine!

Oh! If we only had other organs which would work other miracles in our favour, what a number of fresh things we might discover around us!

16th May. I am ill, decidedly! I was so well last month! I am feverish, horribly feverish, or rather I am in a state of feverish enervation, which makes my mind suffer as much as my body. I have, continually, that horrible sensation of some impending danger, that apprehension of some coming misfortune, or of approaching death; that presentiment which is, no doubt an attack of some illness which is still unknown, which germinates in the flesh and in the blood.

17th May. I have just come from consulting my physician, for I could no longer get any sleep. He said my pulse was rapid, my eyes dilated, my nerves highly strung, but there were no alarming symptoms. I must take a course of shower baths and of bromide of potassium.

25th May. No change! My condition is really very peculiar. As the evening comes on, an incomprehensible feeling of disquietude seizes me, just as if night concealed some threatening disaster. I dine hurriedly, and then try to read, but I do not understand the words, and can scarcely distingush the letters. Then I walk up and down my drawing-room, oppressed by a feeling of confused and irresistible fear, the fear of sleep and fear of my bed.

About ten o'clock I go up to my room. As soon as I enter it I double-lock and bolt the door; I am afraid – of what? Up to the present time I have been afraid of nothing . . . I open my cupboards, and look under my bed; I listen – to what? How strange it is that a simple feeling of discomfort, impeded or heightened circulation, perhaps the irritation of a nerve filament, a slight congestion, a small disturbance in the imperfect delicate functioning of our living machinery, may turn the most light-hearted of men into a melancholy one, and make a coward of the bravest? Then I go to bed, and wait for sleep as a man might wait for the executioner. I wait for its coming with dread, and my heart beats and my legs tremble, while my whole body shivers beneath the warmth of the bedclothes, until all at once I fall asleep, as though one should plunge into a pool of stagnant water in order to drown. I do not feel it coming on as I did formerly, this perfidious sleep which is close to me and watching me, which is going to seize me by the head, to close my eyes and annihilate me.

I sleep – a long time – two or three hours perhaps – then a dream – no – a nightmare lays hold on me. I feel that I am in bed and asleep . . . I feel it and I know it . . . and I feel also that somebody is coming close to me, is looking at me, touching me, is getting on my bed, is kneeling on my chest, is taking my neck between his hands and squeezing it . . . squeezing it with all his might in order to strangle me.

I struggle, bound by that terrible sense of powerlessness which paralyses us in our dreams; I try to cry out – but I cannot; I want to move – I cannot do so; I try, with the most violent efforts and breathing hard, to turn over and throw off this being who is crushing and suffocating me – I cannot!

And then, suddenly, I wake up, trembling and bathed in perspiration; I light a candle and find that I am alone, and after that crisis, which occurs every night, I at length fall asleep and slumber tranquilly until morning.

2nd June. My condition has grown worse. What is the matter with me? The bromide does me no good, and the shower baths have no effect. Sometimes, in order to tire myself thoroughly, I am fatigued enough already, I go for a walk in the forest of Roumare. I used to think at first that the fresh light and soft air, impregnated with the odour of herbs and leaves, would instil new blood into my veins and impart fresh energy to my heart. I turned into a broad hunting road, and then turned towards La Bouille, through a narrow path, between two rows of exceedingly tall trees, which placed a thick green, almost black, roof between the sky and me.

A sudden shiver ran through me, not a cold shiver, but a strange shiver of agony, and I hastened my steps, uneasy at being alone in the forest, afraid, stupidly and without reason, of the profound solitude. Suddenly it seemed to me as if I were being followed, as if somebody were walking at my heels, close, quite close to me, near enough to touch me.

I turned round suddenly, but I was alone. I saw nothing behind me except the straight, broad path, empty and bordered by high trees, horribly empty; before me it also extended until it was lost in the distance, and looked just the same – terrible.

I closed my eyes. Why? And then I began to turn round on one heel very quickly, just like a top. I nearly fell down, and opened my eyes; the trees were dancing round me and the earth heaved; I was obliged to sit down. Then, ah! I no longer remembered how I had come! What a strange idea! What a strange, strange idea! I did not in the least know. I started off to the right, and got back into the avenue which had led me into the middle of the forest.

3rd June. I have had a terrible night. I shall go away for a few weeks, for no doubt a journey will set me up again.

2nd July. I have come back, quite cured, and have had a most delightful trip into the bargain. I have been to Mont Saint-Michel, which I had not seen before.

What a sight, when one arrives as I did, at Avranches towards the end of the day! The town stands on a hill, and I was taken into the public garden at the extremity of the town. I uttered a cry of astonishment. An extraordinarily large bay lay extended before me, as far as my eyes could reach, between two hills which were lost to sight in the mist; and in the middle of this immense yellow bay, under a clear, golden sky, a peculiar hill rose up, sombre and pointed in the midst of the sand. The sun had just disappeared, and under the still flaming sky appeared the outline of that fantastic rock which bears on its summit a fantastic monument.

At daybreak I went out to it. The tide was low, as it had been the night before, and I saw that wonderful abbey rise up before me as I approached it. After several hours' walking, I reached the enormous mass of rocks which supports the little town, dominated by the great church. Having climbed the steep and narrow street, I entered the most wonderful Gothic building that has ever been built to God on earth, as large as a town, full of low rooms which seem buried beneath vaulted roofs, and lofty galleries supported by delicate columns.

I entered this gigantic gem, which is as light as a bit of lace, covered with towers, with slender belfries with spiral staircases, which raise their strange heads that bristle with chimeras, with devils, with fantastic animals, with monstrous flowers, to the blue sky by day, and to the black sky by night, and are connected by finely carved arches.

When I had reached the summit I said to the monk who accompanied me: 'Father, how happy you must be here!' And he replied: 'It's very windy here, monsieur'; and so we began to talk while watching the rising tide, which ran over the sand and covered it as with a steel cuirass.

And then the monk told me stories, all the old stories belonging to the place, legends, nothing but legends.

One of them struck me forcibly. The country people, those belonging to the Mount, declare that at night one can hear voices talking on the sands, and that one then hears two goats bleating, one with a strong, the

The flower raised itself three yards from my eyes

other with a weak voice. Incredulous people declare that it is nothing but the cry of the sea birds, which occasionally resembles bleatings, and occasionally, human lamentations; but belated fishermen swear that they have met an old shepherd wandering between tides on the sands around the little town. His head is completely concealed by his cloak and he is followed by a billy goat with a man's face, and a nanny goat with a woman's face, both having long, white hair, and talking incessantly and quarrelling in an unknown tongue. Then suddenly they cease and begin to bleat with all their might.

'Do you believe it?' I asked the monk. 'I scarcely know,' he replied, and I continued: 'If there are other beings besides ourselves on this earth, how comes it that we have not known it long since, or why have *you* not seen them? How is it that *I* have not seen them?' He replied: 'Do we see the hundred-thousandth part of what exists? Look here; there is the wind, which is the strongest force in nature, which knocks down men, and blows down buildings, uproots trees, raises the sea into mountains of water, destroys cliffs and casts great ships on the rocks; the wind which kills, which whistles, which sighs, which roars – have you ever seen it, and can you see it? It exists for all that, however.'

I was silent before this simple reasoning. That man was a philosopher, or perhaps a fool; I could not say which exactly, so I held my tongue. What he had said had often been in my own thoughts.

3rd July. I have slept badly; certainly there is some feverish influence here, for my coachman is suffering in the same way as I am. When I went back home yesterday, I noticed his singular paleness, and I asked him: 'What is the matter with you, Jean?' 'The matter is that I never get any rest, and my nights devour my days. Since your departure, monsieur, there has been a spell over me.'

However, the other servants are all well, but I am very much afraid of having another attack myself.

4th July. I am decidedly ill again; for my old nightmares have returned. Last night I felt somebody leaning on me and sucking my life from between my lips. Yes, he was sucking it out of my throat, like a leech. Then I got up, satiated, and I woke up, so exhausted, crushed and weak that I could not move. If this continues for a few days, I shall certainly go away again.

5th July. Have I lost my reason? What happened last night is so strange that my head wanders when I think of it!

I had locked my door, as I do now every evening, and then, being thirsty, I drank half a glass of water, and accidentally noticed that the water bottle was full up to the cutglass stopper.

Then I went to bed and fell into one of my terrible sleeps, from which I was aroused in about two hours by a still more frightful shock.

Picture to yourself a sleeping man who is being murdered and who wakes up with a knife in his lung, and whose breath rattles, who is covered with blood, and who can no longer breathe and is about to die, and does not understand – there you have it.

Having recovered my senses, I was thirsty again, so I lit a candle and went to the table on which stood my water bottle. I lifted it up and tilted it over my glass, but nothing came out. It was empty! It was completely empty! At first I could not understand it at all, and then suddenly I was seized by such a terrible feeling that I had to sit down, or rather I fell into a chair! Then I sprang up suddenly to look about me; then I sat down again, overcome by astonishment and fear, in front of the transparent glass bottle! I looked at it with fixed eyes, trying to conjecture, and my hands trembled! Somebody had drunk the water, but who? I? I, without any doubt. It could surely only be I. In that case I was a somnambulist; I lived, without knowing it, that mysterious double life which makes us doubt whether there are not two beings in us, or whether a strange, unknowable and invisible being does not at such moments, when our soul is in a state of torpor, animate our captive body, which obeys this other being, as it obeys us, and more than it obeys ourselves.

Oh! Who will understand my horrible agony? Who will understand the emotion of a man who is sound in mind, wide awake, full of common sense, who looks in horror through the glass of a water bottle for a little water that disappeared while he was asleep? I remained thus until it was daylight, without venturing to go to bed again.

6th July. I am going mad. Again all the contents of my water bottle have been drunk during the night – or rather, I have drunk it!

But is it I? Is it I? Who could it be? Who? Oh, God! Am I going mad? Who will save me?

10th July. I have just been through some surprising ordeals. Decidedly I am mad! And yet!

On 6th July, before going to bed, I put some wine, milk, water, bread and strawberries on my table. Somebody drank – I drank – all the water and a little of the milk, but neither the wine, bread, nor the strawberries were touched.

On the seventh of July I renewed the same experiment, with the same results, and on the 8th July, I left out the water and the milk, and nothing was touched.

Lastly, on 9th July I put only water and milk on my table, taking care to wrap up the bottles in white muslim and to tie down the stoppers. Then I rubbed my lips, my beard and my hands with pencil lead, and went to bed.

Irresistible sleep seized me, which was soon followed by a terrible awakening. I had not moved, and there was no mark of lead on the sheets. I rushed to the table. The muslim round the bottles remained intact; I undid the string, tembling with fear. All the water had been drunk, and so had the milk! Ah! Great God . . .

I must start for Paris immediately.

12th July. Paris. I must have lost my head during the last few days! I must be the plaything of my enervated imagination, unless I am really a somnambulist, or perhaps I have been under the power of one of those hitherto unexplained influences which are called suggestions. In any case, my mental state bordered on madness, and twenty-four hours of Paris sufficed to restore my equilibrium.

Yesterday, after doing some business and paying some visits which instilled fresh and invigorating air into my soul, I wound up the evening at the *Théâtre-Français*. A play by Alexandre Dumas the younger was being acted and his active and powerful imagination completed my cure. Certainly solitude is dangerous for active minds. We require around us men who can think and talk. When we are alone for a long time, we people space with phantoms.

I returned along the boulevards to my hotel in excellent spirits. Amid the jostling of the crowd I thought, not without irony, of my terrors and surmises of the previous week, because I had believed – yes, I had believed – that an invisible being lived beneath my roof. How weak our brains are, and how quickly they are terrified and led into error by a small incomprehensible fact.

Instead of saying simply: 'I do not understand because I do not know the cause,' we immediately imagine terrible mysteries and supernatural powers.

14th July. Fête of the Republic. I walked through the streets, amused as a child at the firecrackers and flags. Still it is very foolish to be merry on a fixed date, by Government decree. The populace is an imbecile flock of sheep, now stupidly patient, and now in ferocious revolt. Say to it: 'Amuse yourself,' and it amuses itself. Say to it: 'Go and fight with your neighbour,' and it goes and fights. Say to it: 'Vote for the Emperor,' and it votes for the Emperor, and then say to it: 'Vote for the Republic,' and it votes for the Republic.

Those who direct it are also stupid; only, instead of obeying men, they obey principles which can only be stupid, sterile, and false, for the very reason that they are principles, that is to say, ideas which are considered as certain and unchangeable in this world where one is certain of nothing, since light is an illusion and noise is an illusion.

16th July. I saw some things yesterday that troubled me very much.

I was dining at the house of my cousin, Madame Sablé, whose husband is colonel of the 76th Chasseurs at Limoges. There were two young women there, one of whom had married a medical man, Dr Parent, who devotes much attention to nervous diseases and to the remarkable manifestations taking place at this moment under the influence of hypnotism and suggestion.

He related to us at some length the wonderful results obtained by English scientists and by the doctors of the Nancy school; and the facts which he adduced appeared to me so strange that I declared that I was altogether incredulous.

'We are,' he declared, 'on the point of discovering one of the most important secrets of nature; I mean to say, one of its most important secrets on this earth, for there are certainly others of a different kind of importance up in the stars, yonder. Ever since man has thought, ever since he has been able to express and write down his thoughts, he has felt himself close to a mystery which is impenetrable to his gross and imperfect senses, and he endeavours to supplement through his intellect the inefficiency of his senses. As long as that intellect remained in its elementary stage, these apparitions of invisible spirits assumed forms that were commonplace, though terrifying. Thence sprang the popular belief in the supernatural, the legends of wandering spirits, of fairies, of gnomes, ghosts, I might even say the legend of God; for our conceptions of the workman-creator, from whatever religion they may have come down to us, are certainly the most mediocre, the most stupid and the most incredible inventions that ever sprang from the terrified brain of any human beings. Nothing is truer than what Voltaire says: "God made man in His own image, but man has certainly paid Him back in his own coin."

'However, for rather more than a century men seem to have had a presentiment of something new. Mesmer and some others have put us on an unexpected track, and, especially within the last two or three years, we have arrived at really surprising results.'

My cousin, who is also very incredulous, smiled, and Dr Parent said to her: 'Would you like me to try to send you to sleep, madame?' 'Yes, certainly.'

She sat down in an easy chair, and he began to look at her fixedly, so as to fascinate her. I suddenly felt myself growing uncomfortable, my heart beating rapidly and a choking sensation in my throat. I saw Madame Sablé's eyes becoming heavy, her mouth twitching and her bosom heaving, and at the end of ten minutes she was asleep.

'Go behind her,' the doctor said to me, and I took a seat behind her. He put a visiting card into her hands, and said to her: 'This is a looking-glass; what do you see in it?' And she replied: 'I see my cousin.' What is he doing?' 'He is twisting his moustache.' 'And now?' 'He is taking a photograph out of his pocket.' 'Whose photograph is it?' 'His own.'

That was true, and the photograph had been given me that same evening in the hotel.

'What is his attitude in this portrait?' 'He is standing up with his hat in his hand.'

She saw, therefore, on that card, on that piece of white pasteboard, as if she had seen it in a mirror.

The young women were frightened and exclaimed. 'That is enough! Quite, quite enough!'

But the doctor said to Madame Sablé authoritatively: 'You will rise at eight o'clock tomorrow morning; then you will go and call on your cousin at his hotel and ask him to lend you five thousand francs which your husband demands of you, and which he will ask for when he sets out on his coming journey.'

Then he woke her up.

On returning to my hotel, I thought over this curious séance, and I was assailed by doubts, not as to my cousin's absolute and undoubted good faith, for I had known her well as if she were my own sister ever since she was a child, but as to a possible trick on the doctor's part. Had he not, perhaps, kept a glass hidden in his hand, which he showed to the young woman in her sleep, at the same time as he did the card? Professional conjurors do things that are just as singular.

So I went home and to bed, and this morning, at about half-past eight, I was awakened by my valet, who said to me: 'Madame Sablé has asked to see you immediately, monsieur.' I dressed hastily and went to her.

She sat down in some agitation, with her eyes on the floor, and without raising her veil she said to me: 'My dear cousin, I am going to ask a great favour of you.' 'What is it, cousin?' 'I do not like to tell you, and yet I must. I am in absolute need of five thousand francs.' 'What, you?' 'Yes I, or rather my husband, who has asked me to procure them for him.'

I was so thunderstruck that I stammered out my answers. I asked myself whether she had not really been making fun of me with Dr Parent, if it was not merely a well-acted farce which had been rehearsed beforehand. On looking at her attentively, however, all my doubts disappeared. She was trembling with grief, so painful was this step to her, and I was convinced that her throat was full of sobs.

I knew that she was very rich and I continued: 'What! Has not your husband five thousand francs at his disposal? Come, think. Are you sure that he commissioned you to ask me for them?'

She hesitated for a few seconds, as if she were making a great effort to search her memory, and then she replied: 'Yes . . . yes, I am quite sure of it.' 'He has written to you?'

She hesitated again and reflected, and I guessed the torture of her thoughts. She did not know. She only knew that she was to borrow five thousand francs off me for her husband. So she told a lie. 'Yes, he has written to me.' 'When, pray? You did not mention it to me yesterday,' 'I received his letter this morning.' 'Can you show it me?' 'No . . . no . . . no . . . it contains private matters . . . things too personal to ourselves . . . I burned it.' 'So your husband runs into debt?'

She hesitated again, and then murmured: 'I do not know.' 'Thereupon I said bluntly: 'I have not five thousand francs at my disposal at this moment, my dear cousin.'

She uttered a kind of cry as if she were in pain and said: 'Oh! oh! I beseech you, I beseech you to get them for me . . .'

She got excited and clasped her hands as if she were praying to me! I heard her voice change its tone; she wept and stammered, harassed and dominated by the irresistible order that she had received.

'Oh! oh! I beg you to . . . if you knew what I am suffering . . . I want them today.'

I had pity on her: 'You shall have them by and by, I swear to you.' 'Oh! thank you! thank you! How kind you are.'

I continued; 'Do you remember what took place at your house last night!' 'Yes.' 'Do you remember that Dr Parent sent you to sleep?' 'Yes.' 'Oh! Very well, then; he ordered you to come to me this morning to borrow five thousand francs, and at this moment you are obeying that suggestion.'

She considered for a few moments, and then replied: 'But as it is my husband who wants them –'

For a whole hour I tried to convince her, but could not succeed, and when she had gone I went to the doctor. He was just going out, and he listened to me with a smile, and said; 'Do you believe now?' 'Yes, I cannot help it.' 'Let us go to your cousin's.'

She was already half asleep on a reclining chair, overcome with fatigue. The doctor felt her pulse, looked at her for some time with one hand raised towards her eyes, which she closed by degrees under the irresistible power of this magnetic influence, and when she was asleep, he said:

'Your husband does not require the five thousand francs any longer! You must, therefore, forget that you asked your cousin to lend them to you, and, if he speaks to you about it, you will not understand him.'

Then he woke her up, and I took out a pocketbook and said: 'Here is what you asked me for this morning, my dear cousin.' But she was so surprised that I did not venture to persist; neverthless, I tried to recall the circumstance to her, but she denied it vigorously, thought I was making fun of her, and, in the end, very nearly lost her temper.

There! I have just come back, and I have not been able to eat any lunch, for this experiment has altogether upset me.

19th July. Many people to whom I told the adventure laughed at me. I no longer know what to think. The wise man says: 'It may be!'

21st July. I dined at Bougival, and then I spent the evening at a boatman's ball. Decidedly everything depends on place and surroundings. It would be the height of folly to believe in the supernatural on the Ile de la Grenouilliere . . . but on the top of Mount Saint-Michel? . . . and in India? We are terribly influenced by our surroundings. I shall return home next week.

30th July. I came back to my own house yesterday. Everything is going well.

2nd August. Nothing new, it is splendid weather, and I spend my days in watching the Seine flowing past.

4th August. Quarrels among my servants. They declare that the glasses are broken in the cupboards at night. The footman accuses the cook, who accuses the seamstress, who accuses the other two. Who is the culprit? It is a clever person who can tell.

6th August. This time I am not mad. I have seen . . . I have seen . . . I have seen! . . . I can doubt no longer . . . I have seen it! . . .

I was walking at two o'clock among my rose trees, in the full sunlight . . . in the walk bordered by autumn roses which are beginning to fall. As I stopped to look at a Géant de Batille, which had three splendid blossoms, I distinctly saw the stalk of one of the roses near me bend, as if an invisible hand had bent it, and then break, as if that hand had picked it! Then the flower raised itself, following the curve which a hand would have described in carrying it towards a mouth, and it remained suspended in the transparent air, all alone and motionless, a terrible red spot, three yards from my eyes. In desperation I rushed at it to take it! I found nothing; it had disappeared. Then I was seized with furious rage against myself, for a reasonable and serious man should not have such hallucinations.

But was it an hallucination? I turned round to look for the stalk, and I found it at once, on the bush, freshly broken, between two other roses which remained on the branch. I returned home then, my mind greatly disturbed; for I am certain now, as certain as I am of the alternation of day and night, that there exists close to me an invisible being that lives on milk and water, that can touch objects, take them and change their places; that is, consequently, endowed with a material nature, although it is imperceptible to our senses, and that lives as I do, under my roof.

7th August. I slept tranquilly. He drank the water out of my decanter, but did not disturb my sleep.

I wonder if I am mad. As I was walking just now in the sun by the riverside, doubts as to my sanity arose in me; not vague doubts such as I have had hitherto, but definite, absolute doubts. I have seen mad people, and I have known some who have been quite intelligent, lucid, even clear-sighted at every concern of life, except on one point. They spoke clearly, readily, profoundly on everything, when suddenly their mind struck upon the shoals of their madness and broke to pieces there, and scattered and foundered in that furious and terrible sea, full of rolling waves, fogs and squalls, which is called *madness*.

I certainly should think that I was mad, absolutely mad, if I were not conscious, did not perfectly know my condition, did not fathom it by analysing it with the most complete lucidity, I should, in fact, be only a rational man who was labouring under an hallucination. Some unknown disturbance must have arisen in my brain, one of those disturbances which physiologists of the present day try to note and to verify; and that disturbance must have caused a deep gap in my mind and in the sequence and logic of my ideas. Similar phenomena occur in dreams which lead us among the most unlikely phantasmagoria, without causing us any surprise, because our verifying apparatus and our organ of control are asleep, while our imaginative faculty is awake and active. Is it not possible that one of the imperceptible notes of the cerebral keyboard has been paralysed in me? Some men lose the recollection of proper names, of verbs, or of numbers, or merely of dates, in consequence of an accident. The localisation of all the variations of thought has been established nowadays; why, then, should it be surprising if my faculty of controlling the unreality of certain hallucinations were dormant in me for the time being?

I thought of all this as I walked by the side of the water. The sun shone brightly on the river and made earth delightful, while it filled me with a love for life, for the swallows, whose agility always delights my eye, for the plants by the riverside, the rustle of whose leaves is a pleasure to my ears.

By degrees, however, an inexplicable feeling of discomfort seized me. It seemed as if some unknown force were numbing and stopping me, were preventing me from going farther, and were calling me back. I felt that painful wish to return which oppresses you when you have left a beloved invalid at home, and when you are seized with a presentiment that he is worse.

I, therefore, returned in spite of myself, feeling certain that I should find some bad news awaiting me, a letter or a telegram. There was nothing, however, and I was more surprised and uneasy than if I had had another fantastic vision.

8th August. I spent a terrible evening yesterday. He does not show himself any more, but I feel that he is near me, watching me, looking at me, penetrating me, dominating me, and more redoubtable when he hides himself thus than if he were to manifest his constant and invisible presence by supernatural phenomena. However, I slept.

9th August. Nothing; but I am afraid.

10th August. Nothing; what will happen tomorrow?

11th August. Still nothing; I cannot stop at home with this fear hanging over me and these thoughts in my mind; I shall go away.

12th August. Ten o'clock at night. All day long I have been trying to get away, and have not been able. I wished to accomplish this simple and easy act of freedom – to go out – to get into my carriage in order to go to Rouen – and I have not been able to do it. What is the reason?

13th August. When we are attacked by certain maladies, all the springs of our physical being appear to be broken, all our energies destroyed, all our muscles relaxed; our bones, too, have become as soft as flesh, and our bodies as liquid as water. I am experiencing these sensations in my moral being in a strange and distressing manner. I have no longer any strength, any courage, any self-control, not even any power to set my own will in motion. I have no power left to will anything; but someone does it for me and I obey.

14th August. I am lost! Somebody possesses my soul and dominates it. Somebody orders all my acts, all my movements, all my thoughts. I am no longer anything in myself, nothing except an enslaved and terrified spectator of all the things I do. I wish to go out; I cannot. He does not wish to, and so I remain, trembling and distracted, in the armchair in which he keeps me sitting. I merely wish to get up and to rouse myself; I cannot! I am riveted to my chair, and my chair adheres to the ground in such a manner that no power could move us.

Then, suddenly, I must, I must go to the bottom of my garden to pick some strawberries and eat them, and I go there. I pick the strawberries and eat them! Oh, my God! My God! Is there a God? If there be one, deliver me! Save me! Succour me! Pardon! Pity! Mercy! Save me! Oh, what sufferings! What torture! What horror!

15th August. This is certainly the way in which my poor cousin was possessed and controlled when she came to borrow five thousand francs off me. She was under the power of a strange will which had entered into her, like another soul, like another parasitic and dominating soul. Is the world coming to an end?

But who is he, this invisible being that rules me? This unknowable being, this rover of a supernatural race?

Invisible beings exist, then! How is it then, that since the beginning of the world they have never manifested themselves precisely as they do to me? I have never read of anything that resembles what goes on in my house. Oh, if I could only leave it, if I could only go away, escape, and never return! I should be saved, but I cannot.

16th August. I managed to escape today for two hours, like a prisoner who finds the door of his dungeon accidentally open. I suddenly felt that I was free and that he was far away, and so I gave orders to harness the horses as quickly as possible, and I drove to Rouen. Oh, how delightful to be able to say to a man who obeys you: 'Go to Rouen!'

I made him pull up before the library, and I begged them to lend me Dr Herrmann Herestauss' treatise on the unknown inhabitants of the ancient and modern world.

Then, as I was getting into my carriage, I intended to say: 'To the railway station!' but instead of this I shouted – I did not say, but I shouted – in such a loud voice that all the passers-by turned round: 'Home!' and I fell back on the cushion of my carriage, overcome by mental agony. He had found me again and regained possession of me.

17th August. Oh, what a night! What a night! And yet it seems to me that I ought to rejoice. I read until one o'clock in the morning! Herestauss, doctor of philosophy and theogony, wrote the history of the manifestation of all those invisible beings which hover around man, or of whom he dreams. He describes their origin, their domain, their power; but none of them resembles the one which haunts me. One might say that man, ever since he began to think, has had a foreboding fear of a new being, stronger than himself, his successor in this world, and that, feeling his presence, and not being able to foresee the nature of that master, he has, in his terror, created the whole race of occult beings, of vague phantoms born of fear.

Having therefore read until one o'clock in the morning, I went and sat down at the open window, in order to cool my forehead and my thoughts, in the calm night air. It was very pleasant and warm! How I should have enjoyed such a night formerly!

There was no moon, but the stars darted out their rays in the dark heavens. Who inhabits those worlds? What forms, what living beings, what animals are there yonder? What do the thinkers in those distant worlds know more than we do? What can they do more than we can? What do they see which we do not know? Will not one of them, some day or other, traversing space, appear on our earth to conquer it, just as the Norsemen formerly crossed the sea in order to subjugate nations more feeble than themselves?

We are so weak, so defenceless, so ignorant, so small, we who live on this particle of mud which revolves in a drop of water.

I fell asleep, dreaming thus in the cool night air, and when I had slept for about three-quarters of an hour, I opened my eyes without moving, awakened by I know not what confused and strange sensation. At first I saw nothing, and then suddenly it appeared to me as if a page of a book which had remained open on my table turned over of its own accord. Not a breath of air had come in at my window, and I was surprised, and waited. In about four minutes, I saw, I saw, yes saw with my own eyes, another page lift itself up and fall down on the others, as if a finger had turned it over. My armchair was empty, appeared empty, but I knew that he was there, he, and sitting in my place, and that he was reading. With a furious bound, the bound of an enraged wild beast that springs at its tamer, I crossed my room to seize him, to strangle him, to kill him! But before I could reach it, the chair fell over as if somebody had run away from me – my table rocked, my lamp fell and went out, and my window closed as if some thief had been surprised and had fled out into the night, shutting it behind him.

So he had run away; he had been afraid; he, afraid of me!

But – but – tomorrow – or later – some day or other – I should be able to hold him in my clutches and crush him against the ground! Do not dogs occasionally bite and strangle their masters?

18th August. I have been thinking the whole day long. Oh yes, I will obey him, follow his impulses, fulfil all his wishes, show myself humble, submissive, a coward. He is the stronger; but the hour will come –

19th August. I know – I know – I know all! I have just read the following in the *Revue du Monde Scientifique*: 'A curious piece of news comes to us from Rio de Janeiro. Madness, an epidemic of madness, which may be compared to that contagious madness which attacked the people of Europe in the Middle Ages, is at this moment raging in the Province of San-Paolo. The terrified inhabitants are leaving their houses, saying that they are pursued, possessed, dominated like human cattle by invisible, though tangible, beings, a species of vampires, which feed on their life while they are asleep, and which, besides, drink water and milk without appearing to touch any other nourishment.

'Professor Don Pedro Henriques, accompanied by several medical savants, has gone to the Province of San-Paolo, in order to study the origin and the manifestations of this surprising madness on the spot, and to propose such measures to the Emperor as may appear to him to be most fitted to restore the mad population to reason.'

Ah! I remember now that fine Brazilian three-master which passed in front of my windows as she was going up the Seine, on the 8th day of last May! I thought she looked so pretty, so white and bright! That Being was on board of her, coming from there, where its race originated. And it saw me! It saw my house which was also white, and it sprang from the ship on to the land. Oh, merciful heaven!

Now I know, I can divine. The reign of man is over and he has come. He who was feared by primitive man; whom disquieted priests exorcised; whom sorcerers evoked on dark nights, without having seen him appear, to whom the imagination of the transient masters of the world lent all the monstrous or graceful forms of gnomes, spirits, genii, fairies, and familiar spirits. After the coarse conceptions of primitive fear, more clear-sighted men foresaw it more clearly. Mesmer divined it, and ten years ago physicians accurately discovered the nature of his power, even before he exercised it himself. They played with this new weapon of the Lord, the sway of a mysterious will over the human soul, which had become a slave. They called it magnetism, hypnotism, suggestion – what do I know? I have seen them amusing themselves like rash children with this horrible power! Woe to us! Woe to man! He has come, the – the –

what does he call himself – the – I fancy that he is shouting out his name to me and I do not hear him – the – yes – he is shouting it out – I am listening – I cannot – he repeats it – the – Horla – I hear – the Horla – it is he – the Horla – he has come!

Ah! the vulture has eaten the pigeon; the wolf has eaten the lamb; the lion has devoured the sharp-horned buffalo; man has killed the lion with an arrow, with a sword, with gunpowder; but the Horla will make of man what we have made of the horse and of the ox; his chattel, his slave, and his food, by the mere power of his will. Woe to us!

But nevertheless, the animal sometimes revolts and kills the man who has subjugated it. I should also like – I shall be able to – but I must know him, touch him, see him! Scientists say that animals' eyes, being different from ours, do not distinguish objects as ours do. And my eye cannot distinguish this newcomer who is oppressing me.

Why? Oh, now I remember the words of the monk at Mont Saint-Michel: 'Can we see the hundred-thousandth part of what exists? See her: there is the wind, which is the strongest force in nature, which knocks men down, and wrecks buildings, uproots trees, raises the sea into mountains of water, destroys cliffs and casts great ships on the breakers; the wind which kills, which whistles, which sighs, which roars – have you ever seen it, and can you see it? It exists for all that, however!'

And I went on thinking: my eyes are so weak, so imperfect, that they do not even distinguish hard bodies, if they are as transparent as glass! If a glass without tinfoil behind it were to bar my way, I should run into it, just as a bird which has flown into a room breaks its head against the window-panes. A thousand things, moreover, deceive man and lead him astray. Why should it then be surprising that he cannot perceive an unknown body through which the light passes?

A new being! Why not? It was assuredly bound to come! Why should we be the last? We do not distinguish it any more than all the others created before us! The reason is, that its nature is more perfect, its body finer and more finished than ours, that ours is so weak, so awkwardly constructed, encumbered with organs that are always tired, always on the strain like machinery that is too complicated, which lives like a plant and like a beast, nourishing itself with difficulty on air, herbs, and flesh, an animal machine which is pray to maladies, to malformations, to decay; broken-winded, badly regulated, simple and eccentric, ingeniously badly made, at once a coarse and a delicate piece of workmanship, the rough sketch of a being that might become intelligent and grand.

We are only a few, so few in this world, from the oyster up to man. Why should there not be one more, once that period is passed which separates the successive apparitions from all the different species?

Why not one more? Why not, also, other trees with immense, splendid flowers, perfuming whole regions? Why not other elements besides fire, air, earth, and water? There are four, only four, those nursing fathers of various beings! What a pity! Why are there not forty, four hundred, four thousand? How poor everything is, how mean and wretched! grudgingly produced, roughly constructed, clumsily made! Ah the elephant and the hippopotamus, what grace! And the camel, what elegance!

But the butterfly, you will say, a flying flower! I dream of one that should be as large as a hundred worlds, with wings whose shape, beauty, colour and motion I cannot even express. But I see it – it flutters from star to star, refreshing them with the light and harmonious breath of its flight! And the people up there look at it as it passes in an ecstasy of delight!

* * * *

What is the matter with me? It is he, the Horla, who haunts me, and who makes me think of these foolish things! He is within me, he is becoming my soul; I shall kill him!

29th August. I shall kill him. I have seen him! Yesterday I sat down at my table and pretended to write very assiduously. I knew quite well that he would come prowling round me, quite close to me, so close that I might perhaps be able to touch him, to seize him. And then – then I should have the strength of desperation; I should have my hands, my knees, my chest, my forehead, my teeth to strangle him, to crush him, to bite him, to tear him to pieces. And I watched for him with all my over-excited senses.

I had lighted my two lamps and the eight wax candles on my

mantelpiece, as if with this light I could discover him.

My bedstead, my old oak post bedstead, stood opposite to me; on my right was the fireplace; on my left, the door which was carefully closed, after I had left it open for some time in order to attract him; behind me was a very high wardrobe with a looking-glass in it, before which I stood to shave and dress every day, and in which I was in the habit of glancing at myself from head to foot every time I passed it.

I pretended to be writing in order to deceive him, for he also was watching me, and I felt – I was certain that he was reading over my shoulder, that he was there, touching my ear.

I got up, my hands extended, and turned round so quickly that I almost fell. Eh! well? It was as bright as at midday, but I did not see my reflection in the mirror! It was empty, clear, profound, full of light! But my figure was not reflected in it – and I, I was opposite to it! I saw the large, clear glass from top to bottom, and I looked at it with unsteady eyes; and I did not dare to advance; I did not venture to make a movement, feeling that he was there, but that he would escape me again, he whose imperceptible body had absorbed my reflection.

How frightened I was! And then, suddenly, I began to see myself in a mist in the depths of the looking-glass, in a mist as it were a sheet of water; and it seemed to me as if this water were flowing clearer every moment. It was like the end of an eclipse. Whatever it was that hid me did not appear to possess any clearly defined outlines, but a sort of opaque transparency which gradually grew clearer.

At last I was able to distinguish myself completely, as I do every day when I look at myself.

I had seen it! And the horror of it remained with me, and makes me shudder even now.

30th August. How could I kill it, as I could not get hold of it? Poison? But it would see me mix it with the water; and then, would our poisons have any effect on its impalpable body? No – no – no doubt about the matter – Then – then?–

31st August. I sent for a blacksmith from Rouen, and ordered iron shutters for my room such as some private hotels in Paris have on the gound floor, for fear of burglars, and he is going to make me an iron door as well. I have made myself out a coward, but I do not care about that!

10th September. Rouen, Hotel Continental. It is done – it is done – but is he dead? My mind is thoroughly upset by what I have seen.

Well, then, yesterday, the locksmith having put on the iron shutters and door, I left everything open until midnight, although it was getting cold.

Suddenly I felt that he was there, and joy, mad joy, took possession of me. I got up softly, and walked up and down for some time, so that he might not suspect anything; then I fastened the iron shutters, and, going back to the door, quickly double-locked it with a padlock, putting the key into my pocket.

Suddenly I noticed that he was moving restlessly round me, that in his turn he was frightened and was ordering me to let him out. I nearly yielded; I did not, however, but, putting my back to the door, I half opened it, just enough to allow me to go out backward, and as I am very tall my head touched the casing. I was sure that he had not been able to escape, and I shut him up quite alone, quite alone. What happiness! I had him fast. Then I ran downstairs; in the drawing-room, which was under my bedroom, I took the two lamps and I poured all the oil on the carpet, the furniture, everywhere; then I set fire to it and made my escape, after having carefully double-locked the door.

I went and hid myself at the bottom of the garden, in a clump of laurel bushes. How long it seemed! How long it seemed! Everything was dark, silent, motionless, not a breath of air and not a star, but heavy banks of clouds which one could not see, but which weighed, oh, so heavily on my soul.

I looked at my house and waited. How long it was! I already began to think that the fire had gone out of its own accord, or that he had extinguished it, when one of the lower windows gave way under the violence of the flames, and a long, soft, caressing sheet of red flame mounted up the white wall, and enveloped it as far as the roof. The light fell on the trees, the branches, and the leaves, and a shiver of fear pervaded them also! The birds awoke, a dog began to howl, and it seemed to me as if the day were breaking! Almost immediately two other windows flew into fragments, and I saw that the whole of the lower part of my house was nothing but a terrible furnace. But a cry, a horrible, shrill, heart-rending cry, a woman's cry, sounded through the night, and two garret windows were opened! I had forgotten the servants! I saw their terror-stricken faces, and their arms waving frantically.

Then, overwhelmed with horror, I set off to run to the village, shouting: 'Help! help! fire! fire!' I met some people who were already coming to the scene, and I returned with them.

By this time the house was nothing but a horrible and magnificent funeral pile, a monstrous funeral pile which lit up the whole country, a funeral pile where men were burning, and where he was burning also, He, He, my prisoner, that new Being, the new master, the Horla!

Suddenly the whole roof fell in between the walls, and a volcano of flames darted up to the sky. Through all the windows which opened on the furnace, I saw the flames darting, and I thought that he was there, in that kiln, dead.

Dead? Perhaps. – His body? Was not his body, which was transparent, indestructible by such means as would kill ours?

If he were not dead? – Perhaps time alone has power over that Invisible and Redoubtable Being. Why this transparent, unrecognizable body, this body belonging to a spirit, if it also has to fear ills, infirmities and premature destruction?

Premature destruction? All human terror spring from that! After man, the Horla. After him who can die every day, at any hour, at any moment, by any accident, comes the one who will die only at his own proper hour, day, and minute, because he has touched the limits of his existence!

No – no – without any doubt – he is not dead – Then – then – I suppose I must kill *myself!* . . .

THE MUMMY'S FOOT
Théophile Gautier

I had entered, in an idle mood, the shop of one of those curiosity-venders, who are called *marchands de bric-à-brac* in that Parisian *argot* which is so perfectly unintelligible elsewhere in France.

You have doubtless glanced occasionally through the windows of some of these shops, which have become so numerous now that it is fashionable to buy antiquated furniture, and that every petty stockbroker thinks he must have his *chambre au moyen âge*.

There is one thing there which clings alike to the shop of the dealer in old iron, the wareroom of the tapestry-maker, the laboratory of the chemist, and the studio of the painter – in all those gloomy dens where a furtive daylight filters in through the window-shutters, the most manifestly ancient thing is dust; – the cobwebs are more authentic than the guimp laces; and the old pear-tree furniture on exhibition is actually younger than the mahogany which arrived but yesterday from America.

The warehouse of my *bric-à-brac* dealer was a veritable Capharnaum; all ages and all nations seemed to have made their rendezvous there; an Etruscan lamp of red clay stood upon a Boule cabinet, with ebony panels, brightly striped by lines of inlaid brass; a duchess of the court of Louis XV nonchalantly extended her fawn-like feet under a massive table of the time of Louis XIII with heavy spiral supports of oak, and carven designs of chimeras and foliage intermingled.

Upon the denticulated shelves of several sideboards glittered immense Japanese dishes with red and blue designs relieved by gilded hatching; side by side with enamelled works by Bernard Palissy, representing serpents, frogs, and lizards in relief.

From disembowelled cabinets escaped cascades of silver-lustrous Chinese silks and waves of tinsel, which an oblique sunbeam shot through with luminous beads; while portraits of every era, in frames more or less tarnished, smiled through their yellow varnish.

The striped breastplate of a damascened suit of Milanese armour glittered in one corner; Loves and Nymphs of porcelain; Chinese Grotesques, vases of *céladon* and crackle-ware; Saxon and old Sèvres cups encumbered the shelves and nooks of the apartment.

The dealer followed me closely through the tortuous way contrived between the piles of furniture; warding off with his hand the hazardous sweep of my coat-skirts; watching my elbows with the uneasy attention of an antiquarian and a usurer.

It was a singular face, that of the merchant – an immense skull, polished like a knee, and surrounded by a thin aureole of white hair, which brought out the clear salmon tint of his complexion all the more strikingly, lent him a false aspect of patriarchal *bonhomie*, counteracted, however, by the scintillation of two little yellow eyes which trembled in their orbits like two louis-d'or upon quicksilver. The curve of his nose presented an aquiline silhouette, which suggested the Oriental or Jewish type. His hands – thin, slender, full of nerves which projected like strings upon the finger-board of a violin, and armed with claws like those on the terminations of bats' wings – shook with senile trembling; but those convulsively agitated hands became firmer than steel pincers or lobsters' claws when they lifted any precious article – an onyx cup, a Venetian glass, or a dish of Bohemian crystal. This strange old man had an aspect so thoroughly rabbinical and cabalistic that he would have been burnt on the mere testimony of his face three centuries ago.

'Will you not buy something from me today, sir? Here is a Malay kreese with a blade undulating like flame: look at those grooves contrived for the blood to run along, those teeth set backwards so as to tear out the entrails in withdrawing the weapon – it is a fine character of ferocious arm, and will look well in your collection: this two-handed sword is very beautiful – it is the work of Josepe de la Hera; and this *colichemarde*, with its fenestrated guard – what a superb specimen of handicraft!'

'No; I have quite enough weapons and instruments of carnage – I want a small figure, something which will suit me as a paper-weight; for I cannot endure those trumpery bronzes which the stationers sell, and which may be found on everybody's desk.'

The old gnome foraged among his ancient wares, and finally arranged before me some antique bronzes – so-called, at least; fragments of malachite; little Hindoo or Chinese idols – a kind of poussah toys in jadestone, representing the incarnations of Brahma or Vishnoo, and wonderfully appropriate to the very undivine office of holding papers and letters in place.

I was hesitating between a porcelain dragon, all constellated with warts – its mouth formidable with bristling tusks and ranges of teeth – and an abominable little Mexican fetish, representing the god Zitziliputzili *au naturel*, when I caught sight of a charming foot, which I at first took for a fragment of some antique Venus.

It had those beautiful ruddy and tawny tints that lend to Florentine bronze that warm living look so much preferable to the gray-green aspect of common bronzes, which might easily be mistaken for statues in a state of putrefaction: satiny gleams played over its rounded forms, doubtless polished by the amorous kisses of twenty centuries; for it seemed a Corinthian bronze, a work of the best era of art – perhaps molded by Lysippus himself.

'That foot will be my choice,' I said to the merchant, who regarded me with an ironical and saturnine air, and held out the object desired that I might examine it more fully.

I was surprised at its lightness; it was not a foot of metal, but in sooth a foot of flesh – an embalmed foot – a mummy's foot: on examining it still more closely the very grain of the skin, and the almost imperceptible lines impressed upon it by the texture of the bandages, became perceptible. Those toes were slender and delicate, and terminated by perfectly formed nails, pure and transparent as agates; the great toe, slightly separated from the rest, afforded a happy contrast, in the antique style, to the position of the other toes, and lent it an aerial lightness – the grace of a bird's foot – the sole, scarcely streaked by a few almost imperceptible cross lines, afforded evidence that it had never touched the bare ground, and had only come in contact with the finest matting of Nile rushes, and the softest carpets of panther skin.

'Ha, ha! – you want the foot of the Princess Hermonthis,' – exclaimed the merchant, with a strange giggle, fixing his owlish eyes upon me – 'ha, ha, ha! – for a paper-weight! – an original idea! – artistic idea! Old Pharaoh would certainly have been surprised had someone told him that the foot of his adored daughter would be used for a paper-weight after he had had a mountain of granite hollowed out as a receptacle for the triple coffin, painted and gilded – covered with hieroglyphics and beautiful paintings of the Judgment of Souls,' – continued the queer little merchant, half audibly, as though talking to himself!

'How much will you charge me for this mummy fragment?'

'Ah, the highest price I can get; for it is a superb piece: if I had the match of it you could not have it for less than five hundred francs; – the daughter of a Pharaoh! nothing is more rare.'

'Assuredly that is not a common article; but, still, how much do you want? In the first place let me warn you that all my wealth consists of just five louis: I can buy anything that costs five louis, but nothing dearer – you might search my vest pockets and most secret drawers without even finding one poor five-franc piece more.'

'Five louis for the foot of the Princess Hermonthis! that is very little, very little indeed; 'tis an authentic foot,' muttered the merchant, shaking his head, and imparting a peculiar rotary motion to his eyes. 'Well, take it, and I will give you the bandages into the bargain,' he added, wrapping the foot in an ancient damask rag – 'very fine! real damask – Indian damask which has never been redyed; it is strong, and yet it is soft,' he mumbled, stroking the frayed tissue with his fingers, through the trade-acquired habit which moved him to praise even an object of so little value that he himself deemed it only worth the giving away.

He poured the gold coins into a sort of mediaeval alms-purse hanging at his belt, repeating:

'The foot of the Princess Hermonthis, to be used for a paper-weight!'

Then turning his phosphorescent eyes upon me, he exclaimed in a voice strident as the crying of a cat which has swallowed a fish-bone:

'Old Pharaoh will not be well pleased; he loved his daughter – the dear man!'

'You speak as if you were a contemporary of his: you are old enough, goodness knows! but you do not date back to the Pyramids of Egypt,' I answered, laughingly, from the threshold.

I went home, delighted with my acquisition.

With the idea of putting it to profitable use as soon as possible, I placed the foot of the divine Princess Hermonthis upon a heap of papers scribbled over with verses, in themselves an undecipherable mosaic work of erasures; articles freshly begun; letters forgotten, and posted in the table drawer instead of the letter-box – an error to which absent-minded people are peculiarly liable. The effect was charming, bizarre, and romantic.

Well satisfied with this embellishment, I went out with the gravity and pride becoming one who feels that he has the ineffable advantage over all the passers-by whom he elbows, of possessing a piece of the Princess Hermonthis, daughter of Pharaoh.

I looked upon all who did not possess, like myself, a paper-weight so authentically Egyptian, as very ridiculous people; and it seemed to me that the proper occupation of every sensible man should consist in the mere fact of having a mummy's foot upon his desk.

Happily I met some friends, whose presence distracted me in my infatuation with this new acquisition: I went to dinner with them; for I could not very well have dined with myself.

When I came back that evening, with my brain slightly confused by a few glasses of wine, a vague whiff of Oriental perfume delicately titillated my olfactory nerves: the heat of the room had warmed the natron, bitumen, and myrrh in which the *paraschistes*, who cut open the bodies of the dead, had bathed the corpse of the princess – it was a perfume at once sweet and penetrating – a perfume that four thousand years had not been able to dissipate.

The Dream of Egypt was Eternity: her odours have the solidity of granite, and endure as long.

I soon drank deeply from the black cup of sleep: for a few hours all remained opaque to me; Oblivion and Nothingness inundated me with their sombre waves.

Yet light gradually dawned upon the darkness of my mind; dreams commenced to touch me softly in their silent flight.

The eyes of my soul were opened; and I beheld my chamber as it actually was; I might have believed myself awake, but for a vague consciousness which assured me that I slept, and that something fantastic was about to take place.

The odour of the myrrh had augmented in intensity: and I felt a slight headache, which I very naturally attributed to several glasses of champagne that we had drunk to the unknown gods and our future fortunes.

I peered through my room with a feeling of expectation which I saw nothing to justify: every article of furniture was in its proper place; the lamp, softly shaded by its globe of ground crystal, burned upon its bracket; the water-color sketches shone under their Bohemian glass; the curtains hung down languidly; everything wore an aspect of tranquil slumber.

After a few moments, however, all this calm interior appeared to become disturbed; the woodwork cracked stealthily; the ash-covered log suddenly emitted a jet of blue flame; and the discs of the pateras seemed like great metallic eyes, watching, like myself, for the things which were about to happen.

My eyes accidentally fell upon the desk where I had placed the foot of the Princess Hermonthis.

Instead of remaining quiet – as behooved a foot which had been embalmed for four thousand years – it commenced to act in a nervous manner; contracted itself, and leaped over the papers like a startled frog – one would have imagined that it had suddenly been brought into contact with a galvanic battery: I could distinctly hear the dry sound made by its little heel, hard as the hoof of a gazelle.

I became rather discontented with my acquisition, inasmuch as I wished my paper-weights to be of a sedentary disposition, and thought it very unnatural that feet should walk about without legs; and I commenced to experience a feeling closely akin to fear.

Suddenly I saw the folds of my bed-curtain stir; and heard a bumping sound, like that caused by some person hopping on one foot across the floor. I must confess I became alternately hot and cold; that I felt a strange wind chill my back; and that my suddenly rising hair caused my nightcap to execute a leap of several yards.

The bed-curtains opened and I beheld the strangest figure imaginable before me.

I beheld the strangest figure imaginable

It was a young girl of a very deep coffee-brown complexion, like the bayadère Amani, and possessing the purest Egyptian type of perfect beauty: her eyes were almond-shaped and oblique, with eyebrows so black that they seemed blue; her nose was exquisitely chiselled, almost Greek in its delicacy of outline; and she might indeed have been taken for a Corinthian statue of bronze, but for the prominence of her cheekbones and the slightly African fullness of her lips, which compelled one to recognise her as belonging beyond all doubt to the hieroglyphic race which dwelt upon the banks of the Nile.

Her arms, slender and spindle-shaped, like those of very young girls, were encircled by a peculiar kind of metal bands and bracelets of glass beads; her hair was all twisted into little cords; and she wore upon her bosom a little idol-figure of green paste, bearing a whip with seven lashes, which proved it to be an image of Isis: her brow was adorned with a shining plate of gold; and a few traces of paint relieved the coppery tint of her cheeks.

As for her costume, it was very odd indeed.

Fancy a *pagne* or skirt all formed of little strips of material bedizened with red and black hieroglyphics, stiffened with bitumen, and apparently belonging to a freshly unbandaged mummy.

In one of those sudden flights of thought so common in dreams I heard the hoarse falsetto of the *bric-à-brac* dealer, repeating like a monotonous refrain the phrase he had uttered in his shop with so enigmatical an intonation:

'Old Pharaoh will not be well pleased: he loved his daughter, the dear man!'

One strange circumstance, which was not at all calculated to restore my equanimity, was that the apparition had but one foot; the other was broken off at the ankle!

She approached the table where the foot was starting and fidgeting about more than ever, and there supported herself upon the edge of the desk. I saw her eyes fill with pearly-gleaming tears.

Although she had not as yet spoken, I fully comprehended the thoughts which agitated her: she looked at her foot – for it was indeed her own – with an exquisitely graceful expression of coquettish sadness; but the foot leaped and ran hither and thither, as though impelled on steel springs.

Twice or thrice she extended her hand to seize it, but could not succeed.

Then commenced between the Princess Hermonthis and her foot – which appeared to be endowed with a special life of its own – a very fantastic dialogue in a most ancient Coptic tongue, such as might have been spoken thirty centuries ago in the syrinxes of the land of Ser: luckily, I understood Coptic perfectly well that night.

The Princess Hermonthis cried, in a voice sweet and vibrant as the tones of a crystal bell:

'Well, my dear little foot, you always flee from me; yet I always took good care of you. I bathed you with perfumed water in a bowl of alabaster; I smoothed your heel with pumice-stone mixed with palm oil; your nails were cut with golden scissors and polished with a hippopotamus tooth; I was careful to select *tatbebs* for you, painted and embroidered and turned up at the toes, which were the envy of all the young girls in Egypt: you wore on your great toe rings bearing the device of the sacred Scarabaeus; and you supported one of the lightest bodies that a lazy foot could sustain.'

The foot replied, in a pouting and chagrined tone:

'You know well that I do not belong to myself any longer – I have been bought and paid for; the old merchant knew what he was about; he bore you a grudge for having refused to espouse him – this is an ill turn which he has done you. The Arab who violated your royal coffin in the subterranean pits of the necropolis of Thebes was sent thither by him: he desired to prevent you from being present at the reunion of the shadowy nations in the cities below. Have you five pieces of gold for my ransom?'

'Alas, no! – my jewels, my rings, my purses of gold and silver, they were stolen from me,' answered the Princess Hermonthis, with a sob.

'Princess,' I then exclaimed, 'I never retained anybody's foot unjustly – even though you have not got the five louis which it cost me, I present it to you gladly: I should feel unutterably wretched to think that I were the cause of so amiable a person as the Princess Hermonthis being lame.'

I delivered this discourse in a royally gallant, troubadour tone, which must have astonished the beautitul Egyptian girl.

She turned a look of deepest gratitude upon me; and her eyes shone with bluish gleams of light.

She took her foot – which surrendered itself willingly this time – like a woman about to put on her little shoe, and adjusted it to her leg with much skill.

This operation over, she took a few steps about the room, as though to assure herself that she was really no longer lame.

'Ah, how pleased my father will be! – he who was so unhappy because of my mutilation, and who from the moment of my birth set a whole nation at work to hollow me out a tomb so deep that he might preserve me intact until the last day, when souls must be weighed in the balance of Amenthi! Come with me to my father – he will receive you kindly; for you have given me back my foot.'

I thought this proposition natural enough. I arrayed myself in a dressing-gown of large-flowered pattern, which lent me a very Pharaonic aspect; hurriedly put on a pair of Turkish slippers, and informed the Princess Hermonthis that I was ready to follow her.

Before starting, Hermonthis took from her neck the little idol of green paste, and laid it on the scattered sheets of paper which covered the table.

'It is only fair,' she observed smilingly, 'that I should replace your paper-weight.'

She gave me her hand, which felt soft and cold, like the skin of a serpent; and we departed.

We passed for some time with the velocity of an arrow through a fluid and grayish expanse, in which half-formed silhouettes flitted swiftly by us, to right and left.

For an instant we saw only sky and sea.

A few moments later, obelisks commenced to tower in the distance: pylons and vast flights of steps guarded by sphinxes became clearly outlined against the horizon.

We had reached our destination.

The princess conducted me to the mountain of rose-coloured granite, in the face of which appeared an opening so narrow and low that it would have been difficult to distinguish it from the fissures in the rock, had not its location been marked by two stelae wrought with sculptures.

Hermonthis kindled a torch, and led the way before me.

We traversed corridors hewn through the living rock: their walls, covered with hieroglyphics and paintings of allegorical processions, might well have occupied thousands of arms for thousands of years in their formation – these corridors, of interminable length, opened into square chambers, in the midst of which pits had been contrived, through which we descended by cramp-irons or spiral stairways – these pits again conducted us into other chambers, opening into other corridors, likewise decorated with painted sparrow-hawks, serpents coiled in circles, the symbols of the *tau* and *pedum* prodigious works of art which no living eye can ever examine – interminable legends of granite which only the dead have time to read through all eternity.

At last we found ourselves in a hall so vast, so enormous, so immeasurable, that the eye could not reach its limits; files of monstrous columns stretched far out of sight on every side, between which twinkled livid stars of yellowish flame – points of light which revealed further depths incalculable in the darkness beyond.

The Princess Hermonthis still held my hand, and graciously saluted the mummies of her acquaintance.

My eyes became accustomed to the dim twilight, and objects became discernible.

I beheld the kings of the subterranean races seated upon thrones – grand old men, though dry, withered, wrinkled like parchment, and blackened with naphtha and bitumen – all wearing *pshents* of gold, and breastplates and gorgets glittering with precious stones; their eyes immovably fixed like the eyes of sphinxes, and their long beards whitened by the snow of centuries. Behind them stood their peoples, in the stiff and constrained posture enjoined by Egyptian art, all eternally preserving the attitude prescribed by the hieratic code. Behind these nations, the cats, ibises, and crocodiles contemporary with them – rendered monstrous of aspect by their swathing bands – mewed, flapped their wings, or extended their jaws in a saurian giggle.

All the Pharaohs were there – Cheops, Chephrenes, Psammetichus, Sesostris, Amenotaph – all the dark rulers of the pyramids and syrinxes – on yet higher thrones sat Chronos and Xixouthros – who was contemporary with the deluge; and Tubal Cain, who reigned before it.

The beard of King Xixouthros had grown seven times around the granite table, upon which he leaned, lost in deep reverie – and buried in dreams.

Further back, through a dusty cloud, I beheld dimly the seventy-two pre-Adamite Kings, with their seventy-two peoples – forever passed away.

After permitting me to gaze upon this bewildering spectacle a few moments, the Princess Hermonthis presented me to her father Pharaoh, who favoured me with a most gracious nod.

'I have found my foot again! – I have found my foot!' cried the Princess, clapping her little hands together with every sign of frantic joy: 'it was this gentleman who restored it to me.'

The races of Kemi, the races of Nahasi – all the black, bronzed, and copper-coloured nations repeated in chorus:

'The Princess Hermonthis has found her foot again!'

Even Xixouthros himself was visibly affected.

He raised his heavy eyelids, stroked his moustache with his fingers, and turned upon me a glance weighty with centuries.

'By Oms, the dog of Hell, and Tmei, daughter of the Sun and of Truth! this is a brave and worthy lad!' exclaimed Pharaoh, pointing to me with his sceptre, which was terminated with a lotus-flower.

'What recompense do you desire?'

Filled with that daring inspired by dreams in which nothing seems impossible, I asked him for the hand of the Princess Hermonthis – the hand seemed to me a very proper antithetic recompense for the foot.

Pharaoh opened wide his great eyes of glass in astonishment at my witty request.

'What country do you come from, and what is your age?'

'I am a Frenchman; and I am twenty-seven years old, venerable Pharaoh.'

'–Twenty-seven years old! and he wishes to espouse the Princess Hermonthis, who is thirty centuries old!' cried out at once all the Thrones and all the Circles of Nations.

Only Hermonthis herself did not seem to think my request unreasonable.

'If you were even only two thousand years old,' replied the ancient King, 'I would willingly give you the Princess; but the disproportion is too great; and, besides, we must give our daughters husbands who will last well: you do not know how to preserve yourselves any longer; even those who died only fifteen centuries ago are already no more than a handful of dust – behold! my flesh is solid as basalt; my bones are bars of steel!

'I shall be present on the last day of the world, with the same body and the same features which I had during my lifetime: my daughter Hermonthis will last longer than a statue of bronze.

'Then the last particles of your dust will have been scattered abroad by the winds; and even Isis herself, who was able to find the atoms of Osiris, would scarce be able to recompose your being.

'See how vigorous I yet remain, and how mighty is my grasp,' he added, shaking my hand in the English fashion with a strength that buried my rings in the flesh of my fingers.

He squeezed me so hard that I awoke, and found my friend Alfred shaking me by the arm to make me get up.

'Oh you everlasting sleeper! – must I have you carried out into the middle of the street, and fireworks exploded in your ears? It is after noon; don't you recollect your promise to take me with you to see M. Aguado's Spanish pictures?'

'God! I forgot all about it,' I answered, dressing myself hurriedly; 'we will go there at once; I have the permit lying on my desk.'

I started to find it – but fancy my astonishment when I beheld, instead of the mummy's foot I had purchased the evening before, the little green paste idol left in its place by the Princess Hermonthis!

ACKNOWLEDGEMENTS

The publishers gratefully acknowledge permission to reproduce the following stories and extracts:

THE LANDLADY from *Kiss Kiss* by Roald Dahl. Reprinted by kind permission of Michael Joseph Ltd and Penguin Books Ltd.
THE RIDDLE by Walter de la Mare. Reprinted by kind permission of The Literary Trustees of Walter de la Mare and The Society of Authors as their representative.
THE MONKEY'S PAW by W.W. Jacobs. Reprinted by kind permission of The Society of Authors as the literary representative of the Estate of W.W. Jacobs.
THROUGH THE DOOR from *The Phantom Roundabout* by Ruth Ainsworth. Copyright © 1971 Ruth Ainsworth. Reprinted by kind permission of Scholastic Publications Ltd.
A KIND OF SWAN SONG from *Shades of Dark* by Helen Cresswell. Reprinted by kind permission of Helen Cresswell.
THE CLOCK TOWER GHOST from *The Clock Tower Ghost* by Gene Kemp. Reprinted by kind permission of Faber and Faber Ltd.
BAD COMPANY by Walter de la Mare. Reprinted by kind permission of The Literary Trustees of Walter de la Mare and The Society of Authors as their representative.
THE WELL by W.W. Jacobs. Reprinted by kind permission of The Society of Authors as the literary representative of the Estate of W.W. Jacobs.
THE SWAN CHILD from *A Whisper in the Night* by Joan Aiken. Reprinted by kind permission of Joan Aiken and Jonathan Cape Ltd.
THE RED ROOM from *The Complete Short Stories of H.G. Wells* by H.G. Wells. Reprinted by kind permission of A.P.Watt Ltd on behalf of The Literary Executors of the Estate of H.G. Wells.
THE BLADES by Joan Aiken. Reprinted by kind permission of Joan Aiken and Jonathan Cape Ltd.
SWEETS FROM A STRANGER by Nicholas Fisk. Copyright © 1978 Nicholas Fisk. Reprinted by kind permission of Nicholas Fisk.
THE HITCH-HIKER from *The Wonderful Story of Henry Sugar* by Roald Dahl. Reprinted by kind permission of Jonathan Cape Ltd and Penguin Books Ltd.

The publishers have made every effort to trace copyright holders. If we have omitted to acknowledge anyone, we should be most grateful if this could be brought to our attention at the first opportunity.